THE GAMMA QUADRANT

Naero's War, The Citation Series

Book 4

Mason Elliott

THE GAMMA QUADRANT

Naero's War, The Citation Series

Book 4

by

Mason Elliott

High Mark Publishing

High Mark Publishing
www.highmarkpublishing.com

Seattle & Portland, Los Angeles, Chicago, London

THE GAMMA QUADRANT

by
Mason Elliott
Createspace Trade Paperback Edition
© 2016 by Mason Elliott. All rights reserved.
Published by High Mark Publishing
ISBN 978-1-930451-24-7
Watch for other titles by this author in the future.

Cover Art by Michael McAfee
mcafee.mic@gmail.com

Edition Notes

If you do not see this edition note here in this spot on the copyright page and on the very last page of your eBook or print version of this title, then you are not getting the final, polished version of this novel that the publisher, editors, and author intended for you to receive. Please contact either the publisher or the author via their emails or websites if you do not see the following update code:

High Mark Publishing Update Code D0632A

Become a fan of my books.
Please join my Readers List:
http://bit.ly/1L2QpUL

Thanks, from Mason Elliott

1

The night before the mission into the Interdimensions, Naero had a dream where the stars fell.

If they did not actually fall out in space, then their light was being extinguished, one at a time and then in whole bunches. What did it all mean?

It was as if the darkness itself had come to life, like some predatory thing, and was penetrating and devouring them from within.

Then a very bright star appeared, placing itself before all the rest as if defending them. It came against the darkness, but in the end, it too was finally overwhelmed and it was consumed. All of the rest quickly perished, until there was only silence, darkness, and death.

The last thing Naero recalled before she started up out of her nightmare was the weeping and tormented cries of children, all suddenly silenced.

After all that, she found it very hard to get back to sleep.

For her, such dreams were almost always a warning of some kind.

Despite bad dreams, on the morrow, Naero and her strike force slipped into the Interdimensions for only the second time.

Shalaen and several more cautious, even frightened Yattai stayed close together.

The energized aether of the various folds and pocket dimensions they zipped through were all brightly colored, each in their own way, with varied, fractal patterns and bursts and splashes of Cosmic energies.

Yet with their third eyes, and all of their heightened senses from being in their energy forms, all of the joined realms they passed through pulsed and reeked with Chaos, destruction, slaughter, and subjugation of the resident sentient beings within.

Something was very wrong.

Thank goodness not all of the Interdimensions were linked.

Many might yet have survived the sweeping tide of violence that had struck hard in these places.

From the information that they had gathered thus far, these regions of Interdimensions adjacent to the Gamma Quadrant were being ravaged and torn apart by waves of deadly, invading forces.

Unknown until just very recently, the escaped hordes of vile, G'lothc spirits, shades, wraiths, or whatever it was appropriate to name the evil things, had waged a horrifying war. This was clearly a campaign of attrition, enslavement, and destruction that if left unchecked, could spread outward against the energy being races far beyond.

SpaceTime operated with much greater variation in the Interdimensions. Vast distances were traversed much easier by beings in energized, Cosmic forms. Much like the Astral Plane, in many cases such enormous distances could be leaped with the speed and power of thought.

It usually helped to have the conceptual reference of a starting and ending point.

This new enemy war, however, struck hard and without warning among most of the energy being races close to the Gamma quadrant.

Most of the known species of energy beings were being ruthlessly and systematically farmed and enslaved with impunity, to the point of extinction. Who knew how many other energy being races, yet to be encountered were also being attacked in this grave fashion as well?

Now that the majority of the great enemies were once more contained in their prison of near annihilation, a full assessment of the terrible losses suffered among those other, many and elusive interdimensional beings needed to be made, or at the very least attempted.

The Alliance could not simply hang back and cede the newly discovered and vital Interdimensions to the Great Adversary.

Naero's friend Shalaen and her valiant people, the energy beings known collectively as the Yattai, proved to be invaluable new comrades, and offered to assist the sentient, Prime Material races and allies in the known galaxy and beyond.

The Interdimensions were nearly as strange and beyond as one could find, save for the actual Beyond itself.

Naero and Shalaen remarked to each other about what amazing times of terror, wonder, and enlightenment they lived within.

How odd that the Yattai energy beings had once stood firm and stubborn as the staunchest isolationists.

All of that had changed and been swept away by their near destruction at the hands of the great enemy.

Near genocide quickly convinced them that they could no longer ignore the greater threats at hand, to them and others.

Not even near ascended energy beings were safe any longer. In fact, the enemy and its slaves hunted all such beings down now on a wide and regular basis, in order to use them as power sources for Darkforce generators…or for things far worse.

In the uncertainty of the Interdimensions, especially now, they stuck together and maintained their telepathic links to each other. That was the most efficient form of communication.

We have heard grim rumors from among the surviving remnants of the other energy being races, Shalaen informed Naero and her people. *It is said that Nahaxrathrax, the most ancient and most powerful of all the Dakkur Dark Emperors, has taken to devouring energy beings whole, by the hundreds as if they were grapes. He does this horrid thing, not only to increase his vaunted power, but because he enjoys devouring souls. We know of nothing that can stop this monster. And he has also willingly joined with legions of the fell spirits of the G'lothc housed within himself, and added their power, knowledge, and influence to his own malignant force of will.*

Even worse, another Yattai known as Jaeyar added. *He has sworn to somehow bring back The Six G'lothc Champions of the Darkforce!*

Shalaen gasped. *That would be a great evil and disadvantage to us.*

Jaeyar shook his head. *Indeed. It would mean the end.*

Now just wait a moment, Naero said. The Seven Kexxian Dreamers destroyed the Six in their final battle together, millions of years ago. How could such fiends be brought back into existence?

Indeed, Jaeyar told them. *Their mighty physical forms were obliterated, but their dark souls–their evil spirits–still lurk among the G'lothc within their Cosmic prison realm. They wait only for their release at the end times of the Cosmic Prophecies. Even the G'lothc themselves feared the Six–*

3

whom they mistakenly created after many millennia of evolution and genetic and Cosmic manipulation.

For until they stood before the Seven Kexxian Dreamers, the Six knew no equals. They were unstoppable, unmatched in ruthless villainy and depraved atrocities splattered all across several galaxies. Sentients took their own lives in wholesale panic before letting themselves or their children fall under the hands of one or more of the Six. Time and time again, entire populations were tormented and finally wiped out, according to their whims. What monsters they were.

Shalaen wept into her hands, seeing those age old memories in the hearts and minds of her people for the first time. *What mad folly is this? Such horrors cannot be unleashed on the universe again.*

Naero sighed heavily. Alas, I have both seen and sensed the hideous power of the Dark Emperor of the Dakkur. Nahaxrathrax will dare much, and stop at nothing. The enemy has the same insane plan that it has always pursued: destroy all life in the universe. They seek to somehow create or summon the Great Destroyer to accomplish this. That is a great part of what drives the ancient, Cosmic Prophecies.

We and all free sentients must band together and stop him. Like all of our greater foes, the Dark Emperor must be hunted down and utterly destroyed, before he does the same thing to us.

They passed into another realm, and the terror and death that filled it for light years and parsecs at a time sickened them almost instantly, even in their energy forms.

Naero had not thought that possible.

What is this dread place? Naero asked her Yattai friends.

Jaeyar frowned. *This was one of the wide realms of the Laelor, a race of energy beings slightly younger than the Yattai.*

What has happened here? Shalaen cried. *I sense torture and death all around us on a scale that is nearly unimaginable. Countless energy beings perished within this dimension. The aether itself is thick with the after effects of suffering and violence beyond reckoning.*

Even Naero could sense in part what was overpowering the Yattai. Terrible things had taken place here, and the psyonic memory and screams of the fallen still hung in the aether and echoed in the minds of all who passed that way. Spirit beings left horrific scars behind them in their passing.

This entire realm was scarred, scorched, and stained with horror.

It was a place haunted now by destruction and terror.

She also sensed in every way, the passing of the Dark Emperor and his fell servants, as well as something else that she could not yet define.

Where they had passed, the enemy left death and oblivion in their wake.

Now there were only what seemed to be flakes and bits of glowing, energized cinder and ash scattered upon the aether winds. Cosmic bits, shades, and shadows. All that remained of many Laelor energy beings and whatever constructs they had made.

A vibrant, advanced society and culture now forever ravaged and lost.

It was almost as if everything had been disintegrated, but how?

Naero asked. Shalaen, can you tell how many Laelor perished in this realm?

Shalaen glanced at Jaeyar and a few other Yattai, confirming first with them. *By our reckoning, some four hundred and sixteen thousand, three hundred and eighty nine...and counting, Naero. From the energy readings and shadow images left behind, the Laelor made a brave stand, and did their best to hold back the enemy. But the Dark Emperor and his hosts were still far too powerful for them to withstand. Many were taken away as energy slaves. The rest were merely slaughtered, in some terrible way that even we cannot yet comprehend.*

Naero gathered data and readings from Om, the Kexxian AI defensive protocol merged with her mind. As always, his essence came along with her. Their findings together were even more frightening and ominous.

Shalaen, I don't want to alarm you and the other Yattai, but something else was at work here. Even the Dark Emperor and his servants could not have wiped out so many powerful Laelor on their own, so quickly.

Shalaen turned to her. *Then what could it have been?*

I'm sensing some kind of low level, Darkforce energy residue in the aether. That's part of what's making us so sick and uneasy. I fear that this was some new super weapon of the enemy, designed especially to work within the Interdimensions, on an immense scale. Something we haven't seen before. And perhaps more than one kind of it."

What was it? Jaeyar asked.

Naero shook her head. I don't know yet, but by my calculations, these new threats tore the Laelor defenders apart as if they were paper. And they just didn't simply consume the Laelor–these new threats converted them somehow, and made them part of the attacking swarm, or whatever it was that the Dark Emperor unleashed against them. I have never sensed such malignant powers before. They defy definition, but the results are clear for all of us to detect.

Ahh! Shalaen cried out, rubbing her arm suddenly.

Naero rushed over to her to see. What is it?

Shalaen continued to wince painfully. *It's nothing. One of those bits of Cosmic ash. It really burned when it-*

Naero asked, How can it possibly harm your energy form?

She was screaming in pain an instant later, by the time Naero studied the arm wound with a mix of biomancy and teknomancy.

The mote of Cosmic ash flared with modified Darkforce and in another second, had burned through and consumed most of Shalaen's spirit form arm from the elbow down.

Even as it consumed Shalaen's hand, Naero quickly ensnared the particles and froze them solid within a concentrated sphere of countering Cosmic energy. She tucked the sample away for further study and turned back to Shalaen.

Her good friend struggled with the pain.

This was rapidly becoming very frightening.

The clouds of energy infused ash floating nearby suddenly came to life and swept toward them, rushing at them all with menacing focus and intent.

Naero cried out psyonically in warning. Withdraw! Don't let those particles touch you. It's part of an attack!

Naero instantly vaporized the concentrated particle clouds directly around them in a bright flare of Lifespark energy. Such positive energies passed through them all and did no harm. Yet it consumed the attacking, microscopic Darkforce particles, and purified any residual portion of Shalaen's virulent, spreading wound.

Naero's longtime friend clutched her own damaged arm, struggling to regenerate it. *You stopped it! Thank you. The pain was agonizing, N.*

I imagine it was. It appears to be some kind of malignant, Darkforce phage that converts other energy forms into more of itself. That is one major way that the Laelor were crushed so easily.

Jaeyar raised the alarm. *There is another entire nebula of those Cosmic phage particles sweeping straight at us, half a parsec in diameter.*

Even Naero could not take on a swarm that enormous.

Order everyone out of this sector, she shouted telepathically. Flee! If that nebula overtakes us, we'll be completely devoured and converted, just like the Laelor. This is another new super weapon of the G'lothc.

Together they sped out of that region, but it was touch and go for many moments. The phage storm continued to gather speed and pursue them closely, reaching out with long tendrils of Darkforce particles stabbing forward at them with great, deliberate speed.

The phage operated as if it were a living, ravenous collective organism with intent, purpose, and force of will.

At the last instant, Naero and her allies escaped that diseased realm, sealed off the access to it, and then destroyed the portal in that region behind them.

Until they had a way to counter this new threat, no energy beings could ever enter such a place safely again. The phage swarm had to be cut off and kept from infecting and attacking any other Interdimensional realm or separate pocket dimensions.

A large scale cure or defense against the enemy Darkforce phage would need to be developed. If the enemy used this new weapon successfully once, they would clearly press their advantage again.

The Yattai sent the warning out to all of the other known energy being sentients in the Gamma Quadrant and beyond.

Naero brought out and studied the frozen sample of the phage she possessed, with the necessary Cosmic mix and Om's help. The phage was yet another relentless threat that their ruthless and resourceful enemies inflicted upon them.

She and her allies had also sensed other threats yet to be revealed.

2

Naero's personal fixers gave her an instant view of herself from any angle whenever she needed it. Much better than a holomirror.

She needed to change something else, mix something up with her general appearance. Perhaps a splash of blue coloring in her normally jet black hair would do the trick. That trend of color splashing was certainly on the increase among Spacer women, and even some of the men.

Her many reps messed around with their looks all of the time. Why not the original?

Khai might even like a little daring variation in her standard look.

She went ahead and did it, right before reporting to duty.

Naero and her internal Kexxian AI partner Om worked closely with the Alliance labs and Mystic experts to attempt to understand and defend against the newly encountered Cosmic phage of the G'lothc. Shalaen, the Yattai, and researchers from the Oden, Khai's people, joined the team.

The latter seemed very impressed to be working with anyone connected with Khai, The Cosmic Enforcer for the Spacer Mystics. To them he was some kind of throck star.

Being his equally famous wife, they held Naero up on the same level.

As for the new threat at hand, a workable defense or solution needed to be found, and once again, their foes were way ahead of them in the game.

Luckily, Naero had retrieved a sample of the Interdimensional phage just before her own escape, and provided it to the team to study and observe.

Naero chose to confer with Om first, while all of the others took their turns studying the highly dangerous sample.

Researchers bombarded it with many types of Cosmic energy under controlled conditions, most of which the phage quickly absorbed and converted into its own lethal version of the Darkforce. In essence, it consumed everything it could, draining what it came into contact with its ravenous negative energies, and only grew stronger and more voracious, if allowed to do so.

Meanwhile, Naero knew that others among Alliance and Spacer Intel interviewed and questioned the few survivors among the energy beings who had encountered the phage directly or indirectly. They gave their accounts and explained how they had escaped and stayed alive.

Most of them did so by getting away or transporting to other parts of the Interdimensions that had not been infected yet, at the very start of the attack.

Om presented his initial goals and findings.

Naero, nothing major yet, but I am also monitoring all of those interviews among our energy being allies for any new insights through our spy fixer network. I'll let you know if anything new comes up, but the energy beings are understandably just as frightened and baffled by this new threat as we are.

Om, how are our energy being allies responding to all of this?

Not good, N. Khai's people, the Oden, were already in the process of going into hiding somewhere they think they will be safe. The Yattai are still attempting to discover where hundreds, perhaps thousands more of their kind have been spirited away, mostly by the enemy no doubt. As you might expect, everyone is running scared.

And why wouldn't they? Naero gritted her teeth and clenched her fists briefly. No doubt the enemy was feeding off of their new Yattai, Laelor, and how many other captives, using them as batteries and power sources in their Darkforce energy generators

Just one of the many ways that the Great Adversary powered their efforts. Her remaining brother Jan had been trapped and tormented inside such a device once. No sentient being, whether flesh or energy in form deserved such agony.

Om waited for what he thought might be a response from her. Then he simply continued with their link in her mind. *The Yattai, the Oden, and the newly encountered Laelor are still holding out hope that they can locate the members of their race that the enemy subjugated and took away. They are captives, but at least they still live. Once those energy beings are found, the Laelor have asked the Alliance for assistance in freeing any survivors.*

As they should, Om. And as their allies, we are going to help them. But for the moment I simply don't know how. This phage nightmare is certainly a caution.

Agreed. The Interdimensions are still new to us, and this enemy threat must be neutralized. No energy being is safe now. The Laelor have been decimated by the phage. So few still survive. The ones in captivity may be the bulk of all that remain. Before all of this, they were extremely numerous. The loss of their ancient wisdom and knowledge is incalculable.

I know, Om. I have seen the few survivors grieving on their own and among one another–just several dozen. They're still in shock. They had no idea that such a disaster could be inflicted upon them. Their entire culture has been shattered overnight.

They estimate that over half of their entire race was obliterated within a matter of days. They still have no idea how many of their kind were actually captured and taken away.

We have no answers yet, Om. Give me peace for a time, so that I might ponder our situation and rest a bit.

Take all the time you need, N. I am always here when you have need of me.

Naero transported, shook her head, and knitted her hands as she sat down alone in her flagship quarters for a bit to consider all of these matters.

Her nightmare still worried her deeply. Was this all part of it coming true, somehow?

At least some hope remained for the poor Laelor. If they could find a way to counter the phage threat, then the Alliance might locate the captives, and find a way to bring them back to freedom. Yet again, no one knew where the enemy was hiding, let alone keeping all of their slaves.

Another important call chimed in. Naero took it.

No rest for the weary or the wicked.

Naero's team and all of the Allied leaders and advisors present were being summoned for one of High Admiral Klyne's emergency brainstorming sessions.

They came together in the large, primary conference chambers within Naero's Flagship, *The Holy Ghost*. They floated adjacent to the other flagship outside. Klyne's flagship *The Kathmandu* had already docked. Other fleets and ships and personages joined them. Those summoned on board quickly filled the many state rooms, including Aunt Sleak, Zalvano, their daughters Anya and Nuvi, and their new born son, Bren.

Naero went to greet them, hug them, and catch up with them all.

Her young cousins worshipped Naero, and clung to her every word.

Their own psyonic gifts were already emerging in powerful ways. The two girls could already transport nearly without limit, across several parsecs and all throughout the Astral Plain, accompanied by Mystic and energy being escorts, from the Oden and the Yattai.

But because of the increased enemy threats, especially lately, the young twins were now restricted from venturing out on their own.

They hated it.

Time passed so swiftly. Within another year, Sleak's twins would begin their own training with the Mystics as prodigies in their own right.

Naero also met briefly with Janner and his wives, Vejja and Calyxo, their son Amashin, and younger daughter Cliovanna. Clio was a sweet looking little thing who already had a full head of long, red gold hair.

Naero could not stop hugging and snuggling her nephews and nieces when they came within range of her arms.

Jan with kids.

That fact still took a lot of getting used to. But he was probably a great dad.

Sleak and Zalvano sent the twins and Bren along with Amashin and little Clio with Jan's wives and their many other guardians.

Then the attendees rejoined the main throng of adults taking their places in the primary conference room.

For several reasons, including him technically still being a Spacer outlaw, as well as an outcast, Baeven now joined such meetings and conferences openly, yet only as an advanced interactive holo.

A holo could not be arrested.

To show her solidarity with her beloved, Jia did so as well, as did any other interested parties who could not be present in person at such briefings, but still wished to attend.

"I think we'll begin," Klyne announced. "Others can continue to join us as they may."

Even as he spoke, Captain Tyber's holo blipped in, and then the holos of Fleet Captains Chaela and Saemar. They all smiled and waved at Naero and many others.

Another holo joined Ty; Alala took a dark holo form that was deep, flat black, with keen blue eyes to represent her presence at the interactive session.

Om sighed. *Sometimes I'm jealous of Alala. I'm going to have to make one of those advanced holos at some point,* Om noted. *But I kind of like being anonymous and doing my work hidden inside of you, N. I'm still your back up, especially if you lose consciousness. Most still do not know that we are merged together in your mind. That's a very good secret for us to maintain.*

I love you too, Om. Now please shut up for a bit so that I can pay attention.

To save time, Klyne buzzed through the current yet still expanding list, introducing everyone present. Then he dove right into the matters at hand, as was his style.

"Well, my friends, as usual we have our work cut out for us. Terrorist attacks continue to ripple throughout the Alpha Quadrant and are becoming a serious threat. Countless lives are being lost and many systems are being destabilized. We know the enemy is behind these coordinated assaults, but they continue to distract us, sap our strength, and limit our ability to effectively manage our resources and support networks. Yet another classic enemy campaign of chaos and confusion."

Several Alliance Naval and Marine officers gave corroborating reports, pinpointing and detailing the enemy's efforts. Then they provided suggestions as to how these attacks might be anticipated, countered, and suppressed.

Over the next hour, all of these matters were debated and evidence was studied again and again–including spy fixer footage from the new Fixer Net. This new network maintained surveillance on most of the main systems, including the new ones on the expansion borders.

"We're still learning about most of these attacks as they happen or after the fact. We need to detect, intercept, and prevent more of them before they take place."

The brainstorming council made many workable suggestions to help counter the enemy's strategies.

"Now we come to our efforts in the Gamma Quadrant," Klyne announced. "Not only is the enemy here preparing for some kind of massive counter attack strategy within the sectors we know about. But in the Unknown Regions, huge swaths of unexplored interstellar space are already said to be ablaze with wide-ranging wars before we even attempt to enter those areas. Trying to explore those Unknown Regions or search for our primary foes will be something akin to suicide."

Jia provided them with an advanced update on some of the conflicts ahead of them in the Gamma Quadrant Unknown Regions, detailing some of the advanced, sentient alien races and teknologies that they would be running up against. Many of them sounded quite formidable.

Naero waited her turn patiently and joined the discussion at the proper time. "In my role as advanced scout, I can continue to go ahead of our first contact, exploration fleets to study and interact with these new races firsthand. My Mystic shapechanging abilities will be perfect for such infiltration and observation needs. I can also try to discover if our primary foes are at work among these new races as well.

"As we know all too well from our own terrible experiences, the enemy delights in possessing, manipulating, and controlling other sentient races without their knowledge from within and behind the scenes. Perhaps I can expose and eliminate their agents, who usually strive to take over beings in key positions of influence and importance. We can't begin that process soon enough."

Many were in agreement with that.

Shalaen, Tarim, and several Oden, Yattai, and Laelor joined the conference at that moment. It took a few minutes for them to filter in.

In one amusing sideline moment, the energy beings had trouble with the concept of sitting down in a physical chair. So they simply bent themselves or somewhat floated above such odd structures.

Chairs and the formality of sitting remained perplexing to many spirit beings.

Klyne drew them all back to the current conversation that Naero had opened up. Suggestions poured in, but most seemed to be in agreement with Naero's proposal and her initial assessment as to what needed to be pursued throughout the Gamma Quadrant.

There were various suggestions as how to exactly proceed with all of that.

Evolving contact with all of these new races of sentients would continue to remain key. Each one represented a group of potential new allies in the fight against the primary foe who kept pulling the strings behind the scenes.

There was no doubt in Naero's mind.

The fact that all of these unexplored Gamma Quadrant regions and sectors had already been set ablaze in ferocious wars meant that the enemy was indeed hard at work spreading Chaos and destruction there–just as they normally did everywhere.

Unfortunately, even the barely explored Interdimensions were also unsafe now.

After the Alliance had sufficiently dealt with the latest developments in the Prime Material Plane, as if on cue, it was time for Klyne to bring up new business.

"Now, let's go over these new threats. First, we need to address this latest major situation in the mysterious Interdimensions–which we only just started to investigate and explore. What do we know thus far and how can we respond? Beyond that, how can we be proactive as we continue forward, and not just get stuck being reactive."

Shalaen commented first. "The Interdimensions–a series of expanding, loosely connected pocket dimensions scattered throughout and connected with our galaxy and dimension–have come under an unprecedented enemy attack. Thus far these devastating attacks have taken the form of this new enemy engineered, energy being disease, which we and our researchers have named the Cosmic phage, or the 'phage,' for short."

Shalaen brought up several viewscreens and streamed vids and test data across them. "Working in conjunction with frontline forces, Intel, and Mystic researchers, we have determined, so far, that the phage is a robust, insidious, and invasive form of a highly contagious and fast evolving Cosmic negative energy life. It has specifically been developed to attack, break down, and consume regular energy beings. Here I will defer to advanced Cosmic scientist Gyna Haddyn of the Oden."

Gyna took over, a widely respected researcher in that advancing field, especially within the last day or so. The mid-sized, hyper-intelligent woman appeared to be fairly old, even for an Oden. Her short, pale golden hair was shot mostly with various shades of green, which only occurred among Khai's green skinned race in advanced age.

Oden were known to live for a handful of centuries.

Her eyes also glowed green from within, a trait that younger Oden could suppress.

Holoscreens filled with data lit up above and behind her. "The phage operates on several levels," she calmly explained, "like a fast acting, weaponized disease agent. In some ways it acts on contact with another energy being, much like a Cosmic germ or bacteria in the Material Plane. Then in other ways it even behaves like a virus. It does whatever it can to penetrate, break down, consume its victims, and then produce more of itself.

"What's more, the phage can be controlled by its masters, even directed and pulled back, in order for them to seize and enslave energy beings who have been stunned and weakened by phage attacks. There have been many reports of such orchestrated attacks. The enemy beats down all resistance, kills as much of the defenders as the enemy wants, and then moves in quickly to seize the remaining energy being captives for their purposes. As I'm reporting now, the Oden have also suffered significant losses among our population from such encounters."

Deneer from the Yattai jumped in. "The Yattai have suffered nearly twenty-percent casualties, counting those destroyed outright and those taken prisoner."

Haemet from the shock-stricken Laelor floated slowly to an erect position. "Our grave losses approach the ninetieth percentile...or higher. This is a disaster of horrific proportions. For our people, there may be no way back from this that we can perceive. For us, this looks like...extinction."

A sad few moments of stunned silence followed.

Klyne looked around at them all. "How do we respond? How do we meet this threat? What can be done?"

Several partial suggestions poured in.

Naero and Om listened intently, and constantly used teknomancy to rapidly sift through the data that still poured in from the ongoing lab research.

N, fixers might be able to be modified to enter the Interdimensions and flood the phage with neutralizing or negating energies. At the very least— in theory—these energies could slow the phage down, or nullify their effects and confuse them. Later on, a full cure might be developed in order to eliminate the phage entirely. This might buy us the time we need to do all of that.

I agree with you in part, Om. But one huge problem remains. Normal matter cannot enter the Interdimensions without being seriously disrupted and degraded. None of our fixers or tek is equipped to handle or operate in such an energized, extreme environment. Basic matter has no spirit form. Only energy beings do, and like the Astral Plane, in the Interdimensional aether, only energy constructs can be fashioned and maintained to be solid.

Ahh...but the fixers are Kexxian tek, N. Of course they would need to be modified so that they were energized properly, in order to function within such strange environments.

That ability is still beyond us at our current tek level, Om.

All the more reasons to keep searching directly within the KDM for a solution to our dilemma.

Naero finally proposed all of that to the group as a possible direction to go in.

"I will focus my search within the KDM for any data that might assist us in this effort. Although I cannot promise quick results, as you well know."

After further discussion, Klyne gave her, Ty, Alala, Baeven, and Jia the go ahead to pursue such a solution. "Until an answer can be found, any remaining energy beings are welcome to find sanctuary among us, or in the Astral Plane under our protection, and that of the Astral/Dimensional Council."

Haemet of the Laelor raised another important point. "What about the many other energy beings that the Alliance races have yet to encounter? Such as the *Nodani*, or the *Elok*? They and countless others could already be at risk or under attack."

"The Oden have had contact with a race of beings known as the Glos," Gyna added.

"The Yattai have had interactions with other energy beings who call themselves the Prill. No doubt there will continue to be many others."

Klyne held out both his hands. "We will deal with these other beings and try to work with them as we encounter them," Klyne said. "We have sent out warnings with our long range probes and fixers, but we can do little else at this time. I'm quite sorry. The Interdimensions are new to us, and we must proceed with caution, as well as develop defensive and offensive capabilities that will function within those realms.

"Keep in mind, much of this information that we are working with has been gathered and studied only within the expanse of one standard day and counting. But as many have clearly stated, time is also of the essence. We need solutions now, not weeks or months from now. We must do all that we can to develop them. Our enemies will never wait."

Alarms suddenly sounded in the conference room.

Many rose up and scanned all about them, checking in with the fixer net.

They also readied various weapons.

"This is not an enemy attack," Klyne said. "Incoming direct reports of vital new developments continue to reach us at this very instant, overriding the system from many regions. These things are taking place as we speak. Watch them up on the screens."

Reports from several hot battlefronts continued to pile in.

The facts were plain to see. Klyne coordinated the feeds and cut the volume on all of the vids and data flooding in. "As we feared, the enemy is counter attacking across many systems in the Gamma Quadrant. But this time, their old inferior fleets are being backed up and supplemented by new advanced warships of both Dakkur and G'lothc design, whose weapons and other systems are supported by Darkforce energies. Much of this enemy hi-tek is beyond anything we have yet to encounter.

"From the assessments of the initial engagements, the presence of these new warships put the enemy fleets strategically on par with our most advanced formations. Even more–ton for ton, these new enemy vessels that our forces have encountered surpass most of our own warships in raw firepower, defensive capabilities, and maneuverability. They have eclipsed us one on one. Henceforth, at current levels, we will need to come at them in three to one or higher ratios in order to take them down."

Aunt Sleak, still a reserve admiral, broke in. "Have we managed to capture any of these new enemy warships to study and reverse engineer them or any of their systems?"

Klyne shook his head. "Regrettably, no. These new vessels can vanish within seconds. In the one instance where a new frigate sized enemy vessel was sufficiently damaged, it exploded without warning, taking two of our ships with it. The resulting blast was so intense that it disintegrated everything completely within a certain radius. There was literally nothing left to study in the aftermath. Obviously, this is some kind of improved enemy failsafe device integrated inside them to prevent us from capturing and studying their new tek."

Now it was Alala who spoke up. "We have analyzed similar enemy systems on their older vessels, protecting the enemy ion cannons. This sounds like a more advanced version of that. How can these initial reports be believed? The power required would be far more than the level of energies any one ship could possibly generate or contain."

Klyne nodded. "We do indeed need answers to these many questions and mysteries. You and Captain Tyber will be sent out periodically, in further such attempts to try to capture one of these new enemy warships. Please be extremely careful. We cannot afford to lose you, or *The Dark Star*."

Baeven even offered to go along. "When the time is right, the Shadow Fox will assist. I suggest we bring in The Mystic Enforcer, and Naero and her brother Janner as well, and Shalaen and Tarim. Even the energy beings can assist us. We must capture some of these new warships to study them and their advanced systems. We can only assume that there will be more of them; we do the same thing. I believe that this matter is so vital, that we need to rush out and assign all of our champions and heavy hitters to this task. It might take all of us combined to capture just one these vessels and keep it from self-destructing."

Klyne smiled a very grim, grudging smile. "For once, I agree with you, Baeven. This is now of primary importance. Work will continue forward on all other matters. In the future, if the enemy unleashes entire fleets of these advanced warships on a large scale against us, it could spell the end for the Alliance. Baeven is correct."

Baeven grinned back smugly. "First time for everything."

Janner insisted on making another point. "We keep hearing about the threat of this new alien armada from the next galaxy over. What if this is it? What if these ships, just starting to trickle in, are in fact the advanced wave of such an armada? Conjecture states it to be strategically limitless in number. The enemy could flood our galaxy with these fleets and completely vanquish us."

Baeven roared with laughter. "Then in that case, I'd say we're all royally fucked."

Nervous laughter followed, some from Naero herself, knowing her brazen uncle. Others remained silent, not finding the grim humor so amusing.

Naero rose up and shattered the section of the nanotable in front of her with one mighty fist. "This is all part and parcel of what we need to discover. There's so much going on. So much that we still need to know and understand, and the enemy is not going to sit back and let us take all the time we need to figure things out. Clearly they are going on the offensive across all fronts. They will do anything they can to overwhelm us."

3

The brainstorming session continued for hours thereafter, especially with the new threat of the phage, and the advanced enemy warships.

The Alliance held an enormous banquet that evening. As was her want, Naero even took a turn at one of the grilling and cooking stations alongside her favorite fleet chefs, Tolen Kothari and Eugene Blooding.

Cooking gave her time to goof off with many of her crew and acquaintances as they came along.

Together they laughed and joked, cooking up a storm for over a standard hour.

Once her shift was over, she went to enjoy her own meal with Aunt Sleak, Jan, and their families. But Jan and his group weren't there yet.

Those who were present relished a great treasure that Naero brought—a big bowl of Eugene's secret black gravy, as mouthwatering and as amazing as ever.

They dipped shuga bread in it until the precious glop was all gone.

The kids fought over cleaning out the bowl.

Naero turned to her Aunt, "So, heading back to the Alpha Quadrant?"

Sleak grimaced and nodded. Even over fifty, like most Spacers, Naero's only and favorite aunt still looked stunning.

"Unfortunately," Sleak said. "with things heating up in the Gamma quadrant, Zal and I simply can't have the kids here. We're jumping out tomorrow. You and the Alliance can take care of business. We have faith in you."

Zalvano sat down with the two of them, and gave Sleak a long lingering kiss. Both of them smiled and laughed for a moment together.

Naero didn't mind in the least. If Khai had been there, he and Naero probably would have already snuck off for a bit and filtered back. The kids were in good hands.

She had always respected and loved dear Zalvano. What a good guy.

There was never a time in her mind when this brave, reliable, and intelligent man had not been a close part of the family. Now that he and Sleak were happily married and had kids together, him becoming Naero's uncle officially had all just been an added bonus.

All three of them quickly discussed what needed to be said about the growing war. Then topics shifted to various trade ventures her aunt and uncle had in the works back home.

Finally they smiled and spoke about the kids, their favorite subject, watching them play.

"Anya and Nuvi have gotten so big," Naero noted.

Both of them were transport savants. Long red hair and big gray eyes. For some reason their hair even pulsed glowing red at times when they teleported. They could blip here and there at will laughing and screaming as they played with their younger brother Bren.

They made him chase them. Bren was exceptionally quick and fast. He was smaller and two years younger than the twins, but that never stopped him.

Even with their transport abilities, Bren was able to tag one of them here and there. He was that fast and clever.

Like his father and Naero, the young boy's particular Maeris strain gave him very similar violet eyes and dark hair which he wore somewhat long, and an energy level that just didn't quit. Bren kept going until his tanks ran dry and he merely passed out and slept. The young boy did that everywhere.

Usually when he finally dropped, the family just let him snooze.

When he woke up, however, look out! Ben wanted to eat and could fuel up and pack it away almost like an adult Spacer. That kid could eat.

While the grownups had been talking, the girls or Bren would pop in or race over for a hug or a kiss from mom or dad, or even from Naero, their only, most famous, and adored blood aunt.

Any chance Naero had to wrap her arms around them and kiss them was just like being with her own kids. She loved them all so dearly and never wanted to let them go at times. But she had to.

Jan burst in, late as usual with his two wives and their kids, much to the joy of all present.

And as usual, her brazen younger brother and his luscious spouses were clearly adjusting their slinky nanoclothing on the go. They were always late to such dinners and parties, usually for the obvious reason.

Did those love junkies ever let their beds get cold?

Naero rolled her eyes at her younger brother. Haisha, Jan. Give it a rest.

Yet the three of them looked exceptionally happy—and clearly well-sated.

Naero suddenly missed Khai very urgently in that instant, and could only roll her eyes at her goofy brother once again and sigh.

For once Jan's first wife Vejjah Fae was not pregnant. At least she wasn't showing. Her long, white gold hair and dazzling blue eyes always turned heads, not to mention her knock out figure.

But even she could not ever be as exotic as Jan's second wife, Calyxo, princess of the Mahri feline race. Her statuesque, sinewy body and tail were all magnificently striped with glistening fur, that did little to hide her sleek and supple athletic, near human female body.

She even had whiskers and feline ears.

She only wore patches of cloth that might not even be considered a bathing suit among humans, but her luxurious fur covered most of her charms.

The two wives were not lovers with each other. From what they had told Naero, going into much more intimate detail that she ever wished to know. Jan took turns wearing them out.

But only Vejjah could bear the children they all wanted.

Naero had once offered to adjust things using biomancy so that Calyxo could give birth to Jan's offspring as well. The Mahri princess thought long and hard about it, but at last stated that she was quite happy with the arrangement and decided to let it stand.

Thanks, but no thanks.

Calyxo had no trouble loving the kids as her own, and the children already thought having two moms to love them was a huge bonus. She was also more active with the Mystics than Vejjah.

Once the kids were grown up, she had already remarked that she very much intended to become a Mystic Master, and help train the next generations of Mystics from among what she hoped would be all of the Alliance races. Including her own people.

Their son, Amashin, named after Naero and Jan's grandfather, quickly joined Bren chasing the twins as the boys teamed up.

Their daughter, Cliovanna had a mix of Jan's dark hair and Vejjah's bluer-than-blue eyes. She was no longer an infant, but still toddled around, unable to keep up with the older kids.

Amashi and Clio also had to have their share of affection from the other family members. Spacer kids needed a lot of attention.

The evening waxed later, and the kids were sent off to sleep with even more flurries of affection and fanfare.

Delicious Spacer poteen was afterwards brought out and liberally distributed among the adults. It took a great deal to get a Spacer metabolism even tipsy, let alone drunk. Yet with persistence, inebriation was still possible.

Even if it did not last very long.

Naero helped polish off a few delicious bottles of the stuff among her family and old friends with hardly a buzz, yet most of the time she preferred to sip Jett, her old lix standby.

With her in the Gamma Quadrant, Naero missed Khai, Shetharra, and the kids, and their whole family group back in the Alpha Quadrant.

Of course Khai and the Mystics had their hands full back there with rampant enemy terrorism, protecting the exploration expansion, and trying to hide and protect his father's people, the Oden.

The latest reports stated that they were being attacked by the enemy phage as well, in parts of the Interdimensions adjacent to them there. Yet many of those energy beings had already retreated, abandoning their known and secret homes, pocket dimensions, and alternate realities.

At least some of the warnings and protocols worked in time. Any place the phage appeared in had to be evacuated and sealed off.

The Oden had never been as numerous within the Interdimensions as were the Yattai and the Laelor. Many Oden sought sanctuary among the Mystic Homeworlds, but at present, there was no guaranteed safe place for anyone.

Their primary enemies still had the potential to strike anywhere at will, as they had repeatedly demonstrated.

Om distracted Naero at one point before she was about to retire for the night under a heavy guard of Shai and hi-tek spyfixers. *Naero? Are you going to make use of that Kexxian transfer technique we've been*

22

practicing from our meditations and explorations within the KDM? A quick visit back in the Alpha Quadrant could help with the deep homesickness and loneliness you've been experiencing.

Even in the dark, Naero closed her eyes and draped her right forearm across her face. Am I that bad, Om?

Well, to be honest, you have been sighing and acting somewhat melancholy when you are away from other persons. But you have been more or less successful at hiding that from the others, if that makes you feel any better.

Naero grinned sadly and shook her head, dropping her arm down. Nothing gets past you, does it, Om?

I do have the advantage of being merged with you inside your mind. As your people like to say, you are somewhat of an open book.

She chuckled half-heartedly. Seeing Jan and Aunt Sleak and their families helped somewhat. That was nice. But then on the other hand, seeing them made me miss Khai and the kids all the more. Holos and vidscreens only go so far.

So, do you want to give that splitting technique a shot? We did go to the trouble of sending a small portion of your true self back to the Alpha Quadrant to stay near your kids.

All right, Om. Let's try it out. But Ty says he's working on some kind of different tek altogether that will be even better. Anyone will be able to use it.

Yes, yes, but the last time I checked with him, all of that new synthezoid construct stuff wasn't quite ready yet. What we have available to us now will need to suffice.

They made preparations for implementing this new Kexxian psyonic ability.

With the splitting technique, Naero kept a small portion of her true-self back in hibernation, in a cold sleep pod that she and Om could operate remotely through psyonics and their private portion of the medical fixer net.

This wasn't a replicant, which try as she might and as formidable as they were, even her latest reps always fell short of her true self and her most powerful abilities. Nor could replicants maintain a stable, psyonic mindlink connected directly to her over such huge distances.

This fragment of her true self could maintain such a link, only because it was in fact a true part of her actual self…it was her, just far removed by distance.

Yet as she and Om quickly learned, the further away she was from her fragmented self, the higher the strain and the quicker Naero exhausted herself. Great distances could be extremely taxing in a very short time.

To compensate for this, the fragment was normally kept dormant in a secret, heavily guarded life support, cold storage pod. Naero could go into a slightly modified version of an Astral Plane trance or deep meditation sleep, transfer her mind fully into the fragment for a short while, and then remotely wake her fragmented self up and interact with others while far away.

When the strain of the link grew too much, the fragmented self would return to the stasis pod, and become dormant again. Naero's mind would return to her entranced, primary form and wake up, with a need to rest further and regenerate after that.

Om followed her line of thought all along. *That's how it's supposed to work, according to the Kexxian theories, but we've yet to make a real attempt, over such long distances.*

No time like the present, Om. If it doesn't work, it doesn't work.

Hey, N. Like I mentioned before, I really want to set up and try out one of those advanced, interactive holos. Like the kind Alala and the others have been testing out. It might be nice to slink around and check some things out on my own.

Naero smirked. Om could always see her facial features through the cloaked and phazed spyfixernet that was constantly around them. Tell me true, Om. Is there some kind of budding thing between you and Alala?

I do find myself very drawn to her in many ways. We find each other incredibly intriguing. You have to admit, N. Alala and I do have many things in common. We are both highly advanced AI sentient beings. The only two of our kind known to exist, who developed and emerged entirely out of a fusion of machine and interactive advanced sentient interaction and mind growth. Both of us are unique.

Not to worry, Om. When and where possible, we'll arrange some genuine dating time for you and Alala, with your holos. But aren't the open links even more…intimate?

They can be, and we have shared huge amounts of introspection and data on many occasions. A sort of getting to know each other, you might say. Yet then again, data links can in a sense also be too intimate and direct from the right perspective. In a way, becoming actual separate entities with separate forms on the Prime Material Plane could be much more enjoyable for the both of us in a variety of ways.

You're starting to worry me Om. You and Alala are forming a real time, real world relationship? Affection and all of that? What reference would your machine-based love follow? Am I going to lose you to another gal?

Now it was Om's turn to giggle a bit internally. *That is a possibility one day, Naero. And you have no one but yourself to blame. My emotional development and advanced sentient thought and behavior patterns are largely based upon the example of your mind and emotions.*

Naero chose not to remind him that so were Alala's.

And I've had plenty of first hand, unavoidable and observational knowledge of your intense emotions and feelings for Khai. Not to mention your, shall I delicately say mutual, extremely vigorous, and enjoyable physical interactions and exertions?

Why shoot, Om. You're going to make me blush. But seriously, when you love someone, that all kind of goes with it. You go all out for each other. You enjoy being together in every way possible.

Well then, if Alala and I ever do take up physical forms, then it is at least possible that we might have similar feelings for each other, and experiment with real physical pleasures. It would only be a logical progression.

I don't know about that, Om. Perhaps if you find a physical way to procreate, you might even have offspring. Then you wouldn't have to construct kids like the Mechans and other machine peoples. But come on. We're not at those crossroads yet, so let's stay on task here.

Another time then. My consciousness will stay here with our primary form to protect and monitor it, while your mind travels to link up with your fragmented self that we took the time to ship back to the Alpha Quadrant.

Thanks, Om. I always know that I can count on you. Let me ready myself. It will take several minutes to prepare for and make the mind transfer attempt.

Naero settled in and eased her mind into the trance.

It did take longer than she thought, but finally she felt her consciousness swept away.

How odd that an enhanced mind could make a journey across half a galaxy faster and easier than their current, most advanced tek.

Weird, she seemed to sense shadows and echoes of something all around her as her mind sped across the vastness of SpaceTime. What was it she was detecting?

It felt somewhat like the SpaceTime Nexus, yet different.

Ugh! Just as abrupt, she experienced a psyonic, jarring impact as she slammed into the bodily extents of the part of herself left back in the Alpha Quadrant.

When she fluttered her eyes open, her consciousness and strength returned and, after some quick biomancy, she sat up immediately on the medbed in her alternate body.

Top Spacer researcher and physician Lellian Wang smiled and greeted her, the head of the transfer and cold sleep team on the Intel medship *The Angel Wing*. "Greetings, Admiral Maeris. I received your notification. I trust the transfer went well? Your vital signs are all as crazy as normal …for you that is."

Lell was a Clan Chang Spacer in her seventies, keen shining black eyes to match her straight dark hair. Spacers did not show signs of advanced aging until they reached around one twenty.

"Thanks, Lell. I feel great. I brought some new tek and research with me that you and your staff will want to see. How are my kids doing?"

The older woman laughed. "As fit and as rambunctious as ever. Sharrah and her team have them well in hand. Do they know you're coming?"

Naero grinned. "Not the kids. I wasn't completely certain the transfer would work. So it's a surprise."

"You'd better go see them, then."

"Thanks, Doc. That's right where I'm heading next."

The Intel Marine guards at the bulkhead snapped to attention and saluted as Naero slipped past them, giving them a salute.

The Angel Wing was a high security medship attached to Intel Fleet 71, one of the fleets under her command.

One of their primary missions included protecting Naero and Khai's children, especially Shetharra, who was seen as a great hope for the future. Conceived within a star by her mother and father, Shetharra showed signs of wisdom and power far beyond her age. Beyond anything yet known, even when compared to her amazing parents.

Yet Naero also knew very well that greater powers often came with larger problems and concerns regarding the development and control of such abilities.

At one point in the past year, Shetharra had absently injured a playmate very severely, almost without thinking.

She hadn't meant to be careless. She was just impossibly strong, and still very young.

But in truth, she had nearly killed the young boy, a very close friend. She hadn't meant to do so; she was that powerful, and growing stronger with each day.

Almost killing a beloved friend was a serious lesson for one still so very young.

Of course she had healed her friend and even made him stronger without a thought. She did so before anyone else could act. The boy, Aevin James, would have died within seconds if Shetharra had not regenerated him.

Afterwards, the boy was just fine.

Shetharra, however, was not. She felt horrible and hid herself away for days, terrified and grief stricken, very frightened by what she had done—by pure accident.

Naero and Khai took turns holding her in their arms and letting her cry.

Shetharra worried that she couldn't control her powers.

That they would turn her into a monster.

A little eight, nearly nine year old girl worried that she was a monster.

What if it happened again?

What if she got angry at someone and lashed out? What if she actually killed someone, a friend, or worse—a family member?

Naero recalled trying to comfort her oldest child, cradling her in her arms and rocking her gently.

"We can work on all of that, Shetharra," Naero told her. "If you want to practice controlling your emotions and learning to deal with anger, you can't just keep it bottled up inside. That just makes it worse. You have to deal with it. If you want to get angry at someone, your father and I can help you work through your emotions in a safe place. You can't hurt either of us."

She looked up at Khai, who cocked one eyebrow.

"Then there are various forms of meditation, some of which you already know. Or you could spend some time with the gentle Tua again. There are the Yattai. And the Oden, your father's people, know many ways of controlling their powers. You can learn from all of them.

Shetharra blurted out her fears, rambling on.

If she did lose control of her powers, everyone would fear and hate her very quickly, and eventually try to destroy her for the sake of everyone else.

Naero fully understood the situation, and explained her own situation as best as she could to her oldest daughter.

Shetharra at last found hope in that.

If her beautiful, loving mother could control such powers, then there was still hope that she could learn to control hers.

Naero had other concerns that she kept to herself and Khai for the time being.

This could just be the tip of the iceberg.

Would Shetharra develop her own Darkbeast, the same way that Naero and Baeven had done? Would she be able to control it, or would it take control of her? That alone was a terrifying consideration.

Or like Naero's younger brother Janner, would the child be spared such an ordeal?

Some of the Mystics surmised that Janner was spared the Darkbeast, because those leanings went into his insane, twin brother Danner, now deceased. Yet Naero knew for a fact that other Mystics never had to deal directly with their own dark side, at least not one that openly manifested itself in such a terrible way.

In fact, the Darkbeast condition seemed quite rare.

And that held true among the ancient Kexx as well. Even among the mighty, godlike Dreamers, who could control matter and energy at will, they had similar experiences. Some learned to control their Darkbeasts. Others had enough of the harmony within them to avoid such a fate entirely.

Naero moved through her medship at will, passed more guards and check points, and finally strode into the nursery with a huge grin on her face and the start of tears in her eyes.

Her beloved children were beyond the next bulkhead door.

She took a breath and stepped through.

Heads popped up, and her kids recognized her with explosions of glee right away. "Momma. Momma's back!"

Shetharra was still eight, going on nine, a radiant little angel with her hair of white flame, flame that never burned or harmed anyone. Naero and Khai loved all of their kids dearly, yet the first child was always special. They had their favorites, like all parents did, which they tried to keep to themselves.

The twins, Daeyen and Kathron were three going on four and quite a handful. The little trouble makers were everywhere and into everything, and then on to the next adventure, often squealing with laughter along the way.

But as most parents and caregivers rapidly learned, kids were most dangerous when quiet. Staff were constantly tracking Dae and Kath down to find out what mayhem they were causing next.

Yet one factor saved the universe from the twins. They revered Naero, Khai, Sharrah, and their oldest sister with an almost fearful respect and adoration. If any of them said a word to the twins, or even shot them a glance, the twins would scramble to obey and put things in order.

Naero smiled her half smile, hoping that all of that would last for a few years longer.

Allantar was two by then, going on three. He was usually quite happy playing on his own, constructing fascinating patterns and structures with his holographic building tools and units. Sometimes Shetharra would sit and work with him for hours, along with her three energy being tutors, marveling at the infant's savant like gift.

They said the intricate patterns often mirrored high level math, sentient synaptic patterns, Cosmic energy fields, and flows within the Astral Plane and the Interdimensions.

As for herself, Naero even saw the patterns of majestic Kexxian music at times. Only she could see it. Theoretical researchers marveled at the unique structures and were often amazed and baffled by them. All of little Allantar's play sessions we're now recorded and sent abroad for in depth study by visionaries in many advance fields of thought and study.

They had to force little Allan to go out and play with the other kids and do other things. His parents wanted all of their children to experience the phases of life as they grew, to be exposed to new things, and continue to have a well-rounded life and education.

After the greetings and the explosions of hugging and kissing upon arrival, Naero took the next three hours to sit down with her kids and give all of them time to snuggle and catch up, and tell her about their lives and experiences. Then Naero took a quiet nap with them all, in her expanded, round nanobed in her quarters. All of the little Clan Maeris and Williams kids snuggled in and were at peace, tucked in and snuggled around their mom.

The staff stated that they could not gaze upon them all together like that without bawling their eyes out. The sight was so beautiful.

And hour or so later, Naero contained her own tears and laughter, and transported out of her quarters to one of the galleys as she had arranged, letting her little ones sleep.

She immediately began to prepare a meal for her family, something she loved to do and rarely got the chance.

For some reason she keenly missed her mental companion Om in her mind at that instant.

A minute later, Shetharra popped in next to her mom with the girl's three energy being tutors floating protectively around her in their tiny reduced forms. Yet Naero knew that size was relative for such beings. They could easily make themselves as huge as a mountain in and instant.

They referred to themselves as 'the Trio.'

Eight-year-old Shetharra hugged her mother around Naero's slim waist and tucked her radiant head under one arm. Naero loved the sweet child so much she nearly went to pieces, and stooped slightly to enfold her arms around she who would always be her little duck.

Naero suddenly felt a twinge of warning as she held her oldest girl close. She quickly expanded her awareness to check around them.

Nothing threatening seemed to be amiss.

Shetharra smiled wide. "I'm so glad to see you, Momma. Can I help?"

"Sure you can, my little duck. Can you stir this for me?"

"I sure can."

Naero bobbed her head around the Trio. Ziiris was from the Yattai, apparently a cousin of Shalaen's. She or it was a small floating orange and yellow humanoid figure, much as if she had been made of molten metal, yet much like Shetharra's hair, she gave off no heat to the touch.

Not that their charge would have been affected; she was already quite immune to normal heat, cold, and pressure concerns. She was immune even to the intense vacuum of space.

Ziiris whispered something to Shetharra and the Spacer child giggled, stroked, and caressed Ziiris against her cheek.

Naero sautéed the Luranian fowl meat and veggies in a hot pan. The Berollian blue thread rolls would be done in a few minutes.

Yudy was an Oden child only a few years older than Shetharra, who had achieved her energy being form. She bobbed around as a small green orb and pulsed with bright energy when she spoke or used telepathy.

The last of the Trio was Seviya, from the Laelor. Her reduced form was a reddish-pink collection of small glowing bubbles that zipped around.

These energy beings doted on Shetharra, simply drawn to her. Even though they were sent to counsel and teach the Spacer child, they claimed openly that they were learning just as much if not more from their charge in response.

Most everyone who came in contact with Shetharra was amazed by her.

Yet there were always a few who did not understand or feared her. And because of that, some did not like her. But she had to deal with the fear and dislike of others as well.

Naero still worried intensely, and not just as a mother.

That much power in any person was always dangerous.

So much could go wrong, as she well knew.

That was just one of the reasons why Shetharra was being watched, tutored, and studied so closely.

Naero and Khai still wanted to give their oldest girl the chance at having a real childhood, to grow up loved, and given every opportunity to learn and develop as a normal person.

The meal was nearly ready to serve. Naero sent a telepathic signal to Sharrah and the staff to bring the other kids to the mess hall.

Then she checked in with the Trio using a mind link. Everything with Shetharra going well?

Yudy was ecstatic, pulsing her joy with intense flashes of green light. *The light child is a joy to work with. Very advanced and centered for a fledgling energy being so young.*

Seviya concurred. *Light child is well aware of her energies and automatically makes certain that she suppresses her abilities and does no harm to carbon-based flesh people.*

Ziiris hesitated. *Things are going well...for now. But it is my assessment that her powers are still expanding exponentially. Even faster than before. This could very well lead to several major difficulties, and potential dangerous calamities. If Shetharra loses control even slightly, she could bring great harms to others around her. That is a definite risk.*

I am aware of all of that, Naero told them. Let's keep going with the plan at hand, to monitor those potential risks, and keep them under control. That is really what you three are here for, isn't it? That is your true job.

We concur, the Trio said in unison.

The meal went very well, although a bit messy. Thank goodness for self-cleaning nanotables. Little kids liked to spill things and make a mess. Naero and the staff ran herd on the toddlers and baby. Shetharra also helped wrangle her sister and brothers, laughing along with the rest of them at the various sloppy antics going on.

When enough of the delicious meal was actually deposited in the kids instead of all over them and around their proximity, the meal ended. No small task. They then cleaned up the lot and took the kids to a spiral chamber during kiddie time.

Floating around in Zero-g was great relaxing fun for everyone. Shetharra and the Trio enjoyed it immensely. They zipped and bounced around at will.

That night, Naero and her kids slept together again in the big round, expanded nanobed that took up almost all of the floor of her private quarters on the medship.

She would need to say her goodbyes and get back to the Gamma Quadrant the next day, reversing the mind splitting transfer process.

But she awoke at four bells.

Something was definitely wrong.

The Trio appeared.

Shetharra was tossing and turning and moaning slightly. Perhaps it was just a bad dream.

Naero had been plagued by bad dreams and nightmares almost all of her life.

To be safe, Naero transferred her oldest and the Trio to a medical bay, placing her daughter on a medbed that came online. Naero used biomancy and teknomancy to hurriedly make the necessary buffering and expansion adjustments to become compatible with Shetharra's special needs.

"I had a bad dream. My head hurts, Momma. I can't stop it. Make it stop, please."

Naero turned to the Trio, who already swooped down and focused their abilities on Shetharra's skull. Perhaps it was nothing major. Naero had also had powerful headaches in her tweens. But not this young, before puberty.

Seviya said to Naero. "There, that should ease the pain."

Shetharra already drifted off into a deep sleep.

Yudy added, "Perhaps this was nothing more than a sudden Cosmic power spike. They do occur randomly throughout the universe. The light child might be very susceptible to them."

Ziiris noted, "Yet it took nearly all of our considerable energies to reduce the intense pain reactions such a spike triggered. Will it happen again, and will we be able to sooth away the agony next time?"

No one offered an answer.

Naero took her daughter into her arms. Shetharra's head slumped, and her hair and body were soaked with sweat. She had never been like that before.

Ziiris continued. "The limitations of her physical form leave her vulnerable to fatigue. Energy forms do not experience such things in the same way or to the same degree."

"Look, we've been over this. She's going to keep her physical form and remain a dual form being," Naero insisted. "If she gets too used to an energy being form now, she'll never go back to having a physical form. Her regular, flesh and blood body is going to remain her normal, preferred form."

"For how long?" Yudy asked, flashing bright green. "What if she chooses not to?"

"What if her powers make the choice for her?" Seviya added.

"When she comes of age, that choice will become hers," Naero stated flatly. "But not until that time."

Shetharra seemed fine the next day. Naero said goodbye to family and friends, and then returned to Lell's deep sleep chamber to reverse the mind transfer splitting process.

Now that she understood the process fully, it would go much easier next time.

Despite lots of reassuring, Naero still had many other grave concerns.
What if Shetharra did manifest a Darkbeast of her very own?
How could they even begin to control such a thing in one so young?
And what had really happened to Shetharra?
To Naero, it almost seemed like some kind of direct Cosmic attack.

4

Naero returned to her primary body, right in the middle of an all-out fleet battle in the Gamma Quadrant from what she could sense.

She recovered as quickly as she could manage, putting all of her efforts into regenerating and getting over the mind transfer disorientation and fatigue.

Om rejoined her and caught her up while the blasts, explosions, and rocking concussions from the frontline battle made even the largest ships such as hers shudder and shake

Good thing you're back, N. For the last three hours, the enemy has been attacking in force along most of our lines. They're coming right at us and standing toe-to-to, as you Spacers say, against our most powerful warships.

Their new shields are much stronger, and each of their fleets is now being supported by one or more of the new alien warships, armed with new weapons as good as or better than our own. Just as we feared.

Let's transport to the bridge, Om.

They flashed there in the next instant.

But the first thing Naero noticed when she returned to her bridge wasn't the hot battle going on or the 3-D holographic display screens and their data flows.

Naero-Kali, her latest, most advanced rep conducted the battle with calm, swift efficiency.

But Haisha!

What alarmed Naero more was that several of the crew on the bridge appeared to be infected with what at first glance appeared to be some kind of alien parasites.

And she seemed to be the only one who could see or detect the presence of these growing invaders.

She needed to be cautious.

Everyone else seemed oblivious to the things—even Naero-Kali.

It must be the broad range of vision and Cosmic awareness gifted to Naero through her third eye.

Just from her visuals, in the Cosmic spectrum of energies that automatically flowed through her enhanced sight and awareness, Naero cautiously studied them for a time.

All the while, Om raced with her personal fixer cloud with teknomancy in an attempt to modify them to pick up on these extreme energy levels and to be able to detect these scary things, whatever they were.

For the present, she could not give it away that she could see them.

From their reactions, some of them could see her through their hosts.

They're busy collecting data and intel on us, as well, N.

I'm also trying to trace their data streams, see where they are going, and if I can block or intercept them without giving us away.

Good job, Om. I want Klyne and Intel notified the minute we have a way to detect, track, expel, capture, and destroy them. I don't want to hurt the hosts if possible. They seem to be merely observing us for right now. But I sense that they can take control of the host at any time.

They were patches of what appeared to be sticky splatters of dark and light glowing energy being matter. Naero sensed both sentience and force of will, and the Darkforce was somehow involved, so she guessed once more that they were from the enemy.

Haisha, Om. They're like an advanced form of the phage.

Second, third, or fourth generation, I'd say, N. Bred specifically for mind control, I'd guess.

She used a trickle of biomancy, teknomancy, and psyonics, the same combination that had to be used to study other energy beings to explore these infiltrators. But what were these weird things? What was their function and purpose?

It was clear that these nasty things were attempting to feed off of and grow around and within their hosts. Yet because of their stealth and their energy being nature, they could clearly mask their activities from the host completely.

Some of the things were still very small. Some of them had almost covered their hosts entirely, and there were many stages in between. Even the gestation times seemed to vary

Haisha. Next Naero witnessed a smaller one detach itself from a large mass and leap a meter from the original host onto another Spacer who had not bet infested before.

Then she felt a strange sensation.

She could hardly sense it, but one of the lesser things was on the small of her back, doing all that it could to remain undetected.

It slipped up her spine, sending out tendrils of energy being nerve connectors as it did, heading up toward the back of her neck and the base of the skull.

That must be the key. Everyone infected with the things had a blotch of it at the base of the skull.

Clearly these things—these wraiths—were preparing for some kind of mass mind control attack, most likely at a crucial moment in the battle. But apparently they had to spread all over the entire body before they could attempt to take full control.

She glanced back at Naero-Kali, still running the battle. Kali wasn't infected yet, alone on her command platform, but it was likely only a matter of time.

Naero had to act, but how? The infestation was spreading rapidly. These things acted like a virus, or a kind of bacteria. Yet they had a will of their own, as well as the capability to communicate and coordinate their actions collectively with outside forces.

She was watching a complex strategy at work.

Through biomancy they definitely reminded her of a variant of the phage. But these sentient wraiths were even more highly advanced and much more complex in a multitude of ways, clearly designed to take over their hosts, physical sentients, or energy beings. Yet they operated in a far more sophisticated way than the enemy possession wyrms ever could. Those vile things eventually burned out their victims' physical bodies.

These advanced wraiths would not. They could feed off of and control their hosts for as long as the hosts lived, and take over more hosts as they went along.

This was an extremely sophisticated form of psyonic stealth attack.

And from their psyonic readings, they were fully active in their minds and higher intelligence, able to pursue complex goals and activities.

Perfect for taking over other sentients and key personnel.

Om, anything we can use yet? We have one on us. Don't let it link with or take over our mind.

I know what it's doing. Hmmm...almost there. Switch to these energy scan filters I'm bio-teknomancing to you. Then you can see its energy flows directly.

Naero switched over to an even more enhanced version of her sight. It allowed her to study her wraith thing up close, from several vantage points bounced off of the fixers.

She could even watch the thing and its intricate Cosmic energy flows in real time. This was definitely G'lothc-based Darkforce energy being biotek at work.

Her own wraith reached the base of her skull.

That was creepy.

It didn't attempt to invade her mind and brain right away. Once there, it cautiously settled in to slowly draw energies from her at such a slow rate as to be nearly undetectable.

Nearly. The enemy wraith was growing stronger every second, and spreading slowly but consistently from that point to cover her entire body. She winced slightly as it lined the inside of her mouth and nose.

Om and the fixers finally had the answers they needed; his reaction was priceless.

Holy shit, Naero! Do you see exactly what these damn things are?

Indeed. I'm beginning to figure them out, Om.

The fixers calculate that forty-one percent of the crew has now been infected.

As long as the thing did not attempt to take control of her, Naero, Om, and the fixers continued to study her enemy wraith and the others on the bridge while the fleet battles continued.

At first she attempted to retreat somewhere more secure, like a medical bay, where they could stun, capture, and then isolate the wraith spreading over her. She and Om prepared to fight the thing off when and if it did attempt to take her over.

Then she quickly realized that that would not work.

Om, the other wraiths are also linked to each other. They will know when I attack mine, wherever I do so.

Then I suggest we utilize an advanced Kexxian protocol through me, designed to counteract such an enemy attack as these wraith things over a wide area.

37

They prepared their counterattack against the wraiths, before the creepy things could spread throughout the flagship and take over the entire crew.

Naero studied Om's strategy, and continued to monitor the energy being composition of the wraith on her. She was right. It was a highly advanced form of energy being life, related to the phage, which was simple in nature by comparison.

Then she proved their initial hypothesis. The phage and the wraiths were in fact somewhat like replicants—proto versions, less involved versions of the original G'lothc themselves.

According to the confusing genetic evidence, the phage and the wraiths were actually lesser G'lothc, warped to perform these functions.

The G'lothc themselves were biotek weapons—any kind of weapons that they could twist themselves into, on many different levels.

Destroyers.

Here we go!

Om launched his Kexxian based counterattack, frying and exterminating the vile wraiths in a fraction of a second throughout the entire ship.

On an energy being level, there would be a bright flash.

He and the fixers used clever bursts of energy being level flows to disrupt and blast away the wraiths off their oblivious hosts.

Naero did her part. She managed to keep some several dozen of the things frozen, captured in Cosmic energy orbs of frozen Chaos ice for further study

This included the specimen that had been on herself.

To make matters worse, however, the flagship was not the only Alliance warship that was in the process of being infested by the enemy mind control wraiths.

Naero and Om quickly use the fixer nebulae, modified by Om, to bathe the Alliance fleets in Interdimensional energies that first stunned, and then broke down and dissolve the enemy wraiths.

They did this at the same time that they notified Klyne and Intel, and asked for permission to cleanse the Alliance fleets of the infestation.

The response from Klyne shot back, albeit too late. "Proceed immediately."

"Thank you…" Naero replied.

It took four more standard hours for a break in the fighting to take place.

As it turned out, over thirty percent of the Alliance fleets had been infested by the wraiths and expanding.

Immediate warnings flashed out to all of the Alliance forces in the Gamma Quadrant, and were also tight beamed through wyrmholes back to the Alpha Quadrant.

Thankfully it was soon revealed that the enemy wraiths had infested fleets mostly in the Gamma Quadrant, especially near the front lines. Yet some of the wraiths had also made it back to the Alpha Quadrant as well and had started to spread, most notably among Fleet 71, first of all.

Naero pinched her lips together and her eyes narrowed to slits.

The enemy never gave up. It always kept coming at her and her family, in every way they could.

Since the wraiths could also take over other energy beings, further warnings also went to Shalaen and all of their allies from the Interdimensions. They were both warned and sent several different strategies to fight the enemy wraiths on their terms.

Yet another major threat remained. Naero and the Alliance leaders who were still available in that region convened another meeting.

Captain Tyber and Alala were there, presenting their findings that they had made working in conjunction with Jia and Baeven.

Backed by the new enemy warships, the enemy fleets fought on an even level with the Alliance fleets now, and even had a bit of an edge, one on one. The Alliance would need to stack up additional fleets and raw numbers to assure victory in any battle.

Ty combined his research with that of Alala and Jia. They came to the conclusion that the Alliance must make badly need advancements in the structural composition of its warships. There was no time to wait, and they must take the same path that the enemy had done with their new vessels.

This new super alloy in warship armor and construction was a breakthrough and a new game changer. It was the advanced alloy that the Driathans and the Kexx had long referred to as *Ultrium*.

"Ultrium," Tyber explained, "the very same living, self-healing, nearly indestructible super metal that Jia and her people were fashioned from. It has unlimited applications; it can be infused with various energies and purposes. But it also takes staggering amounts of Cosmic energy to produce and manufacture the raw alloy, in quantities vast enough to construct starships, warships, and advanced ship systems."

Jia spoke and told them stories from a past long forgotten. How the mightiest among the godlike Drians and Kexx had used huge, superhot stars as furnaces to produce their Ultrium. They shaped the super metal into the forms, vessels, and miraculous tek that they needed by sheer force of will, imagination, and secret techniques yet unknown.

Aided by the Song of Making, one of the most powerful tools of abject matter and energy Creation that the Kexx and especially the Dreamers could use, Ultrium was utilized to its limits. The Kexx manipulated unthinkable quantities at will and with great ease.

This was the point where tek became equal to what could only be comprehended as magic.

With the naked power of pure Creation at their command, the Kexx at last formed the Starkillers, entire warships larger than the largest planet possible, comprised of some unknown material that was said to be beyond even Ultrium, and filled with the hyperdense, packed Cosmic energies of the universe.

Against such miracle weapons, the numberless G'lothc armadas were slowly obliterated from one stricken galaxy to the next.

It was said the when they had at last met their match, the once invincible G'lothc were first taught the meaning of terror by the fearsome might of the radiant Starkillers that ripped through them.

The mightiest of all warships that had ever been known to exist became indestructible juggernauts, unstoppable titans that struck fear in the dark cores of even the G'lothc leadership. For once they appeared in battle, they spelled out inevitable defeat, no matter how the Great Adversary tried to stop them.

In the last battles with the great foe, entire fleets and massed waves of Starkillers blasted their way into the G'lothc Galaxy to lay utter ruin to that evil species, responsible for the deaths of so many that their numbers shall never be known. True to their name, the Starkiller fleets wiped out even the enemy's fearsome, diseased Darkforce Stars which they had contaminated on purpose.

During the course of that long and terrible conflict over the course of millions of standard years, both sides had utilized many different kinds of Ultrium, for countless purposes. Ultrium was a valuable and ready servant, an energized, living metal on a Cosmic level, capable of many uses, for good or ill.

"Driathans are made of one of the most advanced forms of Ultrium ever known to exist, the truly living metal. And there are secrets of our creation that I cannot reveal, and many that I still do not know. But I will work with my dear friends Captain Tyber, Naero, and Alala to do all that we can to produce Ultrium for the Alliance to use in this war. For if we lose, then our universe is doomed and all will eventually perish."

When Jia ended her tale, Tyber spoke once more. "Thus the enemy has clearly regained the use of such advanced materials in their manufacturing on a wide scale," Tyber concluded. "If we are to have any hope of surviving or attaining victory from this point on, the Alliance needs to switch over and develop the wide spread production and the military use of Ultrium as soon as possible."

Naero and Om had already thoroughly studied what was known about the many versatile properties of Ultrium, both with Jia and the Driathan blank.

She was glad that Jia had budged. Naero had closely protected their findings and kept them secret, guarding that knowledge vehemently upon Jia's private wishes and personal request.

In fact it, the topic of Ultrium remained a sticking point between Klyne, Intel, and Naero. Both she and Jia had adamantly refused to turn the Driathan blank over to Spacer Intel and the Mystics. They had no rightful claim to it.

Naero could not take that chance, or do anything that might bring exposure and destruction down upon Jia and her hidden people.

Besides all of that, Naero still hoped that she and Jia could eventually find a way to unlock the secrets of the blank, and implant and merge the soul of her lost friend Zhen within it.

The same soul that Naero protected within herself, keeping it dormant and safe.

They had not unlocked those vital secrets yet, but even Jia admitted that the blank was somehow attuned to Naero in a way that even the Driathan Queen could not comprehend. Thus their experiments and attempts continued.

Otherwise, Jia would have simply kept the blank hidden away with her and Baeven. Thankfully, as long as no one used any Ultrium knowledge against the Driathans, Jia would continue to cooperate.

Naero understood the basic composition of Ultrium with her teknomancy and biomancy. Actually, most did not know it, but Ultrium was the closest substance to hyperdense and Cosmic infused Ur-metal. Many of their sub-atomic and crystalline structures were almost identical, with only slight but significant variations.

Yet the effects of those variations remained considerable, as much as that between hyper dense collapsed steel and duranadium, and their lesser cousin iron.

Ultrium, for all of its many and amazing applications was almost indestructible, an almost perfect material.

Ur-metal was in fact, indestructible, and had survived the collapse and destruction of who knew how many universes.

That was why Ur-metal was so unique and so rare; perhaps the rarest form of matter and metal ever to exist, throughout all SpaceTime. It occurred on its own in very small amounts, with no known way to manufacture it, even among the ancients. It was supposedly even beyond them and their great knowledge.

But for the time being, the Alliance was on the spot, because now the enemy could develop and make use of Ultrium once more in warship construction, and they could not. This did not bode well for their future plans, military and otherwise.

"Or like the difference back on Old Earth, between wooden vessels, and warships made of metal," Naero suddenly blurted out. "That's what we face, if we do not act upon this new tek."

Once again, the enemy was already way ahead of them.

5

After the latest battles had ended, more or less at a high priced draw, Naero, Jia, Tyber, Alala, Om, and their research teams used every bit of teknomancy at their command to study the composition, properties, and theoretical ways to manufacture Ultrium.

Along with Om and Alala, they carefully examined and analyzed both Jia and the Driathan blank, marveling at how even those two types of Ultrium were very different. A living, functioning Driathan such as Jia was comprised of almost a completely different form of Ultrium, and that was an eye opener. How could that be?

The blank had once been alive as well, but now that it was lifeless, the very composition of the Ultrium had also drastically changed. The fact that Jia possessed life, sentience, force of will, and a soul all added up to make her not only different, but far stronger, and therefore made of Ultrium that was by far stronger and more intricate, even at the level of her raw physical composition.

These results were baffling.

The fact that an energized, living metal such as Ultrium had so many variations, fluctuations, and potential uses also made it nearly impossible to understand and comprehend. In many regards there was no way to call it anything more than simply being alive. It behaved like a sub-sentient, even near sentient living organism, which also just happened to be a highly advance metal alloy.

Naero thought with rage about the enemy's twisted, living machines, the Darkforce generators that fed upon and tormented their energy being hosts, sucking the life out of them painfully and slowly, using them as nothing more than batteries.

Ultrium was like that and yet beyond that. But it remained just a tool. It obviously did not have a complete will of its own.

Yet Naero had seen how even Ultrium could be infused with destructive Darkforce powers just as well as with the Lifeforce. Ultrium magnified and adapted to make use of any kind of energy, malignant or not. Normally on its own, in its raw state, Ultrium metal was incapable of knowing or caring what kind of energy it was infused with. With no exact will or mind, it had no awareness or concern for such matters.

Yet all of this seemed to get very weird when it involved living Driathans.

Naero realized that she had to focus on more than abstractions for herself and the Alliance.

Their priority problem at hand remained. How could they produce large quantities of Ultrium for use in starship construction, ship functions, shields, and weapon systems?

Unfortunately, no one had been able to capture one of the new alien warships. Those vessels were reported to be both highly elusive and self-healing. And if any of them did come close to capture, they exploded without leaving any useable wreckage to study.

Thus Alliance fleets had been successful in destroying and crippling several of the new rival warships, but every time that forces on hand attempted to take control of one of the wrecks, the enemy hulks detonated and were disintegrated with such violent force, that they often seriously damaged or destroyed any other ships near them.

So much for capturing one of the vessels; it seemed impossible at this juncture.

Naero and her development team strove to understand what the ancients meant about forging Ultrium in the furnace of stars.

Only the most powerful energy beings could exist within stars for short periods of time, no more than several hours.

Naero and Khai had done so, and barely escaped with their lives.

Khai only did so briefly if he needed to recharge Yii. That had only been done once. And the creation of the Cosmic sword Yii took the combined force of most of the high level Mystics and the entire Dimensional Council, focused on that single task. They only succeeded after many failed attempts.

Only they and Khai had succeeded at making the first sword of legends. Khai had become one with the Ur-metal of the blade and shaped it into the sword by force of will, pouring his soul into it. Khai and the Cosmic Sword Yii were one.

Only so much Ur-metal was known to exist in their entire universe.

Now they were looking at the daunting task of producing trillions of metric tons of Ultrium, in order to update their fleets and systems in order to have any chance of defeating their enemies. Let alone dealing with the alien Armada in the next galaxy over, just waiting for a gateway that would allow them to flood in and overwhelm the defenders.

Naero and her friends quickly reached the extent of their current knowledge, and that was all but a dead end. Without further information, they were already defeated.

Khai and Naero went over how Yii was forged, and went into a very hot star to try to create Ultrium instead of shaping Ur-metal.

With great effort, they were able to make some Ultrium, but only a few grams—hardly enough to build a destroyer.

Jia herself did not know the complete composition and workings of actually manufacturing this type of Ultrium. That had been a great secret among her creators, the Drians, powerful allies of the Kexx and their near-equals.

It was said that the Drians were overall more enlightened in higher level ethics, philosophy, and the magnitude of overall thought. The Kexx had more of a raw talent for offensive war and direct defense. They were the more practical of the two hyper advanced races.

The Drians were all dreamers to a certain extent, in their own ways. The Kexx were as well, but their seven highest level Dreamers were beyond any powers that the universe had ever witnessed. In the end, even the G'lothc had no understanding or answer for them.

The only thing the hateful G'lothc understood and pursued was all out destruction. They sought the death of all that lived in the universe if they could achieve it, even themselves in the end that they desired. No other purpose drove them, and about that dark and unholy crusade, they were ruthlessly fanatical. If their own existence did not matter, why would they ever pause to care about the existence of others?

The Alliance needed Ultrium desperately, and the means to produce lots of it.

For the time being, only the enemy knew the secrets of such a process. And Naero guessed that theirs was yet another dark and vile method that the Alliance would have no wish to duplicate.

Cracking this tek barrier was a huge problem.

But if the Drians and the Kexx had learned a way to do this thing, then so would the Alliance.

Naero knew where to expand her search: inside the limitless expanse of knowledge within the Kexxian Data Matrix. A matrix of data so near to infinite, that the true problem was always asking the right question, or finding the correct place or direction to look in. Like trying to find one specific planet in the limitless all of the entire universe.

Naero explained the situation to her friends, and many of them kept watch over her as she put herself in the induced trance that would allow her to penetrate the KDM stored within her own DNA.

Once within the KDM, she quickly transformed into her Kexxian spiritmind counterpart, Orean. In her mind, she became the closest thing to a Kexx that she had ever encountered, and merged with that side of her nature.

Only then was she capable of exploring the vast winds and oceans of data, data collected by one of the most powerful race of sentient beings ever known to sweep across the stars.

The KDM was in fact, a legacy of knowledge and enlightenment left behind to the younger races that the Kexx and the Drians had nurtured and protected long ago.

But Naero was just one sentient, trying to comprehend and make use of that great legacy.

From her starting point in the key source of music, Naero sent forth the force of her active will, radiating out into a vista of hundreds of threads and potential leads.

Many times she kept up the search for weeks and months at a time, a few sessions each week. She never found the exact answer to the problem she thought to solve. A few times she had stumbled upon answers and fragments of solutions that came together later. There remained many vital questions she had never gained any inkling about whatsoever.

As with all things she had to start somewhere. But that was also a barrier. She was always beginning, and never finishing.

Even with the basic index to the KDM, there was simply too much raw data to flounder through in order to locate a single correct solution.

Somewhere the secrets of manufacturing Ultrium that the Kexx and the Drians used, almost without effort or thought, awaited her.

Naero only needed to keep struggling in order to find them.

Yet she stumbled on a thread about the G'lothc mind control wraiths without even searching for it, and followed that thread into ocean upon ocean of medical information.

These were simply more oceans of data to thrash around and become lost within.

Yet Naero persisted and she did gain many valuable insights into the enemy wraiths.

Not only could they be destroyed in several ways, but once their Cosmic energy flows were fully analyzed and understood, they could also be immunized against. They could be combatted and prevented from taking hold of the host.

And so could the phage.

They could be defeated like an advanced disease.

Now if she could only have the same good fortune with Ultrium production.

She knew now that she only had to keep exploring and following the various threads to pull all of the proper knowledge and understanding together. Hard work and expanded thought, that was the only way to reach any solution other than blind luck.

Then she actually did stumble upon something else even more grand and lofty.

Working together, the Kexx and the Drians had eradicated all disease and contagion during their time, for millions of years. This was just one of the many impossible things that they had achieved within the galaxies they had explored, warred among, and defended.

Naero stopped just to consider the magnitude of all that.

Under the Kexx, Quadrant after quadrant existed without illness, without disease or any serious maladies on countless worlds. It was as if the infected left hand of Death itself had been hewn off, cast away, and existed no longer to literally plague all sentient beings.

In fact, a new deep secret revealed itself on top of the others.

The Kexx and the Drians spent much of their energies maintaining such immunities among their galaxies.

Even the near endless war against the G'lothc had not required so much from them.

There had also been a grand plan to expand and breed the Dreamers as a new race, and send their mighty offspring throughout the entire universe, both as emissaries of enlightenment and peace, and to the healing of all illness everywhere.

Then the war ended, and both the Kexx and the Drians took their leave of the universe forever, for reasons that still mystified all and remained unknown.

After their departure, disease, sickness, and entropy slowly returned and rose up again in all of their fury.

Naero came out of her trance and back to her friends, sharing with them all of the insights and knowledge that she had gathered.

Om continued tabulating all of the data and comparing it to the little that they already understood. That often led to further valuable insights, much later on.

*

Naero sat in a concentric ring theater, much like a half-dome arena. In the center, she and the audience watched an exceptionally lifelike 3D holographic movie depicting two great empires clashing culturally and on the battlefield.

The setting was some near-human world in the distant past. Fixers worked in conjunction with the advanced projectors, portraying a vivid world of intrigue, emotional depth, and stirring conflict. Heat and cold felt real, if one drew close enough. The wind could be felt when it blew.

Dust and blood, trees, food, and ocean mists could be smelled and tasted upon it. The sweat of lovers and warriors could almost be felt as they strained.

The audience members had the ability to move their seats around in order to experience the spectacle from nearly any angle or vantage point. They were merely prevented from entering the holos and disrupting the movie themselves.

The entertainment extravaganza lasted well over three standard hours, and the last king and queen of the two weary realms finally brought their peoples together to form one nation. This put an end to most of the meaningless violence of an age of ignorance that now lay behind them. The long suffering couple rode wingless dragons off into the sunset along a wave-washed beach under an amazing sky.

The audience clapped and so did Naero.

Yes, it was a bit sappy, but then she still liked a happy ending. It was a movie after all. And she needed a break every now and then from working herself half to death.

Tyber returned his seat to her left, little Galan slumbering in his arms. The little guy probably got bored and drifted off at some point.

The holovid was very long. Almost three hours.

Tyber's face still looked red and wet around his eyes. Naero cried at movies sometimes herself. They got to her.

Then she recalled that the actress playing the last queen had looked a bit too much like Zhen, albeit somewhat more busty than Z, but again, this was a vid.

Tyber sighed and Naero sighed.

Here it came again.

"I miss her, N. I try not to, but I really miss her. You know that."

"I know. I miss her too, Ty."

If Naero could have brought Zhen back to his family right then and there, she would have willingly torn her ears off and scratched out her own eyes.

"Nothing yet?" he asked.

Naero shook her head and looked down. "Nothing yet, Ty. Trust me. I'll let you know. But remember, it might not ever be possible."

"I know that."

He complained that his legs had fallen asleep a bit from holding his sleeping son.

Naero happily took the little boy in her arms and kissed the top of Gallan's head. Tyber got up and stretched his legs a bit.

"Thanks for the holo movie, sib," Jan remarked on her right. For the moment, she'd almost forgotten that Jan and his family had also joined them.

"Good vid," Jan said. "Lots of good sex scenes."

Calyxo giggled and snapped Jan with her tail. She was holding a sleeping Amashi. Vejjah held a snoring Clio.

Naero smirked. "Well sorry, Jan. Next time I'll just download some straight porn for you from the Webnet."

"You most certainly will not," Vejjah protested.

"Humans," Calyxo muttered under her breath. "What is porn, again?" She was dead serious.

That got good laughs from everyone within earshot, as the audience shuffled out of the flagship's holotheater.

Jan will explain it to you," Naero quipped.

"Husband? Tell me what is this porn? Is it humorous? It seems to make everyone laugh."

"Oof!" Jan said. "I will explain later, Cali, my love; much later, in private. You'll catch on pretty quick."

"Very well."

Vejjah turned to Naero and Jan, all smiles. "Hey, it's not that late. Why don't you guys join us in our quarters for snacks, desert, and drinks? We're celebrating. I'm pregnant again!"

"Congrats, Vejjah!" Naero cried, hugging her sister-in-law.

Of course Vejjah was pregnant again. That pretty lady was a regular baby machine.

But when Naero thought about it, she and Khai had more kids than Jan and his wives. She and Khai wanted a huge family. They could afford it.

It wasn't like it was a competition.

"What about hanging with us, Ty?" Naero turned and asked.

You would have thought she slapped him by the look on his face.

"No, thanks. But congrats you guys. I got another full day tomorrow, and Gallan needs to get to bed. Go ahead, N. All of you guys have fun without me this time."

Naero went out with her brother and his family.

She had asked Ty more than once if he ever wanted more of his and Zhen's kids to be born. They were all still there in that little frozen case.

"I'll wait a while still," he had told her.

6

The Alliance continued to fight on across all fronts and continued lines of vital research behind the scenes.

Naero continued in her role as merely part of various offensive and defensive protocols within the Interdimensions. This was just one battle front that they were fighting on.

But the enemy remained a ruthless, determined foe and far from being out of nasty tricks just yet.

Each time that the Alliance tried to counter the phage, the enemy changed key parameters to the self-evolving menace.

Thus the Great Adversary advanced their campaign of farming, subjugating, and destroying the other energy beings wholesale.

The enemy kept the pressure on.

More and more of the new advanced enemy warships continued to come online each day in the weeks and months that followed, supporting the regular enemy fleets, and making all attempts to stop or counter the general enemy push even more problematic.

Naero and the Alliance also encountered just as many if not more variations of the vicious mind control wraiths.

Their enemy kept the energy being races off balance. That seemed to be a vital part of the overall strategy. The energy beings were torn between defending their shining safe zones, and assisting the Alliance against multiple, large scale wraith attacks.

Naero and other strategists quickly determined that they were being jerked around and constantly manipulated, in order to keep them merely reacting to flurries of attacks.

This was little more than a classic confuse and conquer strategy.

They could not allow the remaining energy beings to be captured or destroyed. That meant further Darkforce power for the enemy. That meant that the enemy could accomplish even more of their goals just that much faster with such power at their command.

It was Alala, working with Om, who began to develop a way to infuse the fixers they had with Ultrium and Cosmic energies that would allow them to enter and function in the Interdimensions.

All Kexxian tek seemed to exist to be able to do so.

Once the Alliance had one entire fixer cloud so converted, the process could be both repeated, and greatly sped up.

The inherent nature of the fixers could be used to counteract the phage and at the very least provide a fledgling protective barrier that energy beings and Alliance forces could operate behind or within.

Not only that, but these new fixers could automatically adjust in real-time to the enemy's tricks, pweaks, and shifts of the phage's operational parameters. That would allow the energy beings and their Mystic allies to go back on the offensive against the foe in the Interdimensions, and not just concentrate on defense and attempts to survive.

Other efforts in the Gamma Quadrant re-focused on trying to capture some of the advanced enemy ships for vital study.

Then a new threat suddenly appeared without warning, both in the Interdimensions and the Prime Material Plane.

From all reports, even from Baeven and his crew, an actual Darkforce G'lothc Champion had reappeared in the Gamma Quadrant, bringing overwhelming destruction every place it went. There was no known defense against this Creature from what they could tell.

No existing weapons could harm it.

All Alliance forces were ordered to retreat whenever and wherever this Creature appeared. The thing was that destructive and deadly.

Everywhere the Creature attacked, many Alliance warships and their crews did not return.

Naero studied the vids and other data regarding the Creature. It seemed to be a shapeshifter, and it took a handful of deadly Cosmic energy forms. The Creature was usually humanoid, anywhere from 1.83 to around five meters tall, with what appeared to be multiple limbs and a long prehensile tail. Sometimes it also had prehensile hair or tendrils, and sometimes wings, all infused with lethal Darkforce energies.

It could shrink and expand its size, mass, and density at will.

If this was indeed a vessel for one of the seven lost souls of the G'lothc Champions, it must be unique, and most likely genetically engineered. It matched no known life form or species of sentient being.

It was a true Chimera, a monstrous form of existence created to do one thing very well—Destroy.

All six of the variant, humanoid forms encountered were still vaguely feminine, jet black body with the whip like appendages for a tail and hair. The Creature's five eyes were slitted, with a pair on either side of the nose, and one eye centered vertically up through the forehead. The eyes normally glowed bright, blackish red with destroying Darkforce energies before and while it unleashed one of its devastating attacks.

It possessed multiple physical and energy form attacks, and was dangerous both up close and from a distance.

The thing's primary Darkforce weapons seemed to be a scarlet annihilation beam that could slice through any shields, armor, and entire warships that the Alliance had. This Creature had already demonstrated the ability to destroy dozens of Allied warships in its initial encounters.

The enemy had attempted such a thing before, to find vessels, new bodies for the fallen spirits of the Seven G'lothc Champions.

Had they finally succeeded at last?

All of the evidence supported that undeniable fact.

This was a terrible development indeed.

There was only one point of note in their favor.

Although wherever the Creature appeared, it proved devastating, it did not seem to be capable of remaining in battle for very long.

Not one of its attacks lasted for more than fifteen standard minutes.

One potential weakness was possible.

The thing expended its destructive Cosmic energies at an astonishing rate. It was almost as if the Creature were constantly exploding with raw force, yet without being destroyed by the very forces that powered its naked aggression.

Where and how was it possibly getting such extremely high levels of such unique energies, as if the monster was constantly being bolstered and flooded with them?

The Alliance, unlike the Kexx, had no Dreamers to send against such Cosmic Champion level foes.

Could anyone, even Naero herself and Baeven, stand before the rampant powers of such monsters?

From her Kexxian studies, Naero knew full well, better than anyone, what the Six G'lothc Devils had been capable of. At one point, she herself broke down and wept out of irrational fear.

What if all seven of these ancient abominations were given vessels for their vile souls to inhabit once more? What then?

They who had threatened to destroy all life in seven galaxies before they were finally stopped, beaten back, and obliterated.

Naero calmed herself and tried to reason it out.

Thankfully, these were not the actual, original Darkforce Champions from the ancient days. However mighty these things were, they were still only the shades, the crushed and fallen spirits of their former selves given a new vessel.

And for now, at least, there was only one of them, not all of the Six at once. That was indeed a blessing.

These were initial reports and encounters. They had already studied the thing in depth and found one weakness. They would find others. It remained to be seen just how formidable this new Creature was.

In truth, other than ancient accounts, they still knew so little about the Darkforce Six, other than their names and how the Dreamers slew them at the end of their ancient war. And that read like a legend, little more than a story.

Even Jia had no information to add. The Drians had shielded and protected the Driathans throughout that long and terrible conflict, so that they were largely untouched and unaffected by the war.

Which one was this Creature, if it was in fact one of the Six?

Thus far there was no communication with the thing. It simply showed up and began to lay waste to everything around it. Then as soon as its power levels began to wane, it vanished and went into hiding somewhere.

Yes, the thing definitely had to recharge, ranging from a period of 2.5 weeks, on up to a standard month or more before it showed itself again.

There had been three such attacks thus far, all of them leading to Alliance defeats and retreats in those sectors.

Two days later after the most recent attack, Naero attended another tactical discussion, trying to assess this grave new threat and how they should respond to it.

Initial ideas tended toward having the Alliance Champions band together and hunt this new Creature down and destroy it.

Then Naero received an even more alarming notice of a personal nature, back in the Alpha Quadrant.

Shetharra's headaches and her physical condition had grown progressively worse, also in a relatively short time. Her Cosmic energies were being destabilized by some unknown condition.

It was as if some malignant, outside force was warring against her directly.

The situation had escalated to the point where her very life was now at stake, and she needed to be kept within a Cosmic energy dampening bubble to sustain her physical form and her Lifeforce energies.

7

While they waited for further appearances of the new enemy monster, Naero and Jia worked more with the Driathan blank, trying to find a way to open up its secrets. If they could do that, then perhaps Naero could find a way to imbue the blank with Zhen's now dormant soul, keeping the promise that she had made to both Zhen and Tyber.

Whatever the process was, affecting it still confused and eluded them.

Then Naero hit upon a different radical ideal.

She knew for a fact that Jia had a soul and was also an innately powerful psyonic user.

If Naero trained Jia properly, she wondered if the Driathan queen could enter the KDM with her.

Naero/Orean would act as sort of a psyonic guide. Perhaps Jia might see things that Naero could not. A different view of things—two working perspectives, highly trained in bio and teknomancy might prove more productive. And they could also link minds in order to see what the other saw.

They could share information.

It took two days of various attempts and intense meditation, but at last Naero mindlinked with her friend Jia, transformed in Orean, and carried them both into the depths of the KDM.

At first Jia could not discern much and said that everything around her looked like dark, dense, impenetrable fortresses with impossible walls that would not yield to her in any way.

Naero mindlinked with Jia again and witnessed what the Driathan referred to. Jia was correct. The open skies, seas, and flows that were wide open to Orean were sealed off and completely shut against Jia.

Together they traveled over the breadth of the KDM. Not much changed for Jia at first.

Then she seemed to spot something. She gasped in wonder and led Orean, pulling her along through the flows by one arm. They came to another open expanse. Yet to Orean's mind, there was nothing there but emptiness.

Jia mindlinked with her this time, to reveal to Naero what it was that the Driathan queen beheld when she looked around them.

Haisha! Naero cried. As far as their psyonic spiritminds could take in, they saw a living city of light, and like Orean of the Kexx, Jia was in an instant transformed into Aij, the spiritmind form of one of the near godlike Drians.

Aij dropped to the golden glowing simulated ground with its bright, metallic, golden grass and golden dust for earth. These images rippled out from them in all directions as they took shape.

I am one here! I am one with the thoughts and ideas of my creators! Do you not know what this place is, Orean?

Orean shrugged in her reptilian, Kexxian form. "I have no concept of this place. I am only seeing it through our mindlink, through you. Honestly, I did not even know that it was here. Without you with me, I would never be able to perceive it.

Aij took Orean's hands, barely able to contain her excitement. *This is the Kexxian repository of shared Driathan knowledge. All of this data has been kept here for the sake of my people, to share with them. I feel it rushing into me, in spaces long prepared for me to store and to be able to contain, access, and share such knowledge. With time of course. The rushes of data are so very huge! I can't make out anything specific.*

Orean did rejoice. Now she had someone besides Om who she could relate to on a find such as this, at such levels. The Kexx had recorded the knowledge of each sentient race that they had encountered, and the only race to match them as equals. What a feat, to amass as much knowledge as they did.

In an instant of time, Orean perceived that she would not be alone any longer in her quest for knowledge, wisdom, and enlightenment. Through her eyes and her fertile mind, she could share with Jia all that she had learned and would continue to learn.

They could do so in less than seconds.

And through Jia's amazing mind and consciousness, Naero could now envision the Drian side of things, and behold their deep thoughts and knowledge.

As if in direct answer to their needs, Jia bumbled across numerous references to Ultrium.

Ultrium here. Ultrium there. The Drians used Ultrium for almost everything, just as the Kexx and the G'lothc did.

As it turned out, Naero, the Drians were also masters of utilizing Ultrium in every possible way. And the godlike minds of the Drians could imagine quite a lot.

Even the Kexx were not as thorough or adept at making Ultrium in all of its variations and finding so many applications for each one.

Haisha, how about that, Jia? When it came to the manipulation and use of Ultrium, even the Kexx learned much of what they knew from their friends and allies the Drians.

Only in producing massive quantities of the hyper alloy and forming enormous structures at will did the Kexx surpass their good friends.

Even though Naero had access to general knowledge about Ultrium, there remained so much of it to catalog, sort through, and uncover the practical uses. This alone was an enormous and daunting task.

They came across one method of producing Ultrium for use in hi-tek machines and various instruments, so far advanced, that neither Jia nor Naero could comprehend them, even with their teknomancy.

Early on, N, it appears that the Drians also had great difficulty producing large quantities of specially infused Ultrium for use in many projects, including the creation of what would be their masterwork, and their gift to the universe—the Drians. And next, to a lesser extent, they fashioned fleets of vital warships for the ongoing Great War against the G'lothc.

As many Drian thinkers stated, it was their allies the Kexx who finally made a breakthrough. But in working together, they at last found the solution.

After that, the tables soon turned. For when it came to producing Ultrium in nearly impossible quantities, it was the Kexx who developed a multitude of processes for smelting and forging them.

Aij noted that her people would not have been created by the Drians in the large numbers that they were, without the equally large amounts of the special kinds of Ultrium that their masterpiece required.

Orean and Aij spent many standard hours sifting through the sea of knowledge that both of them now swam in.

Finally they came across three smelting processes for basic Ultrium meant to be used in starship armor, armaments, systems, and shielding. These concepts came from a very early period, one that was at least at a level that Aij and Orean could begin to comprehend. They began to study the wildly intricate advanced materials, schematics for the advanced devices, and their construction and operation.

Much of these processes and the advanced materials, tools, and machines required to make and manipulate them were still beyond the current tek level and basic ken of their present day.

But at least it would be a starting point on the theoretical level.

Orean noted that the actual process for the formation of raw Ultrium required the makers, in what could only be energy being form, to use the intense heat and pressure of a star as a kind of crucible, infusing the super advanced alloy with the Cosmic energies and properties of what was referred to as 'near life.'

The Drians did this with advanced level psyonics and force of will, which to Orean's mind resembled the process of replication, but with teknomancy blended with biomancy and Cosmic energy enlightenment.

When they came to the mention of the Kexxian processes, all that was said was that the Kexx transcended the process and refined it greatly.

The Dreamers and those near to their miraculous levels of energy manipulation not only created, manipulated, and transported large quantities of Ultrium. They went beyond that, to create huge warships, eventually those such as the Starkillers—fully formed out of the star-stuff from which they were forged.

This was done through the mighty Song of Making, one of the great primal powers of Creation and the universe, of which the Kexx alone held the absolute mastery. They later gifted a vital part of it to their brothers and sisters, the Drians.

The greatest of the Kexx only needed to think upon an object or advanced machine they wanted to bring into existence, and then they sang it into being with the Song of Making.

The desired object, however great or small, was simply wished into reality, so great were the powers of the Kexx. At the height of their prowess, they did not even need a star to form such things from it. They could simply focus and create what they wished for at will.

When they finally emerged from their mission, over a day later, Jia used teknomancy to transmit the vast array of data across the screens for their friends to begin to examine and comprehend.

Even Ty, Om, and Alala were absolutely staggered and stunned.

No one could keep up.

Ty attempted to penetrate them with his teknomancy and was left staring and transfixed with his mouth open, stupefied, his spit running in a line to puddle around his feet.

Naero smiled and announced. "This is where we begin to create Ultrium for our needs."

"With what?" Ty finally managed to recover and protest. "We don't have any of these advanced tools, or the refined raw materials and energies needed for any of this. This isn't tek anymore, N. This...this is magic. Compared to all of this, we're still cave people, limited only to fire and perhaps the wheel, or simple pulleys and levers. Haisha! Where do we even begin?"

"Frost, Ty. Relax before you pop a vein or an eyeball or something. We have an edge."

He blinked at her. "And what would that be?"

Naero grinned. "There are upgrades to the Kexxian fixers that will assist us in all of this. Jia and I discovered them together."

Ty's stricken face brightened. "That is good news. That makes all the difference. Let's get started then."

Everyone laughed nervously. Many of the teks still had no clue as to what the hell was going on. Naero hugged her old friend.

She didn't want to say anything yet, but working with the Driathan Queen, they were even closer now to finding a way to bring Zhen back.

Naero could feel it.

*

She had another disturbing dream that night.

Within the aether of what appeared to be some kind of enormous Interdimensional void or Nexus, a malicious form took shape. What looked like a kind of dark spider or jellyfish with countless millions of long, black smokey tendrils reached out with its lethal weapons into the aether void, casting its malignant shadow and absorbing the ambient light.

Millions of Spacer children of all ages, or at least their souls or spiritmind forms, floated in the aether, their soul energies glowing like slumbering stars.

The dark jellyfish thing pierced the veil of each child's soul with one of the dark, barbed tendrils, and began to drain the children of their Lifeforce energies. The aether was filled with their cries of agony, until each scream was cut off.

Naero wailed at the sight of all of those countless little spiritmind corpses floating there in the gloom.

The first of them all to perish was Shetharra, and her dead eyes stared back at her mother, frozen in pain.

Naero woke up with more than a start.

Was it just irrational fear, or could the enemy truly find a way to attack the soul energies of their children? Was such a thing even possible?

Shetharra was suffering from some kind of Cosmic sickness, but both Naero and Khai had survived similar illnesses.

8

Naero did not feel like taking any chances with her oldest daughter's life. She had Fleet 71 and *The Angel Wing* escorted to the most secret, safest place within the Alpha Quadrant. Yet this location was close enough to the Gamma Quadrant and several wyrmholes that would race either of them to the other if the need arose.

Baeven himself had selected this safe place for Naero.

Her oldest daughter's condition was stable and guarded for the time being.

But with everything going on and the enemy threats on the rise, Shetharra and Naero's family had to be kept safe. In her oldest daughter's weakened condition, who knew what could happen if the enemy gained control of Shetharra and the others?

Having loved ones did give Naero a weak spot, and the enemy constantly tried to exploit that vulnerability, or destroy her family outright.

These vile bastards weren't about to stop now.

As proof of that, a new type of enemy mind wraith exploded onto the scene, allied with a new Prime Material version of the enemy phage. They rapidly spread a plague among the Alliance that specifically targeted Spacer children and teens, and threatened to slowly murder them.

The culprit turned out to be a genetically engineered plague of phage disease that slowly broke down young Spacer developing brains and bodies from within.

The disease did not harm adults, but adults could still carry the disease.

The Great Adversary had tried to use biowar agents against Spacers several times before and failed.

That the enemy would directly attack Spacer progeny horrified every race within the growing Alliance. Yet Naero was used to such attacks by then. Just more proof why their ruthless foes deserved to be beaten down and exterminated, wherever they could be found.

The Kexx and the Drians had reached the same conclusion in ancient times during their long war.

Therefore, Naero and Jia continued exploring the KDM and the Drian data oceans as often as they could take the time to go there. Those ancient guardian races had faced these same awful foes, and triumphed against them and the very worst that these terrible beings could unleash.

As Naero and Jia guessed, and as it turned out, there were also many advanced medical uses for Ultrium and its vast seas of super tek data.

With Shetharra's life and the lives of an entire generation of Spacer children and the Alliance now at risk, that gave them just another incentive to crack the Ultrium tek barrier and all of its various benefits and mysteries that awaited.

In the days that followed, Naero and Ty's teams kept at their assigned tasks until finally together, they made a huge, collective breakthrough.

At last they produced the first real, substantial quantities of Ultrium for practical use.

As with Naero and Khai's fledgling efforts, the actual amount that their combined teams first produced was miniscule—just a few grams.

Then, based upon what they learned from that process, they were able to go back in and produce more, a few kilos this time.

Doing so brought *The Dark Star* as close to a star as any Spacer or Alliance ship had ever been, without being destroyed outright. Alala's shields and defenses were strained to the limit.

In fact, with the efforts to produce the super alloy and help keep the test ship shielded, Naero, Shalaen, and over a hundred brave energy beings bolstered the ship's defenses and still nearly perished.

It took them all an entire standard day thereafter to regenerate from their severe injuries, even in their energy being forms.

But they had at last succeeded in smelting and creating real live Ultrium alloy, usable after the Drian fashion—near living metal infused with several stable flows of Cosmic energy

Ty and the others were already arguing intensely about what to do with it, the little Ultrium that they now possessed.

Naero and Jia finally convinced them that there was only one choice. They must use every bit they had to transform one single fixer into a next generation Ultrium fixer.

After hours of failed teknomancing attempts, all of them combined their considerable teknomancy abilities, and finally upgraded one basic fixer according to eighty percent of the Kexxian specs that they understood.

Then they witnessed another surprise.

When activated, the new little fixer immediately went about completing the *remaining* twenty percent of its own newly updated design, all by itself.

At that achievement the development team watched eagerly as the new fixer bridged that teknological gap. Everyone watching struggled to comprehend and keep up with the new miracle advances as the new fixer did things and performed tasks that they could barely understand.

They used teknomancy to study that final phase again and again, revealing wonder after wonder as they continued to learn.

The final result was an advanced fixer design that was now not one, but many generations ahead of their other still amazing fixers.

Not only was this new prototype now capable of operating within a star, but also becoming a small, near-life Cosmic energy machine that could enter and function even within the extreme conditions of the Interdimensions and the Astral Plane.

At first that all seemed like a very small thing for just one little fixer.

Yet that one little fixer could also now replicate and upgrade other fixers to the same new parameters of its updated, unique design.

The replication process went forward immediately.

Then some of those new fixers were further pweaked and modified to perform many other vital tasks, such as producing the tools and advanced materials that they would need to achieve multitudes of other theoretical solutions.

These little Ultrium fixers were just the beginning of a yet another new age.

And one more thing.

From studying multitudes of Kexxian advanced manufacturing and replication techniques, Naero thought she saw a way to cut some corners, and use the new fixers to upgrade a single starship, its hull, and armor into energized Ultrium metal.

The real world applications of this new Kexxian tek breakthrough were mind staggering, and the Alliance had barely scratched the surface of those possibilities.

The medical applications alone would continue to be astonishing. From the start, they could now save and protect the lives of an entire generation of Spacer and Alliance children who were currently under direct attack by an enemy biowar agent.

These new developments brought Shetharra's condition under control and clearly saved her life. Saved her from burning up and dissolving, or expanding too fast and exploding, real risks and perils such as Naero herself once faced, all but alone.

But first things came first. They couldn't get too far ahead of themselves just yet.

The development team used a new advanced fixer cloud the next day to affect the transformation in a new experimental production process. It was just like refitting upgrades to a warship, but in a way never possible or attempted before.

Because *The Dark Star* was already a living, self-aware ship, they felt confident that she and Alala would make the best first subject for such a refit, transformation technique. Alala, Naero, and Ty all knew the exact workings and specs of the unique, hybrid vessel intimately with their teknomancing.

All seemed to be going well, at first.

Then the Cosmic energy levels required to affect the transformation spiked in several unexpected ways and quickly raced out of control.

The fixer cloud did all that it could to absorb the destructive energy feedback that was unleashed.

Naero, Om, Alala, Baeven, Shalaen, and Jan were forced to endure the rest.

They saved the crew, the ship, and Alala, but the vessel was nearly burned out throughout most of its systems and left little more than a contaminated hulk, floating adrift in space, blasted away from the sun.

The new fixer cloud did not survive, and was obliterated, sacrificing itself to save the researchers and crew. There were still multitudes of serious injuries on board *The Dark Star*. Medships and rescue craft posted on standby swarmed on the crew to treat the many casualties.

It was two days before Naero could get out of her own medbed, but she and Om went over what had gone wrong the entire time while she regenerated.

They thought that they now had a way to fix and avoid similar catastrophic risks to the developers. They would still need the advanced fixer clouds to shield them until the last instant, and those clouds would most likely be lost in a similar fashion.

They made another attempt at a variant transformation process the next day.

This time, they not only completed the entire process and jumped out of harm's way before the fixer cloud exploded.

But they also succeeded in transforming the hull and armor of *The Dark Star* into solid Ultrium.

At the same time, other teams of researchers stood by, an army of them. They stood ready and eager to convert all of the warship's systems to the miracles of energized, Cosmic energy infused Ultrium. This also included medical equipment and applications in the medical bays.

Those advances could have not come at a more opportune moment.

Shetharra had relapsed and suffered greatly. Both the physical and energy being forms of the phage born plague had somehow morphed and evolved yet again, and infected her anew, along with many more Spacer children whom they thought they had saved.

The weakest children began to perish first. The current level of Spacer and Alliance medical knowledge had no clear answer.

Yet the KDM might.

More research ships and teams flocked to Naero's location, or waited eagerly for the next breakthrough, as they now came thick and fast.

New devices and machines, new techniques and treatments flooded out of that sector and raced across two quadrants like an expanding Cosmic fire.

They saved the lives of countless Spacer children with each passing second.

Fleet 71 flashed in to rendezvous with Naero's fleets, bringing Shetharra to her mother for the latest new treatment to reverse her decline. *The Angel Wing* was now filled with many suffering Spacer children.

That's exactly when the enemy struck out of nowhere. A strike force of their new advanced Ultrium warships tore open a rent in real SpaceTime, pouring out from that rent from the Interdimensions.

Nebulae of attacking, super modified phage and mind wraiths swept both *The Angel Wing* and *The Dark Star* into the Interdimensional void without warning, just as the two vessels were approaching to dock together.

Jia and *The Star Fox* were already docked with the hospital ship.

Then the rent closed upon them, as quickly as it had opened.

Energized, Ultrium matrix shielding already protected *The Dark Star,* yet the enemy strike force fell upon her immediately and brought multiple heavy attacks to bear against her.

Alala responded instantly, pouring the most advanced fire of the Alliance into the dozen enemy warships hemming her in. Weapons so advanced, that some were still being converted, and others had yet to be tested.

But the two Alliance ships were separated in the course of the fray, pulled apart by the attacking enemy forces. Naero and *The Dark Star* watched in horror at what happened next, to a Prime Material Plane warship or any such object or structure exposed to the energy flows and stresses of the Interdimensions.

The hospital ship *The Angel Wing* had no defenses to speak of.

Immediately it was being torn apart, not only by powerful Cosmic flows and forces, but by the direct attacks from the enemy.

It might break apart or detonate within minutes.

Baeven and Jia attempted to extend the advanced shields of *The Star Fox* over the hospital ship, but *The Angel Wing* was too big.

On top of that, the enemy phage and mind wraiths attacked and swarmed on the stricken craft, doing their utmost to phaze through and get at the fleshy things inside.

Then an impenetrable shield of white fire burst forth from within the ship like an expanding bubble, and held the destruction at bay, pushing back the attackers with an expanding barrier of raw force that destroyed the phage and the wraiths on contact as they hurled themselves against it by the millions.

Good girl, Naero sent out telepathically. My brave little duck!

Shetharra came back across their mindlink. *I'm hurting, Momma. I don't feel good. The dark ones keep hurting me each second. I don't know how long I can hold them off, but if they get through, all of our friends will die. I have placed myself between them. I must hold them back for as long as I can.*

I'm here, my brave girl. Stay strong. I know how strong you are. We'll get you free of them as soon as we can. We're doing everything we can. How long do you think you can hold out?

I don't know, Momma. It hurts so much, Momma. There are so many of them. Make them stop, please!

I'll stop them, Shetharra. You hang in there my duck. I will find away.

9

Naero immediately sent out a distress call to the cavalry, who were stationed nearby back in the Gamma Quadrant, awaiting just such an attack as this. Beacons on board both Spacer vessels transmitted their exact location to any of their friends in either quadrant, or the Interdimensions and the Astral Plane.

The Dark Star and *The Star Fox* were up against two heavy cruisers, two cruisers, four destroyers, two frigates, and two gunships.

Captain Tyber and Alala had already crippled one of the heavy cruisers, and obliterated two of the destroyers outright. But they were taking a lot of fire and could not withstand such an attack for long. Nor could they jump out and leave *The Angel Wing* behind.

That was not an option.

But they and *The Star Fox* were both stealth ships, and vanished off the scanners to continue the fight, giving themselves room in the aether to do so.

Not a second later the enemy's new super Creature appeared on the scene, as if the situation wasn't dire enough. It matched everything they knew about the monster thus far, and it came straight at the floundering, helpless medship as all of the other enemy attacks continued full force.

Alone, Naero transported out to intercept the Creature, transforming into her near Darkbeast form.

They clashed violently in the rarefied aether of the Interdimensions, kicking, ripping, and tearing at each other.

Whatever this thing was, it quickly grew apparent to Naero that it was not only tougher, but stronger and faster than her.

Naero circled, looking for an opening, a weakness, something she could exploit.

She opened her third eye and tried to star tap more raw Cosmic energy, to channel it into more strength and speed for herself.

The Creature clashed with her again, and they punched, kicked, and grappled with each other. Naero got in a couple of flashing spinwheel kicks, rocking the Creature's head back.

It countered with a sweeping strike of its tail that swatted her back, and then drilled her with Darkforce beams from its hair tendrils. Naero transported to avoid what would have been heavy damage.

Next it encased her in some kind of energy draining form that took on the shape of a weird, dark three dimensional fractal.

Naero tried to transport and couldn't.

She barely busted her way out.

They withdrew slightly and the Creature transformed into one of its other modes right in front of her.

The thing laughed and then even spoke at her, its psyonic voice harsh but still somewhat feminine. Yet Naero knew full well that if it was in any way G'lothc, it could take on any form or sound like anything it wanted to.

It even used the voice telepathically.

YOU…YOU ARE THE SPACK BITCH THAT CONTINUES TO TROUBLE US. WE WANT YOU ALIVE, IF POSSIBLE. I WAS GIVEN THIS VESSEL AND THE FIRE OF LIFE ONCE MORE ON THE PRIME MATERIAL PLANE AND EVERY OTHER, IN ORDER TO CAPTURE YOU. YOU MISCALCULATED BY COMING TO FACE ME ALONE, LITTLE ONE. FOR THAT ERROR, YOU AND ALL YOU HOLD DEAR SHALL PAY A HEAVY PRICE.

Who are you? Naero demanded defiantly. What are you, monster?

The Creature drew itself up and laughed once more. I LIVE AGAIN. I AM ELAZETHREK, THE DEFILER, LEAST OF THE SIX, AS IT WAS ONCE SAID. BUT NOW IN THIS MIGHTY FORM, I AM FAR STRONGER THAN I HAVE EVER BEEN. TOGETHER WITH MY DARK BROTHERS AND SISTERS, WE ONCE MADE ENTIRE GALAXIES SCREAM IN TERROR AND AGONY AT OUR DOMINION. WE WERE INVINCIBLE! WE SHALL BE SO YET AGAIN.

Lies. The Dreamers of the Kexx defeated you and all the Six: broke your wills, slew your immortal bodies, and banished you and all of your foul kind to a realm of near oblivion and torment.

Elazethrek reborn glared at her with malignant glee and laughed yet again. AND YET, HERE I STAND; I HAVE RETURNED. WHERE ARE THOSE SELF-RIGHTEOUS FOOLS NOW, SPACK WHELP? THEY BE DEAD AND LONG GONE, WHILE I HAVE AT LONG LAST DISCOVERED A WAY TO RETURN IN TRIUMPH. YOU CANNOT EVEN HOPE TO DEFEAT ME ON MY OWN. WHAT THEN WILL YOU DO WHEN THE OTHER FIVE OF MY KIND JOIN ME SIDE BY SIDE, HOWEVER LONG IT TAKES? WE HAVE TIME, NO MATTER THE GREAT DIFFICULTY IN DOING SO. NOTHING YOU OR YOUR PETTY LITTLE ALLIANCE POSSESSES CAN DARE STAND AGAINST THE SIX ONCE WE HAVE ALL BEEN REMADE, AND ONCE OUR VAST ARMADA JOINS US TO CRUSH AND BLAST YOU ALL INTO DUST AND ASH.

In answer Naero slammed into the Creature, whirling in Cosmic fire with high speed kicks, punches, and power beams from her eyes and sonic attacks from her mouth.

Mind blasts.

Cosmic detonations.

She unleashed attack after attack. No let up.

Technique after technique. Trick after trick.

Elazethrek slammed into Naero with the force of an exploding planetoid. It ensnared her in a net of Darkforce lightning and jolted Naero with shock charge after shockcharge until Naero's teeth rattled and she convulsed, even in her energy being form.

At the last instant Om transported them away before Naero blacked out and shrank down to her normal form.

The Creature hurtled at her again, impossibly fast, as Naero struggled to recover and star tap to replenish her energies.

Elazethrek fell upon her once more, bent on draining all of her remaining energies.

Naero could tell from the shift in the Cosmic flows emanating around the thing. Perhaps that was a weakness that could be exploited. In a sense, this Creature always seemed to telegraph her moves, so overconfident that her overpowering attacks would succeed and overwhelm her opponent.

Naero retreated and transported away once again.

The problem remained that this thing, whatever it was, clearly outclassed her in almost every way.

Where was it getting such enormous amounts of Darkforce energy?

Desperate, she summoned Heartcleaver, her huge Cosmic sword, and tried to hold Elazethrek off with one of her greatest weapons.

All to no avail.

She flailed blows at her opponent, but the Creature blocked strikes with her shielded multiple arms, legs, and tail, even against horrendous bursts of Cosmic force.

It ignored Naero's most powerful abilities, almost as if they were nothing.

The Creature's defenses and even her armored body under all of that dense shielding seemed impervious to Naero's full range of attacks.

Eye of Annihilation! Naero shouted telepathically, opening her third eye wide and launching an all-out effort to destroy the fiend once and for all.

Elazethrek grinned her ranks of vicious fangs impossibly wider.

The thing actually absorbed or channeled those destroying energies away somehow.

One of Naero's most devastating weapons had no effect whatsoever.

Naero just stared for an instant, stupefied and frightened all at the same time.

Elazethrek continued her campaign of threats and premature gloating.

ONCE I CAPTURE YOU, LITTLE SPACK, I'LL ALSO TAKE THE LITTLE SHINING ONE, YOUR OLDEST. THE ONE WE'VE MADE SICK. YOUR OTHER USELESS WHELPS I WILL TORTURE, RIP THEM APART, AND DEVOUR THEM PIECE MEAL, WHILE THEY STILL LIVE AND SCREAM—RIGHT BEFORE YOUR EYES.

For an instant, Naero felt as if she were on fire. She tapped power from every direction on instinct.

She narrowed her eyes at the Creature and used the voice herself. LIKE HELL YOU WILL!

With Heartcleaver and her kicks slashing and smashing like wheels of spinning flame, Naero careened straight into Elazethrek with an amazing speed all her own, finally driving the fiend back.

It cried out in pain, rage, and some degree of surprise.

Naero succeeded in hurting it at last.

Heartcleaver sliced a huge gash, deep down through the Creature's torso.

Anything living or any normal energy being would have been slain instantly.

Yet Naero and Om both sensed that this foul thing was not a true living being—but some horrible form of unlife, a type of horrible existence that defied all normal and rational forms of true life. A terrifying thing that should not really exist, and yet Naero was fighting it, and losing.

Like and yet unlike a true living energy being, comprised almost completely of the Darkforce and its anti-life powers, it sealed up the mortal wound in a flash and shifted into yet another fearsome battle form.

Then it shot at her once more.

YOU'RE DONE SURPRISING ME, LITTLE ONE. LET US END THIS.

A sphere of invulnerable green energy smashed into Elazethrek from her left flank with devastating speed as it crunched into the Creature, sending it spinning away.

Her beloved Khai had joined the fight, coming at once to her aid.

Naero's uncle Baeven appeared, intercepting the thing, slicing at it in his own, near Darkbeast form until huge splashes of Cosmic sparks and gouts of Darkforce energy spewed out. The thing actually shrieked in agony at the wounds Baeven inflicted.

Baeven deflected it once more, spinning in another direction. Elazethrek transformed into yet another variation.

Janner, Shalaen, Jia, and Ra appeared in their energy forms, pummeling the Creature with fresh energy blasts and explosions, rocking it and giving it no chance to recover.

Naero joined in on the combined attack, closing in on the Creature, opposite of Khai.

Hundreds of energy beings from the Interdimensions formed a spherical net of Cosmic energy that quickly collapsed in an attempt to trap the thing within.

Even under such a relentless assault, Elazethrek merely laughed, opened a wyrmhole at will, and slipped away in a blur before anyone else could react.

Naero was alive, but they were still little better off now than they were before.

This powerful, unstoppable, inherently evil thing—brought back from an ancient war millions from years ago—still roamed the stars at will, able to unleash devastating attacks on them and their allies, any time, and anywhere.

Not only that, there were five more of these abominations, each one ten times more powerful than the other waiting in the wings to get out.

Great.

Naero felt it when Shetharra passed out.

She immediately transported to her daughter's side, doing all that she could to bolster the child's strength and energy.

Don't worry, N. Baeven and Khai and the others have destroyed or driven off the last enemy warships. One of the new fixer clouds is covering the hospital ship, keeping it from breaking up. We'll limp it out of here, back to the Gamma Quadrant for repairs.

Thanks, Om.

Shalaen and Jia joined her in Shetharra's medical bay.

Soon the three of them had the child stabilized and resting.

Naero lay upon the medbed with her, enfolding her brave little duck in the protection of her arms.

She tried to sing to her child through their special link.

I had to, Momma. I had to do it. There was no other way.

Naero suddenly grew very worried.

What did you do, Shetharra?

He was going to kill all of us, Momma. I could not let him do that. I had to make him focus just on me. I've blocked the way into this sphere where he found us. Now he has to get through me before he can kill all of the others.

Who, Shetharra? What did you do?

You don't understand, Momma. The sickness just isn't in the regular world; it's coming at us from every place possible. That's how he intends to kill me, and then the others. We have to stop him.

Shetharra. Who is behind all of this?

The worst of the three bad ones, Momma. He's the biggest, nastiest one of them all: The Dark Emperor.

Even as Naero held her child, a fresh wave of the enemy's relentless plague struck Shetharra once more.

10

The attacking disease did not relent. In fact, it seemed to war against Shetharra with renewed fury, as if it had a mind and a will all its own.

Perhaps it did.

How was any of this possible?

Was the Dark Emperor truly behind the driving force of this plague? What was the extent of this mysterious affliction?

But Shetharra's words proved true.

A flood of reports declared that the other Spacer children in more than two quadrants were now recovering.

Had her child actually somehow protected them all by placing herself fully in harm's way, taking on the brunt of the Nahaxrathrax's vile assault?

She considered the ramifications of all of that.

Where could she even begin?

Naero stood by in the Intensive Care medical bay of *The Angel Wing*, watching helplessly over the course of an hour while the enemy inflicted Cosmic sickness warred relentlessly with Shetharra's life forces.

Her oldest daughter.

Her brave little duck.

She felt the same fear and terror that any mother would, and more.

How could they fight a disease such as this, when they couldn't even understand how many levels it functioned on? It even seemed to have a spiritual component. Where did it originate from? How many ways was it attacking her daughter?

For all of their power and knowledge Naero, Jia, and Shalaen all remained stumped, powerless against the terrible energies that were swarming in to try to kill a powerful young child before she came into her full might and wonder. And causing her terrible pain in the process.

Next, Naero burned silently with a terrifying fury, ready to outright murder any monster, being, or force in the entire universe that threatened her family, and her people. If only she could find the right ways to fight them.

Violence she understood.

Yet these beings were ancient of mind and subtle beyond all measure.

They were masters of power, cunning, and deceit.

To defeat and destroy such powerful foes would take more than mere physical force and violence.

She and the Alliance needed to fight these foes and crush them on many different levels.

In the end, Naero realized that this was rapidly evolving into a war of knowledge and enlightenment, perhaps just as it had always been. And still there was something more going on.

This really was a war of right versus wrong, against Cosmic Good and Evil, in every way that mattered.

To her mind, she and the Alliance were in the right. The right to exist was the greatest primary right of all sentient beings.

Everything else ran a distant second thereafter.

If any sentient and their kind were all butchered, mutilated, and murdered, nothing much else was going to matter after that.

All the enemy knew how to do was destroy; it was their very nature, all that they knew or desired. There was no negotiating with such fiends. Naero knew that all too well.

Once she had almost gone mad, and become just like them. They were somehow driven to obliterate everything they came into contact with, as if it were some kind of insane, fanatical mission.

Naero's mind raced in a multitude of directions as she looked upon her beloved child, infected with the enemy's Cosmic contagion, specifically engineered to kill her from within.

Shalaen and many other energy beings present noted that only Shetharra was capable of enduring such an assault this long. Any other energy being known to exist would have perished long ago.

No other Spacer child could have survived such torment.

As it was, Shetharra's quiet battle against the complex enemy disease was something mythic, like something out of legends, the legends from all of the known races as they looked on.

Darkness warring against Light.

Life itself, struggling against the very forces of Death.

There was nothing more that Naero could do—nothing more that any of them could do for now.

Shetharra burned out the Cosmic energy dampening globes at a rate of about one an hour, but that rate was also slowly increasing.

She would reach a point at this rate where she would be consumed entirely by the Cosmic sickness and fever, or else she would explode with a violence no one had ever seen before—much like a gigantic star going nova.

Naero turned to her friends, Jia and Shalaen. "Come with me."

How she wished that Zhen were with them.

She needed her old friend Zhen in this hour.

They had access to all of the Kexxian and Drian medical data dredged up so far concerning healing, disease, and illness. It also covered plague and germ warfare, even of the Cosmic varieties

Yet that was the exact problem.

Those sources of knowledge were so impossibly vast that it might take them all many normal lifetimes to sort out the exact data that they needed to deal with this precise threat.

They still had to try.

Naero and Jia helped Shalaen go into the Astral trance with them. In her energy being spiritmind form, it was almost second nature for her to do so.

They searched the KDM. They searched for two standard days to no avail.

All the while, Shetharra's condition slowly worsened, second by second.

The child of light continued to fight valiantly beyond measure, but she was still slowly losing her grand contest against the surety of death.

At the end of those two days, Naero and even Shalaen were mentally and emotionally exhausted.

Only Jia remained strong, alert, and ready to continue searching. Her fantastic spirit, much like her amazing, living Ultrium body, had been fashioned by godlike hands, and imbued with a mysterious purpose. Jia was immortal and imbued with wisdom and enlightenment beyond even her own understanding.

They went back in as soon as they recovered.

When all things seemed hopeless to Orean, a small pin point of light emerged from her forehead and a voice spoke to her.

Naero? Naero! Is that you in that Kexxian veil? I sense it is you.

Who? Orean asked.

It's me, Zhen. Someone or something awakened me. Where are we? What is this strange dimension? I sensed that I was needed somehow; that you wanted me to be with you. Was my soul still asleep within you? You... you haven't found a way to bring me back yet, have you?

No, Z. No I haven't. I'm so sorry. So far, I've failed at that too. I've failed you; I've failed...everyone.

Well, that's all right. I know it's hard. Don't feel bad. No one else has been able to do that same thing either. I know you'll keep trying.

I will, Zhen. You have my word, and you know what that means to me.

I do. Your word and your honor mean everything to you. Whether you succeed or not is immaterial. I know you'll keep trying, forever if need be.

I will.

How...how are they, N?

Ty and Gallan are great. They're doing well.

That much was true. At least being shielded with his father, little Gallan had so far avoided the enemy plagues designed to infect only Spacer children.

Her anger swelled once again, just thinking of the vile minds that would develop such a weapon on purpose and with the full intent to use it. How ruthlessly practical. Kill off the younger generations, and in a matter of a century of two, by default any war would be over.

Zhen had missed out on quite a lot.

Aij and Shalaen returned to them.

Who are you conversing with? Aij asked.

Who could be here in the KDM besides us? Shalaen added. *Oh, is that Zhen's soul? Did you release it? I thought you were keeping it dormant until—*

I emerged on my own. Hello Shalaen, Jia. But I'm growing weaker. I don't know how long I can remain like this.

You need to choose a spiritmind form to maintain your existence in this place, Shalaen added.

Where are we? Zhen asked once more.

Aij tried to explain. *We're inside the KDM, inside of Naero. I know. It's extremely weird.*

Right. If it's inside Naero, of course it's very weird.

Hey, Orean said.

Shalaen jumped back in. *This is some kind of pocket dimension, or even more like the Interdimensions, or an alternate reality, all to itself.*

They're right, Z. You need to choose a spiritmind form, either Kexxian or Drian in nature. You're not naturally an energy being like Shalaen is.

Zhen's soul orb floated between Orean and Aij, as if choosing between their spirit forms. *Hmmm...not Kexxian, and N's whacked out mind is too weird for me.*

Thanks, again, you quack.

Sure thing, N. No, I think I have to go with a Drian spiritmind form. Aij's mind is more organized and disciplined, more like my own. Even if her entire mind is currently beyond my comprehension.

Aij laughed. *Follow my lead Zhen. I'll help make the transformation easier. I'll have you thinking like a Drian in no time.*

Zhen's soul orb grew brighter and brighter.

Then a slightly smaller Drian spirit form stood before Aij, holding hands with her. Although her spirit form seemed to be shining living quicksilver, she was shaped exactly like Zhen's old material body.

Haisha! Orean gasped.

The shining being looked at Orean and smiled. *Greetings, Orean of the Kexx. Here in this place of knowledge and wisdom, I am Nehz of the Drians. I am all that you knew me to be from before, and now much more.*

Orean couldn't help embracing her. It was beyond hope to have her friend back, even in this form.

Welcome, Nehz. Good to have you with us. I'll explain to you what we're attempting, and what we're up against using our telepathic mind link. That will save a lot of time.

Wait, Aij said. *Nehz, how long will you be able to maintain this spiritmind energy form?*

Nehz paused. *Sixty-two standard days, nine hours, seventeen minutes and—*

Good enough, Orean noted.

Aij smiled. *Like my form, she won't tire. She doesn't have a physical body to return to right now like the rest of us, so she can keep searching for the data we need constantly, during all of that time. She can continue to do so even after we leave to rest. Go ahead with the mindlink transfer, O. Let her know where we stand.*

What happens if I don't return her soul inside of me before that time is up? Orean asked.

Then her soul will go on to the next journey, Shalaen said. *Just as before. But you won't let that happen.*

No. She wouldn't. At least with Nehz helping them now, they could check in with her, assist her when they could, and go on with their equally important lives outside of the KDM's realm of knowledge.

After getting Nehz situated, they returned out of their trance.

Naero cried in Khai's powerful arms that night and he held her close while they talked about the chances Shetharra had and so many other things.

The ongoing efforts to analyze the strange and powerful Creature Elazethrek and discover some kind of weakness in the abomination thus far proved fruitless.

They still knew of no way to either stop or outright destroy the thing.

Naero and Khai had a quiet dinner the next evening with Baeven and Jia, Shalaen and Tarim, and Tyber and Galan, and oddly enough—with Alala and Om.

They invited Jan and his family, but the latter begged off for some reason, saying they were busy this time around. Curious, but no big deal.

Naero was still so upset that she couldn't bring herself to cook, the way she usually did when she and Khai entertained.

Eugene was all too happy to fill in.

Dinner was delicious and wonderful, but a pall of concern and worry hung over the get together.

They spoke together quietly, shifting around in small groups, talking about what else—the war and all of its problems.

Yet everyone avoided talking about Shetharra or asking how she was doing. They knew better.

Ty left early to tuck Gallan in, his ready excuse to be sullen and anti-social.

Naero decided that it was better not to mention anything yet about Zhen's soul helping them on the inside of the KDM.

Khai spoke with hope about all of the information they were getting.

He, Baeven, and Jia discussed how well the new Ultrium infused fixers and ships were performing.

Khai warned Baeven, "Soon we'll have warships on par with *The Star Fox.*"

Baeven laughed. "If only we could. Although that ship isn't technically a warship, it is advanced Drian Tek that still remains far beyond any of us. Even Jia doesn't know all of its secrets, yet; and she merges with it. None of us are as advanced as we'd like to be, against an enemy far more ancient and knowledgeable than we are."

"Perhaps they aren't. We are fortunate," Jia said, "that the enemy's minds were damaged when they originally perished. However they store their information, they lost and forgot much, and are only beginning to retrieve parts of their advanced knowledge and tek to use against us these days."

"Do you think they have something like their own KDM?" Tarim asked.

Naero considered that possibility for the first time. "That's a very interesting question."

"The Drians definitely had something similar," Jia said. "But even the Driathans have yet to find it. Perhaps they took it with them, wherever they went when they left."

"They must have had something like it," Shalaen noted. "Otherwise the Kexx would not have had so much Drian knowledge and tek to record. It stands to reason then, that there must also be a G'lothc data base somewhere, somehow. The Kexx were very thorough about recording every form of knowledge they encountered."

Alala picked up the thread of thought. "Indeed. You said that the Drian wing of the KDM stayed hidden until a Drian attuned mind and soul such as Jia's sensed and unlocked it. Then it would stand to reason that a mind and soul more attuned to either the G'lothc or perhaps the Darkforce might sense and unlock a batch of knowledge centered around G'lothc tek, data, and thought."

Naero still had trouble looking at Alala and Om in their holos as a potential couple. Of course they chose humanoid forms in order to fit in. But today, Alala had chosen a form that looked as if it were filled with stars, except for her bright blue eyes and a human mouth that looked human inside when she spoke. This proved very distracting and disorienting, although Naero and everyone else struggled to avoid it, or saying anything about it.

Om was little better. His form changed colors within at will, and seemed to have lightening going off inside of himself constantly. Talk about distracting.

From time to time, Om would attempt to make some clumsy show of affection toward Alala, who of course had no frame of reference and completely ignored him,

Naero wondered if she should have a talk with Alala, or leave things well enough alone.

Despite the gloominess around them, Naero still felt better having her friends and loved ones around her. They were all working toward the same goals at least.

With the war and things going the way they were, their gathering could not maintain much cheer and broke up early.

Khai and Naero both spent that night sleeping on either side of little Shetharra as she continued to suffer. She was no longer dying, but she wasn't cured yet either.

That made for a very helpless situation for any two parents, whether they were Cosmic champions or not.

11

Naero spoke urgently before the very next Alliance planning session while the research teams continued to pore through all of the vids and scans of the most recent skirmish with Elazethrek. Naero struggled to remember any important details, anything that might help them gain an edge to defeat this new enemy.

Om was also there to help remind her. *The Creature let slip something about how long and complex the process was to give her spirit a vessel to use once more. And then again about what a huge amount of energy it took. It said that it would take just as much time and energy if not more to give form to another of her kind—the Six Darkforce Champions of the G'lothc.*

Jia spoke up. "Look again at the energy reads at the beginning of the attack. This confirms what we observed before."

Baeven grunted. Others saw it as well. "That's a massive amount of specialized Darkforce energy. This Creature is loaded with it—almost as if she's exploding with it from within.

Much the same as you and your uncle, N. But at even high levels.

Sounds like you and me, uncle. And Jan and the others as well, to a slightly lesser degree.

"By comparison, this Creature is similar in some very basic ways to all hyper-advanced energy beings," Shalaen noted. "But the energies are almost completely different, in all of us, to speak true. This thing that we now face is indeed unique in many other ways that we have yet to encounter or understand, both in the type of energies and the impossible levels that it seems to function at."

Naero sighed. "However long it takes, however difficult the process, the fact remains that the enemy has succeeded in giving one of the Six a vessel once again, in these different versions we are now fighting. We must also accept that if they brought back the least of the Six, they can and will eventually bring back the others. How can we possibly defend the Alliance against such impossible monsters?"

No one had an answer.

Naero swallowed hard. For a moment she could not speak any longer.

Finally she could.

"Jia and Baeven might have some inkling about what we're up against. But I'm the only one who has been studying the extensive Kexxian Data Matrix files on what they knew about the Six. Do you have any idea what these fiends are capable of?"

Baeven smiled. "I suppose you're getting ready to enlighten us, N. Don't scare us too much." Everyone present laughed.

"We will find a way to defeat this one, and any others who come our way," Jia said. "We have always found a way to defeat our foes."

"We will? Are you so certain of that? You don't get it," Naero said. "I couldn't beat this thing, and this was the weakest of them in their day. They all might even be stronger now, for all we know. I tried everything I knew, unleashed every attack I have, and I could barely hurt it...just barely. It was the same way with Baeven. He could annoy it, but neither of us got close to inflicting a mortal blow."

"We ganged up on it," Ra noted. "At least together we all managed to drive it off."

Naero clenched her teeth and her fists. "Or else it just decided to leave, to fight us at a better time when it could separate, corner, capture, or kill one or more of us outright. It said it wanted to use my energies to help bring back more of the Six. Face it. We're all just batteries to the enemy— Cosmic power sources to help fuel their efforts. They want to drain all of us. But if they can't do that, they'll settle for eliminating us wherever they can."

Baeven crossed his arms. "If it's after us, if we're its targets, then we need to stick together and protect each other. We have a better chance if we fight this Creature on a combined level."

"I agree," Janner said. "Together we can find a way to take it down."

"I'm still not so sure, Jan," Naero said. "If even one more of these things is reborn, we might not be able to stop them, or chase them off, like we did with this one. And that took all of us teamed up against her."

"Here's something else," Jia noted.

All of them looked at her eagerly, for any sign of hope.

Jia continued. "As we noticed before, the energy levels when it departed were much lower. Notice the decay and depletion rates."

Naero, the Creature was losing energy on its own, at a near critical rate all the while. You and the others had little to do with that. Its own actions were depleting itself. That's a huge flaw that we might be able to exploit.

I can see that, Om. "Everyone, do you realize what this means? Not only do Elazethrek's powers have a limit in their amount, but it is also a matter of duration. The Creature can only stay active at its peak levels for so long."

"Then it must go back somewhere to feed, to recharge and replenish its energies for its next attack."

"If we could find out where it is based," Jan added, "we could attack it while its energies are still depleted. Then it would be weaker and more vulnerable."

"If we could manage to trap it somewhere, somehow," Shalaen said, "then eventually it would run out of power and become helpless."

Naero brought them full circle. "Or, if it is like most of the enemy's whacked out creations, it might even consume itself, implode, or tear itself apart—if it cannot properly feed on the huge quantities of energy it needs to sustain itself and be able to act."

Baeven laughed heartily. "So, if it doesn't slay us outright, we can try to survive against it long enough to at least try to wear it down."

Naero grinned. "One thing is certain. Its powers are not limitless. That's good to know. We might be able to deplete its energies faster and chase it off. Also good to know. But we still don't have the foggiest notion about how to go about destroying it and actually taking it down, even if we did capture the damn thing."

Tyber called out to them over another com link. "Hey my friends, Alala and I might have finally come up with a strategy to neutralize and capture one of their new warships."

That possibility immediately took precedence.

Thus more days followed of desperate attempts to corner one of the new enemy Ultrium vessels. Fleet One and Fleet 73 remained ready to assist the hunters, along with the energy being patrols waiting as a backup, prepared to rush in.

Often the enemy attackers hit and ran, a withering and valuable strategy for them that kept their losses to a minimum and more importantly, made it nearly impossible for the Allies to knock out and capture one of the new ships

Naero advised the hunters to cloak their forces and join the front lines, giving them a chance to lend aid when and where needed, and also get a chance to at least observe, if not get a shot at an actual target.

Finally their persistence paid off.

Aiding an attacking enemy fleet was a new model enemy destroyer of the Dakkur design. A long thick tube of gray Ultrium alloy, the destroyer had main gun nodules located at both ends. These battery arrays could lock onto targets almost within three-hundred and sixty degrees, and were extremely effective.

The scarlet blasts from the destroyer ripped through even the best Alliance shields and armor after just a few hits, and the rate of fire was equally formidable.

The enemy secondary batteries were actually even more destructive up close.

The destroyer in question had seriously damaged about two dozen Alliance warships and was already turning and preparing to jump when Naero's forces uncloaked all about it.

They hammered the vessel soundly and thought that they had neutralized it from the start. All of the destroyer's systems went down, and it had suffered heavy to critical damage.

For all intents and purposes it was a ruined hulk floating helplessly in the black

Naero and Baeven and their strike team went out to secure the ship, search it briefly, and then take it in tow.

They still couldn't take any chances.

Scans showed that all of the alien crew drones were dead. The enemy had now taken to using crews of Ejjai and other alien slaves taken over by the new enemy mind control wraiths.

Such crews did not know fear, fought to the last without question, and followed orders sharply. They were also devoid of free will and could not offer any input or seize upon any sudden advantage or initiative the way that "live" crews could.

There was always a disadvantage to using slaves of any kind.

In such attempts on the enemy's part to run their naval campaigns remotely and micromanage their movements and strategies, there was always a tradeoff that usually worked against them in the end.

Those who fought for both freedom and survival had a definite edge.

The Alliance fleets, not being piloted and led by slaves or witless drones, always seemed to have the real tactical and strategic advantage.

Om warned Naero about the sudden Darkforce energy spike emanating from within the shattered destroyer.

N, it must have self-regenerating AIs on the ship preparing to detonate itself. Think fast.

"Energy drain protocols on my mark!" Naero commanded over their secure link.

Baeven was already attacking, about one instant before Naero. Khai, Janner, Shalaen, and all of the rest joined in.

Whatever controlled the destroyer did everything in its power to transmogrify the energized Ultrium of the captured warship into a massive hyper bomb.

They siphoned the huge energy surges away to prevent a massive explosion.

Where was all of this power coming from? What was the source and how did the ship tap into it?

Naero, attack the ship psyonically. Trust me!

She broke off and did so.

Even as her powerful mindblasts slammed into the ship and its overloading systems, she spotted the trouble, just as Om had.

It wasn't just enemy living AIs controlling the enemy vessel. It was three actual G'lothc minds, in hyper-modified Darkforce generator psyonic pods.

Hyper cyborg shipminds.

Naero attacked them head on with her own powerful psyonic might.

Two of the Ultrium brains she crushed and burn out instantly.

The other shielded itself just long enough to detonate the back half of the vessel.

"Shields. Shields or transport away!" Naero warned.

Even with the combined shielding power of all of the Alliance Cosmic Champions present, the blast was so intense that all of them took damage, and so did the nearest ships of the fleets present.

Shalaen and Janner were stunned and suffered the worst injuries as a result; Jia and Baeven the least. In the last instant, Jia had wrapped herself around Baeven, her own perfect, Ultrium body almost invulnerable to the blast, although a few of her minor systems were disrupted, until she affected repairs and regenerations.

Naero flashed to Jan's side to assist in his regeneration. Ra did the same with Shalaen. They brought their stricken comrades on board *The Angel Wing*.

Success at last, even though it had nearly killed them. But they finally had half of an enemy ship to study and dismantle. Naero also divulged the before unknown psyonic connection of the enemy super warships and their shipminds.

The Alliance now had many new ways to attack and try to capture those advanced enemy warships.

They were lucky that the other half of that Dakkur destroyer had not exploded. Some of them might have actually been killed, and there certainly would have been many more casualties among the assisting fleets.

As it was, an entire new fixer cloud had to constantly drain the captured vessel of energy. The damn thing constantly tried to repower and explode.

When they had the chance to go after another enemy ship, they used improved strategies and techniques.

First, the assigned fleets kept a healthier distance away, even as they initially closed in, based upon the explosive yields of Ultrium hyper bombs, estimations based also on the Ultrium mass of the ships converted to energy.

It was two standard days later that the hunters faced down one of the G'lothc designed tentacle ships, a full sized battleship, which devastated everything that came near it with its glowing, violet and black tentacle cannons.

Naero's fleets remained cloaked, coordinating their efforts to close in, and yet remain out of the line of fire during an intense battle. Not an easy task.

Naero and her Alliance Champion team carefully maneuvered into position.

Then they hit the shielded psyonic shipminds running the battleship with everything they could muster.

The hunter fleets uncloaked and rocked the vessel with big guns from all directions, armed with the latest energy drain beams to deplete the heavily charged Ultrium ship and its systems.

Six of the twelve enemy shipminds shrieked and died almost instantly, ripped asunder and burned out. But the other six shielded and deflected some of the attacks, and then fought back.

The barrage of assaults continued on all levels and blazed back and forth, racing against time.

Even as Naero and Baeven zipped in close, they kept up their psyonic attacks, transformed into their near Darkbeast forms, and ripped into the enemy battleship's main guns. They severed many of the tentacle cannons and flung them away.

These enemy super weapons were almost entirely formed out of structural Ultrium made flexible, but infused with Darkforce energy in a way that had not been thought possible.

Each big gun on the enemy battleships was a living thing, much the same as the Darkforce generators, with a will of its own, kind of. This was living mass and energy on an impossible scale. The guns could target and fight independently on their own, or be coordinated together by their sophisticated, near-hive mind masters.

It was as if each big gun was also an extremely powerful energy being.

A wyrmhole formed out of nowhere and the enemy battleship raced into it.

"Should we follow it?" Baeven shouted.

"No!" Naero screamed back.

"We can locate one of their secret bases!"

He moved to venture in with the retreating battleship.

Clearly they were the only two persons present who could have done so.

Naero wrapped her arms around her uncle and flashed them onto the bridge of *The Dark Star* with Tyber.

Just as the aft of the damaged enemy battleship passed through the wyrmhole, the portal vanished with a dark flash.

"What the hell, Naero?" Baeven protested

"They can't lose either of us. They need us too much, uncle. I made the right call. We have no idea where we would have ended up, or what we would have faced alone. What if it was the Creature? Right now, we can't beat her. Always remember, if one or both of us falls or gets captured. That's it. Game over. Everyone else we know and love will eventually die. Without the two of us, the enemy will kill off all of the others. We can't take that chance."

Baeven shook his head in grudging agreement. "I suppose you're right."

Naero smiled. "No supposing about it. But hey, the salvage and recovery teams are bringing in a bunch of those living Darkforce cannons we hacked off. At least that should tell us something about how to shield against them and such. Haisha! Let's go take a look."

12

Thiolin music played in one of the Sword Rooms on board the flagship.

Naero and Khai joined many of the crew there for some exercise, and brought the kids, minus Shetharra.

Despite still being ill, Shetharra protested, whined, and nearly threw a royal fit. But Naero put her foot down. She left her oldest daughter sulking and angry at both her parents.

Of course once she had failed with her mom, Shetharra then tried the same routine all over again with her father. But he had been on to that act for some time.

Shetharra hated missing sword practice.

To call the Sword Room such was an understatement.

It was an arena complex with many levels of clear, plasteel floors, and walls filled with every kind of sword and practice sword known to exist. The nanowalls and weapon displays shuffled and racked this way and that, presenting its wares to the practitioners to utilize, forming practice nano clothing and armor as needed.

There was even a lix station that rose up and down between the levels, for refueling from sweaty matches, complete with Jett, of course.

Naero and her group occupied one entire floor. She and Khai worked with the kids for a bit, and then just let them play and run around.

Dae and Kath had some small discipline, and with two swordmaster parents, they had their own sets of practice swords designed for their small size and hands.

Allantar was not yet three years of age and he had practice swords, the same way that both Naero and Khai had been raised.

Khai was the Mystic Enforcer, swordmaster without peer—almost.

Naero could still beat him every third time, and with her battle blades she could even fight him to a standstill half the time. But he remained the swordmaster of swordmasters, the best there was.

Naero was content to be a trickster, the Mystic Guardian of Enlightened Change.

Together with the kids they were also a family, and leaders and friends to their crew. All of them protected each other. To the last Spacer the crew of the flagship was proud to work with them.

Naero and Khai made the rounds, watching matches, giving pointers.

Officers Enel Maeris and Surina Marshall dueled with one another in earnest, looking both amused and determined.

They even teamed up to challenge their admiral to a quick match.

Enel seemed content. Surina was happily two months pregnant with the couple's first child—a girl. Naero couldn't help noticing. Biomancy just came too easy to her.

She didn't tell them because they swore to her that they didn't want to know yet.

Tolen and Eugene had left the Galley long enough for one of their required monthly training sessions. They chose energy cutlasses, the flashy practice variety. Tolen was actually quite the hand with one, and from their friendly rivalry, Eugene was getting better all the time.

Passaendra Wilde, Master Engineer Rendar Nelson, and Medical Chief Trudi Cheyenne goofed around enough to fulfill their required exercise quota, but then they merely hung out at the lix bar and talked about old times. Naero had a quick slug of Jett with them. Just one borbble and done.

Then she looked down and saw Shetharra, wielding her twin, scaled down katanas and playing with the kids, Khai, as well as Tyber and young Gallan.

How could her husband be so careless and dumb?

There was her oldest girl, glowing all over, out of her sick bed.

Naero transported right to them.

She yelled at Shetharra. "Young lady, your father may be a stupid pushover, but I am not. Get back to the Medical Center, this instant!"

Shetharra looked hurt. "Mom, I am still in the Medical Center. I haven't left. Uncle Ty-"

"Uncle Ty? What does he have to do with this?" All of them started to laugh, only making her steam and grow angrier.

Khai glared at Uncle Ty. "You'd better tell her and quick," he warned.

"Tell me what?" Naero fumed. Then she reached out and poked Shetharra's shining form.

Definitely not a holo. It had substance, mass, and weight. But that touch also told her that this Shetharra was some kind of...fake. "Haisha. A replicant?"

Fake Shetharra rolled her eyes. "I'm not a replicant, Mom. I can't do that. Only you can."

Tyber was about to bust. "She's a synthezoid construct based upon your daughter's body, N. Shetharra can use it like a holo, and project her thoughts and will through it, but she can also interact with the real world. Amazing, right? Alala and I just perfected the processes involved. She and Om both have one now. Anyone can. It's based on the same process used with the Mystic fighting constructs.

"Even the military is looking into Marines, Allied soldiers, and the Navy using them for remote, dangerous missions. The host can direct the construct warrior from the safety of a bio-pod that remains far away. We can even program extra strength and speed. They can even crew starfighters and warships. Even if the construct is destroyed, the real warrior is never lost, slain, or injured. All they feel is slight discomfort."

Naero was amazed, and she would even be more impressed if all of that other conjecture would work.

The enemy could simply find a way to disrupt or negate the constructs, or the control signals being sent to them.

But the new tek was allowing her oldest daughter to remotely play with her family and friends from her sick bed. And for now, that was a good enough for Naero.

"Good work, Ty. It's okay, Shetharra. You go play. I didn't understand."

Khai kissed his wife. "Hey, you said I was stupid."

Naero turned to him as the kids ran off, placing a hand on his broad chest. "I deeply apologize, my heart. Will you allow me to make it up to you?"

He grinned. "Always. That's the plan I like."

*

Studying the wealth of new data they now possessed left the research teams even more baffled and bewildered than before.

Clearly much of the new or ancient G'lothc tek was still well beyond them, even when they had it staring them in the face.

Their new Ultrium fixers could also only bring them along so far.

Ignorance was still ignorance.

In order to break free from their limitations, Naero brought more of her friends along with her. They entered the soul trance and ventured into the expansive realms of the KDM inside of herself.

Together they would continue the search and explore in logical pairs.

Jia would naturally accompany and guide Baeven.

For the first time, Om and Alala would have energized spiritmind forms all their own—the closest thing known to actual existence, beyond holos and Tyber's new synthetic constructs.

Nor was it known how the KDM would react to any of them. On a mental level, Om was a Kexxian AI construct, so advanced that he was a true mind at his current level. The same could be said for Alala.

Both of them were already well beyond the definitions of true sentients.

Naero would pair up with Ra. She was very curious about how a Shai mind and spirit would interact with the KDM.

She had discovered that both the Ku and the Shai had been the last races to be created, uplifted, and nurtured before the Kexx and the Drians had vanished, so long ago. To her mind, that must make them special.

Then there would be the pairing of Tyber with the spirit mind of his dead wife, Zhen.

At last she had told him the secret, and tried to keep him from expecting too much from such a reunion.

But for Ty, even being able to talk and interact with his beloved Zhen in any form once more, was a risk he was willing to endure.

Clearly such a meeting would be very emotional at first. That could not be helped. But both of them remained excellent minds, with many valuable insights between them. Zhentisa was very ordered and analytical, while Tyber was chaotic and very imaginative in an unconventional way that was still astute and practical. He had proven that many times.

The Alliance still desperately needed answers, and Naero needed all of the assistance that she could pull together. All of their insights combined could not but help their dire situation.

Once they were in the trance, Naero transformed into Orean and guided them in. The initial period of being overwhelmed by the sheer majesty and dimensions of the Kexxian gift passed within a few minutes, under her guidance.

Naero could sense Jan's eagerness and inner turmoil.

Baeven gasped as Aij attempted to help him transform his spiritmind further into a Drian. Yet where Aij's liquid metal form was all silver shining light, Neveab was dark, mercurial, almost gunmetal black and brooding, smoldering Chaos, with even some of the Darkforce mixed in for good measure. His dark eyes now seemed to be lit with scarlet Chaos lightning roiling from within.

If Aij was a goddess of light, Neveab was a dark god of the untainted night of the universe—the void from whence all things emerged

How fitting, Naero surmised.

To a lesser degree, Om and Alala also became something akin to yin and yang all on their own, neither Kexxian nor Drian. Here, as humanoid energy beings in form only, Om was now jet black with a slightly dark aura around him, like some primal titan or demigod. In opposite of him, Alala transformed into a blinding white lantern, shifting and moving about, illuminated and radiant from within. But they remained themselves, and kept much of their personalities.

But somehow they were also neutral, each in their own unique ways.

Shalaen helped Janner transform into a Drian spiritmind form of a shining blue living metal being called Rennaj.

Naero as Orean assisted Ra into adjusting to being Ar, but he remained an insectoid mantid of the Shai race, only converted to a glowing, spiritmind form.

Tyber, try as he might, could not transform into either a Drian form, nor a Kexx. His form stayed humanoid, more neutral like Om and Alala, yet he took on a blue-violet hue with a fluctuating aura that shifted at will from scarlet, to azure, and violet and back again. This too was something new.

They still called him Rebyt.

They had yet to encounter Nehz in her Drian form. Naero knew where she was currently located, and in short while, she and Ar would personally take Rebyt to that place.

First she situated the others and put them all to work.

Most of them had had Orean as their guide at least once before when they had visited the KDM. Orean had already shown them the basics at least once. Some of them would continue to explore the KDM proper. Others would explore the equally near endless archives of the Drian Knowledge Source, the DKS as they referred to it now.

Then, without warning, Nevaeb's very presence unlocked and opened up yet another wide realm of hidden knowledge—the Core of G'lothc knowledge and wisdom that both the Drians and the Kexx had shared as allies.

Something Orean and Aij had long expected to appear.

Yet another entire realm of knowledge concerning what their great foe comprehended, knew, and believed.

Finally Orean and Ar brought Rebyt along with them.

"R, I need to warn you about something again. You need to prepare yourself for this."

"What now, O? Can some of this stuff in here harm us?"

"Yes, but not in ways that you would normally think. But you know very well what I'm taking you to."

He thought a second. "I know you've awakened Zhen's soul out of her dormant state, and you have her mind searching these data nebulae. I-I accept that. I just want to talk to her again."

Orean smiled sadly. "If you can't handle it, I can take you someplace else, R."

"Are you kidding me? I would fight you and every power in the universe to spend one second more with her if I could. Please, please Orean. Take me to her. Take me to her now."

Orean nodded and flashed them to the exact location.

Nehz was floating in the raw data flows with her back toward them. She stiffened slightly and turned her face.

One smile and Rebyt was right with her, no need for words, their spirit minds instantly and completely joined. Their forms almost melded together into one.

Hmm...I didn't think that it would be this easy. I think maybe those two need to be alone for a bit, before they get to work. I'll just send them to the realm of Music.

She flashed them there. Nehz knew her way around by now. Naero had seriously considered bringing Khai inside the KDM with her at some point, for a little spiritmind canoodling.

What would it be like with both of them in Kexxian forms?

Feelings and emotions within were so heightened and intensified here, even for spiritmind forms. It wasn't as great as sex inside a star, but it was pretty close.

Orean guessed that Nehz and Rebyt could use some of that about now. They deserved it.

The wonders within the KDM continued to abound and open before them all.

Each of them reported discovering insights and fragments of something different. It was still taking valuable time, but that was exactly as Orean hoped it would be.

Together they located further medical and biogen warfare data on the countless variations of the enemy phage, and the plague–like enemy mind control wraiths. There was further data on some of the Six Darkforce Champions of the G'lothc. What Orean scanned about these monsters and their many powers and abilities was both enlightening and horrifying.

Elazethrek was often called the least of the Six for good reason.

Each of the Six G'lothc Champions was not just stronger than the one before, but by an entire order of magnitude more powerful.

That did not bode well if another such monster appeared. They were monsters of the worst possible kind. Their acts of Cosmic savagery and atrocity were beyond fear and legend—especially when all of them and their powers were combined.

They had only known fear whenever they faced the Starkillers and the Kexxian Dreamers, who defied them, broke their might, and unmade them as these fiends once were.

Each of them found many references and data rivers that branched out in multitudes of directions concerning the many uses and applications of Ultrium. The energized, super alloy seemed to be the workhorse of all three main races before and during the Great War. They used it for nearly everything.

It finally reached the point where the searchers had more than enough information to attempt to comprehend and apply. Some insights were straight forward and applications could begin immediately.

Others would need to wait, and go through a discovery, comprehension, and experimentation process.

They had a great deal to sort and sift through, but they had clearly done well. The questions multiplied as to whether they could ever apply all of this valuable knowledge fast enough.

After they emerged, Naero and Khai took a few more days to be with their family and watch over Shetharra. Some of the new medical insights could also help her. Naero wanted to see those through.

On a lighter note, understandably, Captain Tyber requested as much time with the KDM as possible.

Yet he grew heartbroken once more, when Nehz explained that her time in her spiritmind form was finite, and once completed, it could not be replicated. Her soul would go dormant once more, and Naero would need to keep it safe within herself.

Tyber would have to face losing her yet again, with no end to their ordeal in sight.

An answer to that problem continued to elude them.

13

Naero and Khai rushed to the energy being critical care ward at three bells.

Khai's face could not have been more ashen, and he was bright green. Naero guessed that she looked just as grim. An urgent summons at that late watch could not be good news.

They flashed in as close as they could and ran the rest of the way swiftly on foot. With all of the Cosmic energy flows around that place, they couldn't take a chance of accidentally disrupting them in any way that might harm their oldest daughter.

The Cosmic energy dampening spheres were now barely keeping Shetharra alive at this point and nearly burning out as fast as the medical fixers reformed them about the suffering child.

As the situation began to death spiral, Naero attempted something that Zhen, Shalaen, and Jia had all suggested.

There was nothing else to try at that point.

Naero flooded her daughter with certain random levels of specifically blended Cosmic energy. In the most extreme cases involving some of the phage infections, this technique sometimes worked as a last resort.

It was no guarantee. Sometimes the being inflicted perished anyway.

Shetharra convulsed violently, but Naero kept up the treatment.

Once begun, there was no turning back.

Naero partially merged with her daughter through their special link, attacking the Cosmic disease within her child directly. She had to break off the mindlink she had with Khai and focus completely on Shetharra. They were counting on the fact that a gifted, eight year-old-child such as their oldest could withstand any damage the technique caused.

If the process did not work, Shetharra would be consumed and perish in any case.

Naero placed her hands on her little girl's thrashing body and took on the Cosmic plague head on, attempting to burn it out completely.

She fought it back on every level that she could conceive of: psyonic, biological, tek, Astral and Cosmic.

Yet she still felt as though she were missing something.

When Naero finished, over an hour later, she fell back spent into Khai's waiting arms, panting and dripping with sweat in her physical form.

She had done all that she could, fighting the invasive, relentless plague as if battling against an actual foe.

It sure felt like an actual foe.

Another respite was the result, but not a complete cure.

Shetharra's eyes flickered open. She smiled. "You saved me, Momma, at least for now. The Dark Emperor was trying to take me again, but you fought him off. You wouldn't let him have me."

Both Naero and Khai had tears rivering down their faces at that point. Naero couldn't even speak for a moment, but at last she swallowed hard, sobbed, and found her voice, as she kissed her daughters small hands.

"He will never have you, my brave little duck. Your father and I won't let him. You are going to live, and one day, these evil ones will tremble and flee in terror at the very mention of your name."

Shetharra whispered weakly, her eyes fluttering. "For I am Shetharra Lythe Maeris...I am the White Tsunami...and the Flame Eternal burns within my heart."

Naero sobbed and covered her mouth with her hands.

"That it most surely does!" Khai cried out, caressing her sweet face with his great big hands as he wept.

"Momma, Papa…the dark powers are still linked with me and will not let go. The Dark Emperor is still waiting, out there and inside me, looking for another way to kill me."

Naero almost broke down, covering her entire face with both hands. "I'm sorry. I did everything I could. I'll keep trying."

Shetharra shook her head. "You tried, and you came close, but you can't defeat it that way completely. You need to understand. It has made itself a part of me somehow, Momma. That is why you can't get rid of it. To kill it off completely, you might need… to let me die, destroy the Dark forces, and then bring me back. Only that will break the hold it has upon me now."

Naero was amazed. "Shetharra, how do you know all of this?"

"When I am close to dying, the Tua and the others come and speak to me. I'm much closer to them then and can hear them better. I can hear them sing to me."

She knew of the Tua. "What others, Shetharra? Who are these others that you speak of?"

"Why, the funny little glowing lizard people, Momma. There are seven of them. They're so funny, and they tell me so many things. They teach me the most amazing songs I have ever heard and their voices are so beautiful that I am drawn to them and the darkness pulls away. They tell me to dream, to dream and to sing as never before…ASHALA! ASHALA JEHO VANEL ELLEL ERUEL KHATAHLETH, ASHALA, ASHALA! JEHO VANEL SHAHIEL JANASHAR! JEHO VANEL, ASHALA. ASHALA!

Naero had a brief vision into a vast, dark void.

In that void, Shetharra was as big as a galaxy and glowing like she was now, like a star. She blocked the way past her into a universe on one side where all of the Spacer children spiritminds were sleeping and glowing softly like stars.

On the other side was a universe of harsher realities, darkness, and death, and a gargantuan monster like a huge black gigantic wyrm lurked in that darkness, and came against Shetharra and her light again and again.

Nahaxrathrax, the Dark Emperor. It was his will and dark powers that were set against the child of light, bent only upon crushing her, and an entire generation of Spacer children beyond.

Naero was viewing spiritual representations of both combatants, metaphors in a spiritual dimension, just another level of hyper-reality upon which this battle was being played out.

Shetharra had told the truth.

She was, in fact, protecting all of the other Spacer children from her fate.

And if she lost, there would be no protection for the others, and all of them would suffer and perish as well.

These were the great odds that were at stake.

Naero blinked, shuddered, shook herself and gasped, returning to the present.

A fierce light awoke within Shetharra as if she were a small star in that medbed. The radiant evanescence quickly spread out all around her, from her small body until the entire room was glowing, even the walls.

Khai gasped and then Naero did the same as the light washed over and passed through them all.

The medical equipment within the room flicked out for an instant, and then restarted again, humming and whirring back to operation once more.

All the while, little Shetharra kept singing her soft but mighty song until at last she drifted off into a deep healing sleep.

For the time being, nearly all of her pain was gone.

Om! Naero cried out within herself. Did you get all of that? Did you and the fixers record all of what just happened?

We did. We have it. But half of the fixers are down, completely burned out. Haisha! Seven levels of the flagship have been temporarily disrupted by this flash or flare, or whatever that was. Systems are coming back online now. Naero...I can't believe this!

Surprisingly, Naero's energies were completely regenerated, when she had been so depleted just moments before. "What are you talking about, Om? What happened?

Shetharra's flare did it, N. It must have. She transformed the Medical Center and most of those seven levels into pure Ultrium!

Naero gasped. That was a *Song of Making*, Om. She just sang another of the Kexxian Songs of Making—part of what only the Seven mightiest Dreamers could use to manipulate and create Matter and Energy out of nothing!

Khai wrapped them both up in his arms.

Baeven and Jia came to them in the Medical Center.

"What is it?" Naero said.

Ty, Jan, and Shalaen joined them seconds later.

"We have new data. The primary enemy Creature we face is not just infused with Darkforce Cosmic energy," Baeven said.

Jia added, "Its host body has also been infused with Ultrium tainted with the Darkforce."

"Elazethrek has Ultrium-laced blood, or fluid, or whatever such a monster has in its systems," Shalaen informed them.

"It's true," Janner said. "We have small fragments of the thing that finally divulged the truth. It couldn't jam our in depth scans forever."

Ty stated, "It's almost sixty-percent Ultrium alloys and compounds. It's as much a super being as Jia…or you and Baeven. And as we've seen, its powers are beyond anything we've ever witnessed. And yet Naero claims that the others of its kind are each infinitely stronger than the one before it."

Naero frowned. "I did not say infinitely, T. I said orders of magnitude greater than the one before, and I assure you, that would be more than terrible enough."

Jia spoke up. "With this knowledge, and time, we'll be able to find ways to defend against this Creature and eventually defeat and obliterate it."

Tyber paled all of the sudden. "Guys? Uh…how did most of the levels around us suddenly become mostly pure Ultrium? Are these scans right? How is this possible?"

Naero smiled down at Shetharra, now asleep. "I've got a little explaining of my own to do," she said.

Even as she finished speaking, alarms began to sound.

Khai reported that the enemy was unleashing yet another major assault, in the Prime Material Plane, the Astral Plane, and the Interdimensions. On all fronts, the great battle raged once more.

Brave Alliance fleets fought with obstinate valor, destroying and being destroyed in the face of the enemy's growing power. Still they fought on.

The Cosmic Champions raced out to join their friends at the nearest forefront.

They flung themselves against ancient tek that they were only beginning to understand, merely to push back their foes, or simply hold them in check.

Naero and her specialized group flashed from battle to battle on all three planes, doing just that, reacting to the enemy and putting out fires where they could.

Elazethrek still did not show itself at any point, and for now, the Alliance forces counted themselves fortunate for that continued respite.

The enemy tried a new tactic, however. They sent huge waves of combined phage and mind wraiths against the defenders along with the fleets of their new warships.

This time, the phage and wraiths exploded violently on contact with great destructive power.

The Alliance countered by sending waves of fixers out before them to intercept the enemy attack waves. These fixers were modified to emit waves of force that stunned the phage and the wraiths, drained them of their tainted Darkforce energies, and then incinerated anything that remained.

The result was more or less another destructive stalemate, as both sides surged forward and back, locked in their deadly contest.

Neither side gained much of an advantage, as of yet, but the losses and the odds continued to tip in their enemy's favor.

Naero took counsel with all of her friends and allies after the battles ended, to see what they could do about changing that momentum.

She also had a very intriguing new Kexxian song to learn, thanks to her oldest daughter.

14

When the tek breakthroughs did come for the Alliance, they often came through in a sudden flooding cascade, a wave of many insights, devices, practices, and utilizations that seemed to burst out all at once.

Tyber located and applied a new way of applying Ultrium tek to various forms of protective shielding. The new Ultrium boosted Kexxian shields absorbed and transformed energy into more stepped up shielding. The principles involved could soon be utilized in personal, vehicle, and starship shields, but the biggest breakthrough of all was actually in planetary and system defense shielding.

The Kexx and the Drians were masters of protecting their worlds with stepped up absorption shields which only grew stronger the more that they were attacked. They even absorbed energy from the planet's sun and grew more powerful, much the same way that Naero startapped.

An immediate program expanded rapidly to distribute such planetary defense systems to worlds in trouble and worlds the Alliance might have to leave behind. This included the slow, stubborn fighting retreat that the Alliance found itself in.

This new tek would give those frontline worlds the best chance to survive, until they could be relieved at a later date during or after the war.

Om and Alala both continued to expand more ways to utilize and further modify the new advanced Ultrium drones. These energized drones could adapt quickly and in large numbers. And they could do so nearly anywhere now, becoming defensive and reactive neutralization nebulae and defensive screens in their own right.

The new drones went up against the enemy phage and wraith clouds all along the front lines.

Nehz located more Kexxian medical files on using advanced medical fixer tek and offshoot machines and treatments that would help against any future plagues directed against the children of the Alliance.

Some of it could also be used to help Shetharra

Naero and Tyber manipulated many new techniques and principles to apply Ultrium related tek to the construction of advanced starfighters.

This took two primary forms.

In the first mode, Naero, Ty, and other teknomancers created Ultrium in the star furnaces and fed the base, energized alloys in long jetting streams into waiting nebulae of construction fixers. These super fixers would then use the raw materials to create new advanced starfighters with many specialized weapons, defenses, and abilities.

The second mode of adaptive construction was completely different.

One teknomancer or a team of them would create a special ionized Cosmic energy field, contained by energy flows around the raw materials in the vacuum of space.

This second process was too dangerous and would not work properly within the relatively unstable environments of different atmospheres. The vacuum of space was more constant and reliable.

Next, the new fixers working within highly charged, rarified fields would transmute the available alloys and materials directly into the actual form of a functioning starfighter and all of its systems into whatever version or design was needed. This included the formation of all of the proper Ultrium alloys—without the need for a solar furnace and a lot of wasted energy.

The latter technique was ten times slower, but in the end it was more economical, because it was much simpler and required far less energy. And the Alliance could compensate somewhat by increasing the number of assisting super fixers.

Both methods utilized many types of Cosmic energies and sustained fields, and had certain advantages and disadvantages.

The second method was exactly how the new phaze starfighters were developed, even though the first prototypes resulted in a number of over eager test pilot deaths.

New synthezoid construct drone test pilots were then used until the tek could be perfected.

Naero and the Alliance could hardly wait until sufficient numbers of these new deadly starfighters would reach the front lines of the war. Their F-75C Super Banshees would scream into action and certainly help even the odds, with more and more of the enemy's Ultrium warships joining the fight.

Yet these were still only starfighters, and not large numbers of the bigger fleet warships. The Alliance still had no practical way to effectively produce the massive quantities of Ultrium necessary for mass warship construction.

The Dark Star was one unique exception, but Naero, Ty, and the few hundred teknomancers in the Alliance were already in high demand. They couldn't spend all of their time simply transmuting Ultrium for warships. They were needed in too many other places and capacities as it was.

Naero knew that they had yet to unlock any of the major secrets of large scale Ultrium production in volume. They still had no idea how the Kexx or the G'lothc were doing so. And thus far there had been no time for her to research and experiment with the new Song of Making that she had learned from Shetharra.

If she used such a power in the wrong way, the results could be catastrophic. She simply had to know more before doing so. Further discussion with Shetharra proved useless. The child did not recall anything more about her fever dream, and she could barely remember the song itself.

Naero set such thoughts aside and continued studying teknomanced specs and data feeds from the new starfighters.

The new phaze shielding was fascinating and quite amazing.

These new Banshees would be impervious to direct or indirect fire, and they had the choice of absorbing any energies that hit them, or simply allow the reactive shielding to shunt any blast right through them as if they were ghosts. The new starfighters could also sweep straight through enemy fleets at top speed, leaving behind clouds of fixers to neutralize and capture the enemy vessels from within, or hi-tek ordnance to blast them to dust.

Tyber turned to working with the Spacer Marines to incorporate phaze shielding into individual battle armor. All of this was generations beyond current phaze armor tek, merely used to pass through solid barriers, such as a warship hull.

Once the new phaze shields were perfected, the Marines would truly be lethal phantoms haunting the Alliance battlefields. Energy blasts and explosions would pass right through them—while they kept fighting without interruption.

Casualty rates would go way down. Battles up in the black or on surface might now last only minutes and seconds, instead of days and hours. All of these new wonders were just weeks and months away from becoming reality.

System after system within the Alliance hurried to install the new planetary defense shields in both quadrants. Flurries of updates and upgrades sped through the military forces like wildfire, while the enemy advance kept on coming.

During one break in the action, Saemar and Chaela were able to join Naero and her kids for a few days.

Khai had just left the day before to perform some brief task for the Mystics.

"I'm sorry we missed that big lunk of yours, sweetie," Saemar said. "That guy's always an eyeful of fun, if you know what I mean."

"I do exactly," Naero said with a laugh.

"I like Khai a lot," Chaela said. "He's good for you, N. He only takes so much of your crap, and yet he's so sweet on you. Just like my Remy in many ways."

Naero smirked. "Thanks, Chae…I think. How is Remy? I'm sorry he couldn't join you and the kids."

"You know him, workaholic." The three friends laughed.

Chaela and Remy's kids, Derron, Jodian, Kaelen, and Pettaerra mixed it up with Dae and Kath, squealing, screaming, and having great fun. The visitors all had the long Viking blonde hair of their mother Chaela to match their blue eyes. A long golden braid hung down each of their backs as they ran and leaped about. They had Chae's good looks and Remy's naturally kind and winning personality.

Aunt Chae and Aunt Saemar were a special treat for the kids, just as Aunt Naero was for Chaela's kids.

They couldn't snuggle and kiss the little ones enough, when the latter stopped moving or came over for some attention.

Naero had plenty of staff on hand, so the two other admirals gave their people some rest. Many of those still chose to stay on hand, just in case, and made merry with Naero's people. Most of them were already good friends with one another.

Ra had even assigned Shai guards to Naero's friends and all immediate friends and family in order to protect and watch over them.

A small group of enemy assassins had gone after Chaela and her family once.

Attacking her and her Shai guards turned out to be an extremely brief and wildly ill-advised career move for those assassins.

Finally the three of them had time to catch up. They talked about the kids. They discussed matters about the Alliance Naval fleets, internal politics.

"Sweetie," Saemar said, "our carriers and crews can't wait to get our hands on our quota of those next generation phaze fighters. Is there any way at all that you can pull some strings and get our deliveries sent to us any sooner?"

"I agree," Chaela piled on. "We're doing everything we can to get ready, N, but we can only go so far with the training simulators. What good are you as our friend if we can't get a little favoritism here?"

Naero laughed and held up both of her hands defensively as her two old friends closed in on her. She even backed away slightly.

"You'll get them when you get them, as part of the new refit rotation. I have no say over that. If I did, trust me, you guys would already be bopping around in them. So don't blame me."

Her friends sulked like spoiled brats who were denied a new toy.

"Come on, snap out of it. Alright, tell you what I'll do. Some of my carriers already have the new Banshees."

Chaela cut her off. "Haisha, so how do you rate?"

Naero shot up one hand. "Just lucky. Hear me out, you hotheads. Why don't I send some of my flights over in exchange for some of yours? That way you and some of your people can trade off and get some flight time in these new rigs. And they are sweet, let me tell you."

Saemar beamed. "Sure thing, sweetie. Sounds good."

Chaela still frowned. "I guess that would work."

"Take it or leave it," Naero said. "That's the best that I can do. Hey, it's only going to be a month or two before the rotation gives you your quotas anyway. Let me know when yours arrive, we can get together, train, and stage some war games. My people will be able to get yours up to speed in the Banshees in no time. At the rate things are going with the war, you know how badly we're going to need them."

Chaela continued to gripe, "And what's this about Tyber's stupid idea to take our fighter jocks out of our ships, and have them pilot starfighters remotely from some kind of mindlink pod? Is he nuts?"

"Yeah, I have my own reservations about the new Synthetic Construct Warrior Initiative," Naero said. "They're calling it SCWI, for short. If it works, it would cut down on casualties."

"Like you said, sweetie," Saemar noted. "*If* it works. I still say too many things could go wrong with that tek. Why, just disrupt the link alone, and all of those remote fighter wings would be floating out in the black, as useless as hell."

"Hang the risks," Chae told them. "A fighter jock knows the risks she or he is taking; it's that edge that makes them better pilots out in the mix with their asses on the line. How are they going to experience any of that while taking a nice cozy soak in some psylink pod back behind the lines?"

Naero sighed. "Look, I hear you loud and clear, ladies. But if it can be made to work, and it saves the lives of valuable pilots, then both the Navy and the Marines are going to go in that direction. So be ready if it does, that's all I say."

Om and Alala joined them and the kids after lunch that day.

They were in their own new synthezoid construct bodies, which normally looked mostly like a Spacer couple in black Nytex togs. Om was male with dark blue skin, short red hair, and orange eyes. Alala was pastel pink skinned with green eyes, and a bob of light green hair splashed with light blue accents.

They were still playing around with the appearances of their constructs, and it was something new every time they emerged.

And Naero noticed something else that continued to change.

As a couple, both of them periodically held hands, and even touched and looked at each other in little affectionate ways.

Was this real progress?

Both Om and Alala had made a study of Spacer and humanoid physical attraction, affection, and courting rituals. But Naero questioned if this was real affection or just mimicry. Were they simply repeating what they had seen others do?

Naero knew that both Om and Alala had feelings and emotions that only continued to develop on many levels. Having physical construct bodies only accelerated that process of growth and development for the two complex AIs

Om claimed that they weren't ready for physical intimacy and relations yet, but with their new physical construct bodies, they both insisted to everyone that they definitely felt affection for each other that was real enough for them.

Then another breakthrough came without warning that afternoon.

Alala kissed Om.

Om kissed Alala back, and soon things appeared to be heating up quite rapidly between them and their two synthetic construct bodies.

Everyone just stared.

The kids noticed and started to giggle.

"Jodi, Pet," Chaela said and pointed, "you and the other kids go play over that way."

Alala and Om were completely absorbed by the impromptu make out session on the love seat they were nestled in.

"N," Saemar told her. "As much as I like to watch—get them a room."

Naero nodded. "Yep. Immediately."

15

Captain Tyber mourned the last day that Nehz was able to sustain her Drian form.

That time was now faded and gone.

Nehz's spiritmind form had dissolved in Tyber's arms and he broke down. "How many times must I lose her again?" he muttered.

Orean held out both hands and kept Zhen's soul orb from escaping, sealing it up safely inside of her once again.

Someday, somehow, Naero had to find a way to truly bring Zhen back to them all, if it were possible.

Today had not been that day, and it might not ever come, but her promise remained firm.

Zhen's disciplined and intelligent spiritmind had served them extremely well over the course of those many days.

While Ty recovered, Naero, Jia, and Shalaen put the finishing touches on a new Kexxian regeneration pod.

As Shetharra's maddening condition took yet another turn for the worse, only the advanced treatments and medical wizardry of the Kexx could help sustain her.

Meanwhile all of the other Spacer and Alliance children remained out of danger, at least for the time being.

In this case, Shetharra's own body worked against her. She was so strong and resilient that the disease that fed off of her and had become part of her grew more powerful also, and used her own strengths and energies against her as weapons.

The Kexxian regeneration pod was made of solid Ultrium alloy of many varieties, just as it was infused with many different kinds of Cosmic energy flows.

Jia told them that in theory, if that pod were converted into being nothing more than a hyper bomb, that it could wipe out all life within thirty parses. Of course the Kexx had numerous safeguards in place to prevent just such a thing from happening. As a species, unlike their enemies the G'lothc, the Kexx were devoted to Life, not Death.

Naero was still amazed by the vast levels of energies warring to keep her oldest daughter alive.

Shetharra responded to the regeneration treatments from the moment they placed her inside the new pod. Her condition stabilized and her strength and focus returned. Even the pain decreased to such a level that she was barely aware of it.

For the first time, they had gotten ahead of the virulent, relentless plague that the enemy infected her oldest child with. They were actually beating it, at least for the present.

To the wonder of everyone except Naero, Shetharra adapted very quickly to the Ultrium device that encased her, and to the Ultrium based, Cosmic energy infused treatments.

In fact, her body seemed to adjust miraculously, working with the treatments and assisting them almost perfectly in both healing and regenerating her diseased spirit form.

Everyone present who was capable used a combination of biomancy, teknomancy, and psyonics to study the fascinating process.

Naero held her child close and they even spoke together and laughed, so improved was Shetharra's condition.

Yet it was still not a cure. Shalaen sadly warned Naero of that fact, and that this would most likely be only another respite.

Jia suggested that perhaps the fixers could modify the regen pod into a containment regeneration suit so that Shetharra could go about on her own once more, and return to her family. Such a suit could sustain the child for weeks, perhaps even months before she might be in danger once more.

Then reports reached them again of increased enemy attacks.

Out in the Gamma Quadrant the enemy had pulled back for a time to consolidate their many gains and regroup. Yet the new planetary shields were giving them fits, right when the foe thought that they would have hundreds of captured Alliance worlds to invade, subjugate, and enslave.

And to feed off of.

Raw destructive power was not always the best tool in the box.

Fearing that this would be a good time for the Creature to turn up again, Naero and her team prepared to return to the front to stand ready for that event.

Naero and Khai had one last day together and with their family. As always, they made the most of what time they had.

Back at the front, the enemy continued its relentless campaign of trying out new tactics and weapon systems of their own during their push.

Thus far the continuing analysis of the enemy tek they had captured revealed several vital secrets. The advanced enemy warships were all, as expected, Ultrium based, Darkforce infused constructs controlled by linked G'lothc shipminds. These shipminds were actually melded at one with the vessels, controlling their every move and function.

The slave crews were also directed by G'lothc mind control wraiths, giving the enemy absolute control, and their new arrays of weapons were extremely formidable.

The most effective Alliance attacks remained those that could hit the enemy vessels on all three levels: structurally, energy, and psyonic. But the Alliance warships were not semi-living entities—at least not yet.

The Dark Star and *The Star Fox* were the only ships that could fit that description.

The main fleets would still rely on their big guns and raw fire power. Improved weapons, shields, and the new starfighters coming online would need to suffice and hold the line for the present time.

Naero hoped that they would all be enough to hold on.

*

Two standard days later, Naero had a rare sparring session with Ra and his father, Mystic High Master Gaviok.

The three of them fought together in one of Naero's flagship's huge arenas, which they had scheduled all to themselves. It took both of the Shai warrior princes combined to press Naero hard enough to give them all a great work out.

The Shai also used the newest synthezoid battle constructs to keep her guessing.

Ra and Gaviok swelled up to their battle size, each about thirty meters tall. When fighting for practice, the color of their mantid forms turned a dark red with patchy black markings.

In war, they went to deepest black with Chaos red highlights on their sharper edges.

As they launched themselves at her in combination once more, Naero took on her near Darkbeast form and met them head on, dodging the lethal swipes of Ra's massive forearms.

Then she shot forward, driving both of her feet into Gaviok's Thorax with all of her force.

That strike drove even the hyperdense Mystic Chaos Master off his feet and sent him tumbling end over end as he tried to recover. He smashed into the far nano stands and the wall, causing great destruction.

Gaviok appeared to be stunned.

The nanoarena would reform within the space of several minutes.

Gaviok's construct bodyguards swarmed at Naero to distract her.

She wiped them out with energized Cosmic sweepkicks and sonic blast screams.

This all gave Ra the opening he waited for.

He sent in his constructs to delay her for a split instant.

Her pulse blast sphere shot out in all directions, taking them down.

With perfect timing, Ra slammed into her hard in an attempt to bring her down and grapple strength to strength.

But Naero flung him slightly back, denying him that option.

Blows flashed in close up as both warriors held their ground.

Naero endured some painful damage in order to set up her own attacks.

With great speed she wheeled into Ra, driving him back with a flurry of punching and kicking combos.

She had him.

This was the endgame take down.

Naero knocked him away and then slammed Gaviok to the ground without even turning to look, cratering him deep into the shattered, splintered nanofloor of the arena. The impact caused those sections of the super battleship to shudder.

She knew all the while that the father had only pretended to be more stunned than he actually was.

"Hold!" Gaviok shouted.

All of three of them laughed together.

Naero was breathing hard. They all shrank back down to their normal, accustomed forms and sizes. Gaviok was always as tall as Baeven, but Ra was normally shorter than her, and she loved him all the more for that.

"Good fight," Ra noted. "The match is clearly yours, N."

"I concede that as well," Gaviok added.

Naero embraced them both in turn. "How I've missed both of you, my great hearts. You shall both dine well at my table tonight."

Her mantid Shai abani turned whitish pink, filled with love and admiration for her, one who was like their own kind to them, though she was a Spacer, like her uncle.

"How much stronger you've become," Gaviok noted with admiration. "You must come back and work with my newest adepts. They need quickening and a good thrashing."

Naero laughed and shook her head. "Alas, Gaviok. Not with the war. You must bring them to me, I'm afraid. Sorry for the bother."

"I have brought some few along in case of that. We shall arrange a time. The war goes badly, then?"

Naero sighed and used Cosmic energy to refresh herself and meld back into her flight togs and personal gear and weapons. "I fear that it is trending that way."

"My queens have finally developed those new genetically altered breeding concubines for planetary defensive support," Ra told her.

"Excellent Ra. I know that we'll need them in the campaigns to come. We can seed them among contested worlds to breed hosts of Shai warriors to assist with any ground wars. They will make superb allies. Thank you both."

They continued talking about the war for a while. Then they switched to Mystic matters concerning the next class of adepts.

"With the expanding war," Gaviok noted, "I don't see how we can possibly produce the large number of Mystics that we will need to support our efforts. The Alliance is simply growing too big. Too many races, too many worlds, and far too many demands for Mystic advisors."

"The Spacer Mystics cannot do it all and be everywhere that Mystics are needed," Ra said.

"I know," Naero agreed. "There's no other way. Adepts will have to be trained from the other Alliance sentients and peoples. The program must be opened up to all who show Cosmic talents and abilities."

"But the Spacer Mystics are still reluctant to open up their secret training methods to outsiders," Gaviok added.

Naero smiled. "They did for you. You're a High Master now."

"That needs to expand, until we have training facilities flourishing across both known quadrants, and not just on the three Mystic Homeworlds."

"You both have my full support," Naero said. "And I will pursue the measure when and where I can. Things that are rigid often change slowly. That is unfortunate."

Baeven and Janner flashed into the arena.

"Here you are, sib," Jan said. "Come on, you're all needed. And here you all are just wasting time, fooling around."

16

Naero contacted everyone she could think of to help her find a way to free Shetharra from the Cosmic disease being inflicted upon her by the Dark Emperor.

She went before the Astral and Dimensional Council. She shared data with Master Jo and the Spacer Mystics. She contacted all of the known Interdimensional energy being races.

All of them were more than willing to assist her, but even collectively, they did not seem to know any more than she did. Such Cosmic diseases were known to exist, but there was no direct experience with one such as this.

This was a Cosmic plague being directed specifically against one individual being by yet another more advanced, ancient Cosmic being. It was being used as a weapon, tailored to destroy one target: Naero's oldest daughter.

Only the KDM made any reference to such types of attacks, and so far, Naero and the Alliance had applied every bit of that knowledge to keeping Shetharra alive thus far.

They continued to search, but they had not come across any data that pointed to an eventual cure.

Naero and Baeven searched together and on their own. Outside of the KDM, with great effort, they went to the Nexus and tried to make contact with some of their alternate selves in other realities. Nothing seemed to work.

Naero tried to link with Shetharra and trace back all of the Cosmic paths through which Nahaxrathrax was attacking the child. But she never seemed to be able to locate them all. And while Shetharra was still engaged entirely in resisting and fighting off the plague itself, such efforts to study the plague only seemed too complex and confusing by far.

But she did confirm one thing.

Shetharra was indeed standing in the way of the Dark Emperor, blocking that focused portion of his malignant intent.

There were in fact some Cosmic dimensions or perspectives that could be focused like lenses of some kind in order to detect, locate, and affect other Cosmic beings.

The enemy possessed some way to zero in on Spacers as a Cosmic race. Using these advanced methods on some rarified level of enlightenment, an advanced being such as the Dark Emperor was more than capable of targeting and inflicting great harm on one particular being, or an entire group, or generation of beings, if they were somehow located and viewed collectively in a vulnerable state, such as childhood.

The strong and the opportunistic preyed upon the young and the weak.

Yet Naero sensed that there seemed to be only one path or vector that could be used to make such attacks. Shetharra had somehow sensed that, and placed herself directly in harm's way, blocking that path and the Great Adversary's lethal efforts.

This door or portal was now closed.

The Dark Emperor could not get at the minds, spirits, souls or whatever else that he needed in order to slay an entire Spacer generation.

Even as young as she was, Shetharra had a great power ignited within her at almost every level. But that power was not limitless, and the dark might of Nahaxrathrax their enemy was very great. So great that there was as yet no way to measure it, or determine how many different levels and ways it came at them.

Naero sent word out to all of her people.

She wanted them all to know and fully understand what was happening.

She made it clear to all of the Spacer Clans, their Mystics, and the Elders. If Shetharra died, they could expect the next generation of hundreds of millions of Spacer children to be wiped out in very short order.

There was no defense.

Because of their ignorance, because they had no way to stop it, the fate of the Spacer race now depended on the strength of a miracle child who was not yet nine standard years of age.

One bright flickering soul who instinctively, by her very nature, willingly and without hesitation stood before the very forces of what could only be Evil incarnate.

With nowhere else to turn, Naero attempted the last thing she could think of. She called upon Womi of the Kahn-Dar, from the ancient race of the great, Interdimensional dragon beings.

She called out to him in the crazy nebulae aether colors, sweeps, and swirls of the neutral Astral Plane, already in her spiritmind form.

She called out to her friend three times.

It took a few moments, but at last the enormous glowing blue serpent flashed in all at once, well over a kilometer in length in his full size. Each of its scales was bigger than she was.

Womi's great shimmering blue eye blinked at her, the size of a small planetary lake.

They communicated through a very close telepathic link that was all their own.

Good to see you, my great friend Naero. You stand before me more powerful than ever, yet you have not reached you limit yet, if you have one.

She could not help it. Naero was so glad to see her friend that she wept on the spot, even in Astral form. And when she reached out to stroke his great cheek, he read her mind and her sorrow through the great bond the two of them shared.

Instinctively, Womi spun down to his tiny size when he was like a bracelet that she used to wear on one of her wrists.

He actually coiled around her right wrist in fond remembrance and blinked and smiled up at her like a living piece of blue jewelry. His joy at their reunion was very great as well. Naero could feel it all around and through them both.

He sensed her anguish, and showed his immense affection to comfort her.

She kissed his small head and petted him as he continued to writhe, and twine himself again and again over her forearm. Womi could purr when he was extremely happy, not unlike a kitten, actually.

And when he was in his full size, Womi's purring roared like thunder across the aether of the planes.

I don't feel all that strong. But look at you. How magnificent. You've gotten even larger," Naero noticed, complimenting him just the way he liked.

Have I? he said. Then the next moment, *Isn't it wonderful? Kahn-Dar continue to grow in size all of their days. What a blessing.*

Please, let us speak plainly, my friend.

I have never known you to speak otherwise, Naero Amashin Maeris.

"I know that you can read my mind, Womi. Have you already deduced why I have summoned you?"

Womi of the Kahn-Dar tittered at first.

Of course, Naero. I read your heart. Your little starchild is in danger, the very radiant older one. A most sad situation. The Dark Emperor bends all of his thought and power against her very existence it seems. He is seemingly devoted to taking her life, and I am sorry to learn that. I have come to love all of your children, even as I love you.

Naero bowed her head to him once more. Thank you, Womi. I know how much you mean that. If only the universe understood the great capacity for love that the Kahn-Dar possess.

Nearly as great as our appetites, I'm afraid. Just one of the many reasons that my people are so misunderstood. Quite tragic, really.

Is there any way that you can help me save her, my friend? I don't even understand the complete nature of this attack and how it is being made. Where is it coming from? How is it being prosecuted? How does it seem that the enemy commands nearly limitless energies to inflict their will? Where do they derive such powers? I would give my own life to end this disease and save my little duck.

Alas, Naero. The deep lore of the Kahn-Dar is not rich about such things. Yet ride upon my back as you did once, show me what you know, and let us explore it together. Perhaps we can find a way, or at the very least learn more than you know now.

Naero flashed onto the top of his head, as he returned to his full size. With barely a thought she formed the construct of seat and lines so that she might sit in comfort and have no fear of being swept off by Womi's great bursts of velocity. It was not intended to rein or steer him in any way. Womi carried her freely, and if she wished to go in a direction, she made it clear to him by will and thought alone.

How is the attack being made against your daughter, Naero?

I have discovered five main paths to it thus far, but I greatly fear that there could be at least one more, if not many others. I simply don't know. That is a large part of my infuriating problem.

Hmmm...let us go smell them or rather let me do so. If these vectors of attack each come from a different place or dimension, perhaps I can sort them out. Kahn-Dar can sniff out masses of energy emanating from any place.

So far, the attacks seem to have come from five separate vectors or dimensions—whatever you wish to call them. The Dark Emperor attacks my child through the Prime Material Plane, the Astral Plane, the Interdimensions, the Cosmic, and even the Spirit Dimension. What have I missed? What am I missing?

Naero, each universe is made up of magnitudes upon magnitudes, and spheres within spheres. There are more ranges and possibilities than any of us can possibly imagine. Some will serve us and our purposes because of the choices we make, and some will serve others for the decisions they choose. Some will serve both, and still others will serve no one, and only exist for themselves on their own, for reasons none can know.

The truth is that there are more universes out there than all the gods could even imagine in their mightiest of dreams.

I ask for none of that, my friend. All the universes can keep themselves. All that I seek is the knowledge to save my daughter, and defend my people. Let that be enough. Please, help me find what I have overlooked.

Together they searched long into the five known dimensions that the enemy was using.

Womi even showed her perspectives where she could witness threads and tendrils of the Dark Emperor's powers going forth on the attack.

She also caught glimpses of her friends and other Alliance Champions, and then of Elazethrek, the Creature. The foul thing hid and recharged, attacked and did great harm wherever it appeared. Then it vanished to regenerate and assail the Alliance again at but another vital point along the wide front.

The defenders of the Gamma Quadrant were slowly being crushed and beaten back by this master strategy.

Yet the Dark Emperor concentrated nearly all his power and force of will in the attempt to destroy a very special young child from afar.

They had yet to locate where the enemy was getting their fearful levels of corrupted Cosmic power to fuel their efforts.

They are summoning these gargantuan quantities of power from somewhere," Womi told her. *"Yet I can perceive neither the source nor the method of transmission. It might even be more than one source or vector. This must be some well-kept secret of the G'lothc that has never been discovered.*

We must find it! Naero insisted.

119

We can only keep looking, my friend.

Womi could not stay by her side forever, and Naero certainly had other matters to attend to. The Creature still had to be opposed and hunted down. The dire losses it dealt the Alliance would soon be unsustainable. There were many other equally important tasks and matters that also had to be addressed.

Naero finally bade her friend from the Kahn-Dar farewell, but both of them vowed to keep searching.

At the front in the Gamma Quadrant, new waves of various types of specialized super fixers joined the fleets as fast as they could be replicated.

Shetharra remained in remission, and accompanied her mother and Jia to one of the new starfighter test flights. The child was almost like her pre-disease self with the constant treatments. The eight-year-old going on nine wore her own advanced Ultrium regen armor, the form fitting shiny silver suit making her look more like a Driathan than a Spacer.

Even Jia commented on it, taking the child into her arms.

Then a strange thing happened.

Shetharra's Ultrium suit began to pulse and glow with a bright, nearly blinding light. That glow or radiant aura quickly spread to Jia, and soon her perfect, shining Driathan form was also blazing with white light.

Then all of the fixers in the starfighter launching bay with them began to catch fire as well, yet none of them were harmed or damaged.

Naero went to Jia, trying to comprehend what was happening. "What is all of this?"

Jia shook her head. "It's not her Cosmic disease, that's for certain. Shetharra is doing this, or at least some part of her. It's reacting with something inside of myself also and producing this glow. I don't know why. It's spreading throughout anything made of Ultrium."

"But is it harming anything in any way?" Naero asked.

All of the new tandem fighters waiting for the test flights quickly glowed with the strange light as well.

Shalaen helped them scan the entire hanger. "On the contrary, the fixers the fighters, and all of the Ultrium based devices seem more powerful than ever. They're operating at peak efficiency, even beyond normal specifications."

Another Kexxian power flare? How was Shetharra triggering such events?

Naero used her own teknomancy. "Yes. Several additional minor modifications and pweaks have taken place automatically via the fixers, as if on their own. None of these changes were authorized or confirmed, because they just occurred. Look at the phaze shields on the fixers. They're operating at twice the normal capacity. I'm guessing that the starfighters will do so as well."

"We'll never know until we conduct the flight tests, Admiral."

Naero recognized the new voice somewhat, but she couldn't exactly place it.

She turned to see a very short and very young fleet fighter wing Captain, with dark curly hair and bright eyes, yet still not as short as herself. The captain carried her helmet under one arm. Naero caught the last name on the helmet and flight suit, filling in the gaps of memory.

Both of them smiled in happy recollection.

Chang. Tiali Wallace Chang. Another distant Cousin of Clan Maeris. Their paths had crossed a short while back. At least it seemed short to Naero.

Chang saluted the very next instant.

Naero returned the salute with great gladness. "Captain Chang, I see that you've been busy, sir. Congratulations are in order, Tiali."

Tiali nodded, smiling even wider. "Thank you, N. That means a great deal to me, coming from you."

They embraced briefly.

"I've kept an eye on you and your career here and there where your name has popped up. You and your units have been extremely well-decorated. You were one of the youngest fighter wing Fleet Captains among the Clans."

"Only Vyktor Ryan from Clan Ryan is younger, by three months."

"A good commander, but not your equal yet, Tiali."

"Thank you, Naero. Again. My pilots and their flight crews would be honored by even just a few words from you, if you have a moment."

Naero grinned and then nodded at the new fighters. "Certainly. I know you have important work to do here, so I'll make it brief. This is my daughter, Shetharra. She's eight, going on nine years old."

Tiali stared at Naero's glowing daughter with wonder. "The Spacechild conceived within the depths of a star. Everyone has heard of her. Greetings Shetharra."

Shetharra wrapped her arms around Tiali briefly and then pulled back just as quickly. "I'm sensing how much you and your people love and respect my mom. That makes me very happy."

Captain Chang grinned and blushed, rubbing her arm with her free hand. "I'm glad, little one. It's all true. You need to know how much your mother and father are loved and nearly worshipped by our people, by the Clans. They are among our greatest champions, and they, like you, are quite amazing in so many ways. You are our paragons. We look up to you all."

The child of light giggled. "I fixed your ships. I'm glad I did. You're very nice. But I would have done it even if you weren't so nice."

Tiali knit her brows. "What does she mean?"

Naero held up her hands while they kept walking. Officers and guards nearby gathered the crews together for a brief address by Admiral Naero Amashin Maeris of Clan Maeris.

"Shetharra, how did you fix Tiali's ships?"

"There were slight design flaws in all of them. None of them would have been critical on their own, but the enemy wraith things hidden inside each starfighter would have made all of the ships explode any way. I couldn't allow that to happen; not to our people, and certainly not to our brave friends who love my mom so much."

Naero held up a moment. "Shetharra, I need to know exactly how you stopped the enemy wraith things."

Her daughter blinked. "I burned them up, Momma. I burned them up with light that they don't like. They can be awfully hard to burn up otherwise. They're very bad things, and even in their tiny little minds, they only think of doing bad things to us and our people. That's why I burned them up. My friends, the little glowing lizard guys in my deep dreams told me what to do."

Naero smiled at that; was it true? "Can you show me? Can you show me the light you used to burn them up with, honey?"

Shetharra grinned wide once more. "Sure I can, Momma. It's very close to the light that's hiding inside Aunt Jia, and inside me—in most of us. The same light that the Tua and my little lizard friends glow with. It's a light so bright that even I have to blink to see it. It's very close to the glow that spread from me and Aunt Jia to all of the shiny metal stuff."

The little girl cupped her hands and an intense bright orb of light the size of a pea appeared, so intense that Naero had to shield them all from it with her hands and her powers, and avert her own gaze.

But she and Om struggled to record the complex frequency of that light, its magnitude and intensity, and all of its Cosmic flow components.

She was certain that it would be vital for the Allies to discover a way how to create such light and learn to apply the fierce forces behind it.

"Very good, my little duck. Well done. Put your light a way and keep it safe."

"I will, Momma. This is a light that won't ever hurt us. It is a light that only harms very bad things."

As Naero and her small entourage strode through the assembled Spacers, a chant grew quickly until it became a roar.

"Omaria. Omaria. Omaria!"

Hundreds of Spacer fists pounded the air in unison, as the chant grew to a great tumult.

Shetharra spoke to her through their near constant mindlink when they were near each other. *Momma, wasn't the Omaria the big exploration ship that Granma Lythe and Granpa Tarthan died in? You've told me so much about them. I wish they hadn't gone away. I know I would have loved them.*

Me too, little duck. Me too. Yes, and they would have loved you with all their mighty hearts—more than you could ever possibly know, so great was their love.

Naero picked her daughter up and held the girl in her arms.

The chanting and cheering only continued.

"Omaria. Omaria. Omaria!"

Haisha! You're crying again, Momma. Here, let me wipe your tears away. I know thinking about your mom and dad being gone makes you sad. If you and papa were gone, I would be very sad too."

It's all right, sweetie. Your dad and I aren't going away like that. Let me talk to these friends of ours for a little while.

Naero held her close and climbed up onto a nearby observation platform while the chanting continued.

Finally when Naero had her feet set, she easily held Shetharra with one arm and drew her energy cutlass with the other, brandishing it aloft in high salute. "REMEMBER THE OMARIA!" she roared, augmenting her words with the voice.

The assembled crowd roared with her.

Meanwhile, Om had the fixers perform a trace scan of the starfighters.

As she guessed, Shetharra had been completely correct. The enemy had infiltrated the construction of those vehicles. This was a new teknomancy tactic for the mind control wraiths—infiltration and sabotage.

Through her, Om alerted Spacer Intel and the Alliance fleets and shipyards about this new threat.

Naero smiled as the roar drew down, allowing her to speak. "My daughter and I are very proud to be among you, our brave people. Thank you for the honor that you have done me and my Clan. You honor us!"

"The honor is ours!" thundered the reply.

"Today we are present at the first flight tests of these awesome new tandem fighters, the TF-78 Ghost Amazons. Very soon, starfighters such as these are going to help turn the tide of the battles that we are now facing."

More cheering.

"I would like to add, that these ships would be nothing without the brave pilots and crews, and wing commanders such as Captain Chang!"

Chang joined them up on the platform, all to more waves of cheering.

"And let me just say that I was trained as a fighter jock myself, as you well know. If they allow me to, and give me an Amazon to borrow, my daughter and I will gladly take flight with you!"

The crowd seemed to go crazy, to have one of their own great Champions flying out in the black with them that day, with them and their beloved captain.

These people love us so much, Momma. I can feel it. Their hearts are filled with love for us, just as ours are for them.

These are our beloved Clans, Shetharra. Our people and our blood. We must always protect them. Never forget that.

I have not and I never will, Momma. I will love you, and I will love them, forever.

17

Naero left Shetharra and her family behind and returned to the war at hand on the front lines. She still recalled kissing all of her children and telling them goodbye.

Out in the black the fighting continued to be heavy and intense.

She and the Alliance Champions played mice and cat with Elazethrek across numerous interstellar war zones and battlefields.

On many occasions they either caught a glimpse of the Creature or just barely initiated their newest energy drain strategy when the thing laughed in their faces and fled once more. The contest grew incredibly frustrating.

Always the cunning monster left a trail of death and devastation in its wake for the Alliance to clean up. There were countless swaths of dead ships and dead crews from among Spacers and all of the Alliance races.

Elazethrek simply existed to kill, mutilate, and destroy all life. The Six were the perfect G'lothc avatars. In the past, they had even slaughtered their own kind in their mad, capricious whims, whenever it so pleased them. The Six could only be controlled so much. The G'lothc themselves feared their own most infamous creations.

On occasion, in some remote area, Elazethrek would sometimes break its normal strategy of hit and run and take its time. On Ruldareth-4 she randomly attacked a Rorg colony world while it was still struggling to install its planetary defense shield.

Ruldareth-4 had been a well-established, large thriving colony of three hundred and ninety million Rorg and growing, concentrated mostly among several megacities.

Elazethrek fell upon them and their world and wiped them out within twenty-one standard hours.

By the time the Alliance forces and their champions received the panicked distress calls and finally reached the distant colony, the genocide was all but complete, and once more Elazethrek was long gone.

Only some few scattered thousands of traumatized Rorg could be found frozen with terror in holes, in caves, and in wild places where they had fled to save their lives.

The Creature's appetite was said to be limitless.

Some she consumed the old fashioned way, by ripping them apart and devouring them whole within a matter of several vicious seconds. The survivors described her as if she were some kind of super ghoul or hyper ravenous demon.

It also converted from one attack form into another at will.

So far, the total on all of Elazethrek's confirmed battle forms rested at seventeen.

Yet other times the Creature mostly attacked planets like Ruldareth-4 from orbit or the sky, simply draining the life force from several hundred kilometers of the planet's surface all at once. First she would make a ring of death many kilometers in diameter and wide, and then consume what life remained inside each circle. There was no escape within.

These attacks left entire worlds scarred, scorched, and devoid of life.

When such a hyper attack swept over a megacity of multiple millions, all of those people burst asunder and were consumed, surrendering their energies over the course of several agonizing moments as they shrieked and perished.

This was the wake of horror the Creature left behind.

Such attacks by their very nature were sweeping and indifferent, none were spared, and all energies were rapidly converted to the Creature's gluttonous use.

Ruldareth-4 had not been the first such Alliance world to suffer this fate, and there was nothing that could be done at present to make it the last.

Naero and the Alliance could only pursue the hunt and continue to improve their tactics and tek as they went.

The Creature remained at large and struck wherever it wished.

*

In her free time, if she could call it that, Naero continued to explore the KDM for all of the secrets and answers that she and the Alliance still needed so badly. She continued to study the new Song of Making, but with little success.

"I have to admit," Orean complained to Aij and the others, "it is definitely more lonely now without the dedicated presence of Zhen's spiritform here with us."

"I miss her good nature, her devoted intellect, and her calm efficiency," Shalaen said.

"Her dry acerbic wit," Aij added.

All of them sighed together. Certainly their new discoveries were way down in light of Nehz's absence.

They emerged from the KDM after many hours of hard work.

Next, Naero took time to consolidate and attempt to apply all of their latest Drian data. She went over the mystery of the Driathan blank once more with Jia and Shalaen. The blank itself was being kept in secret, locked on a shielded medbed within the main security vault of Naero's flagship.

When Khai was available, even he would join her there at such times.

But usually that was just a pretense to canoodle with her. Which Naero also did not mind one bit. They hardly had any time together as it was.

Everyone had their own version of stress relief.

Yet try as she might, even with the important insights of her many friends, together they still seemed far away from doing anything serious to crack this enigma, besides getting the blank to jerk and twitch a little here and there.

Why did it seem that all of these new secrets were so much harder to crack than the many other problems they had faced?

Naero's gut instincts told her that it must have something to do with the ways and the reasons that the Drians created their gift to the universe—the Driathans. Clearly they didn't want just anyone to be able to take over their master creation. The Drians guarded those secrets extremely well.

If their friends and allies the Kexx knew what those secrets were, Naero had not found those data oceans yet. Perhaps there were certain secrets that both ancient allies kept to themselves, for their own reasons.

Naero was alone with the Driathan blank after the others left, as it often happened.

She stretched out next to and even draped an arm over the blank, which she took to calling Nehz, since that had been the name of Zhen's Drian spiritmind counterpart for a time.

A heavy sigh escaped Naero. Why weren't they having any luck, while the enemy seemed confident that…

She sat up quickly and then patted Nehz.

Haisha! Could that be part of answer? The enemy might already know exactly how to take the blank over and infect it with one of their vile spirits. They were the masters of taking over the bodies of other sentients and using them as vessels.

They always seemed to be eager to do just that.

And there was no doubt that a Driathan body would be the ultimate vessel for their needs.

It wouldn't hurt to ask Baeven to explore the G'lothc data portions of the KDM for exactly such knowledge. That might help her in her quest to install Zhen's soul essence into the blank.

Yet that could not be all of it. She began to question her own reasoning. Wouldn't that just lead to another dead end? Many factors still bothered her.

The G'lothc violated and burned out the beings they possessed, almost as an afterthought.

She somehow knew on instinct that such rapacious methods of taking over an unwilling, sentient vessel were certainly not going to be the same way that the loving Drians breathed the breath of life into their greatest of all creations, their beloved children the Driathans, and gave birth to their enigmatic souls.

None of that would ever be done through violence by the loving Drians.

As Jia had attempted to explain many times, the Driathans were not just mere offspring or servants to the Drians.

Not in the least. The Drians were not merely trying to duplicate or re-create more of themselves. Back then, Drians could already procreate among each other perfectly fine. Their farsighted goal was not to make more Drians.

The Driathans were another vision entirely, and created for a far off future that could only be guessed at, long after the Great War and everything was gone—even the Drians themselves.

The Cosmic Prophecies clearly included the Driathans in the fate of the universe. Jia's people had a major role to play.

In a way that was not yet realized—the godlike Drians had created the Driathans not just to replace themselves, but to eventually surpass and even eclipse them.

How could that be possible?

Not even the mighty Kexx had attempted such a feat. They shepherded countless races it seemed, across several galaxies, yet they had no apparent interest whatsoever in leaving behind any version of themselves.

How could these things be? What were the answers? Were the sleeping Driathans truly still in their infancy as a species?

What were they waiting for?

And what, then, could they possibly mature into?

Such thoughts gave Naero both great hope and great concern.

Therefore, she returned to studying Nehz in all five dimensions. But once again, as with curing Shetharra's disease, some key piece or pieces of the puzzle still eluded her. She could almost sense what they were by the logic of their absence. What was she missing?

Suddenly there came a blinding light that pulsed through the entire super battleship and Naero herself.

She gasped.

Another Cosmic spike or flare? From what? Who?

Then she knew.

As if it were the easiest thing to accomplish, Naero's oldest daughter had joined her in the flagship vault.

Naero was attuned to her child and discerned many things all at once through their special link. And her child was attuned to her mother.

Shetharra had clearly sensed the intensity of her mother's turmoil and force of will at work and came to her. The child glowed within her pulsing, shining Ultrium regen suit.

"Hi, Momma. What's wrong? I felt something happening. You're so worried and upset. You still can't get Nehz to open up to you?"

Naero wrung her hands. "No, not yet, honey. I'm so frustrated I can hardly think. She barely responds to anything we-"

Without hesitation, Shetharra stroked Nehz's blank face and kissed her forehead.

Another wave of blinding light zapped everything, and Nehz flowed like quicksilver into a sitting lotus position.

Shetharra calmly curled up in Nehz's open arms as if doing so were the most natural thing in the world. It was always that way with Shetharra and the impossible.

The blank's arms coiled protectively around the child of light and stroked her long hair of white flame.

Naero shot to her feet. "Haisha! Sweetie…how in the heck did you get it do that?"

Shetharra paused and lifted her head. "I don't know. I think you have to keep thinking about who you want her to become, Mom. Stop thinking about it as 'it,' and more like 'her.' You've already been making that switch. Keep it up. Follow your instincts and your heart, like you always tell me."

Shetharra curled up, nestled back down, and let out a deep breath, switching to telepathy through their link as she closed her eyes.

How do you think their creators thought of them, Momma? How did they make them? I'm guessing it all came out of the immense love they felt for the Driathans, using all of their vast powers of Creation.

How could you possibly know any of that, Shetharra?

I keep telling you, Momma. My little glowing lizard friends told me. They've shared so many wonderful stories with me in my dreams. I love them so. You cannot imagine how beautiful they are.

You've spoken to the souls of the Seven Kexxian Dreamers from the beyond, Shetharra. Some of the mightiest beings ever known to exist in this or any universe.

That's silly, Momma. They and the Tua both say that there are forces, beings, and powers in the Beyond who are far greater, and the Fantastic Mystery is beyond anyone's understanding. We're going to see all of that in the next journey, Momma. I can't wait!

But we're not in the Beyond just yet, my duckling. We have so much work to do here, before we take the next journey. So many lives depend on us. Please, ask your friends about the Songs of Making. How come I cannot master the one that you taught me? Why won't it do what I will it to do?

I don't know, Momma. I will try to ask them. I can't get many of their songs to work for me, either, but they tell me to keep trying. Sometimes it helps if you learn other songs first, I think.

Yes, my little duck. You keep striving. Keep dreaming, keep trying and interacting with your gentle spirit friends. Listen carefully to what they are trying to teach you.

Shetharra laughed. *They're so funny, Momma. We laugh together all the time, but I can only hear them best when I am very sick and close to death.*

Have they ever said anything about the blank—I mean Nehz? Can you ask them how to unlock its secrets and bring it to life with a new soul inside?

Like Aunt Jia says, each Driathan is a unique miracle. It's in several of their songs, Mom. Haven't you listened to them? Drian songs are very pretty, too. Many of them make me cry. Many of their stories are so sad.

How they loved each other, their children, and all of the other peoples they protected. There are so many wonderful secrets yet to be revealed.

Naero hadn't had much opportunity to listen to Drian and Driathan music. Perhaps she should take time to do so. She had been so focused on Kexxian music and Songs of Power.

Momma, did you know that the lizard people helped the Drians to create a completely new Song of Making? Then they used that special song only once—to create their shining children, the Driathans. Think about that. If it had not been for the Kexx helping the Drians, the Driathans might not have ever existed.

Everything could always change in an instant.

The young girl opened her eyes and smiled up at her mother.

For Naero, it was like beholding all of the stars of the universe at once.

She smiled back and held out her arms. Shetharra climbed into them.

Naero patted her back. "Come on, little duck. Let's get you back to bed."

They flashed back into the Medical Center, holding each other in Shetharra's medbed. Naero wasn't even sure which of them had transported them; that did not matter.

I feel safer when I'm in the KDM, Mom. And my pain is a lot less there.

"You can't think that way or try to hide there, honey. Your spirit essence might be in the KDM, but your body is still here in the Medical Center, and your pain levels are the same."

Strange. Naero had felt her daughter's light pass through herself on several occasions, but she was not usually suffused in it. Why was that?

Was it because normally, she herself remained tainted by her own Darkbeast?

Then she noticed that back in the vault, Nehz had flowed back into her static prone position there. Shetharra's influence on the blank seemed to be triggered and limited by direct proximity.

Shetharra snuggled within her mother's arms and used her sleepy voice. "Keeping trying, Mom. It might take you a while, but you'll figure it out. I know you. You don't know the meaning of the word quit. You'll find a way. Gallan needs his mom. She'll make a great Driathan with her well organized mind. But I think it will be yours and her capacity for love together that will make the difference and finally bridge the gap."

Naero grinned. "Why do you say that, little duck?"

"Love was one of the Drians' greatest powers, very close to that of the Kexxian Dreamers. It made them all nearly invincible, they were so mighty. That's how they helped each other beat the Great Enemy. The nasty G'lothc hardly have any concept of love, except as a way to manipulate others. The closest they can come to comprehending love is plain desire. How very sad."

"Did the Seven teach you all of that? You know, come to think of it, I've never actually taken you inside the KDM."

"Mom, I've gone there many times. The voices of my little glowing lizard friends and The Tua call me there. I go there whenever I want—it's all inside you through our link. I'm safe there."

"Well, from now on I want you to take me with you whenever you go inside the KDM. I want to attempt to hear what these voices are telling you. I want to see if the spirits of the Seven will speak to me."

"Okay. A lot of it is about the Cosmic Prophecies, and things that happened millions of years ago. I have to admit, I don't understand very much of it."

Naero blinked, and then smiled. "Take me with you, Shetharra. Please. Perhaps we can find some more of our answers together."

Shetharra kissed her. "Okay, Momma. I will."

18

Despite all of their best efforts, the Alliance continued losing the war. They were still being pushed back on nearly all fronts, even without Elazethrek showing up again and again.

The Creature's harrying attacks just made things worse, speeding up the enemy advance.

The Alliance had to do something radical to help turned the tide.

Naero and Baeven led their champion team on an all-out assault to spearhead retaking the Interdimensions.

If they could win there, that might help them stop or at least slow down the relentless enemy progress.

Therefore, the primary goal was to finally push back the rampaging G'lothc phage and eliminate it as a threat.

The Allies felt confident that they now understood the phage enough to defeat it, but it was still backed up by countless legions of G'lothc wraiths, and some of the new enemy warships that could enter the Interdimensions with their energy-infused Ultrium hulls.

After months of experiments and refitting with the new Alliance Ultrium fixers, the Alliance still only had a handful of fleets, and of course the new Ultrium starfighter waves that could also operate there. Yet even those miraculous fighters were not as effective against the new enemy fleets.

One advantage the Alliance did have was contact with a new species of energy being from another far flung portion of the Gamma Quadrant, in sync and adjacent with the Prime Material Plane of the Alliance universe.

The Glos were somewhat gelatinous in appearance, definitely amorphous in their shifting shapes and hues. Each was roughly the apparent size and mass of a large being about two meters in the longest direction. Their offspring or children were lesser gelatinous-looking, plasma-like blobs—lesser versions of themselves who gradually grew to the adult size. The Glos mated in pairs and reproduced by splitting offspring from themselves after mating. The process was quite amusing.

They communicated telepathically with ease, and if they ventured into the Prime Material Plain they could emit intelligible sounds in their odd, wiggly voices. They could learn languages in a brief period of time telepathically.

But it was necessary for them to shield other beings from their vibrant, shifting patterns of Cosmic energy, which could be dangerous and even lethal at times. They were slightly familiar with the Laelor, and had briefly mentioned two other far off energy being races: the Prill and the Elok, but did not know how to locate or contact one another directly.

Fortunately, the enemy had thus far made little contact with the Glos. Naero and the Alliance energy beings relished that, and instantly warned their new contacts about the enemy and their ravaging attack methods.

The Glos were both mildly amazed and somewhat alarmed, yet many of them still felt confident in their defensive capabilities, which did seem formidable.

When asked how long they had existed, the Glos had no answer. They had ascended so long ago that they stopped tracking time for quite a while. They had no knowledge of the G'lothc, or the Kexx or the Drians. It was guessed that eons of isolated immortality had protected them.

They agreed to join the Alliance and assist in the assault, more curious than anything else. Several thousand adult Glos joined in on the attack.

Waves of varieties of phage, supported by their larger wraith counterparts swarmed at the Alliance forces.

The Alliance fixer clouds rushed out to neutralize and otherwise confuse and hold off the majority of the enemy swarm.

The new Alliance phaze-fighters made crisscrossing strafing and bombing runs, blasting the enemy hordes to Cosmic dust.

Casualties still mounted on both sides, but the enemy seemed to be suffering the worst of it by far.

On the Alliance side, any wounded energy beings or damaged fighters would often be quickly overwhelmed, drained of all energy, picked clean, and then completely absorbed. The energy was used by the enemy to create more phage and wraiths almost instantly, in a process of near immediate conversion.

Then the first Glos were killed in a similar fashion. Some of them ventured forward too far on their own, were damaged, and then swarmed on by the wraith-led phage. In no time the blobby beings were devoured and transformed into more foes.

At first all of the Glos halted and behaved as if stunned. War was something they had not recalled in many eons. They still hadn't thought it was possible for one of their kind to be destroyed so quickly and in such a fashion.

Then the Glos went insane.

All several hundred thousand of the remaining Glos swelled up to the size and mass of a battleship and shot forward at incredible speed. Like gigantic amoebae they enveloped large swaths of the enemy hordes and absorbed them.

They took out three quarters of the enemy massed against them in a matter of a few standard minutes, before even the fixer nebulae could act.

But then they also went into a state of torpor, floating helplessly while they finished absorbing and transmuting the Cosmic energies of their huge meals.

Naero and the Alliance forces saw their advantage now, and swept forward to finish off the attacking horde once and for all, leaving the Glos behind under a thin guard.

The remaining enemy forces did not flee nor relent in any way.

After hours of fierce fighting the enemy forces finally broke and fled back through wyrmholes to other distant parts of the Interdimensions that they had conquered. This time, the Alliance zapped those wyrmholes with new tek, freezing them open, and poured through in close pursuit.

The continuous attack kept the remnant of the enemy forces off balance and unable to regroup.

The Alliance pressed the advantage, hunting the foe down wherever they fled and blasting them to perdition. Naero called in further support, rolling the enemy up just as they had hoped.

After more than half a day, they had the nearly-exhausted remains of the enemy hordes backed up to where the ruinous attacks had first begun—on the edges of Laelor Interdimensional territory.

Then a vast rent in SpaceTime opened wide like a sudden wound, nearly a parsec in length.

This was no mere wyrmhole.

"Haisha!" Naero cried to all of her linked forces. "Hurry, finish off destroying the last of the phage and the wraiths. We don't know what is going to come at us next!"

The Alliance forces struggled to finish their first battle, before another could be joined.

Naero's sense of warning went completely crazy.

Massive Darkforce energy burst heading our way, N!

"All shields up! Maximum dispersal. Phaze, jump, or transport out if you can!"

Three quarters of their forces made it out just in time.

The maximum dispersal saved much of what was left, but many were still unlucky.

A wide lash of Darkforce energy raked across half of the original battlefield like vast dark claws. Those claws destroyed anything they touched, whether friend or foe. Such massive enemy attacks were often indiscriminate.

"It's the Dark Emperor!" Baeven shouted.

Naero sensed the great enemy and its terrible might—like a moving, shifting singularity of the Darkforce.

But the evasive thing was already retreating, vanishing after its incredible cataclysmic strike before it could be engaged.

Then Naero and the others sensed other foes jumping in.

Hundreds of advanced enemy fleets entered at extreme range, forming up and racing toward the yawning opening of the SpaceTime rent to pour forward into the Interdimensions from normal SpaceTime.

Elazethrek transported several times in front of them, coming straight at the Alliance.

All six of the assembled Alliance Champions shot forward to engage the Creature: Naero, Baeven, Janner, Shalaen, Jia, and Ra.

Naero gave orders to the rest of their forces along the way. Some who had fled initially now came about. "We'll deal with the monster. The rest of you attack the perimeter of the SpaceTime rent. I've seen one of these before. There will be charged tek nodes keeping it open, maintaining the breach. Destroy those nodes and close the portal before those new fleets emerge, or we're all done for!"

"Is that the enemy Armada we keep hearing about, Admiral Maeris?"

"We should hope it isn't, but either way, collapse that gateway at all costs!"

"On it, sir!"

They engaged Elazethrek right in front of the SpaceTime rent.

"Remember," Baeven told them, "maintain energy drain strategies and attacks. Do everything you can wear it out. Try not to engage it up close or get in the way of the rest of us. If you take too much damage, try to get away and recover."

The team wheeled around the monster, trying to maintain their attacks and keep their distance.

Once again, the Creature's power levels and abilities scanned off the charts. It lashed out at each of them in turn, sometimes missing, sometimes connecting.

It struck at Naero and swatted her away, leaving her partially dazed. She shook it off and transported back in to keep up the pressure, nailing the thing again and again with energy drain blasts and beams.

Elazethrek exploded the aether around Shalaen and almost took her out.

No one could check on her. They left her floating and regenerating behind them with nothing but fixers to protect her.

The mission demanded that they keep fighting, keep Elazethrek busy, and stick to their strategy to wear the damn thing down.

They ganged up on the monster and kept it from going after Shalaen for the kill. They knew what it was trying to do—pick them off one at a time.

Naero sensed Shalaen come to several minutes later and re-doubled her efforts, dodging more attacks.

This was a straight up fight. All of them took a beating and came back swinging. They were being worn down as well, and the thing seemed not to weaken at all.

Om assured Naero that the monster's primary energies were now down to almost sixty percent and failing.

Not good enough.

Not fast enough.

"The strategy is working!" Naero shouted. "Keep at it until we take it down!"

Who was she kidding? They could barely hurt it like this. They couldn't destroy it. More than likely, they'd only chase it off once again.

If they had more time.

The main problem now was that those new enemy fleets were getting closer and closer to shooting through the gateway. That was probably only minutes away by now. Om confirmed it.

Naero called out to their forces over the secure link. "People, that gateway can go down any time now!"

"The enemy tek nodes sustaining it have powerful shields, Admiral. We're slowly cutting through them."

"That's not good enough. Cut through faster. Throw everything you have at them. Use the new infusion negation mines. I don't care if our ships and the fixers take damage at this range. We'll all take a lot more damage if those new fleets fall on us. We can't stop them. Now slam that goddam door shut right in their faces!"

Naero grunted from taking another heavy blast and being tossed end over end.

Even as she recovered and transported back in, the Creature tried something new.

Before their eyes, it exploded, pieces of it scattering in all directions. Strike that. Not in every direction, just right at all of them.

To their amazement, each chunk of the monster re-formed and became another of the same Creature, all on its own, with what seemed to be full strength and abilities.

All six of them now had their hands full fighting an exact duplicate of the monster all on their own.

Om tried to reassure Naero, while she was being battered and pummeled. *It's a nice trick, but all of the replicants don't have any more energy combined than the one before. Now all of that is divided equally between them. Destroy one, and you destroy part of it—for good!*

Great. If you're so smart, Om, then why are these things still kicking our asses?

You've stopped draining its energies and focused on fighting. Renew the strategy.

Not so easy to do, when these things are bent on killing us.

I'll do what I can, N.

Energy drain attacks poured out of Naero once more, even as she fended the monster off. The others couldn't do the same thing, and were barely holding their replicants at bay. Naero called to them over their link.

"Listen everyone. Drive all of these things together and hit them with the biggest energy negation blast we can muster. Flash out at the last instant as it detonates."

"Easy for you to say, sib," Janner noted. "Shalaen and I can barely hold ours off, let alone drive them anywhere."

"New wrinkle then. Get them to follow us into the center. Everyone drive or lure their monster in close with the others, around Jan and Shalaen. Then we blow them all up."

All six of them threatened to smash into one another in total confusion.

Now! Naero shouted.

Spheres of energy negation power erupted one after the other within the same space.

Naero and her people barely escaped the conflagration.

The enemy SpaceTime gate flickered and flashed at the same moment. Then it vanished, as the destroyed nodes imploded.

When it was all over, Elazethrek came back together and floated in the Interdimensional aether, smoking and apparently defeated.

Om?

No detectable energy levels. But be careful. It could be masking them in some way.

Baeven closed in in his near Darkbeast form.

The Creature flashed back to life and impaled Baeven on its right arm, which somehow had shifted into a large, wicked-looking blade. Then it twisted the blade free and booted Baeven away.

Elazethrek grinned and wildly snarled at the rest of them. I FINALLY GOT ONE OF YOU. I'LL BE BACK TO TAKE OUT THE REST OF YOU WEAKLINGS, ONE AT A TIME OR ALL TOGETHER. IT MAKES NO DIFFERENCE TO ME!

They raced at her to take her down, but she formed a wyrmhole and sped through it. The portal winked out and their attacks struck nothing but empty aether.

Jia was the first to reach Baeven. He was already convulsing and dying from being all but gutted.

At least in his energy being form they could all help regenerate him, something that they wouldn't have been able to do in a fight at this level in his physical form.

They were lucky that this battle happened in the Interdimensions.

It still took all five of them pumping Cosmic energies into Baeven to keep him from dying.

19

"It has become clearer and clearer to me and many others," Naero said as she addressed the Alliance joint chiefs, "that we must extend our thinking, just as the enemy has done. In the past few years, we have lost as many battles as we have won, but the overall war continues to unfold and grow larger.

"I believe that in the long term, the enemy holds the advantage over us, and not just in teknology. They continue to plan this war and all of these conflicts far out into the future, over generations and millennia if need be. We have yet to do that. We keep hoping somehow that we will be able to end this conflict within a matter of months or years, at best.

"Everything that we have learned about the G'lothc tells us that they plan their strategies to roll out one after another and eventually overwhelm their foes. We must continue to gather allies, because this is a war that all sentients must fight, if they wish to survive. The Great Adversary and its slaves that we face spare no one."

She paused to drink about half a glass of water.

Transforming back into her physical form from her energy being form required her to stay hydrated. Om had to keep reminding her to eat and drink properly.

"Therefore, in an accord with these findings, Alliance Intel, our Interdimensional allies, and the Astral and Dimensional Council will bring together our brightest minds, our greatest thinkers, and our most brilliant strategists to project into the future, keep up on what we know, and learn from our mistakes to help us survive and surpass the threats that we shall face, now and into the future!"

The Joint Chiefs of the Alliance applauded or cheered, as they were able. Most everyone was in agreement with such long term strategic thinking. This consolidation move was long overdue.

"We have one great advantage," Naero told them in closing. "We can bring in the great thinkers of all sentients to find solutions to our problems. The enemy only has slaves, and drones among their ranks. They do not value the power of the free and unfettered mind and imagination. I say that in the end, this power shall lead us to victory. And once this long war does end, we shall march into an age of peace, knowledge, wisdom, and enlightenment that our galaxy has not known for eons!"

More applause and cheering, both from the room, and the many screens linked to the conference.

Naero lifted her open hands. "Let us all fight and work toward that as our end goal!"

She bowed to the main assembly and returned to her seat of honor. Klyne, Aunt Sleak, and many other dignitaries waited to give their thoughts on the occasion and all of the matters that were being raised.

Klyne took questions on the current state of the war along all of the current front lines.

"Just recently we have won major victories that many of us will not be able to see. Because they occurred in the Interdimensions, only a few of us will be able to appreciate their great strategic value.

"Yet now because of these victories, our allies among the energy being sentients will be able to recover their losses and create more of their kind. They will also be able to support us further in the Prime Material Plane, once we are certain that their series of linked and unlinked pocket dimension realms are secure."

Admiral Rakkit raised the major concern that many commanders fretted about. "What about these new fleets of Ultrium warships the enemy flaunted? When will they engage our forces on the front lines, and what answers and responses do we have to put up against them? Hundreds of these advanced fleets were sighted. Do we know if this is part of the feared enemy Great Armada from the next galaxy over? Are they already here upon us? Is this the beginning of the end, as the enemy has threatened?"

Klyne held up his hands. "Frankly, we don't know. We do not have enough information yet. Intel efforts continue. These new enemy fleets were sighted in these numbers. We can't tell yet if they were constructed in this galaxy or another, in this quadrant or another. We are preparing to engage them very soon, because that seems the most likely outcome. We can always trust that if the enemy has an advantage over us they always unleash it as quickly as possible.

"As for our current response, we still hold the overall advantage in raw numbers, and we have more and more waves of our new Ultrium starfighters joining our fleets on a daily basis. Yet the numbers of regular fighting fleets being converted to Ultrium-based upgrades remains perilously slow. We cannot produce large quantities of construction grade Ultrium for use in large warships fast enough. That is a major problem. Nor do we have any sufficient way of transforming our existing fleets into Ultrium-based upgrades."

Naero frowned. This was not a happy state of affairs and it was her fault. Everyone knew that the enemy was gearing up to give them all a royal butt-stomping once again, and for right now, all they could do was take it and try to survive.

The Kexxian planetary defense shields continued to be their one saving grace. Time and time again, the enemy could capture systems, but not take over the shielded worlds. A large portion of the enemy strategy involved the production of more slaves from the populations that came under their control. In this, the Alliance continued to stymie and frustrate them.

Nor could the enemy mine these worlds for slaves or raw materials at will, either.

As soon as the primary planning session ended, Naero went into a breakout strategy session where they assessed the data and results from their most recent encounter with Elazethrek. The Dark Emperor had also showed himself briefly.

The enemy leaders were powerful, but they seemed unwilling to show themselves now, apparently fearing that the Alliance and its champions would somehow get lucky and take them down. Clearly they planned to bring back more of the Six, the Darkforce champions like Elazethrek, to trouble the universe.

That seemed like a good plan for the G'lothc. Naero feared what would happen if even just one more of those vile monsters did get reborn. One was already more than enough for them to handle.

How would they be able to face two or more of the Six in all out combat?

Elazethrek had nearly killed her uncle Baeven, the strongest of them all, stronger than Naero herself, and that did more than frighten her a little.

The Alliance Champions had made the mistake of thinking themselves strong and powerful before.

There was no other way out now. Each of them had to find any real way to become even stronger if they were going to fight these things.

There was no doubt about it now.

More of these monsters would be sent at them to destroy them, and everything they loved.

*

Time waited for no one. Sharrah had been kind enough, as always, to carry Naero's and Khai's next daughter almost to term. In the midst of the terror they all faced, Spacers and other sentients everywhere continued to mate, give birth to, and do their best to raise their offspring.

Elazethrek would likely need at least a few weeks to recharge before her next devastating attack. That gave Naero the window she needed to give birth to her fifth child.

Chief Medical Officer Trudi Cheyenne and Shalaen used biomancy to transfer the pregnancy back to Naero for the final week or so. In a way it was a nice break to go back to being an expecting mom, despite all of the pain and related issues.

Not to mention the actually agonized joy of the wonderful birth process itself.

Yet it was that connectedness and grounding that allowed Naero to still feel human—to be a human woman with all of those challenges and concerns. She never wanted to forget that or lose that part of herself.

Being a superhero, the Cosmic Champion of Enlightened Change, and an energy being much of the time was just like shapeshifting. It took her away from being human, sometimes too much and for too long.

Biomancy did make giving birth a little better than what it had been for past generations of women, but it was still a literal pain between the legs.

Nothing could really change that completely, and Naero guessed that perhaps it shouldn't. Babies were so important that they should come at some kind of price.

The few hours that she suffered bringing little Selendil Saemar Maeris into the universe proved well worth it. In some crazy way, Naero even looked forward to paying that toll along this life's journey.

Naero and Khai held their child up to the stars and shouted her name out into the black.

Then, as they always did, they expanded their big round nano bed and slept a few days with all of their kids sprawled out there with them and the new addition to the family. Even Shetharra was there with them, in her new, streamlined Ultrium regen suit.

Khai and Naero took turns feeding, changing, and caring for little "Selly" Selendil as needed.

Sometimes they even fought with one another slightly over who was going to care for her, the time with their new daughter was so precious.

They often did so together.

That also gave them quiet time to talk to each other in private.

"Khai, I know the Mystics need you, but I really think that you have to stay with the other Alliance Champions and help us on a full time basis. We really need your help with the Creature. It almost killed my uncle, and you know how tough he is. We can't afford to lose any of us. We need your strength. It could make all the difference."

"I'll talk to the Mystics. If it's that bad, you need me. This threat has to be dealt with once and for all. We need to hunt that blasted thing down and destroy it."

Her husband sighed, let the nanodiaper seal, and the little black Nytex Spacer baby togs after that. "Aww…look at our little bug. She's so snug and wiggly. Gosh, I love all of our kids, but I think I have a new favorite."

Naero laughed, kissed, and patted his big hard arm. "You goof; you say that about all of them when they're babies. I think you just like them when they're this small and helpless. You love it that they can literally fit in the palm of those massive mits of yours."

The man she loved laughed once more. "I do. What's wrong with that, N?"

Khai was a man who cherished being a father. He was definitely hands on in every way with his children, whenever there was time to do so.

But thank goodness for Sharrah and the rest of the staff.

A call to duty could come at any time.

Thankfully, they almost had a fortnight of time with the new baby and the rest of the family before they were summoned away by the endless demands of the Gamma Quadrant war.

20

The new enemy fleets did not attack as feared, for some reason that no one could comprehend. Perhaps they had been from the next galaxy over, and were now cut off once again. If so, then the enemy only seemed to be able to open one of those SpaceTime rents every couple of years. They clearly required a near impossible amount of Cosmic energy.

This time around the Alliance had neutralized several of the nodes and captured them for study, without them all blowing up in a defensive chain reaction to hide their secrets.

Tyber and many of the Alliance teks were still having great trouble deciphering any part of them. Two more of the advanced devices had gone out of control and imploded during the initial examination process, once they could link to any given power source.

Self-aware, living G'lothc tek had an amazing penchant for self-destruction.

At last the Alliance and their champions finally captured a G'lothc heavy cruiser, one of the tentacle ships, using many of the same updated energy drain tactics that they had used against Elazethrek. There was a lesson there as well.

They still weren't seeing massed fleets of the new ships in the Prime Material Plane in the same way that the enemy threatened in the Interdimensions. Naero figured that was only a matter of time.

Why wish for more trouble before it struck?

At present, the new enemy warships continued to replace the older, first generation vessels across the board. The Gamma Quadrant conflict, however, remained a much larger war zone covering a much larger, ever-expanding area. The Alliance was still stuck with exploring new territory, making first contact with new interstellar races, and fighting a vast war in three constantly growing dimensions.

But they were also, nonetheless, approaching the slip point where half or more of the enemy fleets would be comprised of these new warships. These enemy ships were undeniably tougher and more than capable of surviving any fight.

It was estimated that a severely damaged enemy warship could regen, refit, and get back to the front lines within three standard days to one week.

That was near parity with the miraculous refit abilities of the Alliance fixer clouds, who could send an Alliance warship back to the war within a handful of standard days.

At this rate, perhaps in another year or so, all of the enemy ships would be from among their most advanced designs. And that was going to be a major problem.

The Alliance was fighting a slow, mostly organized fighting retreat as it was.

Then it came to light that in the unexplored areas outside of their immense war zone, literally all of the sentient interstellar races they had not met were somehow at war with each other.

How could that be?

This situation had their adversaries written all over it.

As soon as the Alliance began to investigate, they quickly discovered the far-reaching hand of the Great Adversary at work in secret, pitting sentients against each other in order to weaken, wear down, and soften these new races up for future conquest.

This could take place at any time in the future that the enemy was ready to take these unsuspecting sentients head on and crush them, one at a time or several species all at once. Potentially, that also included new Interdimensional races.

It became vital that all of that did not take place, but only so much could be dealt with at one time.

While the primary war continued, Naero and the other Alliance Champions led the campaign to deal with these other growing threats.

Otherwise, the Alliance would move into those new regions of the Gamma Quadrant and find those many sectors already enslaved and turned against them before there was any chance to recruit and bring them into the fold.

Their primary hope now was that Elazethrek had been sufficiently weakened when the monster fled, to lick its wounds and recharge before taking another crack at them. They were trying to make the Creature's recharging patterns work for them

An educated guess as to when and where the monster might attack next was very helpful.

Naero and her team, with the addition of Khai would now make a sweep through several strategic, war torn regions. Their new mission was to covertly alert the new sentients there as to what was really going on across the Gamma Quadrant.

With her shapechanging abilities, Naero was the perfect choice for infiltrating these hot zones and exposing the machinations of the true enemy.

The first sentients the new Alliance task force encountered were the *Gtiin*, a race of near-energy beings on par with the Oden, who had not quite perfected their energy being forms. They were quickly called "the puppet people," because of their unique ability to fragment or separate their segmented, vaguely humanoid, energized body parts and attack with them independently.

Each part of them was an entire, fully functioning entity on its own when separated, and fought with tek, psyonics, or Cosmic abilities. This made each one of them extremely formidable. If only one part of them survived, the entire collective being could be regenerated in about a week or less, depending on the extent of the damage.

The Gtiin also had four separate, interlocking genders: blin, tam, sood, and heth, and required all four to effectively and efficiently conceive and reproduce sexually. Gestation required six standard months, and each parent gave live birth to a single, complete offspring, that in turn took twelve standard years to mature into an adult. The sex of each child was random, or could be selected by medtek and or simple biomancy.

The quad parents could remain together in any combination of mutually beneficial partnerships, or were free to go off on their own and live singly or with others of their kind.

Other than that, Gtiin society was more or less within the societal range of most advanced sentient beings. As parents, they were protective of their offspring within their quad or other partnerships.

At first glance, most Gtiin looked the same: 1.5 to 2.0 meters tall near-humanoids with four eyes in two rows, two flaring, horizontal olfactory slits for noses, and two independent mouths. They could speak in unison with both, or carry on a conversation with one, while eating and ingesting food or lix with the other. Their bald head was on a flexible neck stalk that could stretch and fully rotate in all directions, or detach completely from the body. There were slits around the base of the skull that turned out to be ears.

They were hairless. Their skin was various shades of red, brown, gray, and black. Their genitalia was concealed and protected on their sides. For lack of better terminology, the left side was more female, consisting of a receptacle, while the right side was more male, consisting of a protuberance or series of extending tendrils. Learning their genitalia was the one true way to tell them apart, but because they wore outer garments, this was not always possible.

In order for a quad of Gtiin to conceive, they would need to join together in a square, two pairs face to face, and all in the proper order. This allowed the right protuberances to match up with the right receptacles. Conception occurred sexually as they swung around and waved back and forth while so coupled within the quad, exchanging genetics, pleasurable thoughts, sensations, and energies that came to a peak that could last for an instant or up a few hours in an enraptured stated of being.

Any other joinings were considered lesser relations, and "partial sex." The primary purpose of a quad joining was in fact to reproduce.

Naero instituted a catch and release program on a remote Gtiin colony to learn all of these things and more through covert observation, psyonics, and biomancy on test subjects who were kept unconscious. Usually they were taken for study while they rested, which was about six standard hours each night.

She proceeded to learn how to shapeshift into all of the four genders, and learned from the test subjects how each of the four dressed and acted differently overall from the rest.

Blins dressed conservatively, were quiet, industrious, and very affectionate. Tams were flamboyant, flashy, loud, and outspoken. They lived for the moment. Soods were creative and also very expressive, responsible for much of Gtiin art and music. Singing was a major entertainment for a race with two mouths and two sets of vocal chords. Heths were forceful, neither overly loud nor overly quiet, thoughtful, decisive, and strong willed. They were both thinkers and doers in Gtiin society and often took leadership roles, but they also saw the value in the different ideas of others, and insisted that the other three genders also share duty in leadership roles.

Naero chose to take the form of a Heth, the closest personality type to her own, despite the weird genitalia on either side of her. That was indeed pretty freaky.

Gtiin tek was very advanced, on par with the enemy and the Alliance, and also incorporated Ultrium based warships. That was incredibly interesting

In fact, the Alliance learned a new form or Ultrium production that they had not found inside the KDM as yet. There was even evidence that enemy spies had re-learned this technique from the Gtiin, less than a standard decade ago.

These sentients drew out portions of energized materials from their stars and transformed them into Ultrium base forms to be used in further production. The process combined psyonics and teknomancy in ways that had never been witnessed before.

The powerful teknomancers of the Gtiin literally thought their warships and all of their systems into being. Ships created out of pure thought and force of will.

Gtiin fleets consisted of battleships and carriers. All other fleet operations were handled by clouds of drones of various sizes. They had dispensed with smaller warships such as gunships, frigates, destroyers, and even cruisers.

The sentients that the enemy had pitted the Gtiin against were their nearest neighbors still further awry. This was said to be a strange mammalian race called the Rorg.

It had been an easy matter, from appearances, for the G'lothc to capture and enslave small bands from either side of the conflict with the mind control wraiths and send star ships blasting and tearing through the other species with great destruction and slaughter, until they were eventually taken out.

Naturally, both sides responded in kind against the threat of the other, thinking that they were each justified in doing so against a hyper-violent invader. The enemy had only to use mind control wraiths thereafter to pweak the turmoil here and there in order to keep the war of insane attrition going full force, on both sides.

Once the war was in full swing, the combatants would do the rest.

Little did either race know that they were being weakened and softened up for future subjugation and enslavement by an even more powerful enemy.

Naero made her preparations to let this secret cat out of the hidden, proverbial sack.

In her heth form, she transported down to one of the Gtiin homeworlds that was under direct siege by the so-called invaders, over half of which turned out to be Ejjai, second generation shock troop slaves and drones, and not even Rorg at all.

She and her stealth fixer cloud pinpointed the locations of the thirty-thousand or so mind control wraiths at work on the planet surface, and prepared to expose and exterminate them at the proper time, with the help of stealth fixers and Alliance naval power.

These wraiths controlled key persons on both sides of the conflict.

All of these factors made her task even easier, once she could get the attention of the combatants.

Her golden protective, cosmic aura completely surrounded her, impervious to any weapons present, right up to their largest warships. Naero strode right into a heated battle, shielding herself or whatever she was as a heth, and using the voice in both Gtiin and Rorg.

"CEASE FIRE, ALL UNITS. CEASE FIRE ALL COMBATANTS. LISTEN TO WHAT I MUST TELL YOU ALL. THIS WAR IS A SHAM, A GROSS MANIPULATION. A SUPER-ADVANCED ALIEN RACE IS SECRETLY PITTING YOU AGAINST ONE ANOTHER. ONCE THEY HAVE WEAKENED BOTH OF YOU SUFFICIENTLY, THEY WILL SWEEP IN WITH THEIR FLEETS AND DESTROY AND ENSLAVE BOTH OF YOUR CULTURES! THIS IS WHAT THEY DO. HEED MY WORDS!"

Many stopped fighting, others continued, and some on both sides turned their weapons directly against her.

Heth/Naero continued walking right through massive barrages of direct and indirect fire and ordnance from both sides.

"YOU WEAPONS CANNOT HARM ME, BUT THEY ARE A DISTRACTION. STOP ATTACKING ME, OR I WILL BE FORCED TO NEUTRALIZE THEM."

The attacks lessened, but some still continued.

She sent her invisible fixer clouds out like invisible locusts, dismantling weapons, vehicles, and armor—even disabling entire warships providing ground support. The hapless vessels floated powerless to the ground.

Troops on both sides, in combat armor, meks, and tanks found themselves standing helpless in nothing but their clothing, all of their tek and weapons had been stripped away and rendered inert.

Naero extended the effect out to twenty klicks.

"HEAR MY WORDS. YOU HAVE BEEN DECEIVED AND MANIPULATED. I AM SPEAKING THROUGHOUT THIS ENTIRE PLANET, AND TO ALL OF THE NAVAL WARSHIPS ON BOTH SIDES ENCIRCLING THIS HOMEWORLD. LOOK AROUND YOU. THE REAL ALIEN ENEMY THAT YOU CANNOT SEE HAS SEEDED MIND CONTROL WRAITHS AMONG YOUR LEADERS IN KEY POSITIONS. I HAVE PLACED THEM IN A STATE OF PARALYSIS. I AM REVEALING THEM TO YOU NOW ON WAVELENGTHS THAT YOU CAN DETECT THEM.

DO NOT HARM THE HOSTS. I WILL SHOW YOU HOW TO REMOVE THESE MIND CONTROL WRAITHS. THE HOSTS ARE NOT AT FAULT AND WILL SURVIVE. MOST OF THE WRAITHS CAN BE DESTROYED. BOTH SIDES WILL NO DOUBT WISH TO CAPTURE SEVERAL SPECIMENS FOR FURTHER STUDY."

In some few cases she was still too late.

There were always some on the two sides who overreacted in paranoid terror, and cut down both the innocent hosts and the wraiths at the same time.

Naero had Om and the fixers did their best to protect the hosts, and neutralize weapons throughout the planet and the fleets to avoid a further blood bath.

A tsunami of responses swept her way.

"Who are you?"

"What are you?"

"Release our forces at once!"

"How are you able to do these things?"

"Why do you take the form of a Gtiin heth?"

"why do you pretend to look like us?"

"Why do you take the form of our enemies?"

"Why should we trust you?"

"I AM A FRIEND. I MEAN BOTH SIDES IN THIS CONFLICT NO HARM. ALL OF YOUR QUESTIONS SHALL BE ANSWERED ONCE ALL USELESS FIGHTING AROUND THIS HOMEWORLD HAS CEASED. TRANSMIT THESE FINDINGS TO ALL OF YOUR FORCES IN THIS REGION, ON BOTH SIDES OF THIS SENSELESS CONFLICT. BOTH OF YOUR PEOPLES NEED TO HEAR THESE FACTS, AND ASSESS THIS EVIDENCE. I AM ALREADY TRANSMITTING THE TEK SPECS FOR THE CONSTRUCTION OF DEVICES THAT WILL SCAN, REVEAL, AND NEUTRALIZE THESE ENEMY MIND CONTROL WRAITHS AMONG YOU BOTH. CALL AN IMMEDIATE CEASEFIRE BETWEEN BOTH SIDES WHILE YOU CONFIRM ALL OF THIS NEW INFORMATION."

"This is the High Commander of all Gtiin military forces for this sector. Why should we trust you in any way?"

"I am the Lord Marshall of the Rorg Protectorate Strike Force. I reluctantly agree with my enemy counterpart. If what you say is true, and we are being deceived and manipulated by unseen forces, how do we know that you are not part of it?"

"MY WORDS TO YOU ARE TRUE AND CAN BE PROVEN BY DIRECT EVIDENCE. EVEN UNDER CONSTANT ATTACK BY BOTH OF YOUR FORCES, I DID NOT RESPOND WITH LETHAL FORCE—WHEN I COULD HAVE EASILY DONE SO. I EVEN DID ALL THAT I COULD TO KEEP YOUR PEOPLES FROM NEEDLESSLY KILLING MORE OF THE EXPOSED ENEMY HOSTS ON BOTH SIDES. THEY DID NOT ASK FOR THIS, AND THEY CAN STILL BE SAVED."

"The Gtiin did not request your assistance."

"We do not require the aid of aliens who insist on interfering in our affairs."

"I'M SORRY, BUT I DO NOT HAVE TIME FOR YOUR IMPOTENT STUBBORNNESS, OR YOUR GROSS STUPIDITY. BOTH OF YOUR RACES ARE VERY CLOSE TO BEING HARVESTED AND DESTROYED BY A FOE YOU CAN'T SEE COMING—TERRIBLE BEINGS THAT YOU CANNOT EVEN IMAGINE. I HAVE GIVEN YOU PROOF THAT YOU ARE BEING CONTROLLED BY JUST SUCH AN ALIEN FORCE THAT WISHES TO DESTROY BOTH OF YOUR CULTURES. I BELONG TO AN ALLIANCE THAT OPPOSES THIS ALIEN FORCE THROUGHOUT THIS GALAXY AND BEYOND. WE CAN AID YOU."

"I-I—"

"Y-you—?"

She froze them both in their places and spoke at them directly. "Shut up, both of you idiots! Now is not the time for denial. Your further threats are meaningless to me. You cannot harm me. Do you think that your two races are the only ones suffering from this type of attack? Dozens of other sentient races are enduring the same ordeal, and there are most likely many other sentients that we have not reached yet. Some we may not reach in time. Every moment we delay helps are true enemies. You can help us contact other interstellar species such as yourselves and help reveal this evil plot, so that they will not share in your fate."

"We will fight you with everything-"

"Please don't. Is it not clear that we don't want to fight you? Why would we go to this length? We want to help you against an enemy bent on enslaving and destroying the entire galaxy. Even the entire universe. Can't you see that? Look at the proof we offer you and confirm what I say for yourselves. Must I use lethal force to convince you? Are you so far gone? Is death all that you will understand?

"HAS THERE NOT BEEN ENOUGH SENSELESS DEATH?

"Life is precious to my people. I don't want to kill any of your people, so let's not go in that direction. Must there be further needless loss of life for you to see reason? Study the evidence I am offering you. Calm down and come to your own reasonable conclusions. The Alliance that I belong to is an organization of free sentients gathered together from throughout our galaxy.

"You are free to rule yourselves and your worlds, as long as you do not threaten or harm other sentients. That is our guiding principle. But this galactic alien threat is real, and whether you face it on your own, or with our help, you must do so. We are simply giving you these truths and hope that you will make the best decision for your peoples, and our galaxy as a whole."

Over the next few hours and days, both the Gtiin and the Rorg began to move within a much wider and dangerous universe.

In the end the war between the two sentient races ended quickly, and both sides decided to join the Alliance against the enemy at hand. Like many they were only just beginning to learn about the Great Adversary.

21

After leaving the Gtiin, Naero pushed on to dealing directly with the Rorg. They were six limbed marsupials who were about 1.75 meters tall. They had two pairs of arms and two legs. Gray, brown, or black hair covered their humanoid bodies, and they were a very populous race on their worlds, using their advanced tek mainly for food production and interstellar defense.

Naero stood on the bridge of her flagship, *The Holy Ghost*, giving a tour to amber-eyed Bowda Mozil, Lord Marshall of the Rorg Protectorate Strike Force and his officers. They also traveled with the Alliance task force fleets on a tour throughout the Rorg systems.

Naero had her people put the amazing flagship through its paces, demonstrating several, but not all of its many capabilities.

She always had to keep a few tricks and surprises up her sleeves, just in case.

Bowda and her people seemed sufficiently impressed, especially with the super battleship's astounding rate of fire and the raw damage it could mete out with all of its heavy guns unleashed in an overwhelming barrage.

They vaporized several enemy junk target ships in seconds, making a meal out of them.

"We have never seen such devastating might from a single warship!" Bowda exclaimed. "Your fleets must indeed be invincible!"

Naero frowned, responding in flawless Rorg. "I hate to admit, but the enemies that we face are sending new ships against us even more powerful than most of our own."

Bowda Mozil gasped.

"I quite agree," Naero said. "We're struggling to find parity, even with our superior numbers. The enemy tek advantage remains a serious dilemma."

N, the enemy is preparing to make another move.

Very good, Om. S.O.P. Let's take them down hard and fast when they do.

Affirmative.

They did not have long to wait.

Several Rorg from Bowda's entourage transformed into horrific monsters right before their eyes, bent only on death and destruction.

Many carried phazed micro-atomic devices and fusion bombs. Hundreds of wraiths coordinated an attack on the flagship and its bridge at the same moment.

By the time Naero lifted one glowing hand, and opened her third eye, Om's Kexxian defense protocols already flared and flashed out in all directions.

Black and white energy ribbons minced the attackers into flaring cinders.

Naero's Cosmic blast waves vaporized any stragglers after that, sending their fleeting ashes rocketing back into the Astral Plane from which many of them had emerged.

Bowda and her remaining people were clearly staggered by this flashing performance. "Admiral Maeris, I have heard of such devastating enemy attacks taking place, where none survived. Yet never have I seen such an assault crushed by one individual. How do you possess such powers and abilities? Can my people learn them? Can they be taught?"

Naero smiled slightly. "Some of them can, and I can strengthen and quicken them in others if they are already present, in persons who are of strong mind and will. Do you have any psyons among you? People with mind powers or strange Cosmic abilities?"

Bowda nodded her head. "There are some few. We have tried to train them on our own, but we could use much further guidance and assistance in these matters."

"I will consult with your adepts if I can, and put them in touch with our Mystics for testing and further training. If a talent is there in a person, often it can be nurtured, developed, and strengthened."

All of the visitors seemed visibly shocked and shaken by the attack, and almost equally by the manner in which it was thwarted and defeated. They looked upon Naero with new respect and even fear.

The leader shook her head. "The enemy shapeshifters—their disguises function so well among my people, even my own guards. They are so complete that we could not detect them. How can we defend against such malice and intrigue?"

Naero smile. "There are some ways, and we will share them with you. We will give you equipment and knowledge, with which you can scan among yourselves for such spies and moles. But the enemy is constantly trying to find new ways to deceive us and gain an advantage."

Bowda nodded. "Clearly, we see that now. Yet we have heard rumors that some of your kind are shapeshifters also. Is that true?"

Naero took a female Rorg form almost instantly.

The remaining Rorg jumped at that.

"Some few of us have that talent," Naero said. "But even among us, it still remains very rare. Many of the enemies we face seemed to be born to treachery, disguise, and deception. They come to it almost naturally."

The mouth of their primary guest hung open. "You speak our language flawlessly, as if you are one of us."

Naero shrugged. "So will the enemy's slaves. They are masters at infiltration and mass killing. You must never underestimate them."

"I see," Bowda said. "It must be a fearful thing indeed, that in fighting such foes, you have become more and more just like them."

For an instant, Naero was astonished and stricken by even that partial truth of such a statement.

She had to think on that for a bit.

Was it true?

Was she more effective in thwarting the enemy because she was slowly but surely becoming more like them all the while? Besting them at their own ruthless games?

There had always been a danger in that. Baeven had noted such risks on several occasions. But the full weight of it struck Naero at that moment like a dark epiphany.

In fact, even the Kexx and the Drians had lamented the same concerns in their accounts. That in fighting the long and terrible war across several galaxies, laying waste to entire quadrants, and finally defeating the G'lothc, they had nearly become just like them.

They had begun to think and behave like their despised foes.

And whatever their justifications—they had become the greatest mass killers that several galaxies had ever witnessed.

They followed the ways of the very things they hated and opposed, in order to win, and to keep the Great Adversary from doing the same thing or worse to them and the races they protected. And in doing so, even in their righteous wrath to save the universe, such actions still corrupted them. It left them focused too much solely on hatred and destruction, until they themselves were tainted by such things.

Destruction and the death of multiple species became the ultimate solution.

The end laments of the two mighty, godlike races were fraught with such warnings and unhappy conclusions.

Naero suddenly worried as never before.

Was their great and well-meaning Alliance heading toward a similar fate? What choice did they have, against the same enemy?

She returned to her own primary Spacer form, much to the relief of the shaken Rorg.

Naero spent six days thereafter with the Rorg, going on little sleep, quickening and adding to the Cosmic and psyonic powers of their marsupial adepts. They were grateful beyond the capacity of their language and thought. They were also amazed at the new tek from the Alliance that also came their way freely, which would allow them to detect and deal with enemy efforts at further infiltration among their race, and other interstellar races that they interacted with.

The enemy manipulation was apparently so wide spread and invasive, that Naero feared that they would encounter it everywhere they turned.

Their initial efforts uncovered enemy agents and monsters scattered among mostly the Rorg military, their leadership, and all of their key worlds and populations.

Rooting them out caused a panic among the entire species. Who could be trusted?

As soon as she finished her initial relations with the Rorg, it was time to move on to the next encounter and the next set of challenges.

On the way to yet another mission, Naero had dinner with some of her closest friends: Chaela, Saemar, Tarim, and Shalaen.

The others such as Tyber and Alala were currently unavailable.

Khai was off on dire missions of his own. So were Baeven, Jia, and their rag-tag crew of outcasts and adventurers. It was the same way with Jan and Ra, who had also become good friends and comrades in arms.

They all had other special duties to perform as the Champions of the Alliance.

There was always something for them all to be doing at any given time.

Naero felt fortunate to have this time with this small gathering of friends.

Of course Naero whipped up the food for that evening.

She made Chaela's favorite Spacer broil with delicately seared and spiced selected strips of various meats in an expertly prepared scarlet kareb sauce. They feasted on tender, sweet Khydurian niblet corn on the cob, sky blue kernels with each cob as long as Naero's forearm. She even made a fish and Spum chowder for Saemar and Tarim, a dish that even they could agree on.

Cooking for her family and friends was always a welcome delight, and one of Naero's rare, treasured pleasures.

Tarim and Shalaen were especially canoodly that evening after being apart, and flirted and tittered among themselves for the most part. Their friends quite understood and left them to it without much teasing.

Chaela brought holos of her and Remy's four kids: Derron, age nine, Jodian, age 7, Kaelen, age six, and Pettaerra, age five. They were with their dad back in the Alpha Quadrant, in relative safety and happiness.

Chae and Naero remarked how much their service to the Clans took them away from their loved ones. But it could not be helped.

Matayan crème puffs came out for dessert, and plenty of orange gobra milk, Jett, and Spacer poteen to go around.

"I'm getting a child," Saemar suddenly blurted out.

Naero and Chae tried to cover their faces as they blasted their drinks out of their noses.

"Really?" Naero inquired. "How exactly is that going to fit in with all of your…your other activities?"

Saemar sighed, "Oh, I've cut way back on most of my extra sex these days."

More lix gushed out of Naero and Chae's noses.

"Haisha!" Chaela roared. "Will you at least try to warn us when you drop bombs like that? I do happen to be quite thirsty."

"Well, ya know, sweeties, I've discovered a truth in this here life. If ya spend all of your free time having great sex, after a while it's not so great anymore. To be honest, a gal eventually gets tired and sore after a hundred orgasms or more each day."

Naero blinked and covered her mouth again. "A hundred or more…?"

"Each day, sweetie," Chaela reminded her, with a grin and a finger poke."

Saemar shook her curly auburn head and her cleavage jiggled like ivory gelatin. "It just stops being special, ya know?"

Then their friend leaned in and whispered to them. "Even worse—it starts to feel like work, instead of fun. Haisha, I says. I sure ain't got nothin' ta prove anymore."

Both Naero and Chaela stared and blinked once again, at a complete loss for words.

Saemar knitted her hands together. "After what happened to Zhen, and really what could happen to any of us every day, I wanted part of me and Hikaru to continue on after us, just like your kids will. The universe needs a touch of my blood to stay in the mix."

Naero wrapped her arms around Saemar. Chaela did the same, embracing them both.

"You still don't think that you'll ever find someone else that you'd like to have kids with, Saemar?"

"I've really tried, for years, N. I just can't get Hikaru out of my head or heart. And I don't want to anymore. I've made peace with that. He was the one for me, however things turned out. If I take the genetic samples he left behind and I have his child, it will be like having part of him back with me again. It's a part of the way things could have been. I know that I could love our kids far better than I could someone else's. Seeing you guys so happy with your kids clinched the decision for me. Whatever kind of a mom I can be, I want to be one before my time is up."

Chaela kissed her friend's forehead. "You're going to be a great mom."

Saemar wiped tears away. "Thanks, Chae."

"Crazy as bed beetles, but you'll still be one amazing and fun mom. Kimura Hikaru would be proud to know that you two are going to have kids."

"I'll get with Hikaru's Kimura sept in Clan Mitsubishi to choose a name for our son. Heck, maybe I should just use Hikaru. Why not? I want a girl too. I want to call her Orean, Naero. I've loved the sound of that name ever since you mentioned it, sweetie. Is that all right with you?"

Naero grinned from ear to ear. "I don't own it. Sure, I'd be honored if you did."

They drank a lot more poteen after that than Naero originally intended. Even Tarim drank until he passed out in Shalaen's arms.

Naero waxed philosophical and opened up about her fears of becoming the very things she fought against and opposed.

For her, such possibilities were very real.

Chaela agreed with her and spoke about how they had to guard against giving in to so much hate and violence all around them. Killing couldn't always be the solution.

But Saemar belched and snorted in her debauchery, "N, don't you give that crap another thought. You're still one of the best peoples I know. And I know peoples. You won't become like the enemy, those stinking rat bastards. Bloody murderers. You love us all more than the stars. It just isn't in you. You love the Clans and the Alliance too much. It'd never happen!"

22

On the far side of Rorg space, the marsupials were also embroiled at war against the Garama, stoic, crablike amphibians who had based their lives around logic and reason for millennia.

Yet over the course of the last decade, these advanced sentients had suddenly become extremely warlike and hyper aggressive, manufacturing enormous fleets of warships to pursue ruthless aggression and conquest against all of their interstellar neighbors.

Neighbors that they had formerly lived in peace and harmony with.

To Naero's mind, this had the hand of the enemy written all over it.

No doubt she would find that the G'lothc and their mind control slaves were busy doing what they normally did best—pitting every known race against the other in order to weaken everyone for eventual subjugation and enslavement. That was just what the enemy did.

But getting close enough to the Garama in order to expose the enemy became another obstacle entirely.

They ignored any overtures involving negotiation, they possessed no allies, and they vigorously attacked any foreign starship that came within range of their territory.

Even when Naero shapeshifted into one of their kind and used stealth in order to infiltrate one of the outbound worlds, the Garama somehow detected her almost instantly and attacked her with everything they had— including atomics. She could not get close enough to them or be in contact with them for a long enough period of time to achieve any of her goals.

Perhaps this was the new enemy strategy to combat her efforts at exposing them.

For the present it seemed to be working.

She was not willing to endanger the lives of countless Garama for nothing.

How were they detecting her presence so quickly? She guessed that it had something to do with the Garama's innate psyonic powers. Their brain patterns and neural nets were unique to their highly advances species. Shapeshifting could only approximate so much. She would have to be among them for a while in order to learn more and be able to fully adapt to them.

Naero's normal method was to mimic the outward appearance well enough to get close to a new species, and then further learn about and match their mental patterns, language, culture, and internal characteristics, as needed.

That was no longer reliable. She could not simply approximate.

Then again, the Garama also had an extremely sophisticated sense of smell and taste. Perhaps they could not be fooled in those regards by any shapechanger.

Working closely with Spacer Intel, together Naero and her allies executed a mission to capture a small Garama merchant vessel and study the crew and passengers carefully and in depth within a period of several standard hours.

This would be done without the awareness of the Garama that they had been captured. When the few hours for the research were over, the incapacitated crew and passengers would awake and continue on their way.

The records and data on their vessel would lead them to believe that they had lost consciousness to do a certain type of gas leak that affected them all for several hours. After which, their ship's systems had detected and repaired the dangerous leak, and then refreshed the life support systems in order to revive them.

Those Garama would be none the wiser for their stealth encounter with the Alliance.

Naero chose Captain Tyber, Alala, and *The Dark Star* to assist in the execution of said operation.

Naero and teams of Intel researchers swarmed over the hapless Garama merchant ship after stealth and medical drones gassed all of those on board, and rendered the ship itself helpless, blind, and dumb.

Alala and Tyber directed the effort to wipe all traces of the encounter from the ship's memory banks, security vids, and scans. The research teams and Naero herself wore special hyper clean EV suits that would not leave any odd scent, trace, or even genetic markers for the heightened Garama senses to pick up afterwards.

First, Naero and others fast scanned the ship's logs and used teknomancy also to pore through months of vid records. They studied the merchant ship's trade route activities throughout the Garama homeworld systems.

Then they studied Garama social behavior patterns, culture, and individual personal behaviors, personality types, and activities. The Garama were much like many other advanced sentients in many regards, except for their intense dedication and devotion toward the war efforts, which seemed both standard and rigid among each individual—almost as if each of them had been hardwired that way.

There were no exceptions or deviations and that alone was frightening.

How had they been brainwashed almost so completely? Trillions of beings across hundreds of worlds, and suddenly they were all of one mind about invading, slaughtering, and enslaving their interstellar neighbors wholesale.

Naero was astonished that she found absolutely no trace of enemy mind control or possession. No wyrms, no wraiths, none of the usual parasites of any kind or variety were present.

The mystery continued to baffle everyone.

Then Ty and Alala joined their efforts with only three hours remaining, much to Om's delight. He was still convinced that he was madly in love with Alala. His problem still remained—convincing Alala of that same fact in regards to himself.

For one thing, Alala was not fully convinced as to what love truly was, despite their increased physical relationship.

Plus, she kept telling Om that compared to her, he was, as she put it, a whackjob.

Om laughed and kept pressing his case; he also kept trying to teach Alala to laugh more, and to enjoy a more sophisticated sense of humor.

She kept telling him that he was only further reinforcing her original impression of him.

But in the end, even with Om pestering her with his blatantly romantic overtures, it was Alala who finally parsed out the vile trick that the enemy had played upon the race of the Garama, and the universe.

As it turned out, the genetics of a common cold among the Garama proved to have been the delivery device.

The Garama suspected nothing, and the mental transformation spread quickly merely from exposure. Each Garama did not even have to experience a cold, sniffle, or fever. The mind-altering plague affected each one of them. There was no defense or cure.

One day the Garama thought and behaved one way.

The next they were in lockstep agreement about attacking their neighbors with might and main.

As Alala described the mind plague or mind virus as she finally called it, the attack had been precisely tailored to Garama genetics and their neural nets. Utterly insidious, this was mind control on an entirely new level of depth, complexity, and malignant sophistication.

Naero and Om now remembered skimming across the mention of some such similar enemy attacks on the Kexx and their allies. How the G'lothc relished turning parts of one race's own worlds and populations against the others.

Before the Kexx had cured such madness inflicted upon them, many billions had perished in civil wars that flared up out of nowhere, for no apparent reason.

"How do we reverse the process?" Naero asked.

Alala and Om answered in unison.

"You can't."

Only Alala went on next. "But we might be able to use the same process, the same delivery method to replace the mental shift in attitude with another."

Naero snorted. "But what's to keep the enemy from doing the same thing and replacing one mind pattern with yet another more violent one once again?"

Om jumped in. *The structure of the Garama neural net is very stable. In some regards even simplistic. Despite being high functioning sentients, their brains and minds are extremely vulnerable to this kind of attack. Clearly that is why it was designed for them, to capitalize on this weakness in the first place.*

Alala took over once more. "With some slight biomechanical adjustments, not only can their thought patterns be adjusted to make them more reasonable and less warlike-"

Naero held up both of her hands, palm out. "Hold on. I don't want to play god or change them too much. I just want to get them back to being more of whom and what they were before the enemy made them warmongers. Before the enemy infected them with the kill everyone and everything mindset."

That might be possible. We know what their neural nets were like before, thanks to old medical archives, cadaver medical scans, and samples from the Rorg. And there are several ways that we could close the door on any further attempts at such changes.

"It's vital that we do so," Naero said. "We can't let the enemy do this sort of thing to any race. Haisha! What we need to develop is some kind of harmless, neural vaccine of some sort that can be pweaked to tailor it to any sentient race of any variety. We have enough problems. We can't have the Alliance races infected into killing one another by a neural virus attack."

Within ten standard days, the largest secret fixer assault ever assembled swept through the Garama worlds and their naval fleets.

The transformation and inoculation process took over a week to complete.

Afterwards, in the resulting confusion, the wars with the Garama's neighbors ended almost immediately.

Naero shapeshifted into the form of a Garama and was finally able to complete her mission as ambassador, peacemaker, and promoter of the ever-growing Alliance. This was one of the most exact duplicates of a sentient species that she had ever achieved.

She quickly learned that true Garama could detect a shapeshifter through both a combination of psyonics and physical senses. The neural patterns and the scent variations had to be precise. Otherwise, exposure as a fake was almost certain.

Then there was a learning curve for education and catch up.

Once races such as the Garama were updated on what had been done to them, it became very clear to all who the real enemy was.

No sentient beings with intellect, rational thought, and free will had any desire to be controlled and used like puppets by another.

23

Naero and her forward sweeping delegation and Task Force encountered yet another sentient race, the near human *Klurr*. It was good for the Klurr that their war with the Garama had ended so abruptly.

The Klurr had lost half of their worlds and populations by that time. The Garama were well along the way to systematically exterminating them. Klurr teknology was slightly less advanced, they were not themselves very warlike in nature, and only defended themselves as best as they could out of desperation.

Nor did it help that another more distant, opportunistic species was also taking advantage of the Klurr's weakness to commit invasion and slave raids on the remaining Klurr sectors. This other race was known as the Zadiq, and were said to be near humans with body quills in place of hair.

Naero dealt closely with the Klurr over the next two weeks, finding the expected pattern of enemy phage, mind bugs, control wraiths, and wyrms trying to affect outcomes.

There was one major breakthrough, however. The Klurr turned out to be completely immune to G'lothc mind control wraiths, and highly resistant to possession wyrms. Not only that, but as a proto energy being species, they even showed resistance to the ravaging energy being phage disease.

An entire new field of research exploded all around the Klurr, as the Alliance helped them rebuild and reclaim their horribly depleted worlds.

In the face of the mighty advanced Alliance fleets, after one devastating encounter, the Zadiq raiders fled the Klurr systems and sped far away, back to their own hidden worlds.

Naero attempted to make contact with the Zadiq and find some common ground with them, but they were so terrified from losing half of their warships within a few minutes that they made no response.

All they could do was flee.

She did not mind in the least shapeshifting into the form of a female Klurr and learning their customs and language.

The Klurr were a fascinating sentient mammalian species, with a rich culture, music, art, and cuisine. They were a quite gentle species, and wonderful parents. They were attractive for their own part, their bipedal, humanoid bodies covered with soft fur in patterns of solid black, white, gray, brown, or red, while others had different patterns of stripes and spots.

Their intelligent eyes were black, brown, or amber, their whiskered noses and jaws were still slightly snout like, and their opposable thumb hands ended in dexterous claws.

But what Naero could not bring herself to appreciate in any way was their stink.

During the war, the Klurr had used stench as a major weapon against the acute senses of the crab like Garama, and to great effect.

Naero recalled an Old Terran term for smelly beasts referred to as polecats, which were supposedly legendary for their debilitating stench, which they sprayed on other animals that attempted to harm them.

In this regard, she felt quite certain that the Klurr were the sentient polecats of the galaxy, if not the known universe.

Klurr stink could not be described by the words of any known language to do it justice, or injustice as was more the case.

It reeked beyond anything Naero had ever experienced, and several times she had Om shut down their olfactory abilities to avoid passing out.

She hesitated using her own stench apparatus in her Klurr form.

There were two primary varieties.

On the one hand, Klurr farts were the closest thing to a natural chemical warfare gas that Naero could conceive of. And because of their digestive system, they could dispense it at will.

A single Klurr with the winds, as Spacers called hyper flatulence, could make an enclosed space unbreathable and unlivable within moments.

Then there were the actual scent gland nozzles that each Klurr possessed, located slightly beneath their wrists.

A Klurr could extend those nozzles by flexing their forearms in a certain way, and dispense up to half a liter of the foulest concentrated liquid with pin-point accuracy—for fifteen meters out—several times each standard day.

This noxious spew could even somehow negate shields. It clogged and melted respiration filters on combat armor. It caused horrible chemical burns on exposed flesh, blinded eyes, choked off breathing, caused unconsciousness, and in some extreme cases—respiratory failure and asphyxiation leading to coma and death.

A natural oil that their skin produced neutralized most of the negative effects of the Klurr defensive spray and made them immune. They even had evolved protective membranes in their eyes, nose, mouth, and throat that defeated the chemical make-up of the toxic spray.

Their adaptations were so amazing that Spacer Intel did study them for applications in chemical weapons and bio warfare.

The initial jokes and jibes about stink guns quickly became fact.

The underlying smell of the Klurr was so pervasive, that most sentient beings that could smell elected to deal with them while wearing fully sealed EV suits or even combat armor. The Alliance First Contact teams changed filters frequently and either recycled the suits afterwards, or had them incinerated via decontamination protocols.

Which was all quite a shame, because the Klurr were kindly, noble, generous to a fault, funny, gregarious, and of superb wit. They proved excellent hosts, shared large bounties of excellent food and drink, and were imaginative artists, and superb musicians and singers.

Other than the lethal stench, what wasn't there to love about being a fuzzy, funky, fantastic striped Klurr? In the end, Naero was sad to bid them farewell, and let the follow-up teams come in after her to complete the Alliance naturalization process.

The Klurr proved to be a beneficial inclusion to the Alliance on many different levels.

As Naero raced off to another first contact hotspot, she was greatly pleased to have her beloved Khai join back up with her and brief her on their next joint mission.

They spoke together in private concerning Shetharra's condition, and the potential appearance of Elazethrek once more. The Cosmic Champion containment team was kept close at hand in case the Creature made another attack.

After a few quiet hours together, Naero and Khai met with Captain Tyber and Alala on board *The Dark Star* and compared notes on many of their recent findings, discoveries, and various operations.

Naero and Om even arranged a foray into the KDM for the first time for Khai. Thus far he had always been too busy to make the attempt.

To Naero's surprise, once within the KDM's data expanses, Khai took the form of a very sleek and handsome male Kexx. He was bright green with very alluring golden frills about his head and neck. His Kexxian spirit name became Iahk.

In her Kexxian spirit form of Orean, Naero could not believe the sudden intense attraction that she felt for Iahk. He moved her in ways that she did not know were possible. For the first time, she had insights into what Kexxian mental and physical love must have been like for mated pairs.

How awesome it must have been for them to love one another that much, as that fantastic race apparently did.

Through their intimate link, Naero knew that Khai was experiencing the same passion and wonder that she was while being a spiritmind Kexx.

For his first visit, Khai could do little more than wander around in amazement and follow Orean's lead. Everyone had to start somewhere.

They spent a great deal of time puttering around in the regions of Kexxian Music, after Orean gave him the main tour.

Orean practiced her new song of making, the one that did not seem to do anything. At least it did nothing for her, yet.

With little else to do, Iahk summoned Yii and started practicing sword forms.

But when Orean began singing her song again, the ancient words had an effect on the Cosmic sword of might that was nothing less than astounding.

In Iahk's hands, the sword shook and flared with blinding flashes of light in time with the tune. Within the core of those flashes, which only last for a moment or two, they beheld strange sights.

"What is this?" Iahk exclaimed.

"They're visions. Haisha! They're visions of what might come to pass. Focus on each one. Try to make them out."

In her role as Orean, Naero could control the KDM enough to have it repeat the song she sang back to her, again and again.

In one vision, Khai fought with Yii against a massive darkness that seemed to be trying to engulf and devour him.

Naero had had similar visions about just such an all-powerful hungering darkness many times.

In some of her visions she had been devoured by such madness.

At other times she had become a willing part of it. Such were her nightmares.

This time she watched in horror with Khai as the vision showed him and Yii fighting bravely, but to no avail. At last they were overcome and perished.

One Cosmic sword was clearly not enough against this threat. In order to have any chance to defeat this grave, future threat, both of the Cosmic Swords of legend would be required.

In the next flash, another vision to behold.

A lonely, lifeless world, torn by ancient war.

Yet down upon its scorched and bleak surface, in the center of a few square green kilometers stood what could not be taken for anything else.

There waited the last Ur-metal Cosmic obelisk.

This was a vision of lost, far off Xanathar.

Another flash.

Another possibility.

Wave upon wave of invincible enemy fleets.

Fleets counted in the billions.

In a wave of light they vanished all at once.

Had they somehow jumped from the dark galaxy of the G'lothc nearby?

Were they coming to destroy all before the fury of their blazing guns?

How soon would the Armada arrive?

The music continued, but the visions ended. Yii returned to normal in Iahk's hands. "I'm getting the feeling we don't have much time left," he remarked to Orean.

She smirked in a rather grim fashion. "You too? I thought it was just me. And I can't tell if it's only a few years or decades."

Iahk shrugged. "How could anyone know that? Stupid visions."

He lifted his hands and Yii, calling out to the KDM. "Why can't you tell us something that actually helps why? Why all of these vague riddles, cryptic warnings, and mind games?"

Orean pulled his arms down and hugged him.

"It doesn't work like that, Iahk. Everything is a test. This is our struggle. We have to figure things out on our own. I know it's frustrating."

"Sure is. These powers, whatever they are. They just showed me my death, if I don't achieve the second sword."

"You will my heart. We will find it together. Of that I have no doubts. You have to understand. This is a place of great power. The Kexxian songs are not just songs. They are powers and they are keys that unlock entire ranges of knowledge and wisdom. With such knowledge, the Kexx were able to accomplish nearly everything."

Iahk laughed out loud. "Am I to sing then? Me? You know what a terrible voice I have. Haisha, I'm no singer. That's for certain."

She smiled and laughed with him. "I agree with you, my love. But let me teach you some of the songs—even the most basic of them. It doesn't matter here how good a voice you have. And don't forget, in your spirit form here, you are a Kexx. And they were the mightiest of all singers and dreamers ever known to exist in our entire universe. Humor me. Just try with me."

She re-taught him the seven sacred songs of the Tua, and he sang them with her.

With each song, when he sang it with her, Yii's radiance changed to a slightly different hue, and then back to normal once the song ended.

On a whim, Orean taught him the Song of Making that she knew.

As they sang it together, Yii flared with light once more.

The great Cosmic Sword shuddered and vibrated as if it were some kind of tuning fork.

The peal of a single shining note rang from the sword like a blast wave, and caused all of the KDM to shudder as it faded out into the distance.

A series of glowing stone pillars erupted from the aether at their feet and all around them. They were gray stone set with glowing golden sigils in the Kexxian language.

Orean counted three even rows of seven capped pillars, organized precisely, twenty-one in all.

They were songs. Each had a song engraved in the stone along the pillar's length.

Only Orean could read them, but she quickly taught Iahk how to follow along.

They could barely make out the song on the first pillar and mouth the words together. As they did so, each word of the song and its lyrics would ignite with golden fire and then afterwards fade to blue and back out to nothing.

When they sang the first song, the entire pillar ignited and remained lit up for a while.

Orean gasped and opened her hand.

Within was a tiny pebble, a mote of glowing Ultrium. She knew it.

"Haisha, Iahk. According to these knowledge rivers, we've unlocked all twenty-one Kexxian Songs of Making, from the least to the greatest. These songs are among the most powerful forces of Creation in the entire universe! And now they stand before us, not yet at our command."

171

"Let's try the other one we know," he suggested.

"Good idea."

What they counted as the nineteenth pillar blazed to life when they sang, yet nothing else happened.

Orean thought for a bit.

Iahk was still astonished at the sight of it all.

"From what I understand about Kexxian music and their songs of power," she noted, "I'm guessing that Song 19 won't work for us yet because we haven't mastered Songs 1 through 18. We have to learn, practice, and master them in order. The other songs in between the ones we know only flicker a bit, but Songs 20 and 21 are completely dark to us right now. And they will be the most powerful of all."

Iahk pointed to her hand and the small pebble she held. "Why didn't I get anything like you did?"

She considered that. "You're not a Dreamer yet, like I am, my heart. It takes time, practice, devotion, and meditation. Even so, I can barely make the first Song of Making work. With such songs of power, the Kexx could cure all disease, manipulate matter and energy on almost every level, and create anything that they could imagine. They made pocket dimensions, the KDM—even warships larger than the largest planet, that even the mighty G'lothc lived in terror of. I've been told that they even created an entirely new Song of Making for the Drians to help them create their beloved children, the Driathans."

She looked at the tiny pebble in her hand and laughed. "No wonder Song 19 wouldn't work. Haisha, I think we have quite a ways to go still before we can even hope to fashion anything very grand."

Iahk laughed and embraced her. "Yet it is a start."

Orean could agree with that.

24

The very next day, Naero had to perform a one-friend/admiral intervention on Om and Alala. In a funny way, both of the AI entities were like her older children.

The word going around was that the two AIs had both gone off the deep end.

She transported into their quarters right at noon, fully prepared for anything that she might see or find.

What she found was Alala and Om in their newest synthetic Spacer constructs, passed out in a tangle together in their big float bed.

They were quite naked, which didn't bother Naero that much, but from the zero-G clutter strewn all about, they must have been banging each other pretty hard.

Alala's construct was bright orange this time, with bright green hair, sort of like an Old Terran carrot. Om was purple with red hair splashed with yellow.

Their physical romance definitely seemed to be evolving in interesting directions.

Add all of that to the fact that neither of them had been on duty for the past ten days. Discovering sex obviously had that effect on them. Both beings had placed themselves on vacation, and they still had four more days of their two weeks to go.

Naero did not grudge the two of them anything. But they were also needed as important contributors to certain vital, ongoing research efforts for the Alliance. She understood that humanoid relations and all of the wonderful new physical sensations that went with them were quite a new fascinating distraction to beings that were not used to them.

She also didn't want to see them go bonkers and neglect any of their obligations.

Bottom line, Om and Alala needed to put it all in perspective and keep it in their pants—just like all of the other sentient adults on the team. Even Jan and his gals didn't pull this kind of stunt.

None of them currently had time for a two week love fest in the middle of a war such as this one.

Naero frowned and sighed, thinking wistfully about Khai.

She certainly did not. Not these days.

"Hey, you two," she said, clapping her hands. "Snap out of it. It's the middle of the day."

Om and Alala both groaned and squirmed around slowly.

"Look you two. Finish up your fun and get back to work. We need you guys."

"Oh, Naero," Alala exclaimed, "you can't understand what we're going through. I never thought anything could be this way!"

"This is all so exciting," Om said. "We can't get enough of each other."

"Yeah, yeah," Naero said, "and trust me, I can imagine pretty well. You have to pace yourselves. Just like everyone else, you need to get your assigned tasks done each day, and then go home at night for Bingo-Bango. Haisha, you two shouldn't even need to sleep. How can you be so worn out?"

Om beamed a bright smile. "We found that by giving ourselves the limitation of a Spacer sleep pattern, that the overall sensuality levels are even more enhanced and intense."

"Yes, yes!" Alala said. "It's so much fun wearing ourselves out and then resting for a cycle to do it all over again!"

Naero blinked. "You don't say."

"And the psychological advantage of anticipation for sex is mind boggling!" Om added.

Naero sighed. "Be that as it may, I want you two love bunnies to get it under control. We need you two back at work. The enemy and the war aren't going to wait while you two hump each other to distraction. So get it together and schedule stuff, just like everyone else does. A little denial can make things better when you do get together."

Being AIs, the two love birds also had no concept of shame.

"That does sound like a good idea, Ommy."

Ommy?

"It sure does, La. Okay, N. Give us the rest of today to blang each other-

Naero rolled her eyes. "That's 'bang' each other, you Nimrod."

"...bang each other—and we'll both report for duty tomorrow. We promise."

Wide eyed, Alala bit her bottom lip and nodded her head rapidly.

Naero did an about face and headed toward the door panel. "Great. My work is done here. You two carry on. Just wait until I get out into the damn corridor."

*

The Klurr introduced Naero and her First Contact teams to the *Treel*, lizard people shorter than even herself, standing only .912 meters up to 1.216 meters in height. They were smooth skinned, without feathers or fur, but they were varied in bright hues, with the darker colors on their tops and backs, and the lighter colors on their undersides and bottoms.

They could change color with ease.

A long, slender tail was mostly used for balance, and made up a third of their length when they stretched out. They had large, intelligent heads with big eyes, binocular visions, and smaller snouts that had evolved to have smaller, but still formidable teeth for a successful omnivore. Their adept mouths and vocal tracts could mimic other species, and was useful in learning and speaking many other languages.

Their hind legs were powerful, and Treel were great runners and leapers. With their strong and surprisingly long upper arms and opposable thumb clawed hands, they could manipulate advanced tek and still remained incredible hunters.

Naero shapeshifted into a female Treel with ease after studying them in depth with her acute biomancy. She also learned the mind patterns of their neural nets and gained a growing respect for their culture and all that they had accomplished as a hyper evolved sentient species.

In many ways they were extremely similar to a protospecies of the ancient Kexx, so much so that she and Om both actively searched for some kind of genetic link, but they found nothing definitive.

The Treel had evolved independently and solely upon their own, and simply mirrored the Kexx in all the ways that any successful sentient species might resemble another, and take similar paths on the way to greatness. But the fact that they were lizard-like sentients so much like the Kexx was too uncanny to ignore.

With her in depth knowledge of the Kexx, Naero perceived that it would still take possibly hundreds of millions of years of advanced evolution and progress on many fronts for the Treel to lift their species so high. It was a lofty achievement for any sentients to ever hope to transform themselves into an advanced race as mighty, enlightened, and as beneficent as the enigmatic Kexx.

In any case, the Treel would never progress to that level of heightened existence and enlightenment if the enemy saw fit to enslave and devastate them, just as they were doing to so many sentient beings.

The G'lothc and their slaves were of a single mind and purpose in that regard.

They could only destroy.

That was all that they knew and understood.

Nothing else mattered. There was no alternative. No negotiation.

It was, therefore, with great ease that Naero studied and learned all about the Treel that made it possible for her to shapechange into one of their kind so completely.

That made the first contact with them flow so much more smoothly. They were barely alarmed when she finally revealed to them that she was in fact a shapeshifter, sent to negotiate with them and encourage them to join the Alliance.

On the way to more initial meetings with the rational Treel, on board one of their formidable warships, Naero was suddenly overcome with the nearby energy signatures that could only result from one thing.

Somewhere nearby, in the closest superhot gigantic star, vast quantities of Ultrium alloy were not only being smelted, but manipulated on an industrial scale more vast and intricate. Only a Cosmic energy being such as Naero had become could sense such matters directly by the Cosmic energy flows and levels of awareness.

Even Om was stunned.

Haisha, N! The sheer volume and the rate of construction and sophistication are fantastic. Staggering even!

Om, I've only scanned reports within the KDM about this level of transmogrification of so many various kinds of Ultrium alloy. Only the Kexx, the Drians, and the G'lothc and very few of their allies were ever able to achieve such massive feats of teknomancy. I've never experienced such command of the elements of matter creation and combining.

N, we must learn these processes as quickly as possible and begin to apply them. With the enemy tek advantage, if they can produce Ultrium for their warships at such rates already, it may already be too late for us to catch up at this point.

I agree Om, but we are still in the initial phases of first contact with the Treel. We simply can't ask them to hand over all of their tek secrets to us at the start. They might not ever trust us then.

We could enter that giant star furnace and learn those secrets first hand with teknomancy. Then I would tight beam them to Intel and have our fixers implementing the new processes within so many standard hours. The Treel would never be the wiser. We already utilize Ultrium. They would merely assume that we possess these industrial capacities the same as they do.

Brilliant, Om. I'll ask to retire for a bit and produce a replicant to leave behind to continue our first contact efforts. Then we'll sneak out in stealth mode to learn what we can learn, beam the secrets to our people, and I'll re-merge with my rep when we return.

Their efforts went smoothly, and very soon they hurtled through space in a stealth fighter that Om and their phazed fixer nebula whipped up for them. The star type that the Treel were using for their Ultrium smelting and warship construction was of a specialized class and order of magnitude. Difficult, but not impossible to locate throughout the galaxy.

Such stars were still numerous enough to be easily scanned and located at random among the billions upon billions of stars in a single galaxy of so many amazing varieties.

Naero and Om had all of their energy being protections and KDM protocols up and humming. Penetrating to the core of any star was not for the faint of heart. Were she not an enlightened, Cosmic Champion and a Spacer Mystic Master, she could never hope to attempt such a mad thing. It would prove suicidal many times over before she could even penetrate the star's outer energy fields, let alone its surface.

And to reach the core itself and linger longer enough to discern the Treel Ultrium smelting process would require all of her strength and abilities to manipulate Cosmic energies on her own part.

For the most part, Naero would focus on keeping them from being annihilated. Om would do most of the intelligence gathering and record all that they would need to know for the data feeds.

They reached the point where the vast majority of their fixers could go no farther. Only a few highly specialized Ultrium fixers designed specifically for solar core exploration and manufacturing could hope to accompany them. Nothing was exactly certain with a star of this variety.

Naero and Om knew that by the odds, there was a good chance that they could lose over forty percent of the one hundred or so special solar exploration units.

Such risks were necessary under the circumstances.

Thus they bade their primary fixer cloud farewell, and left those devices posted around the star as outer sentries—waiting, watching, and scanning what they could from a safe distance.

As they drew closer, Naero and Om both observed thousands upon thousands of heavily shielded construction relay platforms and stations arranged at key junctures and Cosmic energy field nodes about the star.

It was nearly a partial Dyson sphere.

They also wove their way through numerous protective fleets stationed around the system and patrolling close by. The solar shipyard was heavily protected.

And with good reason.

N, I've calculated their rate of production to be a new Ultrium warship emerging from each hub every 8.511 standard minutes. Another two standard hours for the vessel to be fully outfitted and have a pre-trained crew and gear brought on board in prep for initial launch and assignment to their fleets and tasks forces.

Naero shook her head.

That's phenomenal, Om. We can't even get close to that with our fixer production clouds.

You're not getting it, N. Each one of these vessels is a gigantic fixer in itself. They're forming themselves and all of their systems out of raw Ultrium protomatter as they emerge, transporting a safe distance outside of the star itself.

Naero suddenly perceived the actual concept that Om was getting at.

Haisha, Om. They're sucking matter out of the star and creating themselves right out in the black, according to their own design specs.

These self-creating ships were only a few steps away from thinking themselves into existence.

Then Naero shuddered, experiencing another vital revelation.

If these Treel fixer ships could create themselves in mere seconds…what could a truly Kexxian-trained mind accomplish?

What could a Dreamer achieve?

Creation. Energy into matter and being.

Thought into reality.

No wonder the ruthless G'lothc could never defeat the miraculous Kexx and their sisters and brothers among the mysterious Drians. The Great Adversary could only destroy, while the two allies had the very powers of

Creation at their command—the enlightened capacity to envision and control almost anything, and then to make it real.

Naero and Om carefully studied the entire construction process, several times over.

N, their communications reveal that most of the nearby systems are training worlds for the crews, shuttled in to operate the various new ships. They arrive according to a regular schedule, and take command of each vessel as it is supplied and made ready.

A very efficient system, Om. We'll be able to learn a great deal from it as well. No wonder they were defeating the poor Klurr.

Not the Klurr. The Klurr were no real threat to the Treel. The Treel are facing a disaster of their own, Naero. They were once the servant race, the makers and shipbuilders of an advanced android species they called the Xaxattar.

The war with their former masters is in fact going very badly for the Treel, and at the far end of their many systems, even their brave naval forces are near the point of collapse.

You're kidding, Om.

Not in the least. At the current rate, the Xaxattar will defeat the Treel in less than four standard years. They can then decide if they wish to re-subjugate or exterminate the Treel, one system at a time. And what appears to be direct enemy involvement through the manipulation of their various mind control agents is not helping things.

The hell with that, Om. We'll have to get in there and put a stop to all of that. These two sentients have no reason to destroy each other. That would be a great loss.

I agree on all counts. It was the Xaxattar who taught the Treel how to utilize this industrial Ultrium tek in order to build their ships for them. Then the uplifted Treel broke away from their former masters and sought their own destiny. The Xaxattar did not dispute the independence of their servants until only recently, when the war erupted between the two.

My guess is when the enemy took over the leaders of the Xaxattar or the entire android race, in order to weaken both sides. Classic enemy strategy.

I would agree with those suppositions. And once again, the enemy could have re-stolen these secrets from these two races.

Om tight beamed the data on the Ultrium production breakthroughs to an astonished Spacer Intel.

Naero checked in briefly with her replicant back with the Treel. Everything proceeded according to plan.

She transformed into a Xaxattar female after studying one of their listening posts and the individuals stationed there.

Amazing as it was, the androids actually had fairly standard male and female sexes and had even been designed to be able to procreate sexually, as many humans and near humans did.

Why do that?

Who had gone to such intricate trouble and why? Why have advanced androids function essentially like mammals? Why not just uplift actual mammals? The Xaxattarans were the most advanced species of machine based life ever encountered, outside of the Driathans.

Then Naero was stunned to see an energy being champion among the Xaxattar, two to three times their size when they transformed, apparently. If Naero had not had all of her defenses up, the Creature could have sensed her presence quite easily. It was comprised of solid black Cosmic energy, from head to foot.

From her assessment, these energy beings were far older than the Xaxattar, and although there was some kind of link, they were two completely different species of sentients.

I think I have it, N. According to ancient Xaxattaran lore, this Kalem, *or Kalim, plural, are from among the guardians of old. It is said that a lost remnant of the Kalim were somehow separated from their former masters, an alien race of great knowledge and wisdom, who were also androids.*

Sounds like the Drians to me, Om. And that would also explain the Drian-like tek for making and manipulating so many Ultrium alloys.

Indeed it would. The Xaxattar honestly believe that the Kalim created them in the image of former masters, as best as they could with their limited command of the tek at their command.

It would seem that the Kalim were Destroyers, a proto-type of some kind of warrior android constructed to serve as soldiers and even leaders in the great Cosmic wars of old.

Once isolated and on their own, the Kalim survivors found their existence lacking and unacceptable. It appears that they did in fact create the Xaxattar in the image of their own former masters, in order not to be alone, and to be among a race that reminded them of their own creators and mentors. As warrior beings, created expressly for battle, they used their abilities to protect and help uplift and advance the Xaxattar as a sentient species.

Being an android who was also virtually human in almost every way was also extremely rare and strange. For some reason, Naero had never been able to transform into a true Driathan like Jia, or inhabit the Driathan blank by entering into it. For her, that was impossible.

Jia had warned her that if she ever did discover a way to do so, it might prove to be a trap. Once her essence was fused with the blank, Naero would herself be transformed and become a Driathan. There would be no way to reverse the process.

Yet Om was correct. She had no doubt that the Kalim created the Xaxattar as some kind of homage to the Drians and their children, the Driathans. Transforming into a Xaxattaran android was the closest thing to becoming a Driathan.

And that was still about as close as taking the form of a primitive cave animal as compared with a modern human, or for that matter, a Spacer.

Naero had no more time to contemplate such things.

She infiltrated the Xaxattarans and discovered precisely how the enemy was manipulating them.

The Kalim were completely unaware of the advanced G'lothc mind control wraiths at work, which had clearly been modified to work on the Xaxattar android brain and mind.

Although the Kalim were immune by their nature to the wraiths, if they became suspicious or learned too much, as energy beings they could be dealt with or even destroyed by Darkforce energy collector drones. Or worse—they might be overpowered and enslaved within one of the foul things as its host and power source.

As usual, the hapless Xaxattaran androids were being controlled, manipulated, and led into wars without their knowledge.

This quickly took on the proportions of an immense task.

To expose and eradicate G'lothc mind control wraiths over dozens of key systems would require numerous fleets, and the assistance of many energy beings.

Naero called in all of her backups, including the other Alliance Champions. To work well, they had to coordinate their actions all at once, and perform a delicate first contact operation in the midst of what was essentially a major battle, coupled with a widespread naval operation.

Too much could go wrong, and the dangerous Kalim super warrior energy beings might get the wrong idea, and attack the wrong people.

And Elazethrek was overdue for an appearance as well.

Naero made initial contact with several key Xaxattaran leaders and officials whom she was certain were not under enemy mind control. They were hesitant and very reluctant to say the least, to believe the facts of what she revealed to them.

Then she isolated and brought them one of their own captive, possessed leaders.

She proceeded to expose and destroy a mind control wraith inside of a female leader, all in a controlled environment set up at a secure location where the Xaxattaran delegation could watch, record, and re-examine the data and the evidence on their own terms.

The host was left unharmed, but weak and unconscious, and would require a few days rest in order to fully recover.

Understandably, the Xaxattar became quite alarmed and even somewhat paranoid. If they could be infiltrated and manipulated so easily without their knowledge, what was real, and what was not?

Naero patiently answered their questions and gave them access to all of the Alliance tek she freely offered them. This would all make it possible to detect the presence of the wraiths at work within their hosts and eliminate them.

Thereafter, the delegation called in a few Kalim, and demanded that Naero repeat the process with another victim under wraith control.

She did so.

The Kalim were even more shaken and concerned, that their great adversary of old had managed to deceive them so well. They raged about their children, their own creations, made vulnerable to the ancient foe.

At that point, Naero explained completely that she was not a Xaxattaran at all herself. She was the vanguard, the ambassador or a grand Alliance organizing against the enemy of all sentient life.

To her dismay, the frightened Kalim moved to attack and capture her.

"How do we know that all of this is not a trick on your part!" one of the ancient Drian battle androids said.

"Surrender," another of them warned, shifting into one of their fierce battle modes. "You are our prisoner!"

Naero shifted back to her own form and phazed completely into an immaterial energy form that could still be seen and heard. Their weapons and Cosmic energy attacks merely passed through her, doing no harm to Naero. Yet they unleashed a great deal of destruction that threatened them and the delegation.

Naero had no desire to harm them or to allow them to hurt each other.

Thus she transfixed all of them where they stood, holding them suspended and frozen in place in midair by a Cosmic energy field attuned to their biometrics and teknometrics.

She spoke to them calmly.

"You cannot hurt me. The Alliance and I have come to aid you in this battle, to be your enemies or take you over. We don't do that. Study the evidence. Join us. You are free to rule your worlds and your people. But you cannot do so while under enemy control.

"We have plans to eradicate the enemy wraiths in short order. Our fleets are already in place. With your permission, we can begin the process within a matter of minutes—to free you and your worlds from this scourge."

She allowed one of the Kalim to speak. Immediately he cast back defiance once again. "You have secret alien fleets surrounding our worlds, and you want us to trust you?"

"I know that this is all extraordinary, but you must see reason in this. We must work together to move quickly. If we withdraw, it will merely take that much longer to get them into position once again. We can proceed without your permission if you force us to, but that will alarm your people and perhaps lead to needless confusion, strife, and casualties.

"If the enemy learns about our presence prematurely, they could do even greater harm, especially with atomics that they have already hidden on many of your homeworlds. We are neutralizing those threats while we speak. After the enemy has been defeated, we can show you all of the evidence. How can I make you see that we are trying to help you all?"

One of the Xaxattarans also remained unmoved when he was allowed to speak. "We have faced many great challenges. We will fight you and all invaders to the last!"

"Oh, please," Naero said. "We want to avoid all of that. We only wish to be your friends and allies." This was getting ridiculous.

Bring in someone that they will listen to, N.

Om was dead right.

Minutes later, Naero transported Jia into their midst in all of her beauty and glorious android perfection.

Naero had had her monitoring the situation all along,

A wave of sudden light emanated out from the Driathan Queen in an unexpected, expanding globe of knowledge and luminescence that washed over the other androids, using teknomancy and biomancy to fully inform and educate them.

Naero released them.

"The Great Mother!" the Kalim shouted, and immediately bowed before her, trembling and shaking at their knees. Many of the Xaxattar were so moved by Jia's presence among them that they seized up and fainted, if androids were capable of doing so.

Jia went to Naero and embraced her. They clasped hands and held them up for all to see.

"I am part of the Alliance. Have no fear or doubt. My beloved sister Naero is part of me and my existence, and one of our greatest champions. Obey her as you would myself. What she has told you about the Great

Adversary is true. We must oppose them in all things and fight as one, side by side with our growing list of noble allies."

A great light was now about Jia.

Never before had Naero seen her friend and sister like this. Before her very eyes, secrets of Jia's Drian creators were being revealed. She now had full command of the Kalim warriors and the Xaxattarans.

Jia went among them and touched each of them as she passed, and those who had been rendered inoperative arose at her touch, imparting her light and all of the knowledge it contained.

All the while she spoke to them in authority. "Join us. Together we shall cleanse your worlds of the adversary's taint. The Great Ones of old created all of us with Cosmic destiny and purpose. The Driathans and the mighty Kalim are but servants and messengers of their eternal love and force of will and design. The Kalim created you, the Xaxattar, in that same spirit. We are all one, secret servants of the Great Mystery, the Grand Design, and the force of will at work for life and sentience in all things."

The eradication of the enemy mind control wraiths began a quarter of an hour later.

As Naero guessed, it took a matter of so many days to complete such a great task, aided by the Alliance, its Cosmic champions, and many of their fleets.

Then dozens of reports flooded in.

The enemy unleashed an immense counterattack all across those sectors.

Naero knew that the enemy had remained inactive for too long.

Baeven contacted her with a grave warning.

"Naero, I've uncovered an important enemy strategy involving the Xaxattar. From long ago, they were already preparing to take over every single Xaxattar world and destroy the Kalim to the last."

"Why do they want with the Xaxattar so badly?"

"To use them all as interim hosts for the G'lothc spirits, until they can locate the Driathans."

"Haisha! We cannot allow that to happen, uncle."

"Agreed. But we must move fast. The invasion process has already begun. Several Xaxattaran worlds have already fallen and are in the process of being converted. Our fixers are installing the Kexxian planetary shields on as many of the other systems as we can."

Vital warnings from Spacer Intel came in.

Elazethrek had appeared in several areas, destroying Xaxattaran and even a few Alliance fleets at will.

The Creature seemed more powerful than ever by the reports.

Even worse, the enemy attacked with huge quantities of their new Darkforce Ultrium warships.

Baeven studied the huge numbers, task force after enemy taskforce, attacking everywhere to the crush the Xaxattarans.

"Uncle? Is this evidence of the first waves of this enemy Armada from the dark galaxy next to ours?"

Even Baeven looked frightened by what they were seeing. "It might be, Naero. We know the enemy all too well. Whenever they launch one of their major attacks, they always hit us with everything they have."

Naero coordinated the movements of the Alliance Champions to intercept Elazethrek.

25

The Alliance was not defenseless.

They responded to the massive enemy assault with all of the might, courage, and force that they could muster.

Thousands of Alliance fleets roared in at top speed to engage and stay the foe, including those of the Treel, the Klurr, and many others who now bolstered their growing ranks. They met the enemy bold and fearless and hammered them to a standstill along every battle line that was drawn.

They achieved these objectives no matter the cost to themselves.

If any within the Alliance did not understand before, they knew now that they fought for their children, for the freedom of the galaxy, and for the fate of all sentient life.

Those were the stakes—everything. All that they held dear was on the line.

Extremely intense naval battles also flared across all of the four hundred and eighty seven Xaxattar worlds.

This was now the hottest focal point of the Gamma Quadrant War.

Vital time was being purchased at the cost of many lives, until the fixer clouds could install the Kexxian planetary defense screens on each world under contention and bring them online.

The enemy attacked to enslave and destroy—to find new and better hosts for their fell masters.

Five doomed worlds had already completely fallen to the enemy thus far.

The G'lothc slew the courageous Kalim and took over the bodies of millions of Xaxattarans by force.

Each of the Xaxattaran bodies their fell spirits claimed underwent bizarre and horrific transformations, reflecting the malevolent minds and essences now encased within.

For the first time in millions of years, a multitude of G'lothc minds now had host bodies and were free once more to defile and rape the universe at their dark whim.

Naero called for their absolute and total destruction at all costs, wherever the wretched destroyers could be located.

"Not one of these lethal abominations can be allowed to survive. Not one. These filth can not be allowed to gain any such foothold at the expense of any race!"

Even as they fought, Naero and Om assessed the wealth of enemy intelligence that Baeven and his people had gathered, at great risk to their own lives.

Her uncle was truly not one to stay idle for very long.

That intel clearly showed that the enemy had planned and plotted almost for an entire standard year to overwhelm and enslave the Xaxattaran android race wholesale, and take over the zillions of them that existed, in order the provide the G'lothc with near immortal host bodies.

With those host bodies they would spread forth in their new Ultrium warship fleets as the leaders of an immense force bent upon galactic domination.

Only the Alliance had any hope to stop them, and in that they were hard pressed and spread thin.

Many other reports confirmed that this could not be the vaunted enemy Armada, still lurking within the dark galaxy.

Yet by comparison, it was the next worst thing.

Clearly the Great Adversary had either re-learned more of the Ultrium mass production techniques from the Xaxattar and the Treel, or had re-discovered them in some way.

Even with those partial secrets in hand, there was now no way for the Alliance to increase their manufacturing in order to catch up to the enemy's current rate of production.

According to Baeven, the enemy's industrial output was staggering, so much so that the foe could not produce enough competent slaves and lackeys to crew them all quickly enough.

Hence the intense enemy push to take over the Xaxattar, giving themselves billions and trillions of leaders and warship crews, within a matter of the next few weeks and months.

Such a plot could not be allowed to succeed.

Then Naero spotted flaws within the enemy plan, and vulnerabilities that they had overlooked.

She contacted Klyne and Spacer Intel immediately to clear a bold new strategy with Alliance High Command.

"Baeven located thirty-three secret enemy Ultrium star furnaces and shipyards, each of them pouring out advanced enemy warships. We need to take all of our reserves and wipe the foe out at those locations while they are still vulnerable. And we must do so quickly, in short order, before the enemy can counter us."

"A mad plan," one of the Alliance admirals noted. "How can we possibly do so? We're already outnumbered and spread too thin. How can we possibly leave ourselves without reserves and execute what would amount to multiple major counterattacks without knowing the enemy's strength in all of those regions?"

Another strategic analyst took up the naysayer argument. "Not to mention that all of those enemy naval shipyards are spread out over one third of the still unexplored sectors of the Gamma Quadrant, strange and dangerous areas that we have not explored yet. Our reserves could go in and never come back out. And we would have no help to send them. Haisha!"

"Haisha indeed," Naero shouted defiantly. "We must execute this plan because we have no other choice. We can not afford to not do so!"

"Admiral. You are insane."

"Am I? Look at the numbers we shall soon face in the field and on the front lines if we do not take action. Look. At. Them."

She allowed the reality to sink in.

"I thought so. Very well. We seize this one chance while it still remains a possible opportunity. Fortune favors the bold! We must take the imitative. Study the intel. The enemy has fully committed themselves where we are now. They would never dream that we already know the locations of these hidden shipyards. I say again, we have this one chance to attack and wipe them out while the enemy is here fighting us.

"If we succeed, we can set their efforts back for a decade or more. They have left only nominal forces behind. They think that they will overwhelm us here with this attack."

"They might at that," Klyne admitted.

Naero grinned. It was a very grim smile as she leaned toward them through her vidlink. "Then consider how much more they shall continue to overwhelm us, every day—every damn second that all thirty-three of those enemy shipyards are pouring out enemy fleets to murder us!"

The orders were agreed upon.

Every last picked fleet of theirs shot into the unknown to strike a heavy blow against the enemy.

Thirty-three coordinated task forces and assault waves screamed into the black and were gone.

The very best they had.

Naero and all of the Alliance turned back to the task at hand, fighting for the survival of the Xaxattar, planet by bloody planet.

The naval battles were horrific, with no quarter or mercy given on either side.

Half of the Xaxattaran worlds were now under the protection of the Kexxian planetary defensive shields, but sufficient ground forces needed to be deployed on each world in order to help the locals defeat any who were already possessed.

That still left over two hundred Xaxattaran worlds that were under direct contention by the invaders.

The battles pitched back and forth on the surface and even more so up in the black.

Naero and the other Alliance Champions aided their fleets as best they could while they awaited the call to go forth to do battle with Elazethrek.

They fully expected her to attack them with each passing moment.

The enemy, however, continued their new strategy. Rather than fight the Alliance Champions head on and get drained and neutralized time and time again, the Creature kept avoiding all direct contact with them.

From the pattern of Elazethrek's growing number of hit and run attacks, the enemy had managed to discern that it would be far better to strike against the Alliance wherever it was vulnerable. The monster could quickly commit enough destruction and mayhem to give the enemy fleets the upper hand.

Then it would vanish and randomly appear in another sector and repeat the same process.

Naero had to admit, both strategically and tactically, that that made more sense for the enemy to use their Darkforce champion in such a role.

Baeven and Naero quickly put their heads together with the other Alliance Champions to work out a counter strategy.

First they tried transporting to the stricken sector whenever Elazethrek appeared.

No good.

They could never respond fast enough, however they tried.

The monster had already struck and gone wherever they attempted to intercept her.

Next, valiant attempts were made to get something traceable on the beast in order for them to track its movements.

All of those attempts failed as well.

Then it was both Jia and Om who simultaneously came up with something after comparing the collected data on all of its attacks.

Each time the monster showed up, destroying everything close at hand, its appearance was preceded by the increasing high energy signatures of the personal wyrmhole projector that it used to get from one battle zone to the next.

This signal would give them several precious seconds to reach that sector right before or right after the vile thing emerged.

And if they could destroy the wyrmhole projector, the Creature could be trapped in that place, and then they might be able to fully drain it of its energies and capture it.

In theory it should work like that. They would put that theory to the test very soon.

Baeven let out a deep breath. "There's something else you all need to know. Shortly after Jia and I split up and explored the Nexus and the Interdimensions and even the KDM with you, Naero, I finally pieced together not one, but two very important discoveries."

They all stared at him for a moment, waiting.

"As we first learned, just as there is an entire section on shared Drian knowledge, there is also another entirely separate pocket dimension of information devoted solely to data and knowledge of the G'lothc.

"Those areas contain everything that the Kexx and the Drians understood about their terrible enemy. Every dark and malignant thing that is known about our great foes and their near matchless tek—much of it stolen and ripped from zillions of annihilated races from several galaxies. The Kexx and the Drians knew everything that the G'lothc were capable of. I am the only one who has been able to bring forth coded data from that place. And just recently, I was able to unlock some of the dark secrets being kept there."

"We must explore that knowledge more thoroughly at once," Janner insisted.

"There remains a deadly catch," Baeven told them. "Every bit of G'lothc knowledge is corrupted and hardwired at the deepest, most integral level. Like the knowledge of the Kexx and the Drians it is indeed alive, after a fashion, yet with a dark will and purpose all its own. In a way, it is still very much part of them.

"To explore it, you must defend against and fight through it almost constantly, as it continually tries to find a way to absorb and dismember you, and make you a part of it—part of its own vile strength. And even when you are finished searching, you must have the strength to fight your way back out. The Kexx and the Drians understood this, and placed heavy safeguards against anyone breaking through to this part of their data oceans. Not many could explore such regions and survive."

Naero already knew the answer, but she still needed to ask the question. "Then how did you get through?"

"That leads me to the first item on my list," Baeven said. "I unlocked these secrets of the G'lothc information because I was destined to. There is also an entire realm of the deepest Kexxian knowledge, and it involves the Cosmic Prophecies. There in that hallowed place, guarding the foulest secrets of their worst adversary stands what remains of the spiritminds of the Seven Kexxian Dreamers.

"I spoke to them, and they answered, telling me many things. I am the Cosmic Champion of Chaos, selected and chosen by one of the three Cosmic Obelisks that the elder races helped establish, long ago. I was meant to find that place. The Dreamers made me stand and pay heed to them.

"We stood for a frozen instant in a place between all SpaceTime—a place that is like and yet very unlike the Nexus that we have seen. Other versions of myself, from all of the other possible universes called out to me there in that place. That is the key to victory, Naero.

"The enemy has sources of their power that we have yet to discover and understand. But we also have sources of great power within ourselves that we can draw from for our purposes as well. If I stumbled upon or was shown such a place once, I feel confident that you or I can find it again.

"As the Defenders of our universe, we can learn to link with and share in the Cosmic might of all of our potential selves—giving us power on par with the Kexxian Dreamers themselves. Yet you must understand. This is it. There is no turning back from this point forward, N. Victory or Death!

Will you stand beside me, Naero Amashin Maeris, my beloved niece, daughter of my beloved sister, Lythe Ivala Maeris? Will you stand with me and face down the full force of our enemies, the might of their powers, and all of the threats to come? There is no guarantee that we shall prevail."

Naero felt tears well up in her eyes.

She came forward and placed her hand upon her uncle's broad breast, feeling the thunder of his great heart. Then she pressed one ear against him to listen, closed her eyes, and embraced him.

She drew back with her accustomed half smile and met his fierce glance with her own.

"We are fighters, you and I. You are my blood, and I believe in you. I will follow you anywhere, at any time, and fight to the death by your side. I am the Cosmic Champion of Enlightened Change, the defender of our universe, chosen by the ancient Cosmic Obelisk. Uncle Kean, I say again. I will stand with you against any foe, force, or power—before the might of Death itself, and beside all of the other champions of our age. Let me say it a third time; we stand as one."

He nodded, "Then let us proceed without fear or hesitation."

Baeven called out to everyone. "The phage, the mind control wraiths, and all of the enemy monsters are linked together. This is yet another test. It falls to us to learn their secrets and defeat them once and for all. Time is limited. All of these things have been foreseen in the Cosmic Prophecies. We must prevail and press forward. If we do not, our entire universe will perish, and all light and existence shall be snuffed out, forever!"

26

When Elazethrek attacked the Elliden sector, the Creature seemed momentarily surprised to find the Alliance Champions ready and waiting for its arrival.

Of course they had only just arrived a few scant seconds before it.

But the Creature did not know that.

The heroes of the Alliance fell upon the monster with everything they had.

It was good that they did so.

Elazethrek had actually seemed to grow in power, with every skirmish they fought with the thing.

Haisha, how was that possible?

Naero, Khai, and Baeven led the initial attack, driving Elazethrek back with impossible blows and combination attacks. Naero and the rest sustained the most powerful assault of energy drain techniques known to exist.

With both Naero and her uncle attempting to get in touch more and more with their alternate universe selves, they were the only two champions who continued getting nominally stronger. Khai and Yii could still stand with them. Wielding the Cosmic sword made him nearly indestructible.

Because of this, he could take punishment that would kill the rest of them.

The others like Jan, Shalaen, Jia, and Ra did their best to improve their abilities and try out new weapons and techniques gleaned from the KDM.

But however they all tried to improve themselves, the G'lothc Darkforce champion still seemed to be slowly but surely surpassing them.

Only through their combined numbers and by adding more energy beings and Cosmic power draining tek kept the playing field somewhat level.

They still couldn't defeat or destroy the Creature.

They had yet to actually harm it in any permanent way.

Together the Alliance Champions made an all-out attempt to not only drain the monster of its energies, but to enmesh it in several Kexxian and Driathan Cosmic energy traps and nets clustered around it with the new fixers.

They planned to capture the Least of the Six, and then study the thing closely enough to be able to destroy it and any of its fell kind. They had to understand these amazing living weapons more and learn what weaknesses they had, if any.

Elazethrek fought to break free and escape, lashing out, ripping through the devices and any attempts to contain it.

Naero took a big risk and reduced herself down to five millimeters tall and loaded with nanoatomics.

She battled her way through the Creature's pulsing personal defenses and located its hi-tek enemy wyrmhole generator.

Another heavy wave of Cosmic energy nearly destroyed her.

She barely shielded herself and deflected the destructive Darkforce energy away from her. All of her shields buckled and failed.

If Elazethrek unleashed another defensive wave such as that, Naero would be reduced to dust in the flash of an instant. She could not raise enough defenses to survive.

Defiantly, she planted all of the nano-ordnance that she had brought and prepared to transport, giving the psyonic signal to the others to do the same.

Everyone had to clear out of that immediate vicinity before the Cosmic blast signatures detonated in a stepped up chain of force blasts.

She detonated them with the largest Cosmic explosion that she could set off and still get away.

All of this a split second before the monster pulsed another defensive energy wave. Naero had sensed it building.

The explosion devastated everything within one quarter of a parsec, and then caused an additional anti-matter implosion as reality around the blast itself broke down and was annihilated.

Naero, Baeven, and their team rushed back in to see if the Creature had been destroyed or, at the very least, severely damaged and stunned.

If destroyed, they still might retrieve any pieces for later study.

To their horror, Elazethrek not only survived such tremendous attack, one that would have slain every one of them, but she laughed at them to their dismay.

Other than smoking and glowing in a few places, it did not appear to be greatly harmed in any way.

And the loss of the wyrmhole generator did not even phase the monster.

The slightly scorched Creature shook itself, opened a wyrmhole with its own innate abilities, and escaped once again.

At that moment Naero grew very afraid.

Only the mightiest of the Kexxian Dreamers had been able to vanquish and destroy the Six Darkforce Champions.

And all of them were lost in the process.

How could the Alliance hope to defeat such invulnerable beings?

What could they do if they had to fight more than one of the things?

How would they ever stand before all of the Six?

These threats would have to be given heavy thought at a later time.

The war continued at its hellish pace.

Billions continued fighting and dying.

And the Great Adversary continued to advance and march on.

With the Creature gone yet again, the fleets of the Alliance called out to their champions once more for aid, from several urgent directions.

*

After the third standard day of the running conflict the Alliance was forced to retreat and regroup in order to avoid having their battle lines broken and even routed in certain places.

And that was without Elazethrek helping the enemy.

While the Creature recharged, the new enemy Ultrium fleets and advanced enemy weapons had definitely gained the upper hand all on their own.

They drove the Alliance fleets back with a vengeance.

Four hundred and fifty-one Xaxattaran worlds now stood safe behind the Kexxian planetary shields.

Nothing the enemy had could break through or penetrate them.

Thirty-six other worlds of the Xaxattar had been lost to the foe, or utterly destroyed and abandoned as a result.

Naero felt lucky that those numbers were less than ten percent.

Things could have gone far worse, but the Alliance fleets were badly battered and had suffered heavy casualties as things were.

New Alliance fleets arrived each day from the Alpha Quadrant, and thus far, three new Ultrium ship building complexes operated constantly, far to the rear, around the appropriate stars.

Twice that many had been constructed by the fixer nebulae in the Alpha Quadrant.

Meanwhile, no word reached the Alliance about their best fleets sent into the Gamma Quadrants Unknown Regions to take out the enemy shipyards that Baeven and Jia had uncovered.

Many feared the worst for all of those brave crews.

Such efforts were very risky gambles, but what choice did they have? Even if those forces could take out half of those advanced enemy shipyards, it might give the Alliance a chance to gain parity.

It was vital now to break the enemy advance and continue bringing in more sentients on board from the Gamma Quadrant. That would continue to swell the Alliance ranks, and save many races which would remain vulnerable to the enemy's devices.

Naero shuddered to consider what could be happening to all of the sentients that they had not reached and would never reach in time. And with almost three quarters of the quadrant yet to be explored, the enemy still seemed to carry the advantage over them.

Haisha and damnation!

At least the new phaze fighters were now standard issue among the fleets—the only overall tek advantage that they truly had.

Even that just wasn't enough.

Each day the Alliance would be launching new advanced Ultrium fleets of its own with new weapons they were developing all the time.

Naero feared that it would all be too little too late.

The enemy still had the numbers to continue pushing them back.

Naero and Khai had a rare dinner with Baeven and Jia, just the four of them in the Fleet Admirals private quarters.

Chief Fleet Chef Eugene Blooding assisted Naero in broiling some fresh Kevadian velta fish in a shielded 3D cooking sphere. The delicious fish were served on beds of deep fried, light purple Bengan tuber chips. These were a lightly salted starch root like a cross between Old Terran potatoes and turnips, with hints of sweet, savory yam or buttery squash.

There were Pingan white grass peas and buttered shuga bread with Eugene's signature black gravy, a perfect sauce on its own or with practically anything else.

For dessert they feast on silly little bobbing globes and strips of tart, zero-G vellato served floating before them and lit by holos. It was a sheer delight to pierce the globes with a wide, brightly colored plasteel straw and suck out the delicious threadlets of succulent, frozen vellato.

They finally lounged across from each other once the dinner was over, sipping their evening drinks.

They had already pweaked the nano lounges in Naero's private quarters into deep cushioned divans and chase lounge sofas. Sweet Spacer thiolin music played all about them.

Naero petted her beloved's long golden hair and caressed his brow as he snoozed with his grinning head resting in her warm lap. Her own long fragrant blue and black hair hung about them like a veil of twilight itself.

Baeven held Jia's goddess-like beauty enfolded in his powerful arms as they both seemed lost in the glamour of each other's eyes. They whispered things to one another that could not be heard by anyone but themselves.

Jia smiled in contented bliss, her vast eyes half-lidded and fluttered with relaxation and sweet passion.

This was a fine relaxing evening, after many days of heavy fighting.

"Thank you, Naero, my sister," Jia said.

"You we're right, N," Baeven said, sighing and stretching. "This is exactly what we all needed."

Naero laughed. "A little R & R was just one of my goals," she admitted.

They somehow got onto the subject of Baeven's crew. "Watch out for Danjen when you manage to run into him," her uncle warned her.

Naero sighed. "What has that furry fool done now?"

"Get this. He's a vidstar now among his people. He keeps acting in these dopey vids, and the all of the fame has gone to his head."

"The Ku are a lot of great things," Naero said, "but they aren't much for high art. Most of their vids are, how can I say it-"

"Stupid, pretentious, lame, idiotic," Baeven noted.

"Yeah, that about covers it. Danjen a Ku vidstar. I shudder to think."

"Wait until he tries to corner you and make you watch one of his goofy ass masterpieces. Just remember, I warned you."

"I appreciate the heads up."

"You're welcome, N. Jia and I appreciate the invite to this nice pleasant evening."

"Well, I can't say I didn't have some kind of ulterior motive. I also wanted to follow up on what you partially revealed to us, uncle, now that we finally have the time to do so. My chambers are under close guard. Let us link our minds together while we are at peace, safe and relaxed. Reveal to us these new Interdimensional discoveries that you and Jia have made. Take us there and show us some of these new wonders."

Baeven sighed again. "Very well. We can attempt to do so while we rest. Everyone prepare the mind trance, just as you would for entering the Astral Plane, or venturing on to the Great Nexus. Such journeys are very taxing, even for us. We cannot stay in these realms for very long. Before we go forth, we shall link all four of our minds and spirits together."

Within several minutes they were out of their bodies, past the Nexus, and racing through the vast sea of the possibilities of all things.

All four of them were closely linked, and Baeven acted as their guide, although he and Jia were still admitted novices at such travels.

"These are the places that our possible selves spoke to us about and hinted at within the gateway of the Nexus," her uncle explained. "I saw them again when the Seven told me about them once more."

The limitless range of possibilities, realities, and universes all around them flickered and flashed, impossible to count or quantify. Infinity simply could not be contained, only glimpsed at.

Jia spoke next. "My friends, there are spheres within spheres, and levels of magnitudes for all that is possible. With the proper focus and mastery, we could behold the entirety of our universe all at once, or focus on one mote of it—one atom within—which is really what our lone galaxy is by comparison."

"Yet one such mote," Baeven said, "affected in the worst ways, by the wrong hands, could poison and destroy the whole, given time. And our universe has nothing but time. Time to flourish on its own, or to be destroyed from within by the malevolent and the ruthlessly persistent. From what I have learned about the G'lothc from inside the KDM, Naero, this is the truth of the Great Adversary. Their far reaching goal is to destroy the universe itself, by any means necessary."

Jia sighed then. "As we learned from our creators," Jia stated, "the enemy is of ancient and cunning mind and knowledge, bent upon these goals of total destruction. The G'lothc already move within wide spheres that we have yet to discover and comprehend. We must continue to explore the limitless realms and possibilities on our own. The Powers That Be have already made contact with you two as the Cosmic Guardians of the Great Cosmic Prophecy. You must continue to find a way to share power with your other selves, for the defense of all. You are not only on a collision course with the G'lothc, but with the Great Destroyer, should that limitless Thing ever arise. And so the great battle is joined."

Baeven pulled them within a certain sphere within an instant. In that place they beheld the continuing contest between radiant young Shetharra and the Darkforce might and malignant will of the Dark Emperor.

"The child of light still holds fast, blocking the way before Nahaxrathrax himself. Past her, through this one place, this one vector, all of the lesser lights of the next generation of Spacer children's spirits lie vulnerable. If their spirits die where they can be attacked in this place, they perish in every other. Perhaps the Dark Emperor merely stumbled upon the vectors of this sphere, this one avenue by chance and sought to take advantage of his good fortune."

"Perhaps it was only a matter of time," Naero added. "Perhaps that foul being or the collection of evil lost souls that he is was drawn to this place by the shining light of Shetharra's bright soul lighting the darkness here. Yet whatever his path, he came at this vantage point and bent his power against it. We have no choice. We cannot allow him murder my oldest daughter and all of the other Spacer children beyond her valiant defense.

"We must find a way to defeat that massive wretch and bar him from this place hereafter. I have learned this much. If a way can be opened, it can also be shut and closed. Only the means remain to be discovered and understood. Khai and I will never stop searching for a way to save our girl and the others, for as long as hope remains."

"As the Cosmic forces once told each of us when we accepted the mantles of being guardians," Baeven said, "by linking up with our alternative selves, we can share in the vast energies of our own limitless possibilities. That is the goal we must pursue in order to match the foe power for power and strength for strength. That is the only way that we can possibly hope to win out against such enemies."

"Yet there are always great dangers as well," Jia warned. "The seas of possibilities are so great that there is always the risk of expanding the mind and self too far or too fast. You could lose yourself, and never be able to reform into what you are. You could become forever lost in the torrents of what might be, and never find your way back to what actually exists in the here and now."

Khai drew Yii, and the great Cosmic sword blazed to life. "It is clear that the enemy uses its knowledge of all of what is and what might be to its great advantage. We must do the same and more. If the great foe can track us and the souls of our children down in such places and attack us here, then there must be similar ways and vectors that we can do so to them.

"We shall hunt them down and assail them just as they pursue and hunt us. They slink, plot, and hide among all that is possible. We must locate and expose their lairs—their hiding places—and bring our power to bear against them where they think they are safest. We also know in theory that they must have huge unknown sources of Darkforce energy that they continually tap into just as we tap into the stars. We must locate these enemy power sources and either destroy them, or at the very least cut them off. If we can separate the enemy from their sources of such power, then our great foes shall be weakened and left vulnerable."

"All of this is easier said than accomplished," Jia noted. "All of us remain but novices at finding, exploring, and comprehending such places. So let's not get too far ahead of ourselves for now."

Linked together, as if to bring home that point, they all felt a sudden weariness wash over them. They had already lingered too long in their current state within the spheres of possibility.

"We must return home for now," Baeven told them. "Let our spiritminds merge with our bodies back on Naero's flagship and awaken. We will still need to rest a few hours and regenerate to avoid feeling ill. Yet each time we venture out to search, we grow stronger and can stay out for longer and longer periods of time. Since there is still so much that we do not know, I suggest we make it a rule that we venture out only in pairs, just as Jia and I have done. In that way, we can assist and protect one another or fetch further help if it is needed."

In another few moments, they awoke within their bodies, feeling the same fatigue as they did within their spiritminds.

Jia snuggled in with Baeven as they shifted around slightly in each other's arms to get more comfortable. "I think Bae and I will rest and regen right here, if no one minds."

"Not at all." Khai's head was still in Naero's lap and her gentle hand rested upon his long golden hair. "I find that notion quite acceptable," he said. "N and I will do the same."

27

The Turmen or Turmeni looked slightly insectoid in appearance, yet this was deceptive. They were not insects in any way, to Naero and others with biomancy powers. Biomechanically and genetically speaking, the Turmen were internally actually closer to near humans and other humanoids.

They stood 1.5 to 2.5 meters in height depending on age, with two pairs of legs and two pairs of arms. They had a stalk-like neck and head, a chest or torso, and an extended lower abdomen section.

Every part of the Turmen body was protected by interlocking panels of a hard carapace like chitin or body armor.

Even the head was encircled by what appeared to be a mantle of such protective panels of varied size. Each arm and leg ended in a dexterous, claw-like hand with four fingers and two thumbs, one on each side, perfect for intricate tool and device manipulation. They were brownish to golden, and had purple-blue highlights and an iridescent sheen to their body panels.

They only had two, very humanoid looking eyes that were very expressive. The Turmeni nose vent was on the top of the head, and the ears or listening nodules were on the uppermost shoulders. Their mouth opened vertically on the neck, beneath the slight chin.

They could speak within a normal range, and their language was easily translated or learned psyonically. They were not energy beings in any way.

Internally, the Turmen vital organs were a bit stretched out here and there, but more or less where they might be expected to be. The big difference was that the Turmen had two hearts and four lungs.

Only a handful of Turmeni chose to return to their worlds with the Alliance scouting fleets.

What they found on the very first shattered homeworld was both disgusting and heart rending.

The brave Turmen had fought with all of their valor and skill, against advanced armies and invaders that they could never hope to defeat on their own.

The second generation Ejjai, the meatships, and other enemy slaves had shown no mercy. Every lost Turmen world thereafter showed the same grim pattern.

The enemy fell upon the native civilian populations again and again and systematically wiped them out with an almost hateful fury that seemed beyond violence. Then the ground attack fleets scorched the land masses into lifeless rock and ash, or else the foe bombed each world and irradiated the surface into slag from orbit.

There was no chance of hiding or escape.

This horrid, efficient process continued from one world to the next in rapid succession. The enemy took whatever they wished and obliterated whatever was left.

Over the course of several months, less than a standard year, the Turmen civilization had fought on and continually cried out into the black for anyone to help them.

No help reached them in time.

The absolute total destruction of an advanced civilization and rich culture was a fearsome thing to witness first hand.

Naero stood among the Turmen survivors who came back with her to view the harsh reality of what had happened to their people. At first they went into numb, stupefied shock as the reports and facts continued to pour in.

When they began to sob, weep, and wail in agony, Naero wept with them, as did many of her battle hardened naval crew.

This was the enemy.

This was what they were.

This was what they did, to everyone.

The great foe had to be stopped, at all cost.

"Broadcast these images and these facts out as far as they will go in every possible format," Naero commanded. "Send the data warnings forth with our probes and our long range, advancing fixer relay nets. If other sentients encounter the enemy that we face, this is what they can expect."

*

After the sorrow of the Turmeni, Naero and the Alliance barely encountered another beleaguered sentient race of centipede like beings in another far off direction, the Yunhu.

The Yunhu were the masters of one hundred and sixty worlds, most of them already under heavy attack by the enemy.

There was no way or time to reach the Yunhu in force.

The Alliance was already in full retreat as things were.

The best Spacer Intel could do was ask Baeven and his people to lead a secret fixer nebula there to help install as many planetary shields as possible, as quickly as possible.

Yet on the ground, the Yunhu would still be facing the full force of the enemy ground units alone.

Naero and Om could not guess how many of those worlds would also fall, and which of them might survive.

Naero sent down as many of her Shetanna reps as she could in the fleeting time allowed. Ra sent down some Shai breeding teams to hatch Shai fighters and assist with the ground wars.

There wasn't a damn thing more that anyone could do about the situation.

To make matters even worse during that time, while Elazethrek recharged, the Dark Emperor stepped in and made several strategic appearances on key fronts.

Hidden within a Darkforce energy vortex, he lashed out against important Alliance positions, slashing through their forces and causing great destruction.

Then he would carefully elude any attempt to engage him directly.

Finally the first full fleets of warships and crews from the new Alliance Ultrium shipyards raced to the front. Each ship, each new fleet was a huge boon.

Their numbers would continue to increase, but the Alliance also wanted to build up a substantial rear guard force to protect the new, far flung production facilities as well.

They did not want enemy strike forces to wipe out the new Alliance production capabilities. Even though that was the same thing they were attempting to pull off against the foe.

This was no rout, yet the front line situation remained a continual, strategic, fighting retreat in many directions. The Alliance continued to survive and bleed the enemy where they could be bled.

Every free moment that Naero and her team had, they spent much of it within the KDM, exploring and gaining new enlightenment and tek secrets. They constantly sought out anything that might give them a better edge against the Great Adversary.

Otherwise, they used the enemy's own tactics against them. Singly and in pairs, the Alliance Champions darted in and out of the conflict, both where the fighting was hottest, and also where the enemy was assessed to be the weakest.

They became firefighters and opportunists. They helped out where the fleets needed them most, and also attacked important targets of opportunity as they arose in a timely fashion.

Then the foe launched a new offensive in the chain of known energy being dimensions adjacent to the Gamma Quadrant.

Once more the enemy had new Cosmic, biomanced forms of their major weapons, the mind control wraiths leading hordes of new strains of the Darkforce phage.

The numerous energy being races were still attempting to recover from the last great battle. Now they were under heavy attack once again.

The Spacer Mystics sent forces to bolster the Alliance energy beings, but many feared that even that would not be enough.

There were more Spacer Mystics now than ever before, and Naero had done all that she could to quicken them, and increase their powers and abilities. The need for them continued to outpace the capacity for the Mystics to train and quicken them.

It was Om who proposed the clear solution.

Naero took it once more straight to the stubborn Mystic Masters.

Within a matter of days, Mystic training was immediately opened up to all Alliance sentients.

The ranks of the Alliance Mystic Adepts swelled ten thousand fold within the first week. The Cosmic talents of all beings of good will were soon being developed in Mystic training camps that were quickly established on thousands of worlds.

Yet all of these efforts would still take time to bear fruit.

Could the Alliance hold the enemy back long enough for these new adepts to prove effective and useful on a large scale?

Then, in the midst of all the turmoil, word finally came back to the Alliance from the secret strike forces that they had sent to penetrate deep into the enemy's territory.

Beyond all hope, those fleets had caught the enemy napping.

They had destroyed or severely damaged all of the enemy Ultrium shipyards. They even left behind stealth fixers to monitor the enemy bases, communications, and commit subtle sabotage to prevent or delay attempts either to reconstruct or to make those facilities operational once more.

The Alliance stealth fixer clouds would become the gremlins haunting and harassing the foe from within.

But the Alliance strike forces had paid a heavy price. Although taken by surprise at first, the enemy had responded quickly and in great force.

Half of the Alliance fleets and their crews had perished valiantly.

The remaining half, battered and damaged, was even now struggling to complete a desperate run back to Alliance lines that no longer existed.

Now the enemy waited for them there, while other enemy forces closed in all about them.

Naero said it first. "They have done the impossible, all that we asked of them and more. We cannot allow them to be slaughtered."

The Alliance heroes could no longer simply open wyrmholes to help leap across the great distances, the same way they went in. Somehow the enemy now possessed and utilized some kind of advanced enemy tek or weapons that neutralized the Alliance wyrmhole projectors across wide swaths of open space.

The Alliance raiders could now only jump from one group of systems to another, leap frogging all the way. The enemy could calculate and cover that entire area with ease and cut them off. No matter where the retreating Alliance ships came out, they found themselves under heavy attack.

The enraged enemy forced them to fight their way out of each system, only to jump once again into yet another hornet's nest.

The only time the hunted had time to refit and repair was while they were in jump space.

By now the enemy knew full well what direction they were headed in, and was always waiting for them wherever they emerged with a running gauntlet of attackers.

Baeven, Jia, Naero, and other Alliance Champions proposed a daring strategy to save the remaining, heroic raiders and help bring them home.

"Just recently," Baeven noted, "our teks have been able to reverse engineer prototypes of the superior wyrmhole tek that Elazethrek has been using. It is immune to most, but not all of the enemy wyrmhole dampening procedures."

Captain Tyber added, "This tek is already being incorporated by all of our new Ultrium warships coming off the line."

This top secret development was still news to some within the Alliance High Command.

Naero always had her fleets converted and refitted with the latest tek, weapons, and the new wyrmhole generators. This was S.O.P. for her command as soon as new tek became available.

Jia joined in. "With these latest advances, Naero and the Alliance Champions can lead five hundred picked fleets behind enemy lines to break up the enemy trap closing in around the escaping raiders.

"Equipped with the new wyrmhole projectors, the relief forces will open multiple wyrmholes in every area possible in order to confuse our opponents and give the Alliance forces every possible opportunity to transport clear of the enemy hunters."

Khai tried to seal the deal on the proposal. "Even the enemy will not be able to neutralize hundreds of open wyrmholes all at once. We can rescue the raiders with minimal losses all around."

Alliance High Command barely approved of the effort after much debate, fearing at first that if something did go horribly wrong, they might lose the relief force and the Alliance Champions as well.

All of the Alliance leaders, however, fully agreed that the raiders had more than fulfilled their duties, and achieved great victory at a very high price. Their courageous efforts had already amounted to enough of a suicide mission.

If all of those ships could be brought back to refit and fight another day, that would also be a huge bolster to Alliance numbers and morale.

Not to mention the fact that enemy warship production had most likely been set back for a decade at least.

Naero's initial assault took almost a third of the enemy trap forces completely by surprise.

On moment the enemy gloated openly over their links about preparing to obliterate the ragged remnants of the Alliance strike force.

And the next they themselves were being decimated by Naero's relief force. Her super battleships and dreadnaughts jumped in close and ripped the enemy fleets from stem to stern, rapid fire giga-cannons blazing in fury.

The Holy Ghost attacked five enemy G'lothc battleships, caught them from behind, and pulverized them.

In the flash of a few blazing minutes, the enemy flagship and the other four had either exploded entirely or were flaming wrecks where they listed.

All of the Alliance ships observed firsthand the various enemy ray emitters being used to neutralize wyrmhole projectors and cancel out existing, open wyrmholes.

Even the new enemy projectors were not completely immune.

But by that time, according to Baeven and Jia's original plan, there were thousands of wyrmholes open, and every enemy ship with a neutralizing emitter on it came under heavy, concentrated Alliance attack.

The battered raider ships, ever valiant, backed through the wyrmholes with their defiant guns still blazing, dealing death even while making good their escape.

Then Naero's relief forces began their orderly retreat.

Close by, *The Shadow Fox* and *The Dark Star* concentrated energy depleting ion fire on a stricken G'lothc heavy cruiser. This was a target of opportunity.

The enemy vessel was yet another of the latest tentacle ships with even newer specs according to the initial scans. It had suffered some kind of massive implosion and had lost most of its power.

As the champions knew well, these ships had to be drained completely of all energy and placed in a type of teknomancy stasis, since they were self-aware and would never stop trying to destroy themselves and everything around them in order to avoid capture.

Naero ordered several of her most powerful battleships to hit the enemy vessel with energy depletion beams to finish the job off quickly.

They did this all while the enemy regrouped and roared back at the relief force.

Naero's own flagship took the captured enemy cruiser in tow and shot through the nearest wyrmhole.

The Alliance relief force had damaged the enemy elements severely upon engagement, rescued the surviving raiders, and now returned with a vital but dangerous prize.

That was a good day's work for anyone.

Naero's team and Intel would relish picking that enemy heavy cruiser apart to learn all of its secrets, piece by piece.

28

"Get back and hold off!" Naero cried.

Her third eye was already open wide.

Om had warned her about the next wave of G'lothc ship AI attacks rippling their way from the main computing bay.

She used telekinesis to shove Jia, Shalaen, and Tyber back with the others, so that she might have full room to repulse the next enemy assault without endangering her friends.

With her Ur-metal short swords drawn and fully charged, she no longer had to hold back.

She flashed around the corner and down the long corridor up ahead.

That corridor was filled with a mass of Darkforce energized tentacles and weaponized appendages barring her way.

The enemy now had forms of the phage and mind control wraiths that were now built within their warships and fully part of their internal defenses.

Naero sliced, wheeled, and kicked her way through these formidable defenses as if she were a spinning wheel of golden Cosmic fire.

She ripped and tore through the forces shooting out from the walls, floor, and ceiling to destroy her.

She sent blasts of incinerating power to eradicate the ship's onboard defenses in front and behind her.

Then Naero followed up with waves of Teknomancy, disrupting and nullifying any attempts at launching other similar attacks in that section.

Over twenty meters of that area were now negated and pacified.

The going continued to be very tough.

Through her links with the others, Baeven and Khai were helping the others suppress similar residual attacks to the rear and from all open sides and access points that they encountered.

The living enemy ship remained both pernicious and persistent in its attempts to kill them. It fought them every millimeter of the way.

As the suppression team penetrated each level of the captured enemy heavy cruiser, they had to both reactivate each section in teknomanced isolation and then fight against its automated defenses at the same time.

Most of all, they could not allow the living-machine G'lothc tek to tap into enough power to be able to self-destruct, and take them all out with it.

This made the takeover of the vessel extremely complex, tedious, and exhausting. Completing such a task could only be done in painstaking stages.

Alala and Om fought side by side, within their newest SCWI morphing, synthezoid hyperconstructs—very similar to the remote, super-adaptoids that the Spacer Mystics continued using and developing to train with. They were just part of the new future ahead of them, used to train the next waves of Mystics, not just from the Spacers, but from all sentients within the Alliance.

Spacer and Alliance Intel were still trying to develop the SCWI adaptoid forms for direct use in the war. Some started referring to them as "Remos," short for Remote Combat Warriors.

Others began calling massed units of the construct fighters instant armies. But much of that was still just theory and conjecture.

Yet in these advanced construct forms, Om and Alala could finally join the fight in the real world.

Both of them unleashed their formidable teknomancy and Cosmic energy powers that Naero had helped infuse them with.

Om still had his own amazing Kexxian defensive protocols to rely upon as well. His Kexxian based offensive and defensive capabilities negated enemy efforts almost at will.

Together the two AIs helped the Alliance Champions battle their way deeper and deeper into the enemy warship's various holds, bays, and systems.

Alala transported directly in front of Khai at one point and took out a deadly fusion beam burst, a lethal, phazed booby trap that might have slain some of the others. Even Khai would have been seriously hurt.

Alala's construct was instantly vaporized when the trap triggered, but with no harm to her actual essence. Since she operated her synthezoid form remotely from a stasis pod, she quickly generated another physical form and rejoined them within five standard minutes.

Om had been shaken, nonetheless, at seeing her construct annihilated right before his eyes. Naero thought it a rather human reaction, especially for him.

Tyber had even suggested that they all use remote constructs to pacify the enemy vessel, as he, Om, and Alala were doing. Tarim was still learning to control a SCWI construct so that he might join them as a floating gunnery platform. It was his wish to help protect Shalaen and the rest of them, with no risk to himself as a normal human.

Naero and the others simply weren't ready for any of that.

They still trusted in their own original forms and powers, rather than some Remo. To use a construct, they would still be forced to give up many of their most powerful abilities. It might be safer, but it would also limit them.

As her uncle Baeven said, to hell with that.

The pacification team struggled on from one objective to the next.

Before they could hope to reach and conquer the main bridge, they still had to pacify and take out the main computing bay and the two back up control bridges. On a living ship such as this, where each part of the vessel was actively trying to slaughter them, the infiltrators could not let down their guard.

Alala swelled up in size, glowing with energy. She continued to drain power from the corridor shaft walls and hammered them back, straining to keep their undulating masses from rippling together and crushing the boarding party.

Naero, Baeven, Khai, Ra, Janner, Shalaen, Jia, and Captain Ty did what they could to disrupt and confuse the Darkforce infused hull in that area.

Alala shouted, "I keep force feeding the ship the crew codes that the enemy uses to allow their slaves to function on these vessels without being attacked and slain! The AI shipminds keep getting trapped within a loop trying to authenticate those codes over and over again."

"I think they know for certain that we're not part of their crew by now," Jia said.

"No, that's still a good ploy. Keep it up!" Ty yelled. "It's still making them hesitate for almost an entire second each time you trigger it. We need that time to continue disrupting them and shutting them down, meter by meter. If that's what will work, keep doing it."

"Look out, N!" Om roared.

He shot past her and became a spinning whir of dark and light Cosmic blades and spinning Ultrium razor ribbons.

Darkforce blasts and stun tentacles exploded from the forward bulkhead without warning and rippled down the remaining length of corridor.

Om tore into them with equal force, both negating and siphoning off their destructive energies.

By her own calculations, even Naero or her uncle Baeven could have been seriously injured by such an onslaught if they didn't have the proper defenses up.

Some of the others might have been slain outright.

Om had saved them yet again and took little damage, which he quickly regenerated.

He kept spinning and sawing through the defenses until he struck the bulkhead and used the stolen energy from the vessel itself to blast right through.

Naero shielded the others sufficiently at Om's warning.

His intense efforts left a glowing, pulsating tunnel of devastation straight through the enemy defenses.

The path to the main computing chamber was now clear for a few crucial moments.

Everyone zipped in quickly, Naero leading half of the team one way, and Baeven leading the other half along the opposite side.

The G'lothc engineered living machine shipminds that controlled the vessel came fully to life and attacked from all directions. Offensive weapons, energized tentacles, and synthetic limbs morphed out of the walls, floor, and ceiling.

Both teams quickly had their hands filled simply with fighting to stay alive, yet alone trying to reach the warship's central core.

That was where the enemy shipminds were cut off, shielded and armored within, in ways that could only be described as a hyper defended vault.

"Where is this ship getting the power to do all of this?" Baeven noted. "All of this should have already been neutralized."

"I know!" Naero shouted back. "Haisha! We drained this damn thing completely when we captured it, but now every part of it comes to life when we enter it and gives us hell. We're missing something. Is it drawing power from us, somehow?"

"Negative," Om yelled. "I can't tell how it's getting this kind of power to resist us. Let me penetrate directly to the core and attempt to locate the power source."

"How in the hell are you going to do that?" Naero said. "There doesn't seem to be one, and yet the ship has all of this energy."

"Easy. By letting it absorb me and take me there."

He sprang right into one defensive mass, enveloping him like a Darkforce amoeba.

Immediately the dark foam seemed to break him down.

"Om!" Naero shouted in horror.

Ra held her back for only an instant.

"My love!" Alala shrieked, charging forward, trying to rip through the enemy defenses.

Om waved her off, grinning weakly as he dissolved. "It's okay, La. Trust me. Try to reach the core from the outside. Keep the shipminds distracted…" His voice trailed off.

Om was gone.

"Trust him, N," Ty shouted to her, Alala, and the rest. "When doesn't Om have a plan?"

Alala nodded. "He's right, N. Om would never sacrifice himself so needlessly. He knows what he's doing."

Naero released a teknomancy blast wave that spread throughout the chamber, cutting down and nullifying enemy constructs and defenses.

"Keep fighting!" Naero yelled.

They charged forward into the core defenses of the shipminds, as the living vessel struggled to rebound and counterattack.

Baeven and his group were hemmed in on the far side for the moment, attempting to break out.

At least between them, they still had the enemy vessel dividing its energies and efforts to defeat them.

A sudden rush of multi-limbed and tentacled mind wraith and phage monsters erupted into larger attack forms, flooding out from several new openings.

This was new.

The Alliance Champions braced themselves.

Naero and others detonated repulsing charges or unleashed Cosmic blasts and energy waves at the right levels to cut down most of these new threats.

Yet it was Khai who finally saved them.

He wielded Yii two-handed, and waded straight into the main thrust of the assault within a sphere of fiery green energy all around him.

The Cosmic Sword of Light whirred and flashed like a drill of destruction through the enemy core.

The enemy construct hordes withered and melted before his onslaught, and both teams battled on towards their main objective, rallying behind the Cosmic Swordsman.

Darkforce generator monstrosities phazed out of the walls and floors, unleashing massive stun bolt attacks.

It was all that Naero, Shalaen, and Baeven could do to shield them all from being outright paralyzed.

The next instant they battled the writhing Darkforce meks to the death.

"Haisha!" Alala shouted, beating at the foes, her gigantic adaptoid hands filled with battered and broken monsters, using them as weapons to bash the others with. Splintered parts and pieces of the monsters rained down and their stinging fluids splattered everywhere.

She damaged the hull of the ship severely where she repeatedly rammed and flattened the monsters into the structure itself. Then she crushed them together into one another, mangling them even further.

Within the space of a few seconds, scores of the vile things were shattered, torn and cut apart, and utterly destroyed.

Just when the Alliance Champions thought that they had reached the actual panels and internal structure of the shipminds themselves, behind the damaged vault walls they ripped open—everything around them shuddered and went still.

"All of the defenses have been neutralized somehow," Jia exclaimed.

All of them confirmed that fact with teknomancy and psyonics. They had defeated the shipminds, but how?

"Did Om do this?" Naero asked her comrades. "It couldn't have been us. We were just about to penetrate the core."

The others looked as confused as she was.

Naero struggled to make contact with Om through their link.

I'm here Naero. I'm in the core. Terrifying, like nothing I've ever witnessed. How could we be so wrong about what our foes are truly capable of?

Everything's all right, Om. You beat them. You shut them all down."

"I did. I had to. I've discovered a connection to the true G'lothc energy source, Naero…or at least one of them. I think that I can discern why these vessels have so much energy and can unleash such destructive attacks."

Naero quickly used her teknomancy to force her way into the stunned structure of the now crippled shipminds, attempting to reach where Om was up ahead of her.

Suddenly she was enveloped in a dark tunnel of Cosmic and Darkforce energy, bathing her in Chaos, pain, and potential destruction, as the latent energies threatened to tear her apart.

She instantly shifted into an energy form and flung up her defenses to resist the destructive forces swelling up all about her.

It was not unlike being inside the core of a dark star, or worse, a small singularity.

She sensed Om ahead of her. I'll join you shortly and we can learn these enemy secrets together, Om. I'm adjusting to the interior of the Darkforce phazed portions of the broken shipminds.

Naero…

I must say, this is amazing. The shipmind interior is much like a pocket dimension of warped and twisted Cosmic energy itself. It all reminds me of the interior dimensions of the KDM in some ways, yet completely different somehow.

N, go back. It's very dangerous here, in ways that I can't even begin to calculate and describe. I've nearly been sucked into the growing vortex several times myself. Even if I don't make it back, don't try to save me. I'm just a construct, remember? Get the hell out of here. Don't come any closer!

Stop it, Om. I'm very close. I can sense that you're right ahead of me. Together we can both-

The implosion struck without warning and warped both of them off into the unknown faster than thought.

There was no way to resist.

The pain was also beyond reality.

It felt as if each atom, even in one of her most powerful energy forms and with all of her Cosmic defenses, was being slowly exploded.

Naero's consciousness struggled to maintain any form of unity and cohesion.

Her own mind expanded at a crippling rate, threatening to blast her existence across the entire universe within the space of nanoseconds, to join and mix with the motes of Cosmic dust everywhere at once.

Yet something held her together.

She located Om near her, just before he was about to perish from the same effects. She quickly merged his spiritmind within herself once again. His construct was destroyed an instant later.

She re-linked with Om almost instinctively, as if it were the most natural thing she could do.

Somehow, having him back within her made things easier, even as she herself continued to expand out of control.

At least she wasn't so alone any longer.

N? You...you kept my spiritmind from returning to my pod. My construct was going to pieces. Haisha! What is this bizarre place, Naero?

I don't know yet, Om. I have no idea how we got here exactly or what this place is. I don't know if there is a way back.

Can't you sense it? The very laws of energy and matter are different here. It's like suddenly being thrust into a geometrically reversed universe of some kind.

A Non-Euclidean universe, Om? That would be staggering.

Something else terrified her suddenly.

Om, why can't I sense my body? Your construct is gone. We know that. I can still think and reason somewhat, but even that's all hazy and fuzzy somehow. What has happened to my physical form? Even my energy form?

Hmmm...we don't seem to have them any longer. Perhaps we don't need them here. Your spiritmind form seems more real here than mine, more stable somehow.

A realm of pure energy and thought, perhaps?

A place of imagination?

Again, it may very well be such a place, N. Either that or our spiritmind forms have expanded so far as to be everywhere in this universe at once.

So you're saying it's a tachyonic universe or another variety of pocket dimension that we have yet to encounter?

I don't know, Naero. I don't have any answers here. But I would guess that since your spiritmind is now in this place, your body remains back on the captured enemy ship.

One thing became a definite worry right away.

How do we get back, Om?

I...I don't know that either, N. Sorry. I don't know anything in this place. It's so difficult for me to grasp concepts. I can't even comprehend exactly how we came here, or what or where here is.

It definitely had something to do with that implosion of some kind, Om. I'm sure of that much. I felt it. I very much had the sensation of being sucked into this place by…by some force, wherever this place happens to be.

All of the possible universes, as they tended to be, were infinitely wondrous, perilous, and incredibly strange, all at once.

She definitely felt several things pulling at her, or perhaps that was just the strange energies of that place still trying to destroy them.

If she were inside the KDM-

She gasped suddenly as if she had been zapped by Darkforce lightning, slapped repeatedly very hard, and then left breathless, all in one instant of SpaceTime.

Naero felt all of these sensations, despite the added sensation of having no physical form.

In that fraction of what was really a torrent of enlightening insight, she began to experience an epiphany of many potential possibilities and solutions as to their locations…and the equivalent perils contained therein, all at once.

One point became incredibly clear to her now.

This place was far from natural. It had obviously been devised by the enemy to serve many of their purposes. This realm was one of their secret constructs in SpaceTime and tainted with their corruption.

Naero didn't feel right.

To be here exposed them and left them vulnerable in ways that she could not yet even imagine.

They might be attacked and destroyed at any instant, if they were discovered.

They had accidentally penetrated a realm that the enemy clearly thought they would never discover.

Mentally, Naero's thoughts and ideas came at her in a flood, a rush that was so great that she began to psyonically babble them rapid-fire, partly to release them and so that she could also begin to share their overwhelming nature with Om.

Naero was drowning in a surging flow of not just conjecture, but also of raw knowledge and conception.

Om, I thought it seemed too familiar in many ways. We're in trouble, very horrific trouble if they sense us here. If he just happens to glance this way. If *He* derives our presence and pin points our location, we're practically at the Dark Emperor's mercy in our ignorance about this place.

Naero, you're overwhelming me with your thoughts and ideas. I can't process them all. Slow down. Slow down! Even through teknomancy and biomancy I can't keep up with your mind.

They stole it, Om. They stole it, just like they always did everything, and twisted it for their purposes. Yet because they did not truly create it, they did not fully understand its structure or purpose.

Naero stopped and giggled both madly and slightly.

It's a rig job, Om. What a pale joke. Why, the Kexxian Dreamers could create such places almost without thought, places of power and majesty beyond all reckoning. They used what were for them mere variations of the Great Songs of Making to bring wonder into being and reality.

Naero, focus, you're ranting. Who made this place? How? What is it? Who stole what in order to create it?

Naero laughed and swept her feeble powers of comprehension all about her in order to confirm her own, nearly inchoate ramblings.

Yes. Of course.

She paused and collected herself as best she could, her formless self and shaken spiritmind still shuddering.

The rampaging flow of the shattered dam of knowledge was now past.

And it had nearly crushed them both.

Om, we're within a pale imitation of something close to the Kexxian Data Matrix.

What? How is that possible?

The G'lothc stole and twisted, and poisoned, and rigged everything that they could from their enemies, the Drians and especially the mighty Kexx. Yet with their limited minds, they could neither comprehend nor achieve the fully expanded use and possibility of the tek they had stolen.

You mean that all of this, this place, this pocket dimension is the result of Kexxian tek that the enemy stole long ago? Then what is its purpose, N?

The Kexx used more advanced forms of this tek to create their masterpiece—their living, knowing, undying gift of love, wisdom, and knowledge to the universe and all who value life and liberty.

Naero paused for a moment and then went on, awash with disgust.

I sense some of what you say, but I still can't see the entire concept at work here, Naero. Why did the enemy create this place? How does it serve them? In what way.

And this is just one such place, Om. There may very well be many others. Many more just like this. Can you not feel it, Om? All around us? That sickening taint of the corrupting energies of the Darkforce. That is what constantly tries to eat and tear at us.

We wondered how the enemy's warships could wield such staggering power and bring such destructive force to bear against us? Well this is how, Om.

Oh, no. No. You're right. I understand now. This is horrible, Naero.

Yes, my friend. Now you begin to see. The enemy constantly fills this place to bursting with Darkforce energy collected and created from countless galaxies, perhaps from the universe itself. This place is a source of near limitless, corrupted power.

Both they and their ships feed upon it and grow stronger continually as a supplemental power source that they only need to tap into. That is why each enemy vessel has special wyrmholes built directly into their drive cores, shipminds, and weapon systems—so that they can access such vast energy sources!

Yes. The Kexx created the miracle of the KDM, and the G'lothc in their penury of imagination, used a lesser version of this same pocket dimension tek. Thus they created little more than Darkforce energy depots for them and their new living warships to access. They use these destructive energies to fuel their plots and attacks.

If the G'lothc ever achieve the vessels they desire for their countless foul spirits, those abominations will become truly unstoppable.

They are near to that, Om. So close that that they hunger for such fulfillment, yet still it eludes them. Follow my keen senses, honed by the KDM. I can project my spiritmind as far as I wish, but I hesitate to do so here. The risk of detection is so great. I can feel it. Now let me try again, as discreetly as I may. Can you not feel them now as they link to this place and feed off of its enormous energies?

Yes. I can sense many enemy warships, drawing energy from this place.

Not just that, Om. I must be careful in order that they don't notice our presence and find a way to come against us. We don't yet understand how to defend ourselves, or how to escape from this place. Both the Dark Emperor and his servant, Elazethrek of the Six also draw strength from this place and others like it from what I can perceive. They hunger for power, and it sustains them like food. Otherwise, they would consume themselves by their own hunger, lust, and hate.

This is why we haven't been able to locate or defeat them, Om. They use vast amounts of such power to mask their movements, avoid detection, and unleash their terrible attacks on the Alliance at times and places of their choosing.

This is how that Creature is able to slip away and recharge itself, time and time again, strike against us, and vanish with such maddening ease.

She gasped as a reflex, even though her spiritmind form did not actually breathe.

Haisha, Om. I can sense the very will of the enemy. With psyonics I can read some of their intense emotions and intentions. Can you feel any of this?

Not yet, N. Open your emotions to me more. Perhaps I can sense these feelings through you.

She attempted to do so.

The Creature is bent upon slaying all of the Alliance Champions—it's all that she thinks about. That is her mission.

Notice, she does think about herself somehow as "she." She sees herself as female, even though she is a monster.

Sorry, N. I'm still just getting the barest surface impressions from you. Nothing directly from the source. Try something else.

All right. I'll focus on the Dark Emperor. Yes, his mind is bent upon something as well. I sense fear, great fear. He and the others are afraid of something. It's...It's...

Naero couldn't believe it.

It's Shetharra Om. That's why the enemy is bent on murdering her. They-

Power within that strange place rippled as if from very far away.

Nahaxrathrax had briefly sensed something odd through his connection to the place and shot a distant glance in their direction.

Naero shut down her energies immediately and attempted to conceal herself.

What was that, N? I felt that.

That was the Dark Emperor, briefly glancing our way and directing a mere fraction of his will toward us.

Naero, there is a wealth of data here that we might be able to eventually use against them. If only we escape and survive this place, in order to return and study it more, and the enemy's connections to it and others like it.

I'm very aware of all of that, Om. Yes, it is vital now that we find a way out, back to the Alliance, before we are discovered and, I'm guessing, easily destroyed.

Here, Naero realized that if she were captured by Elazethrek, the fiend could murder her quite easily.

The fact remained that they were still trapped within this fell place. And more terrible realizations seemed to come to them each moment as they struggled to find a way out.

If a place such as this was like the KDM in any way, the way out should be as simple as it would be complex. She had to return to something she knew very well—as well as she knew herself.

After several hours, when nearly all hope was gone, Naero finally located her anchor that would lead back home.

The first clue was actually through the captured enemy warship. The hapless vessel was still feebly trying to re-energize and regenerate itself. That only confirmed what she had instinctively sensed all along.

After that it was Khai's white hot star of energy that she located and fully recognized, allowing her to immediately rush toward the outlet of escape. As she drew closer, she sensed Baeven, Janner, and all the rest of her family and friends and raced to rejoin them.

Naero and Om made good their escape at last, certain that they would need to return to this place for many reasons, no matter the risk.

She might not have ever found her way back, were it not for what she learned from Khai, Baeven, Womi, and her many other exploration efforts into strange places and dimensions.

The next instant, Naero physically jolted and gasped, coming up against the physical barrier of her body once more, now on a medbed in the infirmary of her flagship.

Khai sat across from her with Janner beside him. Her husband's great sword Yii lay stretched and ready across his knees, gripped in one hand. Khai did not rise up. He only smiled at her, as if he knew she would be back, eventually.

"Took you long enough," Khai scolded her.

Naero winked at him and sat up as if from a mere nap. "There's no time to wait, my love. We need to get with Klyne and the Mystics for a debrief session that's going to be long and somewhat enlightening."

He did stand up at that, absorbed Yii, and helped her down with his powerful hands about her small waist when she appeared unsteady. Her efforts in that strange zone had taken more out of her than she guessed. But she recovered quickly.

She also knew very well how much they both loved him scooping her up and holding her.

"I figured it might be something interesting," Khai noted. "The others worried about you being in some kind of a coma. I figured you were off doing something important."

Janner called on his comunit, arranging the needed debrief session. As they went out of the infirmary together, Naero turned and placed her hand on Khai's chest, speaking to him psyonically through their link in secret.

Khai, I found out how the enemy is tapping into such great quantities of their tainted power, and something more.

What is it, my heart? You look troubled.

While we were trying to locate a way back, I detected how the foe is using these same great quantities of Darkforce energy to continually attack and slowly kill our oldest daughter. That is yet another source of

Shetharra's Cosmic sickness, and why she can never get better. They fear her greatly. Much of their malice is bent on killing her—on making certain that she does not survive. The Dark Emperor has made it his primary goal.

Khai's green eyes narrowed and seethed with sudden fury—the rage of a father who would do anything to protect his beloved children.

Then we shall stop them and find a way to destroy these devils.

Naero smiled briefly up at her dear mate, feeling her own mother's fury burning her in own eyes.

Yes, my heart. We shall find a way. They shall regret the moment that they came after any of our children. For that alone we shall make them pay dearly, by the full might and the weight of our hands, and the force of our combined will.

29

Shetharra's slowly deteriorating condition remained somewhat stable for a time, while Naero and her allies actively sought a final remedy, utilizing some of the new information they had obtained.

If they could only find a way to block the relentless attacks or cut off their sources of energy.

With the advanced enemy warship subdued, at least for the time being, Intel and the Mystics carefully went over the vessel and explored its many secrets in great detail, with teams of teks and other Mystics and energy beings there to protect them from any remaining weird stuff.

Naero wanted herself and the Alliance Champions to explore the strange phantom zones in force next time.

But the fluctuating war in the Gamma Quadrant would not wait, expanding in many directions all at once.

It seemed as if the Alliance Champions were still needed everywhere at once.

Naero's strike force moved to yet another region to encounter the *Glos*, gelatinous shapeshifters and near energy beings on the verge of their first, massed transformation as a species.

This also left the species incredibly vulnerable, and all of the Alliance energy being races marshalled their forces for what they guessed would be another battle royale with the G'lothe wraiths and the ever-evolving enemy phage swarms.

Yet for once, by all of the initial appearances, the Alliance was ahead of the game that was afoot. For all of its reach and power, even the enemy could not assail every corner of the Gamma Quadrant at one time. They could not be everywhere at once.

Yet the situation Naero faced was still complicated and grim.

Enemy elements had infiltrated two other nearby sentient races close to the Glos systems, and of course set them all upon each other in a classic strategy to cause chaos and weaken all three races for eventual subjugation.

The second race enmeshed in the senseless war and strife were the *Dringul*, a mammalian race who were humanoids evolved from a ferret or otter type progenitor.

They were an amphibian based culture centered around oceans, lakes, rivers, and streams. They had only just started to explore and colonize their systems for less than a century, and were very vulnerable themselves. Not being very warlike, they had already endured heavy losses.

The next combatants were an insectoid hivemind race of hyper intelligent, greenish blue beetles. Each *Chibar* was only .608 to .912 meters in length.

It took a minimum of sixteen Chibar to stand up and lock themselves together into a communication pod, to form a collective mind sophisticated enough to communicate with another sentient species. They were natural mimics, and could duplicate many alien voice patterns through complex striculation of their adept mandibles.

A larger pod of two hundred and fifty six Chibar could begin to utilize psyonics. After one thousand and twenty-four of the beetles linked their brain functions, they operated much like hyper aware, super AI computers, and there were collective hive minds beyond that who could think very expansively, take basic energy being forms, and manipulate Cosmic forces. At present, all of them were responding to the warlike threats of the other two species and struggling to increase the size and destructive force of their interstellar navies and ground attack forces.

They would all soon spiral down into an arms race and expanding war that would deplete everyone. None of them could win such a war.

Naero started by first sending in shapeshifted reps of herself to make initial contact and prepare them for the truth of what was really manipulating them.

As was sometimes the case, the Glos attacked and absorbed her replicant ambassador the moment she revealed herself. The Chibar swarmed over theirs and devoured their rep within seconds as well.

Yet Naero learned all that she could about the two races, imprinted on the Lifeforce energy that returned to her from the destroyed reps. These special duplicates were designed so that they would gather and send back data, and not suffer greatly when such things occurred.

And for a first contact situation, even if her emissaries failed and were destroyed physically, at times the new races would learn much about the Alliance and the real threats they were facing. If they read the rep's thoughts or sifted through the brain, the mind, or neural nets in any way, the aliens would quickly discern that the emissary had indeed been telling the truth, albeit too late.

Only the more kindly Dringul were open to reason and gave the emissary rep a chance to really discuss matters with them. Of course, they were frightened also, and made the rep their hostage for a time. Yet it did not take long to convince them by logic and overwhelming evidence as to what was really going on with the three races being driven to madness and debilitating war.

It only took one captured Dringul warship gone rogue, filled with Dringul crew under the complete control of enemy mind control wraiths to prove to them what was happening among all three races.

Naero's cloaked Alliance fleets of her strike force swept in and began neutralizing any enemy presence on the Dringul worlds.

Fortunately, the enemy had only just initiated their standard campaign strategy, which was much easier to head off and put a stop to it.

All of the signs said that it was the same way with the Glos and the Dringul.

The enemy had a slight foothold here and was just ramping up its game.

They were not in complete control of the situation by far.

Within a matter of days, the Dringul worlds were under the Alliance protection of the new advanced planetary defensive screens.

Naero went to the Chibar next, and kept sending entreaties to the Glos.

The higher level beetle minds of the Chibar were greatly amused and intrigued by Naero's claims of alien enemy infiltration of their hive minds.

Convincing them of that fact took much longer than Naero had hoped. But in the end, once the proof was made, the largest hive minds moved decisively, acting faster than Naero could have ever thought possible to eradicate any alien influence over them.

Naero also convinced the beetles finally that it would not be in their best interest to attempt to use a similar campaign against the Alliance itself.

They plainly asked her why not. Why shouldn't they bide their time, join the Alliance, learns all of its secrets, and then absorb it?

Naero quickly informed them that if they made any attempt to become any kind of a threat to other sentient races, similar to that of the enemy, that their race would also have to be dealt with.

When they asked for exact details as to what that would mean, Naero provided several impressive examples of Alliance capabilities, and a few of her own.

If the Chibari became a threat to others, in the end, they might have to be destroyed.

Afterwards, Naero made herself and her mission very clear to the Chibari hive minds.

All sentients had a right to exist, but within reason. They were free to manage their worlds. But if they sought to use aggression against others in conquest and destruction, that would not be tolerated.

"Let there be no misunderstanding," she said. "Warlike destroyers who insist on senseless violence will also be summarily exterminated."

The hive minds complained. "So, the Alliance is taking upon itself to establish and enforce peace based upon the threat of annihilation?"

"Yes. We have never said otherwise."

"How is this your concept of Liberty that you claim to value so much?"

"Peace among rational sentients is the only lasting, logical form of freedom that is sustainable. You must be capable of grasping this fact. The universe, our galaxy, and this very quadrant all remain very complex and dangerous places. Chaos, disorder, and wasteful destruction and terror are certainly not the answer. They cannot be tolerated.

"Yet all of the sentient races must come to recognize that and agree to maintain order and co-existence. Freedom does not mean doing whatever you wish, without regard to the consequences for all. True, enlightened freedom requires that you are free to act in good faith, as long you do not harm or impose your will needlessly upon other sentients."

We still do not understand. These concepts are foreign to our thought patterns. If another sentient race cannot resist or prevent us from pursuing or interests, why should we not displace and as you say, exterminate them? That is our right as a free-thinking race.

Indeed. Only those sentients stronger than us have a right to stop us, or prevent us from engaging our free right to act.

"Very well. Then answer me this. If your concept of Liberty is simply grounded in the fact of who is stronger, then why shouldn't you be destroyed as well? The enemy is more advanced, more numerous, and more powerful than you at this time. Why should the Alliance seek to prevent that? For that matter, if the Alliance is currently stronger than you. Why shouldn't we wipe you all out?"

Perhaps you should. That is your free right to act.

You've threatened as much, if we refuse to operate within the restrictions of your Liberty, as you call it.

"Can't you see? You're too rigid in your thinking. It doesn't have to be that way. Things can be different. Expand your minds and your thinking to accept other possibilities, other possible strategies that do not just boil down to the strong slaughtering the weak. Can't you see how limited that thinking is?"

Possible.

We don't know. This is very confusing. The old mindset is very simple.

"That's exactly the problem. Your thinking patterns need to evolve. Your entire species is driven to evolve and improve itself, correct? That is very clear to see. Much of your energies are devoted to that goal. Am I right?"

Yes.

Agreed. Constant improvement of the spices provides a greater chance for survival and progress for us as a whole.

"Then why shouldn't your minds and your conceptualization skills not change, improve, and evolve as well? Other complex strategies of cooperation and peace among sentients could also help ensure the survival of your species. Why should you simply wait for a stronger species to come along and smash you?"

No response from either of the two.

"If such a species and their slave forces came against you for your destruction, would you not resist them in every way, no matter how futile? Would you not try to hang onto your freedom to act, for as long as you could?"

Of course we would.

The Chibari are brave and selfless. We would resist to the last.

"Then why not join with an alliance of other mutually sustaining sentients to oppose, defeat the threat, and help ensure the survival and mutual Liberty of all sentients of like mind? Would that not be in your best interests? And yet it would only require a slight shift in the complexity of your current thinking.

"Consider this new paradigm. Would not such a shift, such growth be better than simply waiting for another species more powerful than you to happen along and destroy you all upon a mere whim? Have I not demonstrated to you a more logical, effective, and better way?"

You mentioned that this strong species have slaves serving them.

Another possible path to survival would be to submit to becoming more of their slaves.

Naero sighed. "You cannot be serious, after everything we have just discussed. You would choose such a path for your race? Slaves give up their free will, their liberty, and their right to freely act. What is the use of living then? Myself and many sentients in the Alliance believe strongly that we would rather be dead than become the slaves and chattels of such foes. That is why we seek to oppose and vanquish them."

Now who is being futile?

Is this not being too rigid as you accuse us of being? At least as slaves a species would still exist, and perhaps have a chance to overthrow their masters one day. The death of a species is permanent. In that strategy there is no hope of a better way. There is no future.

"Agreed. But is that not an extreme also? And I would certainly try to band with other species and races of like mind for survival, rather than give in at the start before I had exhausted all other options and possibilities. Accepting slavery surely wouldn't be my first choice in order to defeat an aggressor. It would rather be a last resort. Does that not make sense?"

Yes.

We suppose so. You have given us much to consider.

We shall endeavor to examine and study these new ideas, concepts, and possibilities, as you put it, in new light.

At the very least, hostilities ceased between the Chibari and the Dringul.

The beetles couldn't really get at the otter-people anymore in any case, because of the planetary shields.

Naero held off offering them to the insects, as long as they remained on the fence about changing enough to join the Alliance.

The war continued between the Chibari and the Glos, and Naero needed to put a stop to that quickly. The beetles were not going to be the first party to stop the conflict, not while the fighting was still hot.

Naero transformed into one of the gelatinous Glos after much study, amazed instantly by the breadth and complexity of their minds. They were capable of staggering mathematical and Cosmic thought, juxtaposed by being highly creative and sublime artists and experiencing a very broad depth of feeling, perception, and range of emotion, sentiment, and feeling.

The Glos had a fascinatingly rich culture, extremely moving and beautiful even, for a species that many from the outside would only see as pulsating, shifting blobs of energized matter, partially controlled and ambulated by psyonics, thought, and the pure force of will.

Yet their free and expansive minds and their thinking patterns also left them vulnerable to the enemy mind control wraiths, and completely unaware of the invader's potential infiltration and influence.

Fortunately, as with the other two species, the foe had not taken over many of the Glos yet, and were still in the very early stages of their standard pattern of eventual conquest and subjugation.

But the Glos were extremely homogenous and of similar mind. They were also very xenophobic. The only other two sentient interstellar species that they had met thus far were at war with them.

First Naero had to expose the fledgling invaders where they could be located.

Then she could try to reason with the Glos.

Glos were extremely devoted parents and would, without fail, readily sacrifice themselves as individuals to guarantee the survival of their offspring.

Perhaps it was because conception of their young was so tedious and difficult.

Glos mated for life and would often perish if their mate perished. Although they were long lived, they could only try to conceive once every few hundred years, and gestation took half a century, and would produce only one or at most two Glos children.

These children took another fifty standard years to reach adulthood themselves, and had to be cared for and directed much of the time by the doting parents and extended families.

That did not even begin to get into their complex courtships and mating rituals for a couple to become pair bonded.

And then their form of bizarre sexual reproduction involved repeated sessions of absorbing each other in turn, exchanging genetic materials, and then emerging back out of each other. This exhausting process had to be repeated over many entire years devoted solely to reproduction.

Glos sex left them either recovering from the ordeal or preparing for another go around.

Yet it could be said that while mating, the Glos truly became one flesh with each other.

Among themselves, Glos were naturally happy for their kind, and convivial to one another, and especially attentive to their life partners and children.

These near energy beings lived for millennia if not physically destroyed, by accident or war. The Glos knew no crime or violence in their daily congress as a species, but there were unfortunate and occasional mishaps, accidents, and disasters by chance. And now war.

The wholesale, indifferent death and tragedy of war was a new and shocking experience for the Glos, who had long ago done away with such happenings among themselves.

War shocked and moved them to great emotion.

Naero posed as a high level Glos intel officer and quietly "exposed" the growing Alien infiltration as it started out and took over higher ups in the military and government from system to system.

She carefully selected high level leaders who could move and act swiftly to stamp out this terrifying new threat to Glos culture.

Then she revealed that there were also definite signs that the Chibari and the Dringul were also being manipulated by these alien invaders as well.

The Glos remained divided for a time.

Half of them wanted to warn the other races about this threat.

Half of them did not care either way.

Yet others finally prevailed, insisting that these other races might end the war if they were no longer under the control of another more advance species. Certainly the Dringul made overtures that they no longer wanted war.

The Chibari seemed to be waiting and holding back. A cessation of hostilities was negotiated, and all three parties discussed the threat of the invaders. Soon all three parties saw how they had been deceived and driven to make war upon each other.

The enemy plan to enslave or destroy all of them and their systems also became abundantly clear.

It was the Dringul who made peace first, and then divulged their joining the approaching, new sentient Alliance that was sweeping their way.

The larger galactic war against the Great Adversary would soon take precedence.

The reactionary Glos were hesitant to accept this new reality.

It took a deadly phage attack on three of their most vulnerable systems to convince them of joining.

Once the Glos joined, the stubborn beetle hive minds of the Chibari finally saw the wisdom of doing so as well.

*

"Danjen, what in the hell are you doing now, you goof? What's with the strange get up this time?"

He had pulled her aside into a meeting room as soon as they happened to meet.

The crazy ass Ku was dressed up in some weird new costume with a wide ruffle around his neck, strange tights that made his furry legs look all bandy and kooky, and a bizarre, embroidered tunic decorated with strange metal chains, studs, and accents. A puny little dagger and a long skinny sword were on his belt, completing the silly look along with a velvet pouch.

Danjen always had some weird kind of hobby going on behind the scenes that bordered on idiocy and obsession. Then she recalled her uncle's warning.

"Haisha, Danjen. What is that lurid thing over your groin? And where is your loin cloth? Oh, hell no. Is that actually some kind of codpiece?"

He grabbed the damn thing and gave it a quick adjustment right in front of her. "It binds and pinches here and there like you wouldn't believe, N. But it sure makes the Ku babes on our homeworlds swood."

"Isn't the word, "swoon," you Nimrod?"

"Whatever," he said, pointing at the golden metal protuberance with both index fingers. "I'm telling you straight, one glance at this thing and the gals start running."

Naero blinked. "I don't doubt that. Makes me want to run."

He took a bizarre stance and screwed up his face as if badly constipated. What in the hell was he doing? He hoisted his nose straight toward the ceiling and placed his hand over his heart with high melodrama.

Was he actually…posing?

"You're just jealous because you're no longer the only one who has become a vid star—all of those Shetanna action movies? You're a star, and you don't even want to capitalize on all of that fame and money. What a waste."

"Ugh, I think I just urped up some of my own sick." Naero sighed and rolled her eyes. "Danjen, what did you do now, you hairy maniac? Swear to me that it's not porn again this time? Is it? I don't think I could handle all of that ever again."

He shifted and positioned himself on purpose once more.

The fuzzy little bugger was actually posing.

"I still insist that those were tasteful, romantic art piece vids for adult Ku only. They had solid story lines and were never meant to be seen by children."

"Yeah, I heard they made people sick."

Only Ku would rut in public and call it art. In many ways they had no shame. And now they were brazen enough to vid some of their ideas about acting and dare to call it what passed for art among a society of hairy goofballs.

Danjen kept posing this way and that, as if he had an audience watching him, hanging upon his every exaggerated move.

He didn't; it was just him and Naero in the meeting room.

That made it even scarier.

"Everyone's a critic," he tittered, all full of himself.

She put her hands on her hips and shifted her weight. "And in case you've forgotten, I have more than enough wealth and credits than I will ever need. So does Baeven, and so do you if you need any. But your nutball hobbies drive us insane. Remember all of you Old Terran cowboy fantasies? And as for all of those Shetanna movies back in the Alpha Quadrant—I never acted in any of them. Those are actors and doubles. And those movies all used vid footage of me in action during the wars without my damn permission."

"Well, among my people the Ku, I am currently being hailed as one of the greatest lezibians of my day! Women love me."

"No, that word is "lesbians" you twit bag—and that isn't even the right word. You mean "thespians," you puffed up moron!"

"I've made three vids, from original scripts by that new famous vid writer Chog Bekkul. You may not pay attention to Ku homeworld art reviews, but I have been compared to the greats among our entertainers."

Naero could not name a single Ku actor, director, or even any of their idiotic vids. Such things were too localized among lander populations. She did not have either the time or the inclination to pay attention to such trivial things.

That kind of happened when a person was trying to help save both the galaxy, and the universe. And anything the Ku made had to be pretty stupid.

"Very well," Naero said, "so, you're a big time actor now, and all of these hairy females on the Ku homeworlds want you. Are you happy now?"

He struck another pose.

Naero clawed at the very air in frustration.

It was times like this that she wanted to kill him.

"Haisha, please stop doing that before I murderize your stupid, hairy ass, you dumb, furry bastard. It is so pretentious that I want to kill you so bad, and vaporize that hyper offensive cod piece with you still in it. I can't help myself. No magistrate in the galaxy would ever convict me."

Danjen snorted with a haughty air. "I am above your envy of me and your petty insults. Let me just say that I'm not unhappy. Yes, I'm actually quite pleased with myself."

"You don't say?"

Naero sighed again and held both hands over her face, struggling to resist the urge to draw her blaster and shoot him in the cod piece. "Please tell me that you're not going to insist that we watch all three of your vids. If so, take out your blaster, and shoot me through the flipping head, right here and now."

"I suggested to Baeven that we show them all back to back at the banquet tonight as part of the evening's entertainment. Each of the vids is slightly less than five standard hours long."

Naero could not breathe for a second or two and felt her own eyes widen out of control like starship viewscreens. "Five? Each of your vids is almost five hours long? How is that even possible?"

He shrugged. "What can I say? My people like long vids. They make a day of them. They even call it Vid Day. Ku like their entertainment."

"You're all lunatics, that's why. Haisha, it would take almost an entire day to watch them all. Wait…what did Baeven say?"

Danjen looked down and fidgeted with his hands. "Well, first he kind of cursed, I won't repeat his exact words. Then he actually kind of hit me and told me to get the hell away from him."

Naero brought her eyes down to slits and glared his way. "If I hit you, will you leave me alone, Danjen?"

He backed away cautiously around the meeting table. "Ugh, Baeven also said that he would rather sit on Yii and have it shoved all the way up him and out the top of his head before he would waste any more of his time watching another of my wildly sappy vids. But to be fair, he never has had any taste for high art."

"Nor do you. You actually got *Baeven* to sit through one of these five hour masterpieces?"

Danjen cleared his throat and looked nervously away. "Well, perhaps it was only the first quarter hour."

"Now that I can believe, fuzz boy. So what exactly are these vids called and what are they about? How could anyone make a five hour vid about anything, especially with nutball Ku actors?"

"Well, *Typhoon Night* depicts the comical story about two separate shipwrecks, and two unrelated sets of identical twins stranded on the shore of a rival nation. Hilarity ensues when the twins all become separated and ensnared in the machinations of a banished sorcerer, his supernatural agents, the local politics among the nobles, several confused love affairs, a pretentious servant, and an insulted court fool and her drunken allies, all more or less bent upon either romance, or side-splitting revenge."

Naero could only stare at him with her mouth open.

"Naturally, as a lead *thesipian*, I play one of the sets of twins, one of them female, or course, and old Sloom, the shit shoveler who is always trying to clean out the open outhouse slop pit that everyone keeps falling into. Some people don't even recognize me in that role. The makeup job was that good, N! Hee-hee, me as old Sloom on the sly. A classic."

Danjen just kept babbling. "*Dunkerballs the Twenty-Seventh* is an action packed historical adventure with me in the title role, of course, as the courageous Crown Prince of Kracklebutt, set in the pivotal nation of Humperland. My notorious, womanizing father, King Azuresack is dying, after having executed twenty-six of his fifty-two horny wives by poison bedchamber methane. All but the last three survivors he banished back to foreign lands to become bakers, lemur trainers, and codpiece makers.

"I don't have to tell you how things turn out. I rise to the occasion, save the realm, and after much daring do, end up with the three lovely princesses from the defeated enemy nations fighting it out in the mud to be my queen and bear the heir to my crown. He keeps the losers as concubines-"

"Why wouldn't he?"

"Exactly."

Lofty stuff let me tell you, N. The critics wept."

"I bet they did," Naero said. "And the third, Danjen? Please get this over with."

Borgfekka and Yummitips in As You Might Not Want it To Be, a rather long title, even I admit. Two teen nymphomaniacs pretty much screw each other half to death and muck up everything for everyone in this classic tragedy of love, lust, and wanton, gross stupidity and backwards ignorance. Two noble houses never seem to be able to get anything right, no one ever bathes, has a clue about modern hygiene, or safe medical practices. There is a great deal of useless swordplay, needless periodic death, and a virulent plague that almost kills everyone in a bad way, leaving them in puddles of their own explosive, bloody puss that melts the flesh off their writhing, shrieking skeletons. They try to cure the pestilence by casually bleeding each other.

"The young kids in the audience just eat all that gross stuff up, let me tell you. The sloppier the better. They love it. Of course, all of that is digital, as you might expect. They didn't really infect any of the actors with real biogen agents that would act like that."

"Sure. Practical. Good thinking."

"The star-crossed, titled young lovers perish, slowly bitching and complaining while waiting for the forbidden aphrodisiacs that they thought they had purchased for each other to kick in. The love potions turn out to be—you guessed it—lethal poisons mixed up by a drunken apothecary eunuch who didn't have any idea what he was doing. The dying young lovers stumble to the local cliffs in their fevered delirium and fall hand and hand into the sea, where they are promptly gobbled up by voracious costal water weasels."

Naero shot to her feet. "Get out, Danjen. I'm not going to watch any of your insipid vids. They sound really stupid, just rip offs of Old Terran plays by that Shakespeare guy."

"Preposterous. These are original masterpieces, written by the famous Chog Bekkul. They are unlike anything the galaxy has ever seen. The Ku have never heard of this other nobody that you mentioned. What has he done that could ever compare?"

"Yeah, right. So you just take your hairy ass, that sickening codpiece, and the rest of your loopy costume with you when you go. I don't want to hear any more about all of this crap."

"I'll have you know that I brought real life and fire to my role as Borgfekka! And my rutting sessions with the actress who played Yummitips have been widely acclaimed to be the very essence of lust and Ku romance, captured on a vid. We both ended up severely chafed, for the sake of our art!"

Naero came around the table at him, punching her fist into her open palm. "Uh-huh. I'm guessing your porn was probably better. Well start running, fuzz boy. The hitting is about to commence."

From his inspired yelping, Naero got a couple of good smacks in before Danjen got away from her by racing across the outer corridor ceiling. She stopped chasing him after a bit.

Naero hurried back to her quarters to cancel the showing of those vids at the banquet that night, before it was too late for everyone.

She chuckled to herself.

Danjen the Ku vid star. That goofball just didn't quit.

30

Once the highly advanced Glos were part of the Alliance, the other energy beings who helped save them from the enemy phage attacks became fast friends with them in short order.

Energy beings stuck together, especially during the present crisis. There was more safety in numbers.

Under the tutelage of the Spacer Mystics, Shalaen, and the other Cosmic sentients, the Glos quickly succeeded in transforming into their fully infused new energy being forms.

And as it turned out, the Glos soon evolved into amazing healers.

Once they shook off their xenophobia, within the sentient community of the Alliance of free species, they were eagerly welcomed as new members and valued comrades.

Glos culture and good will seemed to explode, pouring forth to share themselves and their many rich gifts with all of the other races in the Alliance who had an interest.

Naero went out of her way to cultivate a growing friendship with a powerful Glos healer called Lah-shubah.

Lah-shubah was a glip, one of the two Glos sexes. Her mate Zoop-vel was a trux, the other gender. But who could tell the difference? Only another Glos, apparently. Among them there did not seem to be any visible sign that marked them as male and female.

Without any outward, physical gentitalia, to anyone without biomancy all Glos looked the same to outsiders—shuffling, shambling human-sized globs and blobs of softly glowing and pulsating gelatinous material.

They were somewhat pear-shaped often, with a blobby head, and they could form appendages and pseudopodia as needed to manipulate their world.

They did have very expressive visual sensory organ patches of body material that resembled two eyes.

Glos consumed food and drink by absorbing it within their body mass and processing it like an amoeba. They did not normally seem to have a mouth or nose. Yet they could create a vocal opening and a voice box if needed to speak with other sentients. They claimed that they had a highly developed sense of smell and taste.

But they still preferred to converse telepathically.

Being gelatinous in nature, their moist bodies collected dust, dirt, and materials as they trundled and shuffled about on their base pseudopods. They actively dispelled waste pellets from their bodies automatically, without much thought to doing so. In their cultures, teams of Glos were always busy collecting these leavings and kept Glos cities clean.

When Glos were around the other Alliance races in non-Gloss areas, fixers had to be assigned to them to collect their odd leavings.

No one was sure whether Glos actually pooped or not, and Naero had no time to investigate Glos physiology any further.

She had no interest in potential Gloss turds either way.

Her Glos friend Lah-shubah fell completely in love with Naero's children upon meeting them, and they her, or it, or her glipness. However her gender could be described.

The Glos healer behaved in, what was to Spacers and other humans, a very motherly fashion.

Thus fair or unfair, Naero began thinking of her new glip friend as a "her" or "she."

To Naero's fearless offspring, the soft, somewhat transparent Glos was a being of new affection and wonder.

In fact, they quickly pushed Lah-shubah down, and to the delight and laughter of all, the Maeris and Williams brood used her for a trampoline and were bouncing in the air giggling.

It was one of the silliest sights Naero had seen in her life. Even poor Shetharra was laughing in her nearby medbed at the humorous sight.

Then Shetharra coughed weakly, and her dark sunken eyes fluttered from the effect of the continuing Cosmic plague.

The Glos healer immediately grasped all of the other laughing kids with a pseudopod and set them gently on their feet.

Faster than Naero would have thought possible, Lah-shubah quickly squeezed over to Shetharra's side and began to examine her within the child's protective, Ultrium containment and regeneration suit.

"How long has your child been like this?" the Glos healer asked.

"Months," Naero admitted.

If a Glos could be shocked, horrified, and still impressed at the same time, all of that washed over Lah-Shubah expressive countenance and the range of her deepest emotions.

"What inner strength she must have. I will do what I can. Yet tell me, what is this dark, outside malignant force that is so maniacally bent upon inflicting this horror on a mere child? Can such evil and depravity actually exist? It sickens me even to draw near to it, but for the child's sake, I must become infinitely acquainted with this terrible force at work. I can barely stand it. Does this wretched affliction bear a name?"

Naero drew in a breath. "It is called Nahaxrathrax, The Dark Emperor. He is a massive, fully grown Dark King Dakkur, almost two kilometers in length. He wields Mystic, Cosmic, and Darkforce powers that are still beyond our ken, one of which is to inflict pain, suffering, and deadly illness upon my firstborn from afar. As yet, we have found no way to stop it."

"From how far away?" the Glos asked.

"From at least a galactic quadrant away or more; SpaceTime seems not to matter to this fell devil. He lurks behind the enemy's defenses, one of their mightiest leaders. No matter how we seek him out to hunt him down and destroy him, he manages to hide from us and elude our attempts with ease."

Lah-shubah examined the child, crying out in pain as if merely touching Shetharra caused the Glos healer immense agony.

Naero sensed that the Glos was an empath healer, and experienced everything that her patient did.

Then the Glos grew angry, and pulsed with a bright light in her energy being form. "It is difficult for me to comprehend the unmitigated evil of this abomination. To do this thing to a child such as this little one? There are no curses in all the universe for such a vile and horrific act. And what a miracle this babe is already. She has all the power and promise of both her parents, and one day it shall blaze a thousand fold for all to see—if she only survives this horrific ordeal."

The healer leaned over to Naero and Khai. "One day she will shatter such abominations beneath her heel and blast them to oblivion with the pure fire that blazes within her. But we must do all that we can to save her now. The next few months shall be crucial."

Taking Shetharra in her arms, Lah-shubah slowly absorbed the small glowing child within herself.

Immediately the Glos was illuminated from within and became nearly transparent, like liquid, flowing crystal.

Naero panicked slightly. "What are you doing? Can she still breathe?"

Lah-shubah smiled. "If this thing you have named cannot defeat her force of will, then nothing that I can do will ever harm her. We are friends, Naero and mate Khai. Trust me. Read my heart and mind; they are open to you. See? She is as safe within me as if she were my own. Now watch as I do all that I can to help her. There is no small risk to myself, but I will not stand by and allow this or any child to be so afflicted!"

Naero felt Khai's large arms suddenly about her as they both looked on.

A struggle began within the Glos.

Lah-shubah went at the Cosmic sickness attacking Shetharra and fought with it directly. Something like dark mist, smoke, or fluid poured out of Shetharra. The Glos healer was drawing it out and concentrating it into a ball or sphere.

The Glos healer suffered greatly for the attempt. She drew the Darkforce corruption out of the child as if it were some kind of actual poison.

As Shetharra's light and strength grew, Lah-Shubah seemed to suffer more and grow weaker.

Finally the healer released Shetharra, slipping the child back into her medbed, the small Spacer girl blazing now with an impossibly bright light.

Yet she bore a gelatinous orb, holding it with both hands upon her breast. Within that orb was all of the malignant enemy poison and sickness that Lah-Shubah had been able to expel.

The Glos healer could barely maintain its form, so spent and weak was she thereafter. She could no longer speak, but through a feeble link of telepathy.

Naero, I have done all that I can. She will be better for a time. I have drawn out all of the malignancy that I can. But alas, I cannot break the dark link that has been established. Only in that way can she be saved. Within months, unfortunately she will grow much worse, and you must fight for her then as her parent. I will try to show you how. For now I must rest for a few days in order to recover my strength.

"Thank you so much, my friend. What shall we do with the evil poison you drew out of my girl?"

Get rid of it. Cast it into the nearest star and destroy it. You or your husband must see to this. Few others would be strong enough to resist it. If unleashed, it could spread from star system to star system on its own vile force of will, wiping out all life. Whatever it touches would die.

Naero placed her hands on their new friend. "Calm yourself, mighty Lah-shubah of the Glos. You are spent. Thank you from our hearts for what you have done for our child."

I would do the same for any child in such need.

"You shall have your rest."

The Glos could no longer move. She had to be folded up, carried away on another medbed, and placed in an adjacent recovery room.

Naero telepathically sent instructions to Khai.

The Cosmic Enforcer carefully took the sphere of concentrated Cosmic poison from the small hands of his first born without hesitation.

Even he, with his great strength, struggled with the heavy mass and power of the densely packed, virulent orb of negative force.

Khai gritted his teeth and transported out to the nearest star to complete his mission.

Naero tracked his efforts until the vile stuff was annihilated.

At last, peace eased her mind.

Shetharra seemed much improved by that time, and smiled and sat up in bed. They even spoke together, waiting for Khai to return.

Naero examined her little duck.

She quietly vowed to herself to fight for her oldest daughter, her children, and her people with the very last of her strength.

*

Naero continued to experiment with the Kexxian Songs of Making within the KDM.

Sometimes she and Shetharra would go there together. They were now up to the Fifth Song of Making, and that had been hard going as it was. Progression with learning the songs and actually accomplishing something with them were two entirely different things.

Naero really only felt confident in using the first three songs. All of the rest were still on a steep learning curve.

And naturally, learning to use the next song in order was far more difficult to master than the one before.

With Shetharra feeling better after her treatment with the Glos healer Lah-shubah, the young girl seemed both happy and content to sing and play inside the KDM during such visits. She liked the data oceans of Kexxian music knowledge and never asked to ever go anywhere else.

Shetharra had a mystical gift to float on the very waves of the music. Even Orean could not do that.

And another strange thing that Naero noticed. Within the KDM, Shetharra was not forced to choose a Kexxian or other form in order to exist there.

She remained herself in every way.

Naero at first had thought that her little duck would take on a Kexxian form as she had needed to in order to interact closely with the KDM.

Yet this was not so.

Shetharra remained Shetharra, who and what she was. She did not need to take on a young Kexxian counterpart to herself called Arrahtehs. That did not seem to be required of her in that unique place.

But then, Shetharra was unique in many ways that continued to unfold and defy all reality.

Naero had hoped to interact with her daughters special little glowing lizard friends, as Shetharra called them. They appeared to the child of light as Kexxian children and playmates. Her mother found that quite fitting, as well as awe inspiring, that such powerful beings would be so naturally drawn to her oldest child and seek to counsel, guide, and help her in her time of great need.

They knew full well the dark forces the child endured against.

Her uncle Baeven had also dealt with the shades of the spiritminds of the mighty Seven Kexxian Dreamers where they kept close watch over the highly dangerous G'lothc seas of knowledge. There they did not take the forms of little children, but of the great and terrible guardians that they actually were—champions of freedom who had never known defeat.

Naero longed to speak with them about many important things, but for some reason, they showed no interest in her and made no effort to contact her directly in any way.

Even when it seemed that her daughter laughed and played with these great beings, and whispered and giggled to them as young children did with their imaginary friends, Naero could sense nothing of them.

She could not see or touch them, hear them, or sense anything about them.

Perhaps the time was not yet right. She struggled to accept that and kept working at learning all twenty-one of the Kexxian Songs of Making. She took that on as part of her sacred mission.

There was an indirect benefit to having Shetharra with her.

Every now and again, her daughter would suddenly tug at her mother's hand and tell her to do something in another way. She would smile and say something like, "My little glowing lizard friends say that you're not doing it properly. The LGLFs say that you should try it more like this."

Then Shetharra would sing a slightly different version of the working tune or sometimes even the pronunciation of the actual lyrics. At other times it was case of inflection or sheer nuance.

Naero looked forward to even these slight hints, giving her insights and possibilities that she might not have discovered on her own.

With the First Song of Making she could produce a small pebble of Ultrium. With the second she could produce a long hair of it, and then a filament or wire. She finally used the Third Song of making to create at first a thin, transparent sheet of Ultrium and then a sheet or plate of the same material.

After that, she shaped that plate with the sheer imagination of her own mind. She could form it into a rectangle, a circle, oval, and then into various 3D fractal and origami forms.

Songs four and five had yet to produce anything, but she did not give up. She kept stumbling forward and learning.

Naero brought Baeven and Janner in with her thereafter, and they tried learning the songs. Jan had some initial success, but the overall process seemed very difficult for him and especially Baeven. She guessed that her uncle was more attuned to Chaos and destruction rather than Creation. The Songs of Making were all about Creation and forming something out of what appeared to be nothing.

She tried the other Alliance Champions and even some of the energy beings and Mystics that she could trust here and there. None of them seemed to have much more of a talent for it than she did.

She did not lose heart.

Naero and her oldest daughter continued their sessions, as often as they could manage the time to do so.

31

Once more Naero and her intrepid strike force moved on to yet another senseless interstellar conflict, this time between a humanoid race called the Dabuki, with their boney, armored heads, and the Nodani, pale and blind near humans who lived without light in what to many beings would be almost absolute darkness.

Both sides had just been recently possessed by the enemy mind control wraiths and pitted against each other.

Yet even as Naero began to work among them, she observed something odd.

The Nodani were in fact energy beings, operating in the darker frequencies of nonlight, as others might see it.

Not only that, but the Nodani detected the presence of the mind control wraiths on their own. Within a matter of days they could not only detect the presence of the wraiths, but also use never-before-encountered dark energy levels of Cosmic force to drive them out and actually destroy them.

The Nodani destroyed these invading aliens with dark spectrum energies at levels and in combinations that had never been encountered before.

Then they went to great pains to reveal these facts to the Dabuki and even help rid their former enemies of the invader possession as well.

The Nodani wore special dark suits to keep from being exposed to any kind of light, which was very harmful to them.

For once Naero came along and operated mostly in a first contact and supportive role for both sentient races, who for the most part had ended the threat of war among them and made peace readily with each other to fight the common foe together.

Naero was fascinated by both races and their intricate cultures. It was a pleasure to relish shapechanging into both species at her leisure, to learn their languages and their ways.

The Dabuki were actually covered in a boney carapace that was essentially armor—a humanoid exoskeleton of bone and tough sinew. The protection was especially thick about the torso, neck, and head. No two carapace patterns were the same, but there were what was called family similarities.

Male and female Dabuki were so devoted to their mates that they actually lived in bliss with each other for six standard decades without any desire to have children. They only became fertile, bore, and raised offspring during the last three decades of their lives before passing on.

Their science and medicine was so advanced that they had little illness among their systems.

Barring accident, violence, or war, almost all Dabuki lived approximately ninety standard years and then died some time during their last year. Knowing that much gave them the surety to live their lives and then set their affairs in order before death claimed them.

Death was something expected and even celebrated by their species.

The Nodani were even more fascinating.

They were energy beings for whom darkness was like bright light to them.

Intense light was harmful and even deadly to this species. They had all of the other humanoid senses, and were also psyonic. They could wield Cosmic energy and even a form of dark Cosmic energy that was not tainted by the Darkforce's destructive, anti-life components.

Their energy forms were comprised of Dark Cosmic matter and energy. They could also operate in a hidden dimension of only two dimensional shapes and forms, like flat shadows without volume or depth.

How very unique and strange.

Exposed to light, their bodies literally melted and broke down quickly, looking pale, colorless, milky eyes—like Old Terran life forms that had evolved underground without light. The Dabuki had actually used weapons against the Nodani that tore them open and exposed them to light.

But to each other, the Nodani were incredibly beautiful, lit from within with faint shades and colors that only they could see or detect. In fact, they were bio-luminescent animals, shining from within at frequencies and ranges of dark light that most other sentients could never experience.

Naero felt honored and privileged to exist among them on their rarified level. The experience was unlike anything she had ever known.

More importantly, they revealed to her levels of existence that she had not thought possible. It was in one of these spectral dimensions that they had discovered the mind control wraiths among their kind, and devised how to expose and defeat them.

This unique ability could be taught to the other energy being races and help them greatly in the course of the war in the extradimensional and Interdimensional regions.

The Nodani parts of the universe were a miracle in countless ways that Naero could never completely imagine or comprehend.

With the Dabuki/Nodani war ended and the situation wrapped up quicker than anyone could have thought, Naero finally had time for her own stuff. More Cosmic enlightenment, Songs of Making, and mind expansion on different levels of her own.

She and some of the Alliance Champions use a modified enemy wyrmhole projector to reproduce the conditions at work on board the captured enemy ship, but with further safe guards, and a clear way back. She returned to the same Darkforce energy depot and searched for other enemy Darkforce pocket dimensions similar to it.

Somewhere, in one of these places, their enemies were lurking.

Naero did her best to mask their presence and not attract attention.

The Alliance exploration teams brought along groups from the other Alliance energy beings, including the Nodani. The idea was to examine these areas from every possible perspective.

First they continued to explore the one that Naero and Om and originally been sucked into.

Then one day, there was no trace of that place that still existed. They could not return to it.

There was nothing to go back to.

Om proposed one plausible explanation. *The enemy must have somehow sensed that their secret had been discovered and then took steps to eradicate it.*

Shalaen and the Yattai searched in the adjacent Interdimensions all about that region. They came back empty handed, and with their final report.

"Something was definitely there once," Shalaen noted. "But we could only detect traces of large quantities of residual Darkforce energy."

"It was definitely some kind of Darkforce energy depot," Khai said. "Yet all evidence shows that it is completely gone now."

Jan, Tyber, and Jia kept their attentions fixed on their special Cosmic attuned instruments, continually using teknomancy to adjust them more and to scan the Interdimensions.

"Can our foes produce these reservoirs of power at will?" Jan asked.

Naero shook her head. "I don't think so, but we really don't know that much about them yet. Creating one would not be very easy, but I suppose they could also reverse the process if they needed to. If something can be made, it can be unmade. Om and I had the sense that the enemy probably has several of these depots out there, in this quadrant alone for them to draw from. It wouldn't make any sense to have just one. That would make them too vulnerable."

Khai frowned. "That would also explain why they have such huge energy reserves at their command for their fleets and Elazethrek."

"Don't forget the Dark Emperor," Jia noted. "That repugnant monster needs huge quantities of power and energy to sustain itself and execute its attacks."

"Like the ongoing attack on my oldest daughter," Naero said.

"Could they have moved this one?" Tyber said. "Could they have just shuffled it to another location?

Shalaen jumped in. "No. If they had moved it, many of us would probably be capable of detecting and tracing that much Darkforce energy being moved around from one place to another."

"All of you are looking at this completely wrong," Baeven told them. "The very nature of all Interdimensional and extradimensional spaces makes them almost impossible to trace or locate, unless you already know exactly where they are. You could search the entire galaxy, the universe, and never stumble upon one. Yet once one opens up, and you go there, you will always know where it is fixed within the folds and layers of the SpaceTime spheres thereafter."

Naero nodded. "The enemy dismantled their depot the same way it was constructed, by the force of will and higher thought alone. They made it into being, and then they unmade it."

Tyber re-calibrated some of his Ultrium sensors and instruments. "There seem to be energy traces streaming off in many directions at once," he noted. "My guess is they siphoned off the Darkforce power they had stored there to other such depots, and then dismantled the pocket dimension itself. There's not very much left to go on."

Baeven still seemed dissatisfied. "If the enemy can use such energy depots to fuel their efforts," he noted, "why can't we?"

Naero smiled sadly and shook her head. "For one thing, most of us don't or can't use the Darkforce. Alas, our ancient foes remain more advanced than us, uncle. The Kexx were the true masters of such arts, and we are only a few days into discovering that such places and capabilities even exist. To create such things even on par with our foes will require many long years of study, learning, enlightenment, and practice.

"Like the Kexxians, we would need Dreamers who fully understand the powers of pure thought and energy matter creation. Even after studying the KDM for a long while, my own level of comprehension of these concepts is akin to that of a child. We're only just able to manipulate Ultrium at the most basic levels."

"All things must begin at some place and go forward from there," Jia declared. "We have the Alliance of Energy Beings; we have the Dimensional Council; and we have the Spacer Mystics and the fledgling Academy of Sentients. You, me, and several others among the Alliance Champions have access to the KDM. This all needs to be expanded and coordinated. We must begin to develop and train our next generation of Dreamers now."

"I agree," Naero said. "But while we're fighting a bitter war? When the simple appearance of another of the Six like Elazethrek would spell the death of us all and the total ruin of the Alliance? First we must survive in order to raise and train our Dreamers."

"Jia is right," Shalaen said. "We must somehow develop to the point where we can do both. Naero is also right. We must survive, carry the fight to the enemy, and find a way to defeat them. But we must also look to our future as well. You, Naero, are by far the closest thing we have to a Kexxian Dreamer. You must be the first."

Naero laughed. "If you only knew what a poor, unworthy specimen I would be, compared to real Kexxian Dreamers. Compared to them and their majesty and glory—all that they could do. Why, I am a wyrm flipping around in the mud by comparison."

Lah-shubah floated up to Naero, and placed a tendril lightly around her. "You forget your oldest child, friend Naero—she who will already surpass you and your mate a thousand fold or more one day. You do not know it. She does not know it as yet, but she is the first of many. And she is already, what you call, a Dreamer, in every potential way that there can possibly be.

"Therefore, it is for you and for all of the future Dreamers that you must struggle. You must fumble about blindly, and stumble, and crawl, and continue to scratch out your poor degree of enlightenment. Whatever knowledge and understanding you grasp, you must pass it on to your children and to all of the Dreamers yet to come, so that it may bear greater fruit among them. What is impossible for you now shall one day be child's play for them. Your oldest child may yet live to see that day, and stand as among the mightiest of them, and so might you as the first."

They were all silent for a time while everyone pondered the Glos's words.

With the weird enemy pocket dimension gone, Naero proposed that they explore the Dimensional Nexus and SpaceTime magnitudes and levels, so that she and Baeven might be able to make more contact with their alternate selves and continue to grow in strength and power.

They might also detect or stumble onto other discoveries.

After that, Naero would lead more and more of them into the KDM as their guide, and continue to fumble about like the blind and learn whatever they could. But she had to screen and trust anyone she brought into the fold.

They would do all of these things and more, for the sake of the future, and for all sentient generations to come.

32

The only breakthroughs they managed were in the areas of energy beings and the Interdimensions. With more energy beings contributing to the Alliance efforts than ever before, and the new Nodani techniques for repulsing and destroying the mind control wraiths and the phage outright, another major campaign was being organized.

This time, the Alliance would surely take back much of the territory they had surrendered to the Great Adversary.

But in order to do that, first they would strike where the enemy thought it was safe, and free countless energy beings that had been captured and enslaved in multitudes of enemy Darkforce generation farms and collector station prisons.

It was hoped that they would also discover more of the enemy Darkforce energy depots and perhaps devise a way to either jam them or shut them down. If they could accomplish any of that, it might cripple the enemy war effort.

Yet as in any military venture, there was always risk.

The Alliance Champions, backed up by even more energy beings, stood poised and ready to face down Elazethrek and even the Dark Emperor if they were forced to. They also had new strategies, forms of attack, and various Cosmic techniques and weapons that they wanted to try out.

On other fronts in the Gamma Quadrant, at least the enemy no longer had new waves of advanced fleets to hurl at them, almost without limit. With their hidden shipyards in ruins, it would be quite a while before those levels of high production would be restored.

The skill and tenacity of the Alliance fleets continued to slow the enemy advance and turn the tide once again.

It was no longer a game of sheer numbers.

The new energy beings also flooded the Alliance ranks. Together with Tyber's new Darkforce detection devices, they had succeeded in locating three major hidden locations where multitudes of enslaved energy beings were pouring great quantities of tainted, Darkforce power into what they surmised to be the enemy energy holding depots.

Yet they still could not locate the actual energy depot dimensions that the Darkforce generators gushed their corrupted powers into. That was very strange. But Baeven had guessed that it might be so.

Naero thought for certain that they would be able to find them as well.

Still, millions of energy beings waited for rescue, helpless, trapped, and tormented within gigantic production facilities on a horrific scale.

That all needed to end.

Even as the strike forces spread out to begin their coordinated assaults, the enemy was at that very moment in the process of ravaging a newly discovered race of energy beings, the Prill.

Half of the Prill were being enslaved and planted inside of generators as hosts. The other half were fighting a losing battle of attrition and slaughter against clouds and clouds of wraiths and phage strains, each more voracious and deadly than the other.

Naero, Baeven, and Janner directed the three part attack from fleets of the newest modified Alliance dreadnaughts and frontline Ultrium battleships racing into the Interdimensions at full attack speed.

Naero drew her energy cutlass and gave the final word to all ships.

"All fleets. Put fire on them! Cut the enemy defenses down in short order. Devastate all enemy forces with extreme prejudice. Give no quarter or mercy to them on this or any other day. Death and annihilation to our foes! They never hesitate to do the same things to us.

"Liberation waves, coordinate your rescue assaults. Bust up and destroy the largest pockets of generators. The Alliance Champions shall deal with the most powerful Darkforce generator meks and titans. Coordinate all fleet firepower against the enemy strong points and alert us as to their type, output, and location. We shall fall upon them in short order."

In reality, the energy being assault waves could handle even the most powerful of the enemy constructs.

The champions wanted to lure out Elazethrek, if possible, and destroy the Beast. They were poised and ready.

Let the Dark Emperor show his horrid visage this time.

They had a few surprises prepared for him, as well.

By then the initial attacks were proceeding very well. There were a few enemy surprises. That was to also to be expected. The Alliance adapted quickly and decisively.

Time and time again, free sentients always fought with a valor and ferocity that mindless slaves and witless bootlickers could never hope to match.

But when Elazethrek and Nahaxrathrax did make their presence known, they held fast to their strategy of avoidance. They would still take no chance at allowing either of them to become trapped in one place and possibly destroyed.

They would make a devastating attack on Alliance forces in one strategic location, and then flee before the Alliance Champions could come against them in force.

The most Naero ever saw of either one was a fleeting glimpse as they vanished, transporting through ready wyrmholes, after leaving death and destruction in their wake.

But the Alliance responded as well.

Whenever either of the enemy monsters appeared, Alliance forces took the most defensive measures possible or fled outright from that part of the battle. They knew very well that the foe was using hit-and-run tactics, and did their best to limit the damage that those fell beings could commit.

Yet many Alliance forces who were surprised and could not escape such surprise attacks still paid a heavy price for being in the wrong place at the wrong time.

In the long term, experts predicted that it was quite possible for the enemy strategy to still succeed. By avoiding the Alliance Champions in direct combat, the enemy was free to destroy the Alliance forces bit by little bit over time.

Death and defeat by a multitude of lesser wounds and disasters.

Tyber and the energy being Alliance struggled to discover a way to consistently detect and predict where either monster might strike next. And also to locate and hunt them down wherever they chose to hide.

If they could even destroy one of the two beings, that might tip the odds in the Alliance favor and spell victory, at least for the present.

The captive energy beings were being rescued and set free by the thousands each second.

Naero concentrated the vast firepower of her fleets against the clouds of wraiths and phage being held at bay by the fixer nebulae, blasting the enemy to dust as they were still confused and reeling.

"Wipe them out. Increase fire from all main batteries and secondary batteries. Bring up the reserves on other vectors. Pour it at the foe until none remain. The Interdimensions are free this day! No longer shall the energy being races be butchered and enslaved. Fight on for freedom!"

Elazethrek attacked a key Alliance strongpoint and lingered there a little too long.

The Alliance Champions were quick to close in on her. Immediately they employed their new attempts to entrap and drain her of her energies.

Then Naero and Om used one of Ty's new scanners to detect at last where she was drawing her great quantities of energy from.

They detected and marked not one, but three Darkforce power depots that the Creature was attached to. There could even be more, but there was no time to search for them.

The enemy monster lashed out in several directions, destroying more Alliance warships and smashing into several champions with a ferocity designed to hurl them back and allow the fiend to make good her escape once again.

Yet even as its wyrmhole formed, Naero and Jan summoned a Cosmic energy construct superweapon, a Remo mek gun platform controlled by Tarim.

He fired its blinding violet beam of raw Chaos and Order energy to disrupt the wyrmhole and disrupt any others for a short while.

In that instant of opportunity, Baeven and all of the other Champions fell upon Elazethrek together and almost took her out.

But the wyrmhole exploded violently, not unlike a small super nova of clashing Cosmic forces. This was a freak detonation of those unstable forces, not a normal implosion as was usually expected.

Friend and foe were scattered, wounded, and stunned by the intense blast.

And in the resulting Chaos, the Creature made good its escape yet again, all by dumb chance.

Yet Naero detected a short term, unstable rift that would only last for a few more seconds. It might possibly take her to one or more of the enemy energy depots where she could send signals back to her friends.

Perhaps they could even trace Elazethrek from there and put her down.

Without hesitation, and ignoring Om's warnings, she transport through the rift—a rent in SpaceTime itself, to see where she would end up among the spheres and folds of potential reality.

Her first impressions were that she wasn't in any of the Darkforce power depots.

It felt more like yet another version of the Galactic Nexus. Dimensional possibilities surrounded her in what seemed to be a universe of vast, energized bubbles of potential reality. Millions upon multiple countless millions of them swelled up and burst all around her in chain reaction after chain reaction.

In some of these potential realities Naero even glimpsed herself. She succeeded, she failed, she lived, and she even died. She witnessed every variation that could be imagined.

It was all incredibly disorienting. Not only that, but the highly unstable, exploding energies threatened to destroy her and mix her energies with their own.

Naero cried out and suddenly felt as if she rose above that wall of bursting and erupting potentials.

Where was she?

It still felt like part of the Nexus, but she looked down upon what could only be her own galaxy, as if from one single vantage point impossibly far above and distant. Her mind and her energy form had expanded nearly beyond her capacity for comprehension.

She was in danger of losing herself forever.

Om stayed speechless and could only mutter unintelligible gibberish.

The sheer scale of things from this vector. The distances she moved within were no longer interstellar, but now intergalactic.

If she had still had breath, she would have been completely robbed of it.

This was a new energy being form for her and a totally new paradigm and frame of reference.

Her enhanced senses focused somewhat more and she made out their nearest galactic neighbor. This was the ruined galaxy that the G'lothc had nearly drained of all life.

This was the place where the great foe had fled and finally been utterly crushed and obliterated during the Great War, millions of years before.

As it turned out, a ruined galaxy was a horrific thing to take in. The terrible scars torn across it by the astonishing weapons of the gods of old were still all too clear to see.

Unimaginable death and destruction had been meted out on a galactic scale.

But the mighty G'lothc had been hunted down for millennia, chased and blasted out of seven galaxies in all, and finally brought to bay there.

There the Drians and most of the Kexxian Dreamers met them in all of their destructive fury of miracle weapons for the last decisive battles.

Now, with their once fierce and terrible bodies long gone, the vile G'lothc souls had survived only on hate and force of will, and sought to come back inside of stolen host bodies to ravage the universe yet again.

Naero could still see and sense it all too readily, with her new expanded enlightenment. Even now, half of the G'lothc galaxy remained devoid of all existence, never able to support any form of life ever again.

She tried to comprehend something akin to that in her own galaxy.

How could she imagine two of their four quadrants, empty of all chance or hope of the Lifespark?

Forever Dead.

Bleak. Stark.

Forever empty.

Not even any stars or star furnaces.

Eternal Death and Nothingness.

In a sense, the G'lothc had gotten half of their epic, malignant wish.

Nothing more than a token victory in their great and ignoble defeat.

They had succeeded in killing half of one entire galaxy off forever—their own. A small taste of the Unlife they wished to spread throughout the universe as the dark gift of their destroying disease.

The death and obliteration of all possibilities.

Then from this new vector, her new vantage point, Naero felt dim connections far down below her.

The first things she somewhat pinpointed in general were her children, foremost in her deepest thoughts. She easily located first Shetharra, and then the others. Then she noted Khai, Baeven, Janner, and all of her family and friends thereafter.

If she wished, she could concentrate and transport directly to them from the magnitude of this vantage point.

But by doing so, she would also give up this new perspective, and from this level within the Cosmic spheres and folds, she was filled with stars and SpaceTime, and felt as if her energy form body was almost as big as a her galaxy itself.

For once she felt akin to the vast potential and hidden Cosmic energies within her. And here she existed at one and at peace with all that she was, and all that she could ever be.

She was nearly expansive enough to contain it all.

Her fear was that once she left this unique paradigm, one that she had only stumbled upon in ignorance, she might never be able to return to it.

Yet she could not stay in this mode of existence. She was needed so badly back with her people. She was a vital part of that reality.

How strange that they all seemed to move upon what to her looked like an incredibly, complex strategy board, very much like the Alliance tactical combat screens during a large battle.

Yet this tactical array dwarfed anything the Alliance had by several orders of magnitude and complexity.

More and more she felt herself drawn back to her own reality with its own limited vectors and perspectives.

Naero struggled to remain where she was, to see what she could see.

She sensed the enemy energy depots.

Haisha! There were not dozens, but hundreds of them.

No, it could not be, in the neighboring broken galaxy, the wasteland of their foes...

Curse the day. It was no myth.

The impossibly vast enemy Armada did most surely await there, lurking like a predatory abomination comprised of countless hordes of enemy fleets, sleeping and slumbering in frozen readiness. They awaited only the signal to awake, pour through, and attack.

They only needed a path to be opened for them.

How would the Alliance ever be able to stand against such astonishing numbers? What was the enemy waiting for?

Just open the floodgates and overwhelm all resistance in a tidal wave of Ultrium warship destruction.

Then Naero sensed them. She roughly located the Great Adversary. Even with their many attempts to obscure their presences and avoid detection, she located The Dark Emperor, and the slightly lesser signature of Elazethrek, forever gorging herself on Cosmic power to maintain its monstrous existence.

It terrified Naero that these two devils that they knew were also working with what might be one or two more other bizarre and hitherto unencountered beings or monsters who were in other ways, just as strong, if not even stronger than the two of them.

What and who were these new potential threats? At present, Naero could not even begin to make them out.

Yet their actions and intentions were all very clear.

The Dark Emperor remained bent almost solely on destroying Shetharra, and, in truth, he was secretly terrified at how the child of light resisted and defeated him with each passing day.

Naero smile at perceiving his frustration. But she also saw that however long the contest took, in the end, Shetharra on her own would eventually succumb and die.

That could not be allowed to stand.

Naero tore her concentration away to see what the other demons were devising in their little pocket hells.

Everything else was but a distraction, a decoy, and a smoke screen.

Almost all of the enemy efforts and the vast bulk of their energies were bent entirely upon re-creating the other five G'lothc Dark Champions.

But even for them, that was a tall order. It had taken them more than four standard decades of ceaseless trying alone to bring Elazethrek back to life in her current form, with the vessel she now possessed.

Each of the Six was stronger than the other by a factor of at least ten. That made six orders of magnitude of Darkforce energy evil.

That was why Elazethrek was often referred to as the Least of the Six. Each was by far greater and more of a threat than the one before.

Naero could barely imagine trying to fight the next abomination in line after Elazethrek. That meant that Asheddethron, the Deceiver would be ten times as powerful as the Creature.

Fortunately, for all intents and purposes, the enemy efforts to re-create the next monstrosity and find it a suitable vessel to sustain its malice still seemed many decades away by comparison.

It appeared that for all of their vast knowledge, there were some things that were still nearly impossible for the G'lothc to achieve.

Yet for how long?

Eventually they might succeed, or even have a breakthrough that would spell disaster for their foes.

How was it that the enemy was so wise and powerful to attempt such advanced things and yet still not possess the power to achieve them?

By reason and logic, there should be equal sources of wisdom and power that she and the Alliance should be able to call upon.

True. They had the KDM, but they were still many years away from fully comprehending its immense mysteries. And even if they did start today, would they ever have Dreamers who could truly stand against the Six, should they all be somehow reborn?

For once Naero's indomitable spirit and her own belief began to falter and fail her.

How could they possible win?

Naero cried out to the universe itself in her current paradigm.

Help! I need help. Haisha! The forces arrayed against us are too great and too powerful. Help me! I don't want to watch as all that I love is murdered and destroyed before my eyes. This isn't fair. We are fighters! At least give us a chance to truly battle against these vast powers that are arrayed against us!

Voices, like her own, seemed to suddenly rain down upon her like pelting hail.

Believe in yourself.
Have faith.
Find within you and others the power you seek.
Do not give in to despair.
We are like you.
We stand with you.
Reach out to us.
We will answer you, in your time of need.
You are with us. We are with you, always.
Remember the words of the Ancient Obelisk.
You and the other must come into your own.
Find the last Obelisk and fulfill your destinies.
The Second Sword must be forged.
The Cosmic Prophecies shall be fulfilled.
Life and Death hang in the balance.
The Great Destroyer is coming.
Never forget that.
You and the others must make ready!

Then Naero felt them, even as she was drawn back into her own reality and her own existence.

They were all of the other possible Naeros in all of the other possible dimensions, universes, and existences.

She felt them around her as if in phantom layers, until they and their energies became as dense as Cosmic metal. Together they were the ancient Ur-metal obelisk itself, with all of their potentials, energies, and the powers of their possibilities combined.

Invincible.

Indestructible.

No force in all the universes ever conceived of could harm them in the end, except for the Great Destroyer of the Cosmic Prophecies.

All of this awareness battered Naero, even as she reduced back down to her own size and scale at a dizzying rate.

Remember, you are the Cosmic Champion of Enlightened Change. You must always find a way to prevail. You cannot despair. Keep striving. Never stop fighting.

I will. I swear it, upon the lives of my children!

She heard another voice, fainter this time.

I am the first. The next possible you closest to you. Remember and call upon me. Link up with me. Together we shall become twice as strong, twice as fast, and twice as powerful. And through our shared powers and abilities, we shall continue to join with all the others and forge our chain of power. Remember me!

When Naero came to, Khai and Baeven had only just located her floating among the wreckage of the battle.

Khai enfolded her in his arms.

"She's here. We found her. She's all right," Baeven relayed to the others.

Naero smiled up at Khai and touched his face.

She felt her lover's strong hands upon her, holding, comforting, and protecting her.

For some reason she thought of their oldest daughter.

In her mind, she thought she could now see a vantage point, a vector from which she could stand and fight for her child's life.

Yet doing so would be very risky, and she was the only one who could even hope to pull it off.

"I am back," she whispered to Khai. "And once more, I have much to tell you all."

33

For the next few weeks after the Alliance victories in the Interdimensions, Alliance forces did their best to consolidate their gains and advance forward.

Naero and the champions always kept busy.

They helped cultivate potential Mystics and Dreamers from every sentient race, whether they were energy beings or not.

Naero herself struggled to define just what Cosmic Dreamers had been among the Kexx, and what they would be now and should be going forth into the future among the known sentient races. What did they stand for? Which values should they focus on? What abilities should they strive for? What would their abilities actually be?

In truth, no one had any answers. Everything was so new to hundreds of thousands of adepts trying to expand their minds and abilities and achieve new levels of knowledge, existence, and enlightenment.

At first all was confusion and Babel.

Progress seemed glacial at best.

Yet the war and the Great Adversary clearly would not wait for them. And the enemy's own master plans and plots continued to grind on, sure to destroy them all.

Naero did find the strange Nexus once again and took Baeven there.

Yet it was not a true nexus at all.

Within minutes, Naero linked briefly with several of her other selves from other dimensions.

Baeven barely linked with one, and they argued, struggled, and even fought.

By sheer chance that other Baeven proved to be quite insane, a real ass wipe.

Her uncle cut off the link and sealed it behind him.

Naero tried to detect the enemy power depots and locate some of them, or the enemy leaders, but this time the entire phantom zone seemed disturbed and hazy, like a still pool that had been stirred up too much and made opaque and muddy.

They couldn't detect a thing, in any direction.

On their way back they took time to study the nearby realm of bubbles of possibility.

There they observed dozens of potential tangents and made several important observations and discoveries to pique their interest.

Most of the bubbles were ephemeral and obviously extremely temporary.

Yet some were permanent to some degree or lasted for a short time before splitting and fragmenting into yet other spheres and bubbles. Fragments of alternate realities or even entire dimensions where things were all very different.

They found many fragments where one or both of them did not exist at all.

In some they were other sexes. Naero was male and Baeven was female. What a hoot.

In others, they were completely different species. That was all jolly fun.

I one in particular version, Naero and Baeven stared at each other, sensing right away that something was definitely amiss.

They both became aware at the same time as they entered that possibility to look around.

They were no longer Spacers with all of their advanced abilities.

Here in this possibility, they were now mere humans.

Just plain, ordinary humans.

Scary.

Naero stared at her hands. Baeven felt his own body as if he were sick.

"Let's get out of this place while we can," her uncle muttered.

"I'm with you. I don't like it here." She was never going back there again, if she could help it.

The countless bubble realities existed by the countless billions. Who knew how many there were? Perhaps there was no way to tally them all.

It would be all too easy to become lost among them.

They emerged and swelled up again into the size and scope of beings filled with a mass of SpaceTime equal in volume to a quarter of a galaxy or more.

Baeven remained curious. "N, How far can our consciousness expand until we can no longer think, reason, perceive things, or still be ourselves?"

Naero blinked. "I don't know if I want to test that. There might not be any limit. Or we might never come back together as ourselves again if we tried. You've only been here once. I've only been here twice. Do we really want to risk that today?"

"I suppose not."

"We need to call this place something. It's definitely not the Nexus we know of, but it is something similar in some ways. The Phantom Zone just isn't right. How shall we refer to it when we bring others here to study it?"

Baeven thought for a moment. "How about: 'The Expanse.' That would seem to fit."

"Perfect. I love it!"

Something moving very fast out of the aether haze suddenly smashed into them.

They were startled more than injured, but even in their Expanse spiritmind forms, there was pain.

"We're under attack!" Baeven shouted.

Naero caught the signature instantly. "It's Elazethrek. She's sensed our presence in this place. Here she comes again, from another direction."

Both of them struggled to transform into their near Darkbeast forms to do battle in.

Nothing happened.

"How can we fight on the scale of this new paradigm?" Baeven yelled.

"We haven't learned how to do that yet."

Elazethrek's combined mass and energy sent them hurtling again, like pins she knocked down.

"Our foe seems to have the knack of it, uncle."

And this time, Naero felt the Creature attempt to ensnare and drain their energies. She felt certain that Baeven sensed that as well.

"Let's get out of here," Naero told Baeven. "We must retreat and fight another day, after we've learned more about how to operate within this strange place."

She felt both of them shrinking down as they passed back into their own accustomed dimension.

Half an hour later, Naero, Shalaen, and Alala worked with Jia once more on unlocking the Driathan blank.

Now they could infuse the entire blank or parts of it with various forms of Cosmic energy. They could get it to twitch, convulse, and respond with movement in many ways.

It always responded to Jia most naturally.

At one point she had it walking like a puppet with invisible strings.

But they still could not unlock its secrets, or fuse Zhen's soul within the miraculous body, and bring her and it back to some semblance of life.

Shalaen summoned several of the Prill, who had been held captive by the enemy for a very long while.

Most of them were still deeply traumatized by their experiences.

Naero and the others continued to ask them about the ordeals they went through.

The Prill could not always speak of those times, even now that they were free. Yet it was still encouraged, when they were ready, and at their own pace.

When Naero and some of the others asked, some of the Prill responded.

The Dark Emperor is a true monster, many of them said, in unison.

He watched as some of us were experimented upon and slowly murdered.

Many of the Prill died, as the enemy sought ways to invade our bodies, erase or souls and minds, and replace them with the infused souls and minds of the G'lothc.

Understand, our great friends. They didn't merely want to possess our bodies against our will.

They wanted to violate us on purpose, and take them over and make them their own, forever. To be as one with them, and wipe us out of existence completely.

"That wanted to shape you into vessels for themselves," Jia noted.

"I'm glad it didn't work," Shalaen added.

No, our bodies rejected them to the point of dying. We could not be made to mesh with them.

Yet to our great sorrow, many of us continued to die outright, despite this failure.

"Why?" Naero asked. "They could still use you in their Darkforce generators. Why did they continue to murder the Prill for no reason?"

A shudder went through all of the Prill present. They could not speak for a long moment.

There was a reason. The Dark Emperor discovered that he enjoyed the way the Prill tasted to him. They had captured so very many of us in the attacks. There were Prill and to spare.

For a long period, various tanks and pens of live Prill, hobbled and crippled so that they could not escape, were kept near him like...like snacks.

He fed upon the Prill the way your offspring eat treats and candy.

Millions of helpless Prill were so devoured, until the Dark Emperor grew tired of the novelty of our taste. Millions of unique and beautiful beings, eaten alive at the sick will of a gluttonous abomination.

He would entertain Elazethrek, the Creature, and a few other monsters who were apparently their peers and allies.

"What did those other beings look like? What were their forms?" Naero eagerly inquired.

We never saw them directly. They either had ways to obscure themselves or were masked with holo projectors.

But the Dark Emperor gave them Prill as a delicacy. Some were also devoured by these horrors. Others were taken away to what fate we know not, whether torture, further experimentation, or enslavement.

Those Prill have never been seen or even sensed again.

Let us tell our great friends about the vast enemy trophy wheels.

"Trophy wheels?" Naero repeated with disgust.

Yes, each time that the enemy defeats a species, they take trophies from among the vanquished leaders or champions of that race or kind.

It is a vast, hi-tek morphing wheel of bodies frozen forever in Space-Time, usually at the moment of their death and defeat, or soon thereafter.

Some of the Prill were added to the Great Wheel of Defeat, for all of us to see.

The inserted a selection of our greatest leaders, thinkers, and warriors. Much to our great shame.

The Great Enemy Trophy Wheel shifts and morphs, showing the defeated of countless species of sentients that the evil ones have crushed.

Naero felt her wrath and fury roar up within her. "Here me, brave Prill. Here me, all of our friends and brave allies. One day we shall hunt these foes down and lay them low. We shall find this Great Wheel of theirs, destroy it, and grind them to dust beneath its shattered weight. All the universe shall know that tyrants such as these, however great and powerful they now stand, shall one day rot with the garbage of past history.

"Those who stand free and who dare to pay the price to accept no chain or yoke shall accomplish these mighty labors. Whether it be done by our hands, or the hands of the mighty children we shall raise up in our place. It shall be done, and the valiant peoples of the Alliance shall know lasting freedom."

Later that same hour, during more discussions concerning the Prill captivity, Naero learned something vital.

The Prill had stumbled upon a way to roughly track Elazethrek's masked energy feeding signatures, since it was constantly feeding.

They also detected where hundreds of her private lairs had been constructed. And they were still being constructed, giving her many secret places to hurtle out from in surprise and attack the Alliance forces, or spy upon them from what could also be used as listening posts.

Naero quickly summoned Tyber with them, they plugged the data and information into his new detection teknologies, and with a bit of teknomancy, soon they were tracking the Creature and attempting to pinpoint its exact location.

They sent word to the other Alliance Champions to gather at once.

And of course, right at that moment, the enemy unleashed another round of heavy attacks across all fronts.

But if they could find, capture, and or destroy Elazethrek, that would be a huge accomplishment.

And for the present, they now had a way to track her location.

In fact, Naero reduced herself down to micro size and transported to the location in full on stealth mode with a cloud of nanofixers. They went to spy upon the monster.

Elazethrek was within one of her horrid lairs.

The shifting, Darkforce energy walls held countless prisoners trapped within, their screams not unlike a form of music and entertainment to the great beast.

The lair itself seemed to be designed as a great ring of spinning, revolving tube cages of many sizes and varieties, all adjacent to each other and moving in different directions.

The immense waves of Cosmic energy that the Creature fed upon each second were staggering.

And all the moving, shifting walls revolving about the monster seemed stuffed and crammed with countless prisoners from many species, both flesh and energy beings.

All of them writhed in the spinning mix, some of them churned and mashed or cut to pieces by the random Chaos of the lair itself that dragged and mutilated them to their deaths.

Sealed within her microstealth armor, Naero could only imagine the reek and the stench of fetid, putrid death and despair within that sick place.

But Elazethrek seemed to feed upon all of that miasma of misery and destruction that hovered around her. The Creature enjoyed it all. It absently fired destructive blasts, beams, and attacks into the helpless sacrifices all around. Because that was just what the enemy were.

It ripped through the very walls and raked, hewed open, and disemboweled the sacrifices sent to it for its pleasure, feeding, and feasting. The Thing readily devoured flesh and energy both.

The abomination dragged some of the offerings out and fed upon them openly, whether they were still alive or dead. It mattered not.

Naero had seen the Ejjai meatships in practice, but this sacrificial chamber of the Least of the Six was one of the most horrific sights that she had ever witnessed.

The memory of which would haunt and infuriate her for the rest of her days.

They must find a way to vanquish and obliterate such malignant foes as these.

Then Elazethrek did something odd.

She ceased her random orgy of tormenting and feeding upon other beings and suddenly focused her full attention upon an enormous holographic comscreen covering one entire section of the lair.

The vast viewport then filled with the baleful image of the Dark Emperor himself.

Its resonating, booming voice echoed throughout the lair until the structure shook and shuddered as if from an earthquake.

"You are ready to advance our plans a generation? Our foes are decidedly distracted. Your decoys shall keep the fools busy long enough."

"Yes, my masters. Yet why not use these energies to bring in the Armada and crush them all outright? Why wait until the Six are reborn?"

"Because, for the time being we cannot yet do both. We have underestimated the capabilities of our foes many times before. Once we have both the Six and the Armada at our command, our absolute triumph and final victory shall be assured. That process begins now. Bring the chosen vessel to us."

"And once we have it, I am free to slaughter those who have thwarted me—I mean...us?"

"Yes, yes. Hunt them all down. Fall upon them individually and murder them all."

"Just think. In a count of so many days, not decades, my brother the Deceiver shall awaken and fight at my side. He who is far greater and stronger than I. How we shall drive the fools before our might and break them. They who dared to stand before our power!"

"Their spawn. Don't forget to assist in exterminating all of the young ones and little ones of their blood lines. Let none escape. The distant aunt and her vile brood. The younger brother and his wives and their brats. All of their bloodlines must be eliminated—completely wiped out."

"I will bring the parents to the brink of death, and keep them just alive enough to witness me running down their offspring, wherever they hide. I will make them look on to see what I do to each one. You swear that I will not need to worry about the eldest?"

"Fear not. She is mine. Within days she will break and I shall feast upon the unproven child's spiritmind as I have never feasted before, and join her fledgling energies to that of my own, ever-growing strength. She shall never live to become a true threat to us."

"Then enjoy it. Feed well, Masters. The others are all mine. I claim their souls and flesh."

"Hold. You cannot. Bring us the bodies, quick frozen, as always. We shall pick over the lot for the wheel."

"That's not fair, Masters! All of this effort and I am not allowed to devour any of them and add their strength to my own?"

"Feast upon a few of the little one's corpses, then. They will not matter. But bring all the rest to us. We must have our spoils for the Wheel of Triumph."

"Very well, my masters."

"And once the meddlers are gone, just think our mighty servant. What a repast shall we dine upon? We will wipe out an entire generation of this annoying spack race. These petty upstarts. Once they are all enslaved or dead, the feasting we shall enjoy on their offspring as a whole shall be as limitless as it will be legendary. Their spawn are in the many millions. We shall breed some remnant of them as food stocks."

"And with the Spacers broken, all the lesser races, species, and interstellar vermin shall break and try to hide themselves from our wrath. A high salute to our grand plans, my masters. Let us proceed and go forth to victory. Victory to the G'lothc and all of their mighty servants!"

Naero did not know what do.

Elazethrek quickly prepared to go forth and fulfill its terrible mission. Was there no way to stop her?

How could Naero take the Creature on all alone?

To attempt to do so was certain death—sheer suicide.

Om raised one possibility. One slight chance.

Naero strove to take it.

First they used the nanofixers to send out several urgent messages.

Then, as Elazethrek was about to depart, Naero smashed into the monster with all her strength, and just barely transported them both into another place that she and om both recalled.

They tumbled together into a picked alternate dimension with very special characteristics that affected all who went there.

Here they were both changed.

In this place they were more or less equals.

Naero needed to strike hard.

She needed to be quick.

Bereft of their advanced powers, both of them rose up, nothing but plain human beings.

It surprised Naero that the G'lothc Champion was herself reduced to being nothing more than a naked human female.

She launched into Elazethrek with all the power she could muster.

And promptly slipped and fell painfully upon her back trying to execute a back spinkick.

The Creature laughed with great amusement and then tried to roast Naero with what would have been some kind of intense, Darkforce assault.

But she just stood there looking stupid, thrusting her two clenched hands before her again and again, still amazed that nothing was happening.

Then the Creature looked around and studied the odd place they were in.

Such confusion and hesitation gave Naero a chance to tackle the enemy bitch and pummel her with a hail of flailing, clumsy blows.

They rolled and wrestled together, jabbing and slapping each other, pulling hair, trying to use elbows and knees, but mostly doing more damage to themselves.

No muscle memory at all. All of Naero's honed fighting skills and techniques—gone. This was what she was reduced to, going from something like a Cosmic superhero or demi-goddess to being a mere weak, scrabbling mortal female with no powers.

But then so was Elazethrek. And the fall for her seemed to be even more of a shock.

Very quickly, both of them were reduced to a mass of tangled matted hair, bruises, scrapes, scratches, bloody mouths, ears, and noses.

Naero finally got her legs around her taller opponent in a weak scissors hold.

Yes, the enemy bitch still had to be taller than her, even here.

Naero got her hands around Elazethrek's throat and began to throttle her, bashing her head against the dirty ground.

For once in her existence, the Creature seemed to panic, and did everything she could, wide-eyed, to break free and get away.

Naero ignored whatever pain and damage the Creature could inflict and struggled to hang on and keep squeezing.

"Not so high and mighty now, are you, bitch? I'm going to kill you, you evil G'lothc fuck. I overheard all of you plans. You aren't going to murder me, my family, my friends, or my people. And you sure as hell aren't going to torture, slaughter, and devour any of my little ones."

Naero gritted her teeth and her own eyes popped.

The Creature clawed, pinched, thrashed, and struck at her something fierce, causing her to bleed.

"Haisha! Do your worst. I will not allow any of that to happen, do you hear me, monster? Not so long as I draw breath. So you just take it here, as even my weak hands choke the living shit out of you!"

Elazethrek's mouth worked in vain. She turned purple. Her eyes began to roll up in her head and her kicking feet drummed and strained, pointing out toes first.

Then she vanished.

Naero fell forward gasping, nearly smashing her own face into the ground as she cried out in frustrated despair.

Who knew where the monster had fled or how?

Naero recovered herself and transported back to her friends, returning to what she truly was.

I almost had her, Om. I was this close to finishing her off. I would have just left her body there to rot and turn to dust.

It was worth the attempt, N. Too bad she got away.

I know, but we kind of know what the enemy's plan is now, as if we couldn't have guessed it all along.

Sure. They want to kill everyone. That's all they ever want to do.

Yep. You got it.

Naero spoke with Jia and Shalaen, who watched over her physical body in her traveler's trance.

She caught them up on everything that had transpired.

But both of her friends still looked worried.

"What is it?"

Shalaen rested a hand on her arm. "It's Shetharra. She's gotten much worse, and the regeneration suit doesn't seem to be working any longer."

Naero hung her head slightly, mind racing, trying not to panic on her own.

She snapped her head up. "What about-"

Jia shook her head. "Lah-shubah is with the child now, doing all that she can, but that treatment is also not working so well. And it will only delay the inevitable for a short time."

"What are you saying?" Naero said.

"We might only have one chance to save your daughter's life, N. The Driathan blank. If we can finally open it up, we might be able to transfer Shetharra's soul into it and meld the two together."

Naero shook her head. "We've never been able to do so yet. And that would leave no chance to bring Zhen back."

"Reports coming in," Jia said. "Elazethrek replicants attacking in several vital areas, causing much damage. Tyber is attempting to pinpoint the real one."

"They're all decoys," Naero said, absently. "Tell the fleets to concentrate their fire and take them down."

Jia still stared at her. "Naero, I do not yet have a child, but do you want to risk losing your older daughter to the enemy? I know you made a promise to your dead friend, but I think even she would understand the harsh choice you now face."

Yes, Zhen would understand completely. "Okay. Let me transport into the flagship's vault and try to prepare the blank, but only as a last resort. Ready?"

Both of her friends nodded.

When they popped into the vault, de-pressurization alarms went off, confusing them at first.

Elazethrek carried the Driathan blank in her multiple arms and tail.

She had just blasted a path of escape out through several levels of the flagship.

"Stop her!" Naero screamed, even as all three of their attacks punched into the Creature, driving it aside for an instant.

But it was heavily shielded.

Naero strove to cut off its massive energy flows.

Shalaen and Om both struggled to block the monster from transporting and escaping with its prize.

Jia glowed with some kind of energy and leaped upon the Creature, causing Elazethrek to shriek in agony.

"You cannot endure my touch, can you, fiend? You know who I am. You know what I am and partly why I was created by my great teachers. You shall never use me or any of my peoples for your evil vessels. This I promise you."

The Creature staggered both Naero and Shalaen with a massive Darkforce shock wave that buckled the vault hull.

Then she pushed Jia away from her and pinned her against the far, ruptured wall with an energy claw. "Wrong, Driathan filth. However you wish it to be so, you have not yet the might and knowledge of the masters who forsook your lesser, weaker kind and left you behind to perish.

"And know this. My masters and the Six know full well how to rip open these forms you think to be so inviolate and sacred, and convert them to our purposes. This one shall be the first, and soon another of my kind shall come against you all. Or perhaps, I shall take it for my own."

The Creature laughed.

"That would be rich. In a few days, after I master this perfect body and grow even more powerful, I shall return to butcher you all."

Elazethrek pointed a finger at Naero as she struggled to rise and fight.

"I'm coming for you first of all, little one. And then your mate, your friends, and at last your little ones. As promised. None shall stop me this time, least of all you. You shall pay for the indignities you made me suffer in that accursed place."

Jia tried to close with her again and zap the Creature with the power the Driathan Queen wielded. She barely got a fleeting hold on the monster's lashing tail, but could not hold on.

Elazethrek cried out in agony again and sped away, making good her escape with the blank. "Enough fools! Damn your tricks. Things shall be far different upon my return. Wait for it and despair!"

34

In all her life, Naero had never felt so terrorized and helpless, for all that she held dear.

There was no way to win now.

No way to defeat this Creature. She and all of her friends knew it as well.

They were finally beaten.

The enemy had won.

Naero steeled herself and smashed her hand into the damaged hull of the vault, tearing through another small section.

No. She would fight to the last, to the death if need be for those she loved. "Everyone focus. Get the Prill and all the others searching for Elazethrek. The Creature must be found!"

Jia shook her head. "Once she fills the blank with either her dark soul or one of the other Six—we've had it. We won't be able to beat them. They'll be unstoppable."

Naero took in another deep breath and turned her head away for a moment, closing her eyes. "It's not over yet. We still have some time if we can get the blank back. Jia, if you can't trace the fiend, can you at least trace the blank? It's still one of your people, even in its neutral, dormant state."

"I'll…I'll try."

Naero continued, trying to think. "Elazethrek herself admitted to us that it might take her anywhere from days to hours to affect the transition. They don't know that we have a partial way of tracking the Creature and possibly the blank itself."

"Let's hope she remains so greedy," Shalaen noted, "and seeks to keep the blank for herself."

"A perfect, indestructible vessel would be extremely tempting for her opportunistic kind," Jia added. "But it will also take her longer on her own to make the switch. But there's something far worse at stake here, Naero."

Naero stared at the Driathan Queen. "Worse than all of us and the Alliance dying, and then the enemy falling upon our helpless children?"

"Far worse, I'm afraid. Once we're out of the way, the enemy will be free to hunt down the hidden Driathans, my people. With perfect, immortal Ultrium vessels, and the hidden knowledge of my kind, they will sweep out from galaxy to galaxy, destroying one after another, and eventually wipe out all life in the universe entirely. All sentient children everywhere shall become their prey."

"For the sake of all, we must find and defeat her!" Naero shouted. "She's probably hiding in one of her rotten lairs. Get Tyber, Baeven, and everyone searching. Find her!"

The Alliance Champions scattered and spread out, many with a host of fixers and energy beings backing them up.

But Naero and Om had to go out alone with only a few fixers, without the clutter of other minds, tek, and links messing with their own highly attuned senses.

They leaped from war zone to war zone, hoping to get some sign or sense of the Creature's passing.

Naero slipped into the strange realities of the bizarre new Expanse, knowing she put herself at just as much risk of detection, capture, or destruction.

A flicker.

Something.

Something that might be the Creature. A faint Darkforce trace energy signature was now gone, as fast as she had just barely detected it.

Yes, one of multitudes of enemy-created pocket zones, just like the ones Elazethrek fashioned into her horrid lairs.

No, something was feeding in that direction. One of the enemy for certain.

Naero knew she had to go in fast and strike hard.

Elazethrek was a master at slipping away. She could escape once more in the flash of an instant.

Naero had to seal off all escape for a short while, and survive long enough for her strategy to work.

If the Creature went directly to the Dark Emperor or one of the other nameless, faceless enemy super-leaders, how would they possibly get the blank back?

But then, they wouldn't let her have the prize for herself.

Let the Creature stay greedy and seek to keep that prize for her own.

There.

Naero transported and pounced.

There was the Creature, focused almost entirely on forcing the Driathan blank open by raw power and melding her own malignant spirit within.

Elazethrek wasted no time and pushed forward with her goal. The monster warred with the blank, but had much of it torn open at last.

It was a disgusting sight. This was one sentient completely violating another sentient form of higher life.

Yet her efforts left Naero's foe extremely vulnerable, filled with many different Cosmic energies at work in delicate levels.

Naero flashed in and detonated several precise Cosmic blasts, right before she herself transported away.

She still took damage, but not as much as Elazethrek did.

And the blank remained indestructible.

The resulting Cosmic feedback and secondary explosions tossed the Least of the Six about, doing more damage to her than the Alliance had ever inflicted on her.

But that would neither slay her outright, nor distract Elazethrek forever.

Naero only had at best precious seconds or minutes to make her move and lock the enemy out of the Blank.

Om assisted her on every level.

With both teknomancy and biomancy, Naero focused all of her knowledge and skill into assisting the blank in rapidly healing the temporary rents and ruptures that Elazethrek had made in ripping and forcing her new vessel open to receive her evil spirit.

Naero quickly and deftly inserted Zhen's soul within the complexity of the Driathan blank, hoping beyond hope that this time, the two entities would finally integrate and properly mesh together.

She just barely sealed the blank off when the Creature recovered, and sent Naero spinning and flying away with a heavy lash of her energized tail.

Om bolstered Naero's regenerations, and kept her conscious.

Elazethrek ignored Naero, and struggled to plunge back into the blank.

Yet now, even when she tried to touch the blank, it resisted.

The same defensive energies that Jia used against the Creature now scorched the monster.

Elazethrek could not bear to touch the blank.

It was effectively denied her, at least for now.

"What have you done, fool? Some petty Drian trick you learned? Curse you and them. Yet I shall find a way to defeat it—after I have ripped the life from your flesh! This is my vessel, mine! I claim it for my own. And neither you nor anyone else is going to keep me from my immortal victory. I shall yet exist and feed on the weak and the defenseless, forever!"

Naero endured a terrific beating thereafter.

She tried to fight back.

She strove mostly just to survive.

35

Naero and Om retreated with the blank to the Interdimensions for a respite, but Elazethrek would find them very shortly, and the one-sided battle would continue until Naero was slain. That was the only logical outcome.

Even before she caught her proverbial breath, Om transported the blank back to Baeven and Jia for them to hide and protect.

Whatever happened now, the blank was safe and out of the hands of the enemy.

Yet now there was no place for Naero to run.

Naero had only one uncertain choice if she wanted to survive.

She had to fully merge with some of her other potential selves from the other dimensions and realities.

She reached deep within herself and her most powerful energy form, finding the place where she and Om struggled tirelessly to unlock just one of her own internal, interdimensional barriers.

She put forth her power, adding it to Om's.

Somehow the energies felt right this time, the proper and precise techniques flowed together, whether out of need, enlightenment, or both.

The first barrier within Naero crashed down and melted away in an instant.

Naero immediately reached out and melded with her nearest other self who just as eagerly waited and strove to connect with her on the other side. The other Naero in that alternate dimension acknowledged her presence at once with joy and understanding of her counterpart's desperate need.

Both of them instantly sensed what they were up against.

Cosmic energies and awareness flooded into Naero, threatening to overwhelm her. She staggered and fumbled back, trying to give herself time to compensate.

But there would be no such time.

Elazethrek emerged in fast pursuit, fresh and ready for the fight to continue. Clearly she had completely recovered from being slightly stunned and flared up anew, right back into her most powerful battle form.

Her crushed and shattered face smiled, popping, crunching and grinding as it clicked and regenerated back together. She gloated and chortled as was her nature.

"Trying to get away in order to recharge, a bit are you? It won't work. I'll track you down whoever you go. How pitiful. All too little, and far too late I'm afraid. You may have surprised me a bit here and there, but this battle is all but over, little one. You've run out of tricks to amuse me with."

Naero set her battle stance, exploding with Cosmic force. "Come on then, if you are so certain. Do your worst, you vile, stinking bitch!"

The Least of the Six grinned and nodded. "Very well then..."

The Creature fell upon her with a fury Naero had yet to witness.

Blows and attacks and blasts engulfed Naero that would have shattered or vaporized entire mountains, had they been unleashed on a material world. Even at her newest peak within the Interdimensions, it was all that Naero could do just to dodge, deflect, and evade the flurry of devastation hurled straight at her.

Elazethrek laughed. "My, what a pretty little dancer you are. So, you wished to see my true power, weakling? Is it to your liking, little one? You are just beginning to understand, aren't you? Even twice as strong–even were you thrice or four times as great–still you are no match for one such as me. My power eclipses you in ways you still cannot comprehend. I'm not going to finish with you quickly, either.

"We're all alone out here. There is no hurry. I'm going to take my time and savor my fun–and murder you slowly."

The very aether around them rocked and shattered by the terrible concussive punches and kicks they traded, thundering and resounding as they connected.

Naero turned a split instant too late and went flying and spinning back several kilometers from and energized kick that engulfed her in a Darkforce blast at the same time.

She was trapped within a fiery comet of destruction, and struggled to survive.

Her shields went down as soon as she put them up.

Her adversary pursued her rapidly all the while, continuing to rant.

"Perhaps I'll tear you apart, piece by piece," Elazethrek mused. "Yet no, I remember now. I was distinctly ordered to kill you and then bring your body back, frozen and as whole as possible, as a prize for the Great Wheel of Triumph. Yet another trophy for my great masters!"

Naero shook off the Darkforce smoldering, immolating all about her. She understood the Darkforce all too well.

Secretly she absorbed most of its raw energy and floated in the aether as if stunned, masking her energies as best she could.

Just long enough for that mouthy bitch to get in close.

"Now let's get the fun started," Elazethrek said eagerly, sweeping in fast with her many spikes and blades fully extended.

Naero transported behind her and nailed Elazethrek with an exploding daisy chain of Lifespark detonations. Impossibly fast kicks knocked the Creature around, enough to daze and dazzle the thing.

Then Naero pounced like a lioness, slashing and ripping at her foe, piling on technique after technique: piercing blast hands, crushing energized splatter wave kicks.

She went all out, tearing into her opponent.

Phazed explosions, transfixing Cosmic rods and Chaos detonations. Spinning energy blades that drained Cosmic force and then exploded. Depleting implosion strikes.

She kept at her opponent's face and head, shattering and smearing it repeatedly. That kept her loudmouthed foe from taunting and wise-cracking all the while.

And at the same time that Naero kept her opponent off balance and trying to recover–she and Om carefully and quickly studied Elazethrek's massive energy flows, and the composition of her vessel. Up close, they quickly perceived many new secrets about the super composed Ultrium-infused body that sustained the Creature's form.

Naero finally understood what gave the evil G'lothc champion spirit the ability to maintain a foothold in the Prime Material Plane, and the Interdimensions.

There! Do you see it, Naero?

I do, Om. The vessel has been genetically engineered and hyper-modified from within at many levels. I understand how they implanted the evil spirit inside her now, the same way she was trying to penetrate the blank. But we've never had the chance to perceive any of this so closely before.

The vessel has been infused with self-regenerating Cosmic energy patterns and Ultrium based life force down to the level of energies within its very blood cells. But now we have an idea how to undo it all and defeat this monster.

Naero shook her head. Not me, Om. Not this time. I'm pretty much spent after all of that. We'll be dead long before we can regenerate enough. Our only hope is to transmit what we've learned to the others through our phazed fixer net. Then we have to get the hell out of-

A massive Darkforce blast wave almost engulfed them.

They attempted to flee; Elazethrek overtook them with ease, cutting them off wherever they turned. Naero went into her partial Darkbeast form and drew Heartcleaver in order to make her final stand.

The least of the Six circled Naero, finally managing to reform properly. "Look at how desperate you've grown. Alas, you used up the very last vestiges of your power, and you still could not take me down, could you? Did you not hear my words? So sad, little one. So foolish and ignorant. And now you have nowhere to run. This time, there will be no escape."

Naero grinned. "You're wrong. I'm not the one who's going to die this day."

More laughter. "Fool. Then you do not know your death when you see it. I cannot die. You cannot kill that which is immortal and indestructible. You possess neither the knowledge nor might enough to stand up to me and destroy my vessel, and cast my spirit back from whence it came."

"You're right. I don't," Naero said.

Elazethrek raised both eyebrows. "Well then, at least you finally admit your ignoble defeat."

Naero charged in once more, with everything that she was.

"That I shall never do!"

With one mighty swing, Heartcleaver chopped off Elazethrek's outstretched arms. Yet at the same time, several Darkforce tentacles shot out and entangled Naero.

They shocked her to her core as she struggled against them.

Her foe dragged her up close, face to face to gloat further. "All alone little one. I will rip your life force energy from you and eat it like succulent fruit."

Multiple explosions and attacks overtook the monster all at once.

Elazethrek shrieked in agony and tried to shield herself, withdrawing.

Naero fought her way free and rammed Heartcleaver right through her opponent's chest and twisted it.

They were eye to eye once again. "I am never alone, you G'lothc filth. Nor need I fight alone. The entire universe shall rally together against your kind, and put you down!"

Baeven was there, along with Khai, Jan, and Jia, Shalaen, Tarim, and dozens of the mightiest energy beings from many Interdimensional races.

Naero gasped.

She had played for time just long enough.

Together, all of them transfixed the G'lothc champion, impaling her upon their powers and weapons, quickly draining her energies away for a change.

The enemy had taught them all very well.

Baeven grunted, "Stop her! She's trying to destroy herself in one massive blast to take all of us out. How do we do this, Naero? How do we destroy her and get away?"

Naero linked with them all telepathically. All at once. Follow my lead. In order to stop her we can only obliterate the vessel. Keep siphoning her power away from her but form it around her in a reflection trap. We must reach her Ultrium based core, a heart of pure, living Darkforce energy is her ultimate source.

"How can we possibly destroy something such as that?" Jan asked aloud. "Haisha! There's no known way to do so."

"Not normally," Jia jumped in. "But Naero and I have faced something like this before. It sounds crazy, but only the Lifeforce itself and the Flame Eternal can kill them from deep within. It is like matter touching anti-matter–the same principle. They cannot withstand such forces colliding."

Shalaen laughed. "I get it. I too have seen this before. Once we get past their defenses, they are extremely vulnerable to positive energies. In essence, we heal them to death from inside with Lifeforce power."

Focus now, Naero told them. We must penetrate to the core and attack. If we are lucky, the vessel will implode instead of detonating all around us. But it can go either way. If the latter happens, we must shield ourselves as best we may and transport out as quickly as possible.

Elazethrek thrashed and struggled like the great monster she was, but the Alliance defenders held her fast and worked their way deep within.

"Fools. Destroy this vessel and I will only find another that is stronger and more powerful yet. None of you are my equal in battle. Look at how it takes a dozen of you weaklings or more to vanquish even my damaged vessel. What will you do the next time when you face two or three Darkforce Champions–or all Six of us at once?"

"Haisha," Baeven said, "do these G'lothc assholes ever shut up?"

Ignore her threats," Naeros said. "She knows she finished now. There it is! There's the core. Flood it with these exact positive energies on my mark and then pull way back. We don't know what the exact reaction will be. Ready? Mark!"

Their foe began to scream and rapidly expand with light from within.

Every one of Naero's allies drew back to a safe distance.

Naero tried to get away herself.

Numerous tentacles ensnared her and held her fast.

"So clever Little One. Fool! At least you shall perish along with my vessel when it explodes, spack scum."

"I don't think so," Naero replied.

She ignited a huge Cosmic energy blast, triggering the even greater detonation of Elazethrek's destabilized host body, and barely transported away, all in the same instant.

The Creature's own erupting powers annihilated and consumed itself, becoming an Ultrium hyper bomb.

For all that, Naero floated in the Interdimensional aether many parsecs away, battered, scorched, and clinging to life.

She had still taken upon herself about one ten thousandth of the damage that was released by such a blast.

While her energy being form floated in the aether and regenerated, Naero left Om in charge and sent her consciousness racing back using the splitting technique. She re-connected with the portion of herself that remained with Shetharra, still on the Allied hospital ship, *The Star Angel*.

With the many insights that she had just gained, she thought that now at last she could finally stand forth in the right Cosmic vantage point to fight for and cure her oldest daughter. Then she could rid Shetharra of the relentless, insidious scourge of the G'lothc advanced energy disease.

For now she more or less understood what the curse truly was, and exactly who and what was behind it. Why it persisted, pursued, and afflicted her daughter with such malignant drive.

Because the curse wasn't just any normal, physical pathogen. It also had psyonic and even Cosmic and spiritual components to it that no one without her level of Kexxian enlightenment, history and knowledge could have ever guessed at or sensed. Let alone perceive it all in any depth to be able to battle against the supernatural source, defeat that direct cause, and reverse and cure its many malignant effects.

Naero merged with her portion of herself that she had left to watch over her daughter.

She gasped slightly, at the rush of advanced Kexxian teknomancy and biomancy information as the correct data bases fully flooded her counterpart's mind and then her own.

They melded together, becoming one and whole again, at least mentally.

Then her spiritmind flashed to her daughter's side and linked with her deep within.

Instinctively, Naero understood the risks involved with what she was going to attempt to do—take on the hyper complex Cosmic disease itself, its originator, and the formidable power that was prosecuting it all with such unlimited might and malign venom.

There was no other way to confront and defeat the plague.

As it seemed to be the way with Naero herself, she would accept the gamble and risk everything.

It could be no less for the sake of any whom she loved, especially her oldest child, who bore a special place in her heart and soul.

A thousand times would she surrender her own life if need be.

Thus it was that if Shetharra died, Naero would be trapped inside of her child, and she would perish as well with her girl.

For both of them the stakes were now life and death.

Naero's spiritmind dove into Shetharra's warring body, mind, and soul without hesitation, fully guessing at who and what she would confront there.

She warred against a form of Death itself by challenging that Cosmic malaise. And as she interposed herself and took the burden of that on, she instantly felt her own self beginning to die in her daughter's place.

Yes, the Dark Emperor himself, or at least a very great portion of him. A vast, cavernous mind and essence that was a full, major component of this Cosmic disease, confirming what Naero had guessed all along.

The loathsome G'lothc and their slaves and minions were in fact all very much like hyper-virulent diseases, inflicted upon the entire universe. This all-encompassing evil was the largest source of the energy disease, and the energy being phage, and the psyonic mind wraiths.

The pattern was clear.

This was one of the deep dark secrets of the G'lothc.

Everything the enemy touched and interacted with was affected in a negative way.

They were all living diseases on every possible level, directed with malice and destructive, malignant force of will.

Shetharra, for all her power and inner might, did not understand any of this. For all of her advanced intellect, in many ways, she remained but a child, as Naero knew well.

How long and valiantly her little duck had battled and resisted—against some of the greatest evils the universe had ever known.

Even her astonishing power and courage would not be enough in the end. How could it be?

All the little girl knew or could comprehend was that to her child's mind, there was something powerful and agonizing invading within her, on so many levels. These terrible threats infected her–heart, mind, and soul–doing its best to end her life, in every way that it could.

Naero wrapped her arms protectively around Shetharra's blazing spirit of white flame, feeling it weakening, yielding, and flickering ever so slightly, yet still inevitably to the dark powers tearing away at her.

Naero whispered to her little duck.

"They shall never have you, my heart. Not while I live to fight them."

She comforted Shetharra's spirit and reassured her child telepathically. *I'm here, my brave little duck. I shall fight for you. You are never alone. I have learned some of the enemy's most terrible secrets, and how to undo them. I've come at last to save you. All of this ends now. Rest and heal. You're going to be all right, my dear one.*

Shetharra leaned against her, clinging to her. *Hurry, Momma. The pain explodes in every part of me. It hurts so much. Why do the dark things want to hurt me so badly?*

Because they fear you, and what you will become one day–their bane!

Naero strode forward, her golden light enveloping her. Her third eye and all of her eyes fully open and ablaze.

She fully interposed herself between the darkness attacking her daughter and drove it off at first by sheer force of will alone.

The agony she endured in Shetharra's place caused her to grunt and grit her teeth.

She nearly dropped to one knee.

This? This was the full effect of what they were doing to her child each instant?

There was no word for something that outdid monster.

No language equal to things that surpassed abomination.

Her fists crackled with Cosmic force.

Naero's eyes went to glowing slits of golden light.

One day. Let that bright day yet come.

How she would make them pay.

She would never stop searching until she discovered a way to finally destroy all of these disgusting fiends. Somehow she would find a way.

Naero called upon all that she was and every Power that might aid or support her.

Her golden radiance expanded well beyond fury. She drove the diseased darkness back with each indomitable and defiant step she took forward. She noted how it had gotten in, and already devised ways to shut it out from that sphere.

The dark, ravenous thing within her daughter pulled back, shrank away from Naero's presence and force of will, and began to grow perceptibly ever smaller.

"The assault of your malignant will is over!" she shouted, putting forth one clenched glowing fist. "It ends now. Begone, Nahaxrathrax! Yes, I name you in defiance, coward, eater of souls. Slink and crawl back to the Cosmic cesspools and sewers of the universe where your hate and malice fester. You shall never have my child, or her bright spirit. I cast you out of her. Begone! And one day, when she comes into her full strength, you shall feel the might of her blinding wrath and be astonished. For the flame that burns within her heart, mind, and soul is pure–that fire which you can never endure nor overcome!

"Come forth then, if you will not flee. Face me and Begone! Gutless slime. I know who and what you are all too well–the entire legion of you! You scum slink in darkness, churning your wretched fear and envy that rots you from within into lethal hate and power. It takes so many active forms. You seek to poison and destroy all things if you may. But you shall not take my children from me. I stand before them in their defense, as I also continue to grow in strength and wisdom. The New Dreamers and I continue to find ways to smite you and strike you down!"

Naero felt it.

Even within her own mind, defending her precious child, the corrupt essence of the Dark Emperor's will stirred and rose up in horror to give answer to her challenge.

Several large slitted eyes, glowing with fell Darkforce energies ignited far above her in the hyperdense gloom. The intense malice the thing emitted all around its presence had the feel of the very core of Evil and Destruction themselves.

SPACK FOOL! YOU ARE ALL NOTHING TO OUR MIGHT. DAY SHALL COME. AND ON THAT DAY, YOU AND ALL OF YOUR PUNY, UPSTART KIND AND YOUR PETTY ALLIES SHALL FEEL THE WEIGHT OF OUR POWER AS IT FALLS HEAVILY UPON YOU. THE FEW WEAKLINGS WHO SURVIVE SHALL

BEAR OUR YOKE AND EEK OUT THEIR SHORT LIVES IN AGONY AS OUR UTTER SLAVES. THIS SHALL BE THE PRICE FOR YOUR INSOLENCE.

Naero strode forward, pressing her advantage, undoing the enemy's work as she did so. The dark presence shrank back away from her as she advanced upon it, the Dark Emperor growing ever weaker and smaller.

Get out! I banish your evil and cast you out forever. You have no place here. Your power in this sphere has been exposed and broken. You are merely a shred of the Dark Emperor's unliving essence, if it can be called such. I have shattered all of your connections, drained your energies, and now I shut you out and seal the way against you for all time! You will not trouble us in these ways ever again, for now we know how to defend against the lethal touch of your foul disease.

WE SHALL TAKE ALL OF YOU AND MAKE YOU WATCH IN HELPLESS DESPAIR AS WE TORMENT, MURDER, AND DESTROY EVERYONE AND ALL THINGS THAT YOU LOVE AND HOLD DEAR. THAT IS THE DARK EMPEROR'S PROMISE TO YOU, NAERO MAERIS. THAT WHICH YOU CALL LOVE MAKES YOU AND THE OTHER FOOLS WEAK AND VULNERABLE. WE SHALL MAKE YOU SUFFER MOST OF ALL!

Naero laughed, openly mocking the Dark Emperor's will. *Haisha! Whether I live or die, I shall never live or stand in fear of you or any of your wretched kind, you filth. Cowards all. Do I not know this truth? You and yours will always attempt to do your worst in any case, because that is what you all are.*

For once, let me ask: what good are you? All you can do is hate and destroy. Even if you murder the entire universe, what then? In the end your evils shall even destroy yourselves. How pitiful and worthless you and your dark pathetic goals are. You would bring about a lifeless, barren existence that even you could never survive to rule over. By your own corrupt, insane choices you are incapable of knowing love, honor, freedom, justice, compassion or respect–or any positive thing that makes life worth living and fighting for. How very futile and sad. Yet I know very well that you will not relent one bit. That is all that you know and cling to in your sick, demented limitations. What horrid wretches you are, and still you remain deaf and blind to your base folly.

YOUR EMPTY WORDS MATTER NOT. KNOW THIS. WE SHALL COME FOR YOU SOON, SPACK WHORE. BEFORE WE ARE DONE, WE SHALL BREAK YOU, SLAUGHTER YOUR FAMILY, AND ADD YOU TO OUR GREAT WHEEL OF TROPHIES, RIGHT BESIDE YOUR–

The vile disease shrank to the size of a small glowing cinder. Even as it continued to spew and rail, Naero stretched forth her shining hand and crushed it in one bright fist, grinding it to nothing.

That was one truth that yet endured, just as her mighty uncle Kean had taught her.

Whenever the enemy strove to strike at her within her mind, her own invincible will always prevailed and reigned supreme.

They would continue to try, but the enemy would never break her in that regard.

Naero withdrew from her merging with her oldest daughter, summoning her physical form, her counterpart that remained there.

Shetharra already smiled up at her and reached out her arms, strength returning to her in every way. But she needed rest.

Verily, the child of light grew stronger with each passing moment.

Naero took her oldest into her embrace and eased her into a deep healing sleep and kissed her sweet face. Let her rest in peace. Shetharra had earned it with many long months of pain and steadfast courage against all odds.

At least now, this danger had been defeated, once and for all.

Before she left, Naero checked on the rest of her family and kissed them all while they slept.

She held the newest addition to Clan Maeris briefly in her arms, little Selendil Saemar Maeris, now only a few standard months old, already with long, blue black hair down to her little shoulders. Although they were now closed in deep slumber, her big eyes were light blue, like many of the skies of unknown worlds.

Khai had made tiny Selly his secret favorite almost from the first moment she had emerged, just as Shetharra was for Naero. No parents worth their hearts could keep from falling in love with their babies.

Naero sighed and blinked through her own streaming tears.

There was always too much to do.

Even more, much of what she had learned would serve Naero and her allies well in many other ways in the future battles yet to come.

More war.

She separated her consciousness again, speeding back to her stricken energy form in the aether of the Interdimensions, and prepared to return to her flagship in order to attempt to work yet another promised miracle.

36

Naero transported back into her flagship as soon as she had enough energy to do so, and shifted back into her physical form.

No small portion of the damage she had endured in her energy form translated back into the flesh.

Had she perished in the Interdimensions or inside her daughter's essence, she would have also expired back in the Prime Material Plane.

Thus she remained beaten up, battered, bloodied–but unbowed.

Naero staggered down the corridor leading to her private quarters.

She and Om consistently and slowly used her flickering energies to close up wounds by priority, stop bleeding, seal up any fractures, regenerate cut, torn, or scorched tissues and deep bruises.

It was important to Naero to remain flesh and blood, despite the many difficulties in protecting and maintaining an advanced, but still mortal physical form.

Om commented directly on that fact.

You know, N. You could go around in one of your energy forms all the time. It would be a lot easier. Easier to protect. Easier to regenerate. More powerful-

No, Om, she told him. Despite all that I have become and learned to control, I still want to do my best to remain a Spacer–in the flesh. A highly advanced Spacer, no doubt, but I want to still be me, not only for myself, but for my husband and my family and friends. I want to still be the Naero they know and love. Not some energy being they won't recognize. Not some evolving demigod who lords its power over them.

To tell you the truth, Om. I like being Naero Amashin Maeris. I like being a Spacer, and a Champion, and an admiral, and a Mystic. And even more than that, I adore being a wife, a mother, a sister, a friend–a leader. A defender of what I feel in my heart and soul should be protected and preserved. I want to love the man I love, have our babies together, and watch them grow up to become Spacers and have lives and ambitions all their own.

I want to do all of that, and more. I want to keep learning and exploring like my parents did. I want to enjoy the freedom to be and do all the things that I want to be and do during the extent of my life. I don't want to fight this war forever. Yet I will not allow any power in this universe or any other take our liberty to be and do all of that from us.

I get it, N. That is why we fight.

Naero shrugged, and paused to lean her shoulder and her head wearily against the solid, cool nanohull of *The Holy Ghost*. She sighed deeply and took in more deep breaths.

Regeneration took a lot out of a person normally. That was why it was often a good idea to lie down during the course of doing so, and usually the healing process went faster.

Naero was still trying to reach her quarters, and she was conserving her energies for something else. Something more important.

When she was ready, she would proceed.

As much as possible, Naero kept her promises when she gave her word.

She smiled sadly.

My people and I will always fight on, Om. That is who we are. That is the blood we come from. Alone or together, we will stand to the last if need be, and strive to push forward.

He wristcom sounded a precise code.

Incoming call from High Admiral Klyne.

Naero started moving again. Around the corner and her goal would be in sight. He wristcom continued to chime.

He probably wants to debrief and get an update on our latest encounter with the enemy.

No doubt. There are several points of interest. I'm preparing a detailed report, as usual.

Thanks as always, Om.

She finally sat down in the empty, hi-sec corridor and took the call.

"Naero," Klyne asked, "you all right? Preliminary reports said things got pretty rough."

"They did. And I think they're going to get rougher."

"Explain? And why aren't you going to the debriefing?"

"Why? Because, I feel like total hell and I'm still regenerating back from the brink of death...if that's okay with you? And I have something very important to take care of as soon as I have the strength; a highly personal matter.

"Don't fume or bluster about protocol, Klyne. Be advised. As soon as I stagger into my quarters, I'm sending you a full report, ASAP, detailing my operations. As you will no doubt hear from some of the others, we have also obtained much vital information about our foes, and their new warships and future plans. Deets will follow, along with my report."

Klyne hissed in a breath through his teeth. "So, can you confirm whether these massive attacks are part of the coming alien armada or not?"

"Sadly, Klyne, they are not. That other massive threat still remains in our future at some point. These new enemy fleets are clearly from the Gamma Quadrant. We might even possibly encounter some more from the Delta Quadrant. Three decades ago, the enemy lurking in our adjacent galaxy merely transmitted the plans and tek for constructing some of these new generation enemy warships to their agents here in our galaxy.

"But up until the last few years, the enemy could not act upon those plans. The foe did not have access to enough Darkforce energy or the necessary energized materials such as Ultrium, to be able to commit to large scale construction of such vessels in great numbers. Now they do, apparently."

"That's bad news for the Alliance, Naero. We'll have to remain hyper-vigilant."

"I quite agree."

"N. It is vital that we find where the enemy has more of these advanced shipyards and take them out. Do we know where any more of them are?"

"Not yet, Klyne. But we have several promising leads, like I said, mostly deep within areas of the Gamma Quadrant we have yet to reach or explore, and locate some possibly even in the Delta Quadrant."

"We all need to pursue these missions at all costs, Naero. Take care of your personal affairs as quickly as you can and get back out there. We need you. But I'm glad that Khai reports your daughter as being out of danger at last. Even when we manage to win an important victory, we still somehow seem to end up no better off than we were before."

Naero smiled her half smile and snorted. "Thanks. Often, it's worse. Our foes are deep, long term thinkers the likes of which we have never seen or envisioned, Klyne. It's their way to always have something new and terrible to hurl at us, while they continue to plan even more and bring it on line against us."

"But we keep learning and growing stronger all the while," Klyne said. "We'll overtake them at some point."

She nodded over the comlink at Klyne. "That is my hope as well. We have more allies joining the fight each day, and there seems to be no end of wonders that are being revealed by the KDM. That will have to be enough for now, Klyne. Much more in a bit, from my report, and then I will be detained for the next few to several hours. I will inform you directly when I am back on the hunt."

"Sounds acceptable, N. Good work. Again, I'm glad little Shetharra is going to be okay. When she grows up, we'll no doubt have another Maeris angel or devil to deal with and assist us when we need her most, just like her mom and others from her proud Clan. Klyne out."

Naero rose up and turned the corner, waving to her twelve Khai guards and sending them all telepathic greetings as she whisked past them and into her private quarters.

She missed Khai and the kids, wishing they were here. The love she felt for them always recharged her more than the most powerful super star.

She smiled at the private Jett dispenser, hit the button, and sucked down a frosty borbble.

"Ahh…" Haisha, that was good. She deserved at least that much.

N, I almost have that report ready. Do you want to scan it before I send it on to Intel?

I'll look it over later, Om. Go ahead and send it on; you know I trust you.

What are you going to do, Naero?

She sighed very heavily once more.

"I'm going to take my defeats and my victories as they come, Om. And when I can, I'm going to do my best to keep the promises that I have made, especially to the people I love the most."

I just sent the report, N. What's next?

Naero rubbed her face, still feeling burned out. Jia will be here within a few hours or to assist me. Please, let me rest until then, Om.

Will do. I'm on watch. All regenerative efforts and protocols shall continue.

She passed out as soon as she curled up on her dark nanofloor. She felt Om raise her nanobed up around her.

Jia shook her gently in what seemed to have been the flash of an instant, yet five standard hours had indeed passed.

Om must have admitted Jia when she arrived.

Naero did feel much better.

"Are you sure you're up to this, Naero? We can keep trying, but I still can't promise anything. The processes involved are still so complex as to remain beyond us."

Naero rose up and embraced the Driathan queen. "Thank you for coming, Jia. I understand, my dear friend. There are never any guarantees. But you are the only one who can help me with these matters. We must keep trying."

They went into Naero's study. The preset lighting came up as before, with the streaming data of all of their other failed attempts posted around them.

The Driathan blank rested on a medbed, as usual.

Yet this time, Zhen's soul actually lay dormant, merged within.

She had managed that much and that alone was a huge step in the right direction.

All they needed to do now, according to Jia, was fully distribute and merge the soul energy within the blank, a complex integration process in itself, and then fully awaken Zhen's consciousness.

They could do nothing else until that much was accomplished.

All of that could take ten minutes, or ten centuries.

"After that," Jia said, "I can assist her in adjusting to her new form, pweaking it, as you Spacers say, and then counseling her on her new existence not only as her new self...but as a Driathan. You understand that, Naero? Your friend Zhen will still be herself, yet she will also awaken to be one of my people now–one of my sisters–a Driathan in all things. She will have a responsibility to my people–her new people–once she is one of us."

"That's fine. If we can awaken her, Jia," Naero asked, "how long will it take her to adjust to most of that?"

"Only a few hours, initially."

"Good. I have Tyber and the others arriving later in the morning. That should work out about right, if we're lucky."

"The full education process on understanding what it means to be Driathan may take several standard months of enlightenment thereafter. It is a grave responsibility, as I said. But I know she can do it. Zhen is so intelligent and quick-minded."

Naero nodded sadly. "Z is extremely smart. She always was. All right, Jia; let's get started."

Jia merged with her mind to study her efforts and the energy flows she put forth. Naero first suffused the blank and Zhen's soul with the Cosmic energy of the Lifespark, using both biomancy and teknomancy to monitor the complex flow of forces in an incredibly precise attempt to expand Zhen's soul throughout her new form, integrate it, and awaken Zhen's consciousness within it in a way that was compatible.

They tried several times over the next few hours to complete the process.

They drew close and closer, yet each time their efforts still fell short.

On the last attempt, they were so close that the blank finally shifted form, like liquid metal, into Zhen's exact appearance, devoid of color.

The shining silver form looked so much like Zhen, down to each hair, her pretty face, and her slender hands. Naero had to stop and cover her face with her own hands and weep.

Her dear friend was almost back among them.

But the new Zhen still wasn't breathing just yet.

"Take heart," Jia said, resting a gentle hand on Naero's shoulder. "We're very close now. Trust me; this is a very good sign. The blank is accepting the soul's form and how the mind sees itself. The two are finally merging properly into one."

They kept trying. They put Zhen on a respirator and continued to infuse her and her new form with the Lifespark.

Still it was not enough.

They were still missing something vital.

Then Naero recalled what she had done when she brought Shetharra and herself back from the brink of death. Yet this was different, and far more intimate in many ways.

Naero wasn't keeping her friend from dying.

She was bringing her back to life.

There had to be a different way to merge with Zhen this time, and make the process work.

She tore the respirator off Zhen's placid face, sealed off the nose, and covered her friend's mouth with her own.

Naero kept the body flooded with life force energy, and breathed the energized breath of life back into her good friend.

Then she jolted Zhen with a pulse of the Lifespark–laced with the fire of the Flame Eternal.

One slight mistake and she could burn out the blank from the inside, and reduce even Zhen's soul to ash, losing it forever.

Naero could even destroy herself.

She breathed out again, flooding her energized breath into Zhen's form.

Another jolt.

This time Zhen convulsed. Her hands and feet twitched and her mouth moved.

Naero dragged Zhen onto the floor, cradling her friend's slender, living metal body in her arms.

They were one now, suffused in the same Lifeforce energies.

It was costing Naero all that she was, and for a bare instant, she too teetered of the knife edge of the forces of life and death.

At last, Naero sensed it all.

Zhen's soul finally expanded, filling her amazing new body to its full extents.

Naero breathed into Zhen a third time, and zapped them both with a final jolt of the life instilling forces–clinging to the very precipice of life and death.

For the barest instant, Naero herself blacked out from her exertions, feeling almost completely drained once again.

When she came back around, Zhen was…breathing next to her.

Haisha! Her good friend Zhen breathed peacefully still cradled in Naero's arms.

Naero called to her, "Come back to us, Z. We love you. We need you." She could speak no more.

Then Zhentisa coughed, and her eyes fluttered open. She stirred and looked up as if she had simply awakened from a long nap.

"N-Naero?"

Naero sobbed and choked on her own explosion of tears.

Finally her voice returned. "Welcome back, Zhen."

Zhen studied her shining silver hands. "N? Where am I…what, am I?" She blinked and thought for a moment.

Jia leaned down, crying as well, and took Zhen's hands into her own.

"You are who you are, and you have become a miracle, Zhen. In more ways than one. You are still all that you were and shall have your life. Yet you are also now a Driathan, a wonder of creation, love, and the pinnacle of all beauty. Your form was fashioned by the majestic hands of loving gods. Remember that you are a gift to the universe and part of its destiny. Always remember that."

"I...I feel so weak, N. Haisha, I want to jump up and dance, cry, and sing, but I can barely move." She coughed. "So...thirsty."

Naero lifted her back onto the medbed, which seemed to go haywire at first, trying to compensate for the advanced form of a living, breathing Driathan. Spacer medtek compensated as best it could, but whatever Zhen had become, a large part of her was now beyond normal comprehension, just as Jia was.

Naero and Om quickly assisted in resetting the medbed with teknomancy, and very quickly it adjusted to monitoring Zhen's normal functions.

Jia laughed for joy. "Don't worry. You will continue to adjust quickly now. A few training adjustments and your new body will respond to your mind completely."

Zhen studied her hands and arms, looking at herself in the mirrors. She smiled. "I'm all silvery, just like Jia. That's nice and all, but...is there maybe a way for me to look...the way I did before? Like a human Spacer?"

Jia grinned and placed a hand on Zhen, merging with her instantly. "If that is what you truly wish. Read the thoughts and processes I pass onto you. Play with and explore them as you wish. These are your own vital abilities now. You can be as you want to be."

Zhen flashed from silver into white, then pink, then blue, purple, and green with the barest thought. "Haisha!"

"Refine it. Picture yourself as you were, as you wish to be. You can adjust your hue, the color of your eyes, your skin, your outer appearance–you can even adjust the texture of your skin and give it the same warmth and feel that you once had. You don't really need to breathe oxygen, but you still can if you want to. You don't have to ingest food and drink either, but you can still enjoy their taste and process them if you choose to do that as well."

Zhen laughed like a playful child, smiling up at them. "Will I...be able to make love to Ty again?"

Jia grinned. "Just as good as you did before, if not better. And you can give birth to the rest of your children to have your family together with him. Driathans have the Lifeforce roaring within them. You will be able to master and control your body as few women can."

"I want to see Ty and our son," Zhen said. She broke down into laughing and crying beyond all control.

Naero covered her face with her hands and nearly started crying again, listening to her good friend's mirth, and knowing what a gift all of that was.

*

They rendezvoused with all of the others at Cyto-4, as arranged.

Naero had the filtered viewscreen up, bathing the mid-sized meeting room in the filtered light of the Cyto system's star and its neighbors.

Such a day as this demanded to be permeated with light.

The room was set for a celebration, and filled with fragrant blooms and blossoms.

Tyber stumbled in first, griping and complaining.

"What's so damn important, N? I've had less than four hours sleep, and I had to bring Gallan along, as you insisted, in a sleep pod."

Without a word.

Without a sound.

Naero transported Zhen in all her graceful beauty right behind Tyber in a brief flash of light. She wore what could only be described as a simple dress made of light fashioned into raiment, hanging softy upon her slender shoulders down to her knees, her delicate ankles and feet bare above the nanofloor.

She was indeed a vision as lovely as the star rise.

Ty put his hands on hips, still focused on Naero. "Well, are you just going to stand there like an idiot and stare at me? Say something. What? What are you crying for?"

Naero laughed and blurted out, "Because, you great blockhead, I've finally kept my promise to you…and to little Gallan."

Zhen clenched her fists and smiled brighter than the star before them all.

"T…Ty?"

Tyber froze and all color seemed to drain from his stricken face and all of his exposed flesh.

When he whirled around to stare wide-eyed at his beloved, he trembled and shook so hard he could barely remain standing.

In fact, he staggered forward and broke down.

Zhen caught him as he fell against her, both of them sobbing beyond all control.

They could not speak.

They both dropped to the floor, clinging to each other, both laughing and crying for all joy.

Naero herself fell to her knees, covered her own face, and wept right along with them.

This was a day for tears to rain down, but none of them would be from sorrow.

After several shining moments, they were not finished yet.

Naero recovered enough to make a quiet call to their waiting friends over the open comlink on her wristcom.

Z and Ty had not moved from where they first came back together.

Saemar and Chaela led the procession with a child's sleep pod between them, along with Tarim, Shalaen, Baeven, Jia, Janner and his two wives, and all of the rest of their many friends and crew.

Shalaen opened Gallan's pod and gently woke the young boy with but a gentle touch. Chaela and Saemar comforted him and allowed him to fully wake up. He rubbed his eyes with his small fists and laughed and giggled with his aunties.

Zhen heard the voice of her son and lifted her head.

Their eyes met.

"Mommy? Mommy!" he shrieked. Galan ran into the arms of his parents and together they made a sweet, tight little family sandwich.

Gallan cried and scolded Zhen. "Mommy, they told me you went far away. They said you might not ever come back."

Zhen and Ty rose up, holding their son between them. Zhen wiped her face. Then she reached out and took Naero's hand and smiled.

"Aunt Naero found me; she kept me safe. She brought me back…when no one else could, beyond all hope, beyond the impossible. She never gave up on me and she kept her word and her promise. We must always thank her for that."

They drew her within their embrace, and the others joined in all around them. Naero smiled wide, the light of the universe blanketing them all with radiance.

This day, she would definitely count among her greatest victories.

THE END

Look for more of Naero's continuing adventures in:

NAERO'S VALOR

And watch for the first book in Mason's NEW SF series:

THE STARWARD SURGE

Please Post A Book Review Right Now

Please post a review of this book where you purchased it, if you enjoyed it.

Just twenty little words are all that is required. Twenty words that say what you liked about this book while it is still fresh in your heart, mind, and soul. Please do so now before something else makes you forget.

Here is the link for *The Gamma Quadrant* if you purchased it on Amazon:

smarturl.it/TheGammaQuadrant

Please click on the link and post your review now.
Done? The author would personally like to thank you very much.

In this busy world, everyone is pressed for time. Our time is so important, no doubt. It has reached the point now where authors of nearly every stripe compete not only for sales, but to garner reviews from their readers. Some authors even stoop to "purchasing" reviews in social media that some services now offer in bulk.

In the publish or perish work of competitive fiction, book reviews from readers are golden, they have now become a commodity even.

Many in the business even consider book reviews as important, or even more important than book sales in some ways. As crazy as that sounds.

So therefore, trust us in this. If you have authors whom you adore, and you want to read more of their books in the future, please post as many reviews for them as you can in all of the forms of social media that you use.

Doing so will help your favorite authors in numerous ways that you cannot even possibly imagine. Never forget that fact. Book reviews matter a great deal.

And if by chance, if you find that there is something about this book that you don't like, and you really do want to help authors, before you slam them with bad reviews, try briefly contacting them instead with your concerns through their contact info that is always readily provided, or through their publisher. Most authors, especially new ones, are usually happy to get constructive criticism that will make their books better. Only hating, online trolls slam authors with bad reviews without giving them a chance. Real pros and fen contact authors directly with any valid concerns. That is the current, accepted etiquette. Please don't be a troll.

<u>Amazon Kindle Review Link</u> for *The Gamma Quadrant*:

smarturl.it/TheGammaQuadrant

Please post one or more reviews for Mason and each of his books, everywhere that you can.

Thank you once again.

Cheers,

Mason Elliott

About the Author

Mason Elliott grew up loving Science Fiction and Fantasy in all of their myriad forms. That love has transferred into his dedicated writing. Like most writers, he lives a Spartan lifestyle and yearns to devote his life even more to his writing. So be a fan, buy his stuff, and enjoy!

Mason's Amazon Author Page:

smarturl.it/BooksbyMasonElliott

Friend Mason on FB at this link:

http://on.fb.me/1qnBfJd

Like and follow Mason on Facebook, where he does most of his blogging at
https://www.facebook.com/masonelliott731

Follow Mason on Twitter at:

http://bit.ly/1nsqOSs

Join Mason's Readers List to get the latest progress on his latest books:

http://eepurl.com/FgQzv

Visit Mason Elliott's website at

http://masonelliott.authorcontacts.com

Become a patron for Mason on Patreon and support his career directly for as little as a dollar a month with great benefits for patrons at every level.

http://patreon.com/masonelliott/

And for even more information on Mason Elliott and his works, visit High Mark Publishing online at:
www.HighMarkPublishing.com

<u>My Super Patreon Patrons Honor Page</u>

Thank you all for directly supporting me with your good faith.

Tracey
Paul
Catherine
Melinda

Acknowledgements

Who can I not thank for a great SF series running so successfully for so long? Gosh I love these books. The usual suspects at High Mark, Jennifer and Josh. My friends and family. My online writing group who back me up all of the time, and kick my butt when it needs to be kicked. A wonderful shout out to the equally wonderful Tracey. That should cover things for now.

Edition Notes

If you do not see this edition note here in this spot on the copyright page and on the very last page of your eBook or print version of this title, then you are not getting the final, polished version of this novel that the publisher, editors, and author intended for you to receive. Please contact either the publisher or the author via their emails or websites if you do not see the following update code:

High Mark Publishing Update Code D0632A

Become a fan of my books.
Please join my Readers List:
http://bit.ly/1L2QpUL

Thanks, from Mason Elliott